Arianna

A Tale from the Eleven Kingdoms

Arianna

A Tale from the Eleven Kingdoms

GC Sinclaire

Printed in the United States of America

GC Sinclaire
Gig Harbor, WA 98329
www.gcsinclaire.com

Publisher's Note: This is a work of fiction. Names, characters, places, and incidents are a product of the author's imagination. Locales and public names are sometimes used for atmospheric purposes. Any resemblance to actual people, living or dead, or to businesses, companies, events, institutions, or locales is completely coincidental.

Arianna: A Tale from the Eleven Kingdoms/GC Sinclaire-- 1st ed.

Print Edition ISBN 978-0-9977915-0-1

Dedicated To:

The Universe

Thank you

Contents

The terminology, as well as measurements, are different in the kingdoms. I have therefore taken the liberty to convert some of them to make it easier to follow this engaging tale.

Arianna

rianna's eyes fluttered open and then fell shut again. Her eyelids felt so very heavy! The effort to open them was almost too much. Once more, she blinked. The images her eyes took in during that brief glimpse started to trickle down to her consciousness. Once they reached there, what she had seen took a little while longer to process.

When it did, however, an immediate alarm reaction sent a jolt of fear through her brain. Her fight-or-flight instinct awoke. Danger signals vibrated through her dazed mind. But, even that was not enough to shake her out of her semiconscious state. Rising up through layer after layer of dense, numbing fog, she finally reached almost full awareness.

Her eyes flew open. Arianna's first sight was of the cloudy sky above her. Next, she noticed wet dark gray stone flashing past her. The jagged rock was covered here and there in pale green lichen and reddish-green moss. Funny that she would take note of such a detail at a time like this.

Where was she? What was going on? It took her somewhat fuddled brain a few more moments to thoroughly comprehend the entire situation. She was falling! This realization was enough to finally catapult her to full consciousness. Why was she falling? And, how had she gotten here? Question after question raced through her mind. She had answers to none.

The logical part of her brain finally took over, and she tried to analyze her situation. Her thinking, however, was still not up to its usual speed. Arianna felt frustrated. Shaking her head in an attempt to clear it, the girl began to evaluate her circumstances as quickly as she could. Her knees were almost level with her horrified gaze! What a most undignified position! The air was rushing past her with incredible swiftness and her waist-long hair was streaming out above her like a wind-whipped flag. Her dress was obscuring her vision straight ahead.

Looking up, she saw a rock ledge above her. That must have been the place she had fallen from! She needed to see how far below the ground was and get a look at the place she was plummeting towards and fast. Since she had already dropped for such a long way, time to help herself might be running out. Carefully, she straightened herself out and turned her head and shoulders.

Her honey-colored hair began to whip into her too pale face. Tears sprang to her eyes and obscured her vision. She was usually very proud of that shiny golden mass. Right now, however, it was more of an annoyance than an asset. It was seriously getting in her way. Impatiently gathering together the strands of unbound hair, Arianna finally managed to glance over her shoulder. She shuddered, and her eyes grew huge as she took in the sight.

She seemed to be falling from very high up! There were woods below, but the individual trees were still too small to make out clearly. Unless she could stop her momentum, there was no way she would survive hitting the ground tumbling from such heights! On the other hand, still being this far up left her some time.

How had she gotten into this predicament? And, where was she? This entire situation was very strange! Going by the rapidity of the rough rock racing past her, she knew that she was falling incredibly fast. But she was still such a long way up! How could that be? Arianna had expected to hit the ground at any moment now! Maybe there was a chance to save herself after all. But how? She was flashing past that cliff face at such tremendous speed!

Her horrified gaze was drawn once again to the dark forest below. For a moment, she watched in fascinated terror. The trees now looked like little toy trees. They were most certainly getting increasingly closer!

Fear constricted her throat. Her heart was frantically hammering in her chest like a drum, so fast and hard that it hurt. Tears of desperation started to overflow her large sea-green eyes but were instantly whipped away by the speed of her descent. She had to think! Why was her brain so muddled the one time she needed it most? What had happened to put her in such a state?

Shaking her head, she pushed those thoughts aside. This was not the time to figure out what was going on or to give in to her fears! The priority right now was to think of what she could do to save herself. There had to be something! If she wanted to live, it was time to take action! Determinedly Arianna started to push down the panic which was threatening to take away what wits she had left.

Never in her life had Arianna given up without a fight. She was not about to this time. Despite her youth and station, she was no stranger to adversity. Even into a young princess's charmed life, misfortune dared to intrude at times. The death of her mother had not only left her without her best friend but had eventually put her in a position where she had had to fight to continue her training. She had never blamed her father but in a way she had lost both parents that day. At least for a while.

Immediately after the accident and for a long time after, her father had been so lost in grief that he was barely able to keep up with the daily demands of the kingdom. He had isolated himself and had been inconsolable. His wife had been the love of his life. As a result, the children had been left on their own to deal with the loss of their mother. It had been Arianna who had to make sure to inform the relatives of her beloved parent's passing.

Her aunt, Queen Margaret of Re'adeen, her mother's sister, had come as soon as the message reached her. When she arrived, the kids had been in a sorry state. It was up to the aunt to comfort the mourning youngsters and help them adjust to the tragic loss. Eventually, it was agreed that she would stay. Margaret took over the raising and education of the young children. At first, all went well for Arianna. It was not long, however, before the queen discovered some of the secret schoolings the young princess had been privileged to all these years.

Being all lady and feeling that her sister's exploits had led to her death, Margaret had been aghast at the unconventional training her niece was receiving. She had felt it was about time the girl learned to behave like a proper princess, a part of the education which in her eyes had been sorely neglected. Fierce determination and compromise on Arianna's part, as well as some serious convincing of the lady, finally won her the approval to continue those studies. It had been a good thing that the overprotective aunt never discovered all the varied subjects her secretive niece was dabbling in!

Pushing away those memories, the princess flipped herself around. Arianna let go of her hair and spread out her

4

arms and legs hoping to slow her incredible momentum. It worked! Almost immediately she noticed a slight decrease in the speed of her rapid descent and for once, she was glad she was wearing a dress. Now, what else could she do? All those years she had spent learning could not have been in vain!

The brief recall of her life made the princess realize how much she wanted to survive. There were adventures she had always dreamed of and so many new things yet to learn. She was still so young and had so much to look forward to! If she had anything to say about it, there was no way she was going to die before she had ever even fully lived. Arianna wanted to experience love in her life. So far the only romantic involvement she had was with that amazing young man in her dreams. She had yet to experience those kinds of feelings for real.

There just had to be something she could do! She was a sorceress after all, wasn't she? Why couldn't she think of anything? Taking deep, relaxing breaths, she began to quiet her anxious mind. She resolutely shoved all those racing thoughts aside. Calming herself, Arianna succeeded in pushing down the still growing panic which threatened to consume her. She managed to center herself. Stillness washed over her, and she could now assess the situation from a more detached state. All of a sudden it felt like the floodgates opened and memories began to wash forth.

Some part of her, deep down inside, became aware that she was actually asleep! This, however, did not take away from the terror of this unchecked fall. She now remembered having had similar nightmares before. In all the previous dreams, however, she had tumbled for just a very brief period before waking.

Even those short nightmares had been enough to affect her significantly, especially after her mother had died in a fall.

Each time she had awoken covered in sweat with her heart racing and her hands trembling. Somehow those dreams had triggered something primal within Arianna and had left her shaken. None of the previous ones had been as bad as this one. Never before had she been able to make out the trees clearly in the dark forest below or had had the time to do so.

This whole episode felt very different. She had not only fallen a far greater distance, but this dream was somehow more real and 'lifelike'. That made it so much more terrifying than any nightmare she had ever had before. Arianna was afraid that unless she could find some way to stop her descent or wake up, she would inevitably impact the rapidly approaching ground.

The princess was only too aware that the shock of dying in the dream would overwhelm her body and mind. It would stop the heart of her sleeping form. Her life would end just as sure as if she had taken the fall for real. There was no way she was going to allow that to happen! She firmly believed that there was always a way out of every situation. Why should this one be any different?

Was she not a devoted priestess of the Exalted Goddess? With all that knowledge and the skills she had acquired since she was a small girl, there had to be something she could do! She had so much to live for and what of her father? He had not been able to comfort his children, but they and the kingdom had been the only things keeping him going after their mother's death. Everyone had been terribly worried about him, and it was evident that he still missed his wife every day, even now, years later. Losing his eldest daughter might just be more than he could bear. There had to be some way to save herself and spare her beloved parent further grief!

Once again, Arianna resolutely brought her mind back on track. Doggedly the girl started trying out different ideas which were now flooding her fevered brain. She just had to stop this fall! First, she tried grabbing at stones in the cliff flashing past, but her speed was still too great. The jagged rocks gave her no purchase and left her fingers bloodied.

Even the enchantment meant to glue her to the wall brought no result. Then, she whispered an incantation to make herself as light as a feather. That should allow her to float down. Nothing! Next, she uttered a spell which would turn her into a big bird so she could glide down. She had done this many times before and, to her, it was such simple magic. But once again, nothing happened. How could it be that all her attempts would fail so miserably?

Something was countering her efforts! There was some dark power at play here. Where she had been frightened before, anger was now starting to grow. Oppose her magic! We would see about that! She had always been able to get around most spells. Why should this be any different? The princess was now more determined than ever to find a way to defeat this magical trap.

Arianna gathered all her significant powers and "willed" herself awake. Nothing! She tried again, despair giving her additional strength. Then once more. Despite her best efforts, she was still falling. Nothing had worked! The forest below was approaching at a steady pace and with it, her imminent death. She could feel the wind streaming past her too pale face, and started to smell the pervasive odor of woods and sun-heated rock. The ground was getting way to close. She was running out of time!

The young woman, still a girl in many ways, tried to think desperately of something else she could attempt. She felt just as helpless as she had at the news of her mother's death.

With all her magical abilities she had not been able to save her beloved parent. How could this happen again? Disbelief and anguish at her inability to rescue herself washed over her. Her whole body started shaking with gut wrenching sobs. Bitter tears ran down her blanched cheeks. Why did nothing she tried work?

Arianna was a very independent person. Even as a small child she had wanted to do everything herself. Her training over the years had given her the tools to be almost entirely self-reliant. If there was a way to do something without having to ask for help, she would find it. It was hard for her to face the fact that she was utterly defeated. She had tried everything she could think of. No other way to stop this terrible dream came to her despondent mind. Arianna reluctantly had to admit that she was out of her league.

The princess would have preferred not involving the Lady. She loved and served her Goddess with devotion and pleasure and knew that help was always available to her. Even being told that she was welcome to call on her loving deity anytime had not changed Arianna's firm resolve to stay as self-sufficient as possible in all aspects of her life. She felt that the Goddess was so kind and sweet and did not need to be bothered by her as well. There were so many others always vying for the deity's attention.

Usually, she succeeded quite well on her own. Arianna had to admit, however, that this time, she was out of options. It rankled her pride that she had to trouble the Exalted Lady. In her mind, it was like admitting defeat and weakness. Something was blocking her, however, and she was not strong enough to overcome it by herself. In the grace of her Goddess lay her one remaining hope.

That she would have called on the Lady on anyone else's behalf without hesitation, never occurred to her.

Subconsciously, the princess felt that being a sorceress changed the equation and that the rules were different for her. She should be stronger and more able to help herself than the average person!

With a heavy heart, she now turned to her divine benefactor. "Please, my beloved Goddess, Lady of the Radiant Light, bright Brigit, please help me! Please stop this nightmare, let me wake up! Please, do not let me die this way!" she prayed fervently. "You have never abandoned me in the past. Please save me now!"

Having sent out her desperate plea for help, she went back to crossly mulling over the grim situation. The falling nightmares she experienced before had been so brief that she had never even had the chance to try stopping the fall or waking herself up so she had no idea if it would have worked. They most certainly had not prepared her for what she was facing now. If this was just a dream, why could she not affect it, change it somehow?

In the past, she had other dreams she had not been able to influence, but those were far different from what she was facing right now. She had been more than happy to go along with those, to let them unfold and see where they would lead. They had been so genuine, so intense, and full of fun and surprises. In those dreams, she had met the winged boy and had watched him grow into a handsome man over the years.

Knowing that what she was experiencing was not real had allowed her to open up more than she normally would. She and the boy had become friends and confidants. In some ways, those dreams and this horrible nightmare seemed similar even so they were worlds apart. Both were more life-like and had affected her more than any of her other dreams. She could not only see and hear but also touch, sense, and smell. The impression of realism made this even more terrifying because it felt like she was actually there.

The winged boy dreams and the falling nightmares had been her steady companions for many years now. After her mother's death, the boundaries between her dreams of the youth and her everyday life had blurred for a while. In her sleep, she had taken refuge in his world from the grimness of life in the castle and cried bitter tears in his mother's arms. His people became as real to her as those surrounding her in the waking hours. Only after her aunt, Queen Margret, arrived did things get better at home.

Arianna had shared her grief with her friend and his people and the solace she had received had felt so genuine that she had started to wonder. Over time, she had come to know so much about his world, and they had shared so many different adventures. Also, there was the fact that he and his people seemed to have real lives which continued in her absence. Were they more than just mere dreams? Were they an astral projection? Or was she truly there? Could it be that she was leading an alternate life while she was sleeping?

One experience finally answered some of her many questions but in turn, raised many more. At least, she was now sure that those nighttime visits were more than just dreams. They did affect her in her waking life! She and her friend had been out climbing on one of the peaks near his home when she slipped and severely bruised her arm. It had hurt something fierce even after she had healed the worst of the injury. The pain had been only slightly less upon awakening, and it had lingered for days. She had even had a bruise!

What truly frightened the princess was that the nightmare she was having now felt just as lifelike. Arianna was certain that, if she hit that forest floor and died from the impact, the pain and terror of her dream-death would kill her for real. Glancing down again, she noticed that the ground was coming up fast now. Sadness filled her. She had tried everything she could think of to keep this nightmare from reaching its inevitable conclusion. Nothing had worked, not even her plea to her goddess. Why was this happening to her? Who was blocking her powers so effectively? And why?

Wait! Could it be that this was not a dream at all but a 'Sending', a magical trap for the unsuspecting dreamer? Those were nasty and usually sent by some magic wielding practitioner of the Dark Arts. A 'Sending' was crafted in such a way that it came to a very particular conclusion and was almost impossible to escape. That would explain her inability to affect this event in some way! It seemed that this one would end with her imminent demise. Why did someone direct this at her? And who hated her so much that they wanted her dead? What had she ever done to deserve this?

As her wisdom and knowledge had grown, Arianna had learned to abide more and more by the rule 'Do as you will but harm none.' To her, this included everybody and everything. Her beliefs and practices had made her a better person. She was respectful and kind to all, and her people loved her. To the outside world, she appeared to be just a sweet, but little wild, princess.

The reality, however, was much different. Arianna was much more than that. She had manifested her first magical abilities shortly after her birth. Her mother had immediately taken steps to ensure that she was trained, and her capabilities kept a well-guarded secret. In their kingdom, as well as some of the neighboring ones, magic was acceptable when used by sorcerers or witches. But a sorceress princess? Unheard of!

Arianna had learned to take advantage of 'coincidences' to hide her magic. She would help where she could and when she felt it was to the benefit of the person or persons involved. Often, this could be accomplished by ordinary means and without anyone ever knowing of her contribution. Over the years, she had made a difference in many peoples' lives. It made her happy to be able to do so.

The more the princess learned, the closer she had grown to nature and the more loving and peaceful her heart had become. The feeling of being one with fate, one with the Divine, of heading in the right direction, and going with the flow of life felt so wonderful that she truly felt out of sorts if she allowed some occurrence to remove her from this state.

With her beliefs came a deep respect for all life. To Arianna, animals and plants had feelings and souls and were deserving of her love and respect. For a while, this had left her with a bit of a dietary conundrum. She had felt guilty every time she ate anything at all. She was finally forced to face the fact that she had to eat if she wanted to live. Therefore, she had chosen what she regarded as the lesser evil. Most of the time her meals consisted of vegetables, grains, fruit, eggs, and on occasion, fish. Animal flesh became something she only touched on rare occasions and then only when her body seemed to crave it. She always made sure to thank the plants and animals for their gift of life and for nourishing her.

Queen Anna had encouraged her daughter to acquire other skills princesses' usually do not indulge in. Arianna had secretly learned to defend herself, track, survive in the wild, and hunt. The procurement of meat from wild game was part of everyday life in their kingdom. Her first kill had been a beautiful buck. Seeing him proud and magnificent one minute and then dead and lifeless at her feet the next had left the girl in tears. It had driven home the value of life, any life. Her mother's untimely death had reinforced this. Now, she would only hunt if she saw no other option or to spare an injured animal its pain. She would use every part of the body she could and always made sure to comfort and thank the departing spirit.

The kingdom considered itself relatively enlightened, but meat on the table still represented a sort of status symbol. Only those too poor to afford it would do without. Arianna would never push her beliefs on any other but, over time, her deep respect for life had not gone unnoticed by her family. Seeing her thrive on the near meatless diet, her father and aunt had decided to cut down on meats served at their table. At first, this had caused some grumbling among a few of the servants but, after they had been assured that this was the family's choice and would not be forced on them, peace reasserted itself.

Since Arianna had been very conscious of her actions towards others for several years now, she could not fathom why someone would want to kill her. She could not remember ever doing something so awful to anyone that they would want this kind of revenge on her. Her father was also a well-loved and fair king. Who could possibly want to harm him or his children? Was anyone else in her family having this horrible dream? And, if they were, might she be able to help them?

Reaching out with her powers, she touched each of her family members' sleeping minds. She found them all resting peacefully, dreaming of far more pleasant things than she. A deep sigh escaped her, and she was greatly relieved. Just to make sure she checked on her favorite maid but found the young woman serenely asleep as well. They were all safe! It seemed this dream was aimed directly at her and only at her.

What had attracted it? It took a lot of effort and time to create such a nasty 'Sending'. Why would someone go through all this trouble just to end her life?

A glance at the woods below told her that her time had almost come and that the end was near now. Arianna reached out to her Goddess one final time. "Thank you, Exalted Lady, for my life, for all the love you have given me, for all the help I have received from you over the years. I give my life into your hands and relinquish all control to you, bright Brigit. If it should be your will, please save me, if not, welcome me to your loving embrace. Blessed be!"

The ground was now so close that she could make out the dark green needles on the trees below and the moss and ferns covering the forest glade which seemed to be ordained to become her final resting place. Resigned to whatever fate had in store for her, Arianna closed her eyes and surrendered herself completely to her destiny. Deep peace began to fill her mind and soul. The frantic beating of her heart began to slow.

Suddenly, she sensed the air being stirred by something like wings. Soft feathers brushed her serene face. Then, a sudden sharp nip at her earlobe jolted her. Welcome blackness washed away her senses. She seemed to float aimlessly in a sea of nothingness. Arianna gladly embraced this total absence of fear and despair and became one with the peacefulness surrounding her. She drifted along in tranquil contemplation until she became aware of a gentle but persistent tug.

Once the princess took note of the disruption, its strength seemed to increase. She opened her eyes and became aware that she was no longer resting without direction but moving towards the source of this tug. With every passing second, she was being pulled faster and faster.

Arianna watched with astonishment her rapid progress towards a swiftly growing bright light. Soon, the luminescence was of such pure whiteness that the girl had to close her eyes to protect them. At first, she feared that the brightness would consume her, but instead it enfolded her in its warm and loving embrace.

The girl felt complete comfort and absolute love surround her and gladly allowed it to flow through her. "Welcome, my child," a soft voice greeted her, and a gentle hand caressed her check. Arianna instantly recognized the touch of her Goddess and opened her eyes. She found herself in a beautiful temple overlooking high mountains and fertile valleys. The sanctuary's white pillars were made of the purest marble and the floor inlaid with rose quartz and amethyst. She was seated on a soft pink cloud with the arms of her Lady around her.

Pulling back a little, the princess looked up at her goddess and asked. "My Lady Brigit! Am I dead?" "No, little one, but had I not been able to intervene, you would have been. All your spellcasting was keeping me from assisting you! Did it ever occur to you to ask for my help just a little sooner and to place your trust in me? This was indeed cutting it a bit close!" came the Goddess stern reply.

For a moment, Arianna was taken aback. Realization dawned on her. She had kept the Lady from being able to help her by trying to do it all on her own, by using only the powers she possessed herself instead of calling on the magic available to her through her benefactor! Her arrogance and insistence on self-reliance had almost gotten her killed! Her personal powers had been nowhere near strong enough to break her free from that nightmare.

For the first time, she truly comprehended that it was not weakness to include her loving deity in her spells. "My Lady, thank you for rescuing me! I thought I could deal with it on my own and did not want to bother you. I tried, but nothing worked! My life is yours!" Arianna answered with a heart filled with wonder as well as profound gratitude.

The beautiful lady regarded her with eyes full of compassion. "No, my child! Your life is your own. But, in future, please remember to send me a quick prayer before trying to fix things on your own! I was almost too late this time! Are we not a team, you and I? Invoking my name will give greater power to your castings. You are my priestess, and you should be doing your workings in my name and imbued with my magic. Or, do you think you have become as powerful as I am and do not need my assistance?" the Lady firmly chastised her overly self-reliant disciple. "Oh no, my Lady! I am no goddess! I just did not want to bother you!" the girl replied shamefacedly.

The flame-haired Goddess sighed in exasperation. "Child! How many times will I have to tell you that calling on me is what you are supposed to do! It is no bother to me. There was great evil sent your way this night. Only once you completely surrendered yourself into my hands was I able to defeat it. Do you want to continue working on your own or will you let me fully into your heart? Will you work through me and with me as you should as my priestess from now on?"

Arianna's face paled. The goddess's words had been gentle and kind, but the young woman had not missed the underlying threat. For the first time, she began to grasp what it meant to be a priestess of the Exalted One. "My Lady, please forgive me! I did not understand! I would not know what to do without you to turn to, without your help and love, your comfort and counsel. I promise to include you in all my craftings from now on!" the girl vowed ardently.

Holding Arianna at arm's length, the Goddess studied her intently. "Good! And make sure you do not forget!" she retorted with mock severity. When she saw the young woman grow even more pale, she leaned forward and tenderly pulled the princess back into her arms. A feeling of oneness, of immense love, of incredible power, started to envelop Arianna. She now realized that she had always held back before. For the first time, she let go of her own Ego and completely surrendered herself to her Goddess's love. She fully and consciously opened her heart and embraced all the Lady had to offer. This love and with it the knowledge of her Deity's immense power took root in her very core. For Arianna, it was an awakening, and she was amazed at the difference she felt within herself. How much she had learned this very night!

Sitting back, the beautiful Goddess gazed at the young woman fondly. "You deduced correctly, by the way. What you experienced tonight was a 'Sending', a wicked one at that. Once you were sucked in, there were no means of escape. It was being fed by your own powers. The harder you tried to escape, the stronger it grew. The spell was designed to use your fears against you and end your life so that your gifts could be passed on to the senders." Arianna gasped and looked at the Lady in horror.

Such a dreadful possibility had never occurred to the princess. The spell had been even worse than she had realized. "Only your complete surrender to fate and my grace saved you. The ones who created it are a group of women led by a very powerful black witch. The 'Sending' was not meant for you specific, it was attracted by your magic. I have made sure they will never know who they had trapped. When the enchantment collapsed, its power backlashed onto its makers. I fear not all of them will have the strength to survive this," the Lady continued.

Listening to her Goddess, Arianna had gone white as a sheet. How naïve she had been! Just because she would not harm another did not mean that there were not others out there who would. It had been her misfortune to fall into their trap. "Are you alright?" the Lady asked with concern. Arianna swallowed and nodded.

"The leader of this group sees any woman having strong magic as a rival and is determined to gain all the power she can and leave no one to oppose her. Your lives will intersect soon, and you need to prepare yourself well!" the Lady continued. "Fate can be a hard teacher. Hold the ones you love the most close, for soon, you will have to leave them behind. Be careful and use all that you have learned with cunning, hide your gifts and knowledge well, and do not confront this evil openly. Be the girl they think you are and do not let them see your real strength. I wish I could spare you the trials coming your way, but the events have already been set in motion. Always remember, I am with you, and I love and cherish you."

Before she could even thank her Goddess, Arianna once again found herself floating in that serene sea of darkness. A sense of profound well-being and comfort flooded her entire being and, for the moment, forgotten was all that had troubled her. She could feel the Lady's love with every fiber of her being. New strength washed through her. An immense sense of gratitude filled her heart. The princess drifted in the peaceful void for what seemed like an immeasurable amount of time, growing calmer and more strongly joined to the Divine. New knowledge rose up from within her, and her connection to the All-Mind grew stronger than ever before. Being here felt so good, she never wanted to leave.

At first, she managed to disregard the insistent pull by her physical form, but eventually, it could no longer be ignored. Once she reentered her body, the memory of the 'Sending' rose up once more. The shock of that horrible nightmare and last minute rescue began to overwhelm her. Arianna was jolted awake and found herself in the darkness of her familiar room. Her heart was racing, and she was bathed in sweat. Her breathing came in short bursts, and her whole body was shaking. The princess sobbed with relief at still being alive. Tears of terror but also of pure joy were relentlessly running down her now flushed cheeks. Deep love for her savior filled her.

The warning the Goddess had given her came back to her mind. How could she best get ready for what was coming her way? Arianna kept going over the Lady's words. Something, someone who meant her harm was coming into her life. It seemed she needed to hide her actual capabilities and extensive knowledge of all the varied subjects she had been privileged to learn.

Some of that should not be too difficult since, to begin with, a lot of the training had been done in secret. Her mother had started it that way, and her schooling had become even more clandestine after she made the compromise with her aunt and father. She had just been grateful that they allowed her the freedom to continue such learning at all.

Pushing back her soft down covers, the princess lay there panting until the lingering terror of the so very horrific 'Sending' started to subside. Her body and mind began to calm, and she became aware of her surroundings. Soft light was illuminating the darkness around her. The silver rays of the rising moon were working their way across her chamber on silent feet. Soon the tall windows of the tower room allowed the shimmering radiance to wash her entire bed with its bright, peaceful glow and Arianna started to relax.

A soft rustling drew her attention. Immediately, her whole body tensed up again, and she was back on alert. Looking around, the princess spotted an enormous white owl sitting on the window sill staring back at her. That had to be the largest owl she had ever seen! The huge bird regarded her solemnly for a moment longer and then flew off into the night on silent wings.

Remembering the sharp pain she had felt right before being catapulted out of the spell, Arianna reached up to examine her earlobe. Her fingers felt something wet, and when she held them into the silvery moonlight, she saw that they were covered in blood. That feathered creature had bitten her! That was what had jolted her out of the deadly 'Sending'! The Lady must have enlisted it to assist her. Racing to the window she called a soft "Thank you!" after the rapidly disappearing apparition.

Shivering in the cold night air, Arianna went back to her bed. Her thoughts returned to the words of the Lady once more. Whatever she was being warned about was not going to be good. The princess felt a deep sense of foreboding. So she would have to rely on herself soon. She could handle that. But, it had sounded to her as if she would be leaving behind her family and friends. That was much worse. Sadness filled her. She loved this castle and its inhabitants and would miss them all dearly. However, she had been taught how to survive on her own and had an excellent idea what she would need to do so. First thing in the morning she would get her things together and be ready for whatever was heading her way.

Still, the prospect of the unpleasant fate the Goddess had warned her of filled Arianna with apprehension. How she wished Kyrill, her winged friend, could be here with her right now! He had been in her life for so long that she had come to rely on his presence whenever she was troubled. The first time she had met him in a dream was on the night of her 9th birthday. He had been so gallant, so handsome and mysterious even then, and she had liked him immediately.

From then on, every year on her birthday she would see him once she was asleep. Once his people set up a hut away from the Aerie as a focus, she was able to visit him anytime she wished and did so often. He always came to her when she was upset and needed his support. When her mother had died, she had cried herself to sleep every night. And, every night he had been there for her. He and his family had been a great comfort in that terrible time of loss.

At first, they had just been friends, but as they grew to know each other better over the years, friendship had changed to attraction and then the beginnings of love. To her, he was the most handsome and fascinating man she had ever encountered. None of the boys or young princes she met in her waking hours had been able to compare.

Arianna had fallen in love with Kyrill's warm brown eyes, his sharp aquiline profile, and his dark brown hair which nearly touched his powerful shoulders. He often wore it parted on one side, and when it fell across one of his eyes, it gave him the look of a dashing adventurer. She had been amazed the day he had shown her his wings and loved the stories he told her about his secluded mountain home. What would she not give to lay eyes on such a wondrous place! Because of his people being very reserved, they had always met away from the Aerie, in the hut which had been set up for just that purpose.

She had realized early on that those dreams were different, they were so real that it felt like she had lived them. Arianna was an active participant and could always remember them vividly once she awakened. Eventually, on the advice of her mentor, the princess had started writing them down. He gave her a special book just for this purpose, and she discovered that she could remember more and more details as she was putting the stories on paper. How this was possible was beyond her understanding, and even her tutor had been at a loss to explain.

Arianna and Baladazar, her teacher and friend, had spent many an hour looking for some reference to the winged people in the wizard's immense library. They had just about given up when they finally found mention in one of the most ancient books. The well-worn tome had described the different kinds of people in their world, present and past, and amongst these were humans with wings. According to this source, the flying people had been shapeshifters and descendants of pairings between humans and magical birds. These amazing beings were able to switch from full human to full bird and many stages in between.

The book had been so very old, and it had stated that no one had seen the avian tribes for many years. They were thought to have fled from persecution by the ever increasing human population into the desolate mountains far to the Northwest. Reading this had filled Arianna with deep sadness. How she would have loved to meet Kyrill and his people!

If her friend was real, he was far, far away. With that kind of a distance between them, how could she ever find out if he existed? In any case, the princess saw little chance that their path would ever cross. There was always so much going on at her home, and her father was busy most of the time. She did get to travel around the kingdom with him on occasions, but it had been years since Arianna had even been to her grandparents' place in the next kingdom over. Remembering Kyrill's gentle touch and loving words, Arianna finally drifted off into a restless slumber.

~

It was not long before she began to dream and he was there, holding her, comforting her. When she felt sufficiently calm, she told him of the misfortune which had befallen her this very night and all she had learned from her Goddess.

The young man was deeply concerned, and the couple discussed the best options for getting prepared for the upcoming situation. Once they had made a tentative plan, the girl finally managed to find some tranquility. Her sleep deepened and her body relaxed. Being here with him felt so peaceful, so right that Arianna fervently wished that she could stay in his arms in that serene mountain place forever.

~~~

Chapter One

An Unwelcome Proposal

It was a beautiful spring morning at Castle Maridar. The fortress was a welcoming dwelling, bright and inviting and filled with cheerful and pleasant people. The town of Maridee had grown up next to the stronghold and spread out to the west and south. Fertile fields and lush woods surrounded the place on three sides and the sea on the fourth.

The palace was located in the orderly kingdom of Maridanmar. Its closest neighbor to the northwest was the mountain realm of Re'adeen. Southwest lay the territory of Larandar, to the south the large domain of Lothrien, and to the east and north, the restless Salten Sea.

Maridanmar's sovereign, King Roderic, was just and fair and the people of the realm mostly happy. The marriage of the then prince to the beautiful Princess Anna of Re'adeen 20 years ago had established a lasting bond between these two kingdoms. This made them a force to be reckoned with. The monarchs had decided to send out invitations to join with them and, being tired of war, several other rulers had accepted their proposal. Peace treaties had been signed, alliances had been formed, and a time of harmony began for the 'Eleven Kingdoms'. War and the frequent squabbles leading up to it became a thing of the past.

For some time now, going on seven years, the threat of violence hung in the air once more. Many had cursed the day the beloved King Randolf had died under mysterious circumstances, and the much despised Prince Vargos had become King of Lothrien. The incident, which led to the unfortunate father's death had been too bizarre and caused nagging questions in the other rulers' minds. Had it truly been an accident or something more sinister? Had the son grown tired of waiting for the throne and had taken things into his own hands?

The father had been an honest and peace-loving monarch, but the son was nothing like him. The new king was petty, deceitful, and according to those who had dealings with him, without even a sliver of a conscience or honor. There were rumors that he was involved with the Dark Arts and that his dragon of a housekeeper was more than she seemed.

Most of the other kings did not put it past Vargos to have somehow caused his sire's deaths. This notion alone left them all wary of this newest member of their ranks. The man's actions since his ascendancy to the throne had only reinforced those feelings. The wily sovereign had quickly created the biggest army in the land which had allowed him to make himself the 'de facto' ruler of all.

Having this kind of a tyrant as an overlord was a recipe for trouble. It was, therefore, a blessing that Castle Maridar was a fortress, as were all the castles of the surrounding kingdoms. Most of them had been built long ago when frequent disputes between the realms had led to wars. As it was customary at the time, one domain or another would end up laying siege to the home of a fellow king. An efficient defense had been the first priority in the building of any town or palace since no king liked being conquered.

Maridar's large compound consisted of four tall, easily defendable towers adjoining one large building. The castle was protected by thick walls designed to act as a last defense and could be held with a small force. In spite of having been built to give shelter in case of war, the place was pleasant with light and airy rooms and a rather cheerful atmosphere. The entire complex sat on a rise and was enclosed by a well-maintained moat, steep cliffs which dropped down to the sea, and the town of Maridee.

King Roderic had never relaxed his vigilance. Even in times of peace, the castle was kept at the ready for the townspeople to come in and find shelter in the event of an emergency. And, just in case, the fortress was always prepared to withstand an unexpected siege. That was still a carryover from more turbulent times but being a wise and circumspect man, the cautious monarch had never let it slip.

During the reign of the king's father, more walls had been built for additional protection. The fortifications did not just encircle the royal residence but also the town which surrounded it. The son had 'improved' on these defenses during his rule. Peace, however, had reigned in the kingdoms for so long that the gates were always kept open during daylight hours. The town and castle were a welcoming place for all weary travelers.

It was the 2nd day of Avril when all that changed. The day was so delightfully sunny and the feeling of spring in the air so pleasantly cheerful that no one was prepared for what was to happen on this fateful day.

~

The sun had barely risen when riders began to come into sight. At first, two individuals, later assumed to be scouts, were spotted. Then, more and more men emerged from the forest. The travelers were lined up in pairs and looked like soldiers or guards.

As the concerned town sentries watched, the column grew longer and longer. A carriage appeared and then more warriors. No flag of any kind was in sight; it seemed this group did not care to identify themselves. The dire news was immediately taken to the king who put the castle and town on high alert. He ordered all gates closed since the approaching force was good sized and no guests were expected for the next few days.

Was this friend or foe? The column was around a hundred men strong, large enough to lay siege to the fortress. Since no friends were anticipated, the inhabitants were accordingly alarmed. The castle and kingdom were a respectful kind of place. Everybody knew that anyone planning a visit would have sent a rider ahead to inquire if this was a convenient time for them to grace the castle and its occupants with their presence. It was common courtesy to do so and acknowledged by all those who considered themselves part of polite society in the Eleven Kingdoms.

This bunch, on the other hand, seemed to have no manners at all. They were not even displaying their flag, a show of blatant disrespect. Nor did the uniforms of the riders give any clue to which Lord they might owe allegiance to. No one with good intentions would approach the town in such a way. Apprehension grew as the column came closer and it became apparent that this group of soldiers was divided into three companies. A front guard with scouts, the men guarding the carriage, followed by a rear guard and three wagons. What could this lot possibly want in their kingdom?

It was past mid-morning when the first men of the column neared Maridee. The guards could now make out that the soldiers did have a flag, but were purposely keeping it rolled up. At a safe distance outside the town's defenses, the company in front peeled off and took up position to the right of the road allowing the riders guarding the coach to continue forward towards the gates.

Those troops also came to a stop well away from the castle, almost as if an invisible line had been drawn somewhere there in the sand. The rear guard took up position in the field to the left of the road. All the soldiers stayed mounted and on alert, ready to defend themselves at a moment's notice. The air was charged with their hostility, and the castle guards were exchanging nervous glances. Who were these men and what did they want?

An officer from the middle company rode forward. He stopped right in front of the city gates and demanded entry in the name of King Vargos. The town guards in return asked the captain to identify himself and for a presentation of the colors to verify the group's allegiance. On the soldier's signal, the flag was finally unfurled displaying the dark and ominous insignia of the much-feared king. Trepidation in the hearts of the city's defenders grew since any contact with the tyrannical monarch had always been to their disadvantage.

An exchange between the city guards and the soldier, a captain called Angus, ensued. The officer of the day, not wanting to take responsibility for allowing even one of these men inside the town, dispatched a runner to the castle to get orders directly from the king. Soon word came from their

Lord. Only the captain and the soldiers guarding the carriage would be allowed to enter. The rest of the force were to remain in the field outside and wait for their comrades to return.

The gates were opened, and a group of around 30 men was allowed inside before the guards quickly barred the heavy doors once more. An escort of King Roderic's men waited to conduct the guests to the castle. The visitors lined up and fell in behind them. First came soldiers, and then a little dignitary splendidly dressed and riding a magnificent horse. All these riches could not disperse the impression that the man looked amazingly like a very large toad. Next followed the carriage, then more fighters.

The small, pompous gent acted like a person of great importance. Not knowing his status or who he was, King Roderic's guards conducted him to the castle with all the ceremony befitting a monarch. It was evident how much the man enjoyed this. His unpleasant features were spread in a strange looking grin. It almost appeared as if the fellow's face had forgotten what it was like to smile and his features could only contort themselves into this kind of bizarre grimace lacking any trace of actual joy. The closer they got to the castle, the more did his fat little body inflate with pleasure at being treated as a person of such standing.

The town's people had watched the soldiers passing through their midst with stern disapproval but had half-heartedly cheered when their king's runners had bidden them do so. King Vargos's troops, here, in their town! The evil despot's reputation was known to all, and many would have rather spit on his men or hidden in their houses than cheered for them.

Fear at the mention of that much-cursed name had spread through the kingdoms over the years like a growing disease. Seeing his fighters heading for their castle filled most of the townsfolk with a distinct sense of foreboding. No good ever came from a visit from these soldiers. The citizens' whispered speculations only halted long enough for the warriors to pass. What could that tyrant possibly want from their beloved king?

~

The diminutive man in front of the carriage puffed himself up more and more as he was being cheered on by the people of this pleasant little town. He was relieved to be in a realm where the king appeared to have better discipline than most. The dignitary disregarded the hostile glares coming from the cheering faces and basked in their feigned adoration. Any agreeable greeting was better than the usual stony silence or the rock, rotten fruit, or vegetables which seemed to come shooting at them out of nowhere in most places.

He, Sebastian, was his king's envoy and for once, he was being treated as was befitting his station. The honor accorded to him filled his withered heart with warmth and pride, and when he and his group was greeted with a trumpet fanfare at the castle's front gates, he nearly cried. The emissary was almost sorry for the horrible request he had been ordered to make of these so very nice people.

~

Not long after the envoy was conducted into the king's presence, the monarch called for his eldest daughter, Princess Arianna. The girl had been instantly filled with a deep feeling of utter dread and had waited as long as she dared before finally obeying her father's request. The young woman's sense of unease increased to almost unbearable levels when she entered the throne room. Her knees began to shake.

The princess was sure that the summons had to do with their unwelcome visitors. She had heard about the horrible death of King Vargos's last wife a few months back. The emissary of that ghastly king paying them a visit and then her being asked to come to the throne room could only mean one thing.

King Roderic, seeing her ashen face, instantly rushed to her side and gently guided the shaking princess to a sitting area nearby. He was only too aware that his young daughter could sense trouble ahead. Arianna was very sensitive and well versed in magic. Her gut feelings were telling her that something very unpleasant was about to take place. Was this the event the Goddess had warned her about?

Putting on a brave face, the girl decided to try the cheery approach. Maybe this would alleviate what was to follow at least a little. "Good morning, father! How are you today? Isn't it a perfect day? The first really warm day this spring!" "Good morning, Arianna, yes it is a nice day," the king answered, but his face was set in a frown. "Leave, all of you, and close the doors!" the king bellowed over his shoulder. Arianna was taken aback. There had been very few times in her life she had seen her parent in this foul a mood. She waited until all the guards and courtiers had left then turned to him. "What is it, father? Has something happened?" she asked apprehensively.

Her dad looked at her somberly. His handsome face was pale and his startling light blue eyes were dark with concern. Even his light brown hair seemed to have lost some of its sheen. King Roderic was a fair and kind man and what he was about to do went against everything he believed in. How could he best break this devastating news to his oldest child? "My daughter, my beloved Arianna, listen to me," the king started gently. He was trying to reassure her, but his words had the opposite effect. Now she knew she was really in trouble! The girl sat quietly next to her father. When he enfolded her chilled fingers in his large hands, her trepidation grew further. This had to be really bad!

The last time he had talked to her like this had been on the day her mother died so many years ago, a day she had never forgotten. It had been a bright and sunny morning when the queen had gone out riding with a couple of her guards. Just like this day, it had also been the first pleasantly warm spring morning. A snake sunning itself on the mountain path to the upper lake had caused the queen's horse to spook. Arianna's mother had been a superb horsewoman, but those skills did not save her that day. Both she and the horse had gone over the side of the cliff and, mercifully, neither had survived the fall.

Her dad was usually calm and always extruded a quiet air of authority. He very seldom got upset over anything. The princess had been watching him carefully. Her father seemed almost as distressed as on that horrible day the queen had died. His forehead was wrinkled with worry, and his mouth looked pinched. She figured that it must be really awful news for him to behave this way and felt a sinking feeling in the pit of her stomach.

The king was trying to gather his thoughts. How could he best tell this bright young woman the destiny he was forced to condemn her to? It did not help that she looked so much like her mother! Anna had been beautiful with waist long reddish blond hair and mischievous bright green eyes. He missed her terribly, especially right now. How could he make Arianna understand that he had no choice in this matter? If it were up to him and at all possible, he would spare her this fate. But, how could he doom an entire kingdom to save one young princess?

His daughter could be willful, and these dreadful words had to be said in just the right way if he wanted to gain her cooperation. Discarding several options, he decided on the most honest and direct approach. "Sweetheart, King Vargos has sent an envoy asking for your hand in marriage." The king saw his daughter visibly pale and felt her begin to tremble. The princess's worst fears had been confirmed.

The sovereign of Lothrien, King Vargos, was a cruel and hard man. His kingdom, which he governed with an iron fist, was much larger than theirs. So was his well-trained army. The despised ruler had a standing force much greater than King Roderic's and the other neighboring kingdoms. The unpleasant monarch was the most powerful of them all and would stop at nothing to get what he wanted. None of the other royals dared to stand up against this vicious tyrant who was well known for being unbending, uncompromising, and relentless when he wanted something. And, now it seemed that he wanted young Arianna.

King Darian of Wymara, the father of the last bride, Princess Alyssa, had not wanted to give his daughter to this dark and brooding man, but his hand had been forced as well. News of terrible events had a way of spreading, even when one tried to suppress them. It was well known that King Vargos's first two wives had died an appalling death under rather mysterious circumstances. King Darian had not wanted a similar fate for his beloved daughter, but Vargos had threatened to invade the kingdom and to take the princess by force if need be. The cruel ruler had done just that when the father of his first wife Sara, King Georg of Daladion, had refused him.

The once thriving kingdom south of Wymara had been overrun by Lothrien's army in record time and before they could even mount a defense. Thousands had died, and the castle and every town in the monarchy had been destroyed, the realm laid to waste. King Georg had been publicly executed and his body treated with the utmost disrespect. The tyrant had made sure that the news of what had been done to Daladion spread even to the furthest reaches.

Word had gotten around that to Vargos all life, other than his own, was cheap and that he would punish any who crossed him. Any ruler trying to take a stand against him might end up with a rebellion of his own people on his hands. Knowing all this, the beleaguered King Darian had seen no way to deny the evil despot without putting his entire kingdom at risk. He had been forced to sacrifice his daughter for the continued survival of his people. The death of his child just a year later had left him a bitter and broken man who was unable to forgive himself for not taking a stand.

"Arianna, I am so very sorry, but I am forced to accept. If I do not, Vargos will bring war to our doorstep. He laid his first wife's home to waste, burned the castle and the fields, and hunted down and killed her entire family. He beheaded her father, King Georg, and hung his body from what was left of the castle gates as a warning to all of us. I not only have a responsibility to you but also to the rest of our family as well as the people of our kingdom. I would like nothing more than to spare you this fate, but I do not know how," the devastated father explained.

"If I refuse, thousands will die, if I accept, I effectively sentence you to a nightmare life and maybe even an early death. I am well aware of the fate which awaits you, but what else can I do? My one comfort is that you are a resourceful young woman, strong and capable well beyond your years. You can handle situations most others could not. I am incredibly proud of you and know you will do your best.

I am so very sorry, my beloved child," King Roderic continued.

Tears were shimmering in the king's eyes. He was a compassionate man and always tried to see things from all sides. He knew his daughter well. The monarch had allowed her to be trained in a variety of subjects as well as in woodcraft and weaponry. At his wife's request, all this had been done in secret. It was not acceptable for a princess to learn such things and it could have ruined any chance of an acceptable marriage for this lively young girl.

His daughter, very much like her mother, had never been overly interested in the typical activities expected of a young princess. After losing his beloved wife, the king had not had the heart to force his determined offspring into learning more of the domestic tasks than her Aunt Margaret absolutely insisted upon. He would have never undermined the lady's authority, but had been instrumental in Arianna being allowed to continue her training when his sister-in-law discovered the other schooling the girl was receiving.

King Roderic had calmed the outraged queen and eventually convinced her to let things go on as they had for many years. It had not been easy, but he had finally been able to make the aunt understand how much this training meant to his daughter. His wife had encouraged and worked with Arianna from an early age on, and these activities were the last bond the young lady had to her mother. Forbidding them to the deeply hurt child would have been devastating. A compromise had been struck which had provided the added benefit of keeping the girl even busier than before. The extra classes in womanly duties kept his eldest so occupied that she had little time to focus on the terrible loss of her beloved mother.

Now he was glad that he had supported this unorthodox training since it would allow Arianna to survive where few other princesses could. He feared that she would need all her extensive skills before this was all over and done with. The king knew that his daughter loved their people. He could tell by her saddened face that she was ready to make this awful sacrifice for her family and kingdom. He had never been more proud of her than at that moment.

~

King Roderic, however, was not prepared to allow her to pay this terrible price. He could not openly defy that monster of Lothrien. Secretly, however, he could encourage his beloved child to think of a way out. And, the monarch was determined to provide her with the means to do so. If it were done right, Vargos would not be able to place blame on him or his kingdom. This ruse might safeguard them all and would buy Roderic time to make some alliances of his own. It would also allow the rest of the family to set out for a place of safety. The oppressed lord might not be able to stand up against the despot, but that did not mean that he had to turn his daughter over to that cruel tyrant without giving her a chance.

The troubled father's heart ached at the shocked and desperate look on his daughter's face. He pulled her close to him as tears started to spill down her face. "Shhh, little one. You are made from a different cloth than those other unlucky princesses. You can survive where they did not. You are the bravest, smartest young woman I know, you will be fine!" he tried to console her.

Pulling Arianna closer and burying his face in her hair to prevent anyone from realizing what he was up to, he whispered. "Listen to me and listen well. We might be spied upon even in here so keep up the crying. I do not want you to go through with this, do you understand?" His daughter gently squeezed his hand. He could feel the shaking of her body slow, but her desperate sobs were still echoing around the chamber.

The princess had grasped immediately what her father expected of her. She very convincingly kept up the pretense of being utterly devastated by the news. "I want you to go along with this farce willingly until you get out of this kingdom. I will send guards along until you get to the border. That way, no blame can be placed on this realm. Once you have escaped, it would help if you could make them believe that you are dead. I know the rapport you have with wild animals, I am sure you will think of something. Keep going north until you reach your mother's kingdom, then head for the mountains there. Remember Road's End?" Once again Arianna squeezed her father's hand.

The king continued. "When you get there, look for an old man named Olaf. You met him long ago. He will help you reach the Hidden Castle. Avoid being seen as much as possible and trust your instincts. You are the most capable young woman I know, so much like your mother, you will find a way. I am so sorry I cannot defend you or help you more, my love. Make sure that you see Baladazar before you leave today, he has some things you will need. Take the secret passage, no one must know."

"King Vargos has spies everywhere, even here in this castle and especially right now that we have come to his attention. Do you understand? I am sorry that this is the best I can do for you. It might still bring war to my door. I do believe that the other kings will come to my aid if I am unjustly attacked, but they would not if I openly defied that tyrant. They all fear him. Stick to the plan, please, since I require that time to get defenses in place and send your sisters and aunt to safety," King Roderic whispered urgently.

Arianna gently pressed her dad's hand letting him know she understood. The king was stroking her long, shining hair. He was muttering platitudes more loudly now, talking to her as you would to a distressed child. During her father's whispered words, hope had grown in the girl's heart. The young woman understood that her dad had no other option and that this daring plan would prevent her from ever returning home. She had contemplated such action herself but had discarded the notion for the benefit of the kingdom. The princess was grateful that it gave her a chance for a more pleasant life than she would have had at Darkmoor Castle. She was prepared to do whatever was necessary to avoid the horrible fate which would await her as King Vargos's bride.

Father and daughter remained embraced for a few more moments, taking comfort from the closeness. They were both aware that these were most likely the last minutes they would have alone together.

Finally, King Roderic gently released his oldest child. "Come, let us get this over with. You will be on your way to your husband this very day so go to your chamber and freshen up, put on a dress fit for travel, and say your good-byes to your sisters and aunt. Your future husband has sent a maid for you, so I am sorry to say, yours will be staying behind," the King said loudly.

"Do not forget Baladazar," he whispered while kissing her forehead. "Yes, father," Arianna replied audibly while giving his hands one last squeeze. She visibly pulled herself together, curtsied, and then left the room with her head held high.

~~~

Chapter Two

Saying Good-Bye

In the young princess's chambers, her usually happy maid Greta was sullenly packing her mistress's belongings into a large trunk. She was almost done and was just about to put Arianna's jewelry case in the chest filled with dresses and shoes. "Greta, wait!" Arianna said gently, taking the box. "I wish to wear some of it to look beautiful for my new husband and give a couple of the pieces to my sisters to remember me by," she explained to the anxious maid. "Am I going with you, Princess? No one told me to pack anything! Are you to go all alone to that horrible place?" Greta asked her mistress, eyes wide with distress and pooling with tears. The young woman was not just a servant but had been her confidante since early childhood. Seeing her obvious unhappiness, Arianna embraced her longtime friend.

"My future husband has sent a maid along for me, Greta. Seems he has thought of everything." She said bitterly. "I will miss you and your smiling face, and all the laughter we have shared. I want to give you a piece of my jewelry, as a memory of better days. I think this pendant will look pretty on you. The stone is an amethyst and its purple color will look lovely with your blond hair and violet eyes." "Thank you, miss! I will cherish this and always wear it! I just wished there was something I could do for you!" Greta replied with tears in her eyes. The young women embraced one final time before the maid fled out the door sobbing. Taking the jewelry, Arianna went looking for her sisters.

As she figured, the younger girls were in the solarium playing games. She was the oldest of five children. Their mother had loved nature and the sea and had named the children accordingly. Her name, Arianna, could mean either *Silver Goddess, Star,* or *Pure of Heart.* Her only brother's name, Dylan, stood for *Son of the Sea.* He was just eleven months younger than she and was at this time being fostered by King Richard at Corydee Castle in Larandar. Her three sisters all had water names. Dionna, meaning *From the Sacred Spring*, Mareena - *From the Sea*, and Genna - *White Wave*. They were each about a year apart, the youngest, Genna, had just turned seven at the time of the tragic accident of their beloved mother, Queen Anna.

King Roderic had been tremendously grateful when their aunt, Queen Margret of Re'adeen, took over the raising and educating of his offspring. The queen was his wife's older, widowed sister. Grief had left its mark on her. She was very different from their happy and high-spirited mother, but she genuinely loved the children.

~

Margret had lost both her husband and teenage son in a terrible accident and had never wed again. The two had been the loves of her life and since her kingdom was prosperous and the coffers well filled, she had seen no reason to remarry. Therefore, she had determinedly turned down any suitor appearing on her doorstep, and there had been many. The queen was a beautiful woman, tall and slender like her sister, with auburn hair and cornflower blue eyes. A good looking woman together with a well to do realm had been an irresistible draw.

Growing up, the lady had been very envious of her much younger sister. Anna had been born when Margaret was 16 years old. The new baby had been a welcome surprise to King Rudemont and Queen Irena of Re'adeen. The couple had given up hope for another child long ago. The infant had been doted on and spoiled, much to the disgust of her older sister. Having been an only child for so many years, the young woman was terribly jealous and resented all the care lavished on 'the brat', as she had taken to calling her younger sibling. She felt that her parents should have been taking care of more important matters, such as looking for a husband for their oldest daughter, instead.

The unhappy princess had felt pushed aside and forgotten and when she did not find a suitor that year or the next, she had blamed all the attention wasted on that baby. If her parents had not been so preoccupied with that brat and had put a little more effort into procuring appropriate suitors, she might have met someone. They had not even accompanied her to all the balls at the neighboring kingdoms. Instead, they had sent her aunt Selda, her mother's younger sister, along for a couple of the dances when the baby was ill. In Margaret's eyes, it was all the fault of that small nuisance that she had not met the man of her dreams. She had almost hated the tiny intruder.

As it was, Margret did meet a handsome prince later that year at a tea party she attended with her aunt and was married early the next. Her parents went all out, and it was a lovely wedding. Feeling a bit more charitable towards her younger sibling, she even let the toddler be part of the ceremony as a flower girl. The small child had been so cute and had shown such love and adoration for her older sister that Margaret had been unable to keep disliking Anna. So on her wedding day, she had finally opened her heart to her little sister. Over the years, a tight bond formed between the two so very different siblings.

Having been raised a very correct princess, Margaret was aghast at the unusual way the youngster was allowed to grow up. It seemed that her parents threw all the conventions of proper child rearing out of the window when it came to their youngest child. Secretly, however, Margret envied her younger sister's confidence in demeanor, her ability to ride a horse bareback, to hunt, to fish, and to defend herself. While she had been mostly confined to the castle growing up, Anna roamed the countryside and accompanied their father on hunting and fishing trips.

King Rudemont had allowed his youngest daughter to receive a well-rounded education that would have done any prince or princess proud. She could out track and outshoot most of the boys, but was just as comfortable serving tea to royal guests. Also, the monarch had realized very early on that the child was gifted in magic. He and his queen had secretly furthered her education in this field as well. The indulgent father loved his precocious child and always found some reason to take Anna along on his travels around the kingdom. The two would return and report how fabulous a time they had had and talk about all the things they had discovered on their way. After a while, they had even managed to convince Queen Irena to join them.

~

The death of her younger sister had hit Margret hard. When King Roderic had asked her if she would like to stay and help him with the children for a while, she had immediately traveled back to her home, packed up her things, put her trusted steward and parents in charge, and moved to Maridar Castle. The youngsters were all very sensitive and had been devastated by their mother's passing. The love and understanding their aunt showed them helped to slowly heal that terrible wound. Being part of a family again had allowed Margaret to mend from her losses as well. She grew to love her nieces and nephew as much as she had her deceased son and raised them as if they were her own.

The lady was a patient and tolerant parent, and she wanted the best for her charges. At first, she had been too preoccupied with grief to take note of all of Arianna's carefully hidden exploits. Eventually, however, she had discovered some of her niece's 'secret' training. At first, Margaret had blamed that kind of schooling for her sister's death and would not hear of the princess following in her mother's footsteps. King Roderic had to have some serious talks with her before she began to come around. The girl's pleas and remembering how well her sister had actually done with her varied learning, had finally swayed her. She did insist, however, that in return for continuing with all that covert education, Arianna's instructions would also include subjects every princess needed to know.

Margaret believed in doing things properly. Once she had committed to this course of action, she set out to make sure it was done right. She was reasonably certain that Anna had already started training Arianna in magic, but the lady now felt that had her sister received more extensive schooling on the subject, the accident might have been prevented. Upon her insistence, Roderic approached their court wizard, Baladazar. The king politely requested that the old mage should begin teaching the girl more than just basic magic. The training was to be done in secret. The magician had acted a bit sheepishly at first. He had finally confessed to his monarch that Queen Anna had tasked him with intensely training the princess several years ago. The only response King Roderic had to this revelation was to laugh. Leave it to his late wife to have thought of everything.

~

The Queen of Re'adeen dearly loved all the children, but this wild, oldest child painfully reminded her of her beloved sister whom she missed very much. The three younger girls were such demure and quiet young women, very unlike the way Anna had been. They would have never asked on their own to learn some of the things their sister was so enjoying. The lady, remembering her own envy of her youngest sibling's carefree life and amazingly diverse capabilities, got it in her head that it might help cheer up the saddened children to get outside and study something different. Margaret, therefore, insisted that the younger girls should learn at least the fundamentals of surviving on their own out in the woods in case of an emergency.

Arianna was delighted by the idea of passing some of her knowledge on to her sisters and happily took them in hand. On outings away from the castle, the older girl taught them how to track game, how to kill and dress it, and how to catch and clean fish. She showed her younger siblings the best way to start a fire, helped them understand the meaning of the different sounds and sights of the forest, made a fun game of blending in with their surroundings, and much more. The girls had protested at first but ended up having a fabulous time since Arianna had a knack for making learning fun. Little did any of them know that this would one day save their lives.

~

"Arianna!" the younger girls exclaimed excitedly as their sister entered the room and rushed up to embrace her. Margaret, seeing her oldest charge's pale face, hurried to her side. "Child, what is it? What has happened?" Throwing herself into her aunt's arms, Arianna began to sob. The queen led the princess to one of the couches and sat down beside her. Wrapping her in a tight embrace, she gently rocked the girl, all the time stroking her long hair, just as she had done so many times after the children's mother had died. Slowly the tears subsided. "Now tell me, what is going on?" Margaret asked again. Looking up, Arianna was about to share the morning's news with her when King Roderic entered the room. Taking in at one glance his crying oldest daughter and her worried siblings and aunt he sighed. "King Vargos demands her hand in marriage, and I see no way to refuse him. Please say your good-byes, child, and do not forget that errant I gave you!"

Margret gasped in horror at his words. Having heard all the stories circulating about this cruel king, she understood that King Roderic's hand was being forced in this matter, but she did not like this turn of events. The lady quickly responded to the monarch's hand motion to join him in the adjacent room. Once the door was closed behind them, the king slumped and hung his head in defeat. Seeing the devastation on his face, the queen went to hug the unhappy father. Roderic, returning her embrace, buried his face in her hair. They stood such holding each other in silence for a long moment, each taking comfort from the others presence.

Being careful not to be overheard or observed, King Roderic whispered into the lady's ear. "Arianna will not wed King Vargos. She will get away from his courtiers once she is out of our lands. I have told her to escape and make it look like she has met with a violent death by a bear or wolf perhaps. Or has taken a deadly fall, anything to shake them off her trail. Do you know what this means?" Margret's sharp intake of breath told him that she understood the consequences of such a course of action for the unfortunate girl as well as the danger this could create for them all.

The dismayed aunt was relieved to hear that Arianna would escape the horrific fate of becoming this brutal king's next doomed wife, but her heart instantly filled with fear for the rest of the family. She understood that there were no good options left to them, and all they could do was try to get through this dreadful situation the best they could. The lady felt deep sadness at the imminent parting with her beloved niece. Her oldest charge would not be able to return home as long as King Vargos ruled or lived. She fervently hoped that the girl would be able to make good her escape and fake her death. No matter what happened, that tyrant would be furious and not only at his men. He would also blame Arianna's family and possibly demand one of the younger sister's as his wife instead.

The lady's heart could not bear the notion of any of the children being subjected to that monster. Margaret was greatly relieved when she heard the king whisper "Get the girls ready for travel tonight, pack lightly, I mean very lightly. Take only what you absolutely need. You must leave unobserved, in your wood clothes, and with only Anders for protection. I no longer know who I can trust in my own home, but I do believe I can trust him." Roderic paused for a moment, and a thoughtful expression crossed his face. "On second thought, I think I will send Baladazar with you too. His life is in danger as well. Can you get yourself and the girls to the Hidden Castle where you will be safe?"

Before she could answer, he continued. "If I can arrange marriages for the girls with some of my neighboring king's sons, I would have allies, and we might yet survive this. I will send news of this enforced marriage to the other rulers along with requests for an alliance by marriage just as soon as Vargos's thugs have left the castle and are out of sight."

The Queen of Re'adeen thought for a moment. The Hidden Castle had been the family's sanctuary for generations, always kept secret except for a select few trusted servants and soldiers who were stationed there to ensure that the place was maintained and guarded. It was a small, but impenetrable fortress built into the very rock of the mountain and defensible with even a negligible force. It was always kept well stocked, and she had made sure that this remained this way. It would be the perfect place to take the children to keep them safe.

The lady realized that her nephew would be in danger as well. She needed to have Roderic sent Dylan to meet up with them on the way. "Together with Anders I can get us to the castle, but Dylan should join us, he will not be safe from Vargos's wrath in Larandar," she finally whispered. The queen knew that she needed to keep the younger princesses hidden until they were old enough to be married to make sure that the girls would escape the fate of their sister. Giving the king one last reassuring squeeze, Margaret stepped back. She returned to the solarium to say her good-byes to the child who was so very much like her beloved sister. Her heart was aching, this felt almost like losing Anna all over again.

~

Arianna, in the meantime, had given each of her siblings a piece of jewelry which could be easily hidden under their clothes. To Dionna, she had given a pendant with a beautiful green stone reflecting her sister's sparkling green eyes. Mareena had received an arm ring to be worn on her upper arm, well out of sight, set with her sister's favorite stone, light blue aquamarine. To Genna, she had presented a pendant with her birthstone, a sky blue sapphire.

Following a hunch, the princess had spelled the items several days ago, right after that horrible dream. "These pieces of jewelry have been imbued with magic. For safety, wear them hidden and always keep them with you. Please, do not sell them or give them away unless the need is dire. As long as these items are in your possession, I will be able to find you! Do not forget!" Arianna urged her siblings. "I love you and one day, I will see you again! Take care of each other and auntie," she continued. "Thank you, Arianna, for these beautiful gifts, and we will always keep them with us, we promise!" the girls responded sadly. The sisters hugged, tears rolling down their faces.

The distraught princesses turned as one as the door opened and Margret came back into the room. She walked over and embraced Arianna. "Be strong, my little dove, and fly true, like your mother would have. You are so much like her, strong and resilient and always able to find your way in life. You will be fine. And, thanks to your teachings, so will your sisters," Margret whispered. "Please, Auntie, take Greta with you. She has always been my true friend," Arianna pleaded, keeping her voice low. "If that is your wish then I will, I promise," the queen replied softly.

Holding her niece at arm's length, Margret looked deep into her eyes. She smiled at the beautiful young woman before her. "Have courage, my darling! You are the bravest girl I know and if anyone can handle that king, you can. You will be all right, and it will all turn out well in the end, just have faith! We will all miss you, but maybe one day soon your husband will let you come visit. We will see you again, until then, know that we love you," the queen continued loudly before stepping back.

"Thank you, Auntie. I will miss all of you very much as well and love you. May I ask a favor of you? I have this pendant. It was my mother's. I do not want to take it with me, please, would you keep it for me?" Arianna replied. "Oh, child!" Margret exclaimed as she saw the necklace. With a nod, she gave Arianna permission to place the beautiful emerald pendant around her neck.

The lady remembered her sister wearing this same piece of jewelry most of her life. It had been her favorite, and she had worn it almost every day, even on that fateful day. "I would be honored to keep this for you! I know how much this means to you! Are you sure you do not want to take it with you?" Arianna, unable to speak, could only shake her head. Her face was wet with tears. Her aunt embraced her one last time just as her father entered the room. The unhappy princess knew it was time to go. Her jewelry case she left sitting on the table. She had no intent on taking it with her only to have to leave it behind.

Arianna faced her sire and nodded. Drawing this painful good-bye out any longer would only hurt them all more than it already had. When her sisters and aunt were about to follow them, the king held up his hand. "No, please stay! The less these vultures see of you, the better. I am sure you have things to do?" King Roderic asked kindly.

The monarch exchanged a knowing look with Margret as he pulled closed the door. "Have you said good-bye to everyone? Vargos's people are in the banquet hall, and I bet they are getting impatient. I will go ahead and stall them for a bit longer. Go wash your face and get ready to go, child! Make sure you have everything you need. I will take them to the throne room and send for you in about 15 minutes," the king told his apprehensive daughter, reminding her with a look that she still needed to see the wizard. "Yes, father," Arianna replied rushing off to her rooms.

~

Her chamber appeared unoccupied, and the packed trunk was gone. Quickly, Arianna locked the door. After making sure the room was indeed empty, she rushed over to the fireplace. Twisting the candle holder to the left caused a door to open in the paneling, revealing a hidden passage. A staircase was leading up into the dark space. Closing the door behind her, the princess raced up the steps. She knew this flight of stairs like the back of her hand and needed no light. Time was of the essence. Baladazar was in his apartment waiting for her, and she rushed into his arms. "You will need a few things, my child, and we do not have much time," the old wizard told her, disengaging himself.

"Here, put these on under your dress when you get back to your room! They will help keep you warm out there in the woods," he ordered handing her a pair of leggings. "It will take two days to reach the border. Gunther, the captain of the guards, will be part of your escort. He will stash some of your brother's clothes, a knife, and a bow for you a little way over the border. He will leave you signs so you can find them. This packet contains a sleeping powder, completely tasteless. It cannot be detected even in water. If you need to, use illusion, do whatever you must. It is imperative that you get away the night after you leave this kingdom. Otherwise, you might not get another chance. If they believe you dead, perfect, if not just make sure they do not catch you. We will be prepared for the consequences by then. You know where to go?" Baladazar asked. Arianna nodded and took the package from the old man. She hugged him one last time and turned to go back to her room.

"Wait!" the wizard called after her. "Take this ring, child!" he said pulling an ornate band off his little finger. "Thank you! But Baladazar! That is your most potent charm! What if you need it?" Arianna protested when she realized how precious a gift he had just handed her. "I am old, child! You, my dear, have your entire life ahead of you. Besides, I have other tricks up my sleeve. Get going, young lady, before they get suspicious!" Arianna slipped the ring on her finger. She quickly gave the old wizard a last grateful hug.

~

The princess rushed down the stairs into her room, closing the panel behind her. She washed her face, pulled on the leggings and a clean dress. Following a gut feeling, the girl placed the ring and sleeping powder into a charmed pouch she always wore around her neck. She made sure that the leggings were well hidden by her stockings. It would not do to have them show under the dress. Just in time! A knocking on the door announced the arrival of Greta, coming to fetch her. Taking one last look around the room she had grown up in and which had been her sanctuary for so many years, she opened the door.

"It is time, lady," The young woman told her unhappily. "Thank you, Greta, and please take good care of yourself. I will miss your cheerful company and you stuffing me into dresses even when I did not feel like it at all," she told her faithful friend, confidant, and companion of many adventures. The two young women had been very close for years and had practically grown up together. In any other marriage, her maid would have gone with her to her new home. That they would be so cruelly parted one day neither had ever expected.

The maid started to walk alongside Arianna as she entered the hallway, but the princess stopped her. "Please, this is something I need to do alone. Look after Auntie and my sisters for me!" Greta turned to her mistress. Tears were brimming in her eyes as she hugged the princess. "The servant they sent for you is a witch, pull your powers deep inside you. Do not let her sense more than just a tiny bit of what you can do. Take this and use it on that woman, it will dull her senses. Good luck, my dearest friend!" Greta whispered urgently. She quickly pushed a small package into her mistress's skirt pocket before rushing off down the hall. Arianna looked after her in wonder. She would have to examine the bundle later, now was not the time.

So that king had sent a witch to keep an eye on her, had he now? That meant they might suspect that she had some abilities. She had been trained in secret so no one should know how much she could do and what aptitudes she did possess. In any case, she would have to play this very carefully. Many people had some gifts, and they often ran in families. If this woman detected no ability in her at all, she might become suspicious.

Arianna decided that appearing to have a small amount of latent power which seemed untrained and undisciplined would be best. That might prevent the witch from suspecting her true capabilities. The princess firmly set her shields in place in such a way that only a tiny hint of her magic was able to trickle through. She squared her shoulders. Lifting her head proudly, the young noblewoman made her way to the throne room.

~~~

Chapter Three

The Journey Begins

Everything after Arianna entered the throne room turned into a blur. She was presented to King Vargos's envoy, the pompous rather short man named Sebastian. His facial features and build reminded her of a big ugly toad, and even his hair was kind of mud colored. The emissary rudely looked her up and down with mean, squinty eyes, almost like you would a horse you were planning to buy. The princess could sense his dislike of her and wondered why he would feel that way. How could you loathe someone you had never even met?

Upon hearing of her acceptance to marry his sovereign, the envoy motioned to his soldiers. Arianna was immediately surrounded by her future husband's guards. In their hurry to get to her, the men crudely shoved aside anyone who was in their way. Two of them roughly grabbed her by the arms. No one had ever dared to touch her like that! The girl felt like she was being treated more like a prisoner than a royal bride. If this was an indication of things to come, she could not wait to escape.

King Roderic's jaws clenched seeing his daughter manhandled like that. He wanted to order those bullies to get his hands off her, but that would have been akin to a declaration of war. He hated feeling this helpless and was even more determined than ever to put an end to Vargos's tyranny. In an attempt to diffuse the situation, he issued a polite invitation to lunch which was irritably turned down. The princess was barely given time to utter one final good-bye to her infuriated father before she was pushed out of the door. The emissary and his guards quickly hustled her off to the waiting carriage where a loud dispute ensued between the king and the offensive little man.

While the envoy and Arianna's father were arguing, Greta came rushing out. Her resolute friend determinedly pushed her way through the soldiers until she reached the princess. Several of the men were treated to her sharp elbows or had their feet savagely stomped on. "Here you go, Pet! If they will not give you time for lunch, at least, you will have something to eat on the way. Looks like somebody forgot to teach this lot some manners!" Greta said loud enough for all to hear. She shot the fat little man a dirty look. How dare he treat her princess like this?

Giving her beloved mistress one last hug, the brash young woman stepped back and winked at the princess. Tossing her long blond braid over her shoulders, she headed back towards the castle entrance. Arianna noticed with amusement how the guards seemed to just kind of melt out of her friend's way. One soldier, caught unawares, did not move fast enough and was doubling over after Greta's passing. How she loved that woman! She would miss her dearly, both as a maid as well as a friend.

The envoy was not happy that her father's men were to accompany them on their way. King Roderic, however, insisted and had finally prevailed. The ugly little man's features were contorted with fury and his face bright red. "Get in that carriage!" he angrily hissed at the princess pointing at an attractive vehicle drawn by four magnificent horses. Just as she reached the top step, the man gave her a vicious shove sending her flying into the coach. He slammed the door shut, and they were on their way. By the time Arianna had picked herself up, they were clattering across the drawbridge. There had been no chance to even wave good-bye. The princess watched her home, and the town disappear in the distance with great sadness. She knew that as long as King Vargos lived, there would be no chance for her to return without bringing disaster to her kingdom.

~

King Roderic was standing on the castle steps watching the carriage harboring his precious daughter disappear into the town. He was seething with rage. Seeing his beloved child treated like that had pushed him beyond his tolerance. The king no longer cared about the consequences. Something had to be done about that monster Vargos! The irate father's feelings were reflected in the angry faces of many of the castle inhabitants. How dare these men treat their princess like this!

"Close the castle gates!" bellowed the king. "Place guards on all entrances! Nobody leaves this castle or comes in unless we know them! Send a runner to make sure the same goes for the city gates!" Being happy to have something to do, the guards jumped to the task with alacrity. They had been expecting these commands and the gates slammed shut on the heels of the messenger almost before the king was done issuing his orders.

The lord looked around. "Is anybody outside the walls that you know of?" "Only the goat boy, Sire, but then he is always out. As per your command, all stayed within the castle and the city. Those on the outside were fetched back in." Captain Caleb, the second in command, replied. "Good! Guard captains! Meeting in the great hall! All you others, listen up! There are some among us who are spying for King Vargos. They will betray us for the promise of a few pieces of cursed silver! What they will most likely get is a knife across the throat from that man! That king does not keep his word! Think and think hard about anyone's suspicious behavior and point them out to the guards! Get the castle ready for a siege!" their sovereign ordered.

Being happy that something would be done about the affront that had been perpetrated on them all by the disrespectful and harsh treatment of their beloved princess, the citizens of the castle cheered. Most were only too aware that standing up to the tyrannical monarch might cost them dearly, but at this moment, none of them truly cared. The insults which had been done to them by the men of this cruel despot had enraged them. The residents of Maridanmar loved their king and his family. Princess Arianna had been the one they knew and loved best. She had always been the most approachable of the royal children and had treated all with respect and kindness. If anyone had needed help, the girl had always done what she could. Even if it meant war, the castle's inhabitants would stand with their king.

~

Arianna, in the meantime, was speeding further and further away from her home. Occupying the seat opposite her in the carriage was a tall, striking woman. Could this be the witch Greta had warned her about? The lady's fair, unblemished skin seemed to fairly glow. The exquisite paleness of the woman's face was offset by her long midnight black hair which shimmered blue-black like a raven's wing.

The shining mass was confined in an intricate braid which fell neatly down her back and nearly reached her slender waist. An elegant black dress accentuated the woman's perfect figure. Even her stylish, pointy-toed shoes were ebony colored. Everything about the stranger seemed dark, but also mysteriously enthralling and beautiful. The princess had never seen a more stunning person.

The girl guessed from the other's perfectly smooth skin that she was just a few years older than herself. Her poise and manners, however, were of someone much older. There was an air of superiority about the lady which made the girl feel insignificant and small. The woman was so beautiful that she made the princess feel like she wanted to do anything she could to please her. The moment Arianna became aware of this effect, she realized that she was in trouble. There was powerful magic at work here, and she suspected that part of the amazing looks of this enthralling female were due to an artfully woven glamor.

The woman extruded some strange force of compulsion which was working on Arianna in spite of her being aware of its presence. How much sway must this kind of coercion have on an unshielded person! The princess could only assume that the troops were firmly under the witch's control. She would have to be very cautious since she was fairly certain that the soldiers in this escort would do anything this lady asked without a second's hesitation. Calling on her Goddess for extra power to her shields, the princess managed to shut out the woman's siren-like impact. She breathed a sigh of relief. Now, all she felt was intense revulsion.

Something about her silent companion seemed ancient, evil, and incredibly powerful. If the enchantress was having this devastating an effect on her, a trained sorceress, how could anyone possibly resist this woman's allure? The witch reminded the princess of a spider ensnaring its prey so she could devour it. The thought sent a shiver down the girl's spine. This person was definitely not someone Arianna would want for a friend.

The lady regarded the young woman with something close to pure hatred. Her pitch-black eyes were large and almond-shaped. They dominated a delicate heart shaped face and were the darkest and most piercing eyes Arianna had ever seen in her life. Another involuntary shiver ran down her spine. This woman was striking, but far from pleasant. An angry scowl marred her exquisite features. She reminded the princess of an irritated, mean-spirited governess or a beautiful but malicious bird. "Hello, I am Arianna. How are you?" she politely introduced herself. The mysterious female glared at her so fiercely that the girl thought better of trying to say anything further.

She could feel the magic in this hostile person and was glad for Greta's warning. It had allowed her to shield herself carefully and had hopefully hidden her capabilities from this formidable opponent. Vargos must have heard from one of his spies that her mother, Queen Anna, had some magical abilities. He was said to pay well for information. This gave him a network of informants everywhere. The officious king must have considered it likely that since the mother had powers, the eldest daughter might have some capabilities as well. Knowing that any acceptance of his marriage proposal would be done under duress, he was going to make sure that she behaved herself. Getting away might not be as easy as she had thought, it seemed her husband-to-be had tried to cover all eventualities.

So if escape was going to be a challenge, she would just have to be smarter than her imposing warden and very, very circumspect. How much power did this witch have? Arianna needed to figure that out and fast. Closing her eyes and pretending to rest, she carefully extended just a tiny tendril of her senses toward the other. What she discovered shocked her. This unpleasant lady was not just a witch, far from it! This person was a full-fledged sorceress with a daunting amount of power. Arianna's senses detected an inky blackness of pure malevolence swirling around the woman. She had never met a black witch before but was sure about one thing. This formidable person was definitely not a follower of the light.

The princess immediately withdrew the minute wisp of her powers behind her shields. It would not do to alert this woman to her probing. Her maid Great's words came to mind. It seemed that her perceptive friend had intuited the danger this stranger posted to her mistress. Whatever was contained in that small package must work 'to dull the senses'. There were a few herb mixtures Arianna could think of which did just that. Witchbane was one. But it was a cruel weapon. This vicious powder could deprive any practitioner of magic of their abilities for many months. If the dosage was high enough, the effect could be permanent, leaving the person bereft of touching their powers for life.

The compound was not something Greta would have given her lightly, or Arianna would use unless she really felt she had to. Her maid must have come across the lady somewhere in the castle. Being the daughter of a wise woman, she would have recognized this person as the indulger of dark magic that she surely was. Her friend had most likely gotten the powder from her mother. Good old Greta! Leave it to her to save the day!

The princess was not sure she really wanted to use the herbs. How could she possibly administer such a horrible fate to anyone, even this unpleasant individual? And, Arianna thought, she would have to be careful what she ate and drank herself. Shielding even more tightly, she connected to her Goddess and prayed for insight and help. This situation was one where more than just wits were needed if she was ever to make a clean getaway.

After they had been on their way for a good while, the unfriendly lady opened up a fair sized picnic basket. She laid out a sumptuous lunch on the pull-up table in the middle of the vehicle. Assuming this delicious meal was for them both, the princess reached out to help herself. There was certainly enough food here for two people. Seeing the gesture, the venomous woman raised her hand as if to slap her. Shocked, the princess recoiled. "Eat your own!" the sorceress hissed furiously. The scowling witch started in on the meal, shooting the young girl baleful glares now and then. Stunned, and no longer hungry, Arianna drew back as far as she could into her seat. No one had ever threatened to slap her in her life! She could not wait to be free of this nasty lot!

The princess curled up on her seat and pretended to watch the landscape race past. In reality, she was observing the sorceress. She was amazed at the amount of food this unpleasant person managed to devour. To be able to defeat her, she needed to know as much about this woman as possible. 'Find her strength, find her weaknesses," she could hear Anders's voice echo in her head. They had practiced this extensively and often intensely. There had been times she had complained at the toughness of his training, but now she was immensely grateful to the gruff man.

He had prepared her well for many different situations and had often turned practice into a challenging game. After a princess had been kidnapped in a neighboring kingdom, Anders had focused his attention on teaching her how to assess a situation, evaluate her strength and weaknesses as well as those of the enemy, find the best avenue of escape, make a plan and then execute it. He had turned it into fun and left the princess free reign in how to make good her getaway. The girl had gotten very good and ever more inventive in her methods. Finally, Anders had been satisfied with her abilities and continued with other training. She was happy to have those skills now!

Arianna watched as the nasty woman returned the empty dishes to the basket and then settled back in her seat. The witch brought out a small packet from a pocket in her skirt. The princess's curiosity was instantly peaked. Being careful not to show her interest, she pretended to look out the window and feigned total indifference. Out of the corner of her eye, she watched as the enchantress inserted a tiny spoon into the envelope and placed what must have been a powder under her tongue. From the puckered look on the haughty face, the compound tasted rather bitter. The sorceress then refastened the minute spoon to the package and returned both back to her skirt pocket. First, nothing seemed to happen but then, even this tightly shielded, the princess could feel the slight increase in the witch's magic. So the powder boosted the woman's abilities. Very interesting!

For a moment, the princess felt deep gratitude towards her mentor. Good thing Baladazar had insisted on her acquiring an extensive amount of knowledge on herbology. She should be able to figure out just what kind of a mixture the sorceress was taking. The girl knew of several compounds which could have an enhancing effect. In her mind, Arianna began to sort through them and their methods of administration. There were Buchu leaves to aid in psychic development and Devil's Bit for compelling and commanding, but she did not think that it was either of these. Could it be Masterwort? That herb had good protective qualities and was suitable for power recipes, but something told her that it was not this one either. She had long since learned to trust her instincts. For one, if she remembered correctly, that herb did not taste as bitter as whatever the witch had ingested. What else was there?

The princess went through a list of several more herbs but discarded each and every one of them. They just did not feel right and had different effects from what she had observed. One plant she kept coming back to, however. She had, at first, dismissed it because it was so rare and hard to acquire. The herb was named Dragon's Blood. The aromatic plant was well known for increasing one's powers as well as granting protection, but it was dangerous and extremely potent. It could be used as a powder or a tincture. Arianna remembered reading that it tasted absolutely awful.

Baladazar had taught her how to make compounds with most of these herbs. He had her test a minute amount of some of them so she would know what their effects felt like. She had only been allowed to try them under his strict supervision. Her mentor had warned her against using any of them on a regular basis. He told her that the increase in one's innate power, as well as frequent usage of some of these herbs, could lead to severe dependence. As time went by, more and more would be required to have the same result. The witch must be using this mixture all the time, or it would have worked much faster. If it tasted as bad as the book claimed, how could the sorceress even stand to take it?

~

The carriage rumbled along the dusty road. The pleasant woods of her home were lit up by the early afternoon sun. After a while, Arianna explored the contents of the lunch which the thoughtful Greta had managed to provide her with. Her heart was filled with gratitude for her quick-witted friend.

The faithful maid had packed a delicious meal of pastries, some slices of bread covered with sweet butter and jam, cheese, and fruit. She had also included some waybiscuits which would last for many days. They were excellent for travel, and she had often eaten them in the saddle eliminating the need to stop for a meal. Did Greta suspect she would try to escape? The princess thought she might, her longtime friend was very perceptive and often full of surprises.

The lunch was a little squashed from her tumble into the carriage, but this did not take away from its delicious taste. Several of the waybiscuits and some of the fruit and cheese found their way into the many pockets of her skirt whenever she was sure her companion was not watching. They would sustain her for several days. The biscuits also worked great as treats for some of the wild animals; they seemed to really like them.

Arianna could not wait to be out in the woods on her own, away from these ghastly people. She was now more determined than ever to escape. What must the king be like if his retainers were this unpleasant?

Hour after hour they bumped along in the carriage in silence. Every so often the woman would bring out the package and ingest some more of the powder. It seemed that she needed a boost to her powers every few hours. Or had it just become a habit? The princess thought that Dragon's Blood might have been one of the herbs Baladazar had particularly warned her about. What would this frequent a use of the potent herb do to a person over time? The witch most likely would suffer severe withdrawal if she ever ran out, maybe worse. Abrupt discontinuation of a compound like that had the potential to cause such severe pain it could make a person go into shock and, in extreme cases, might even cause death. This kind of fate was not something the princess wished on anyone.

~

Not until they had pulled in for the night had the girl been able to take a closer look at the traveling arrangement. What she saw, was not to her liking. The long column of King Vargos's soldiers was divided into three distinct companies. A forward guard, the ones surrounding the carriage and protecting her and the witch, and a rearguard. Gunther and his men had been pushed to the end of the caravan and as far away from her as possible.

Arianna was kept under close guard once she disembarked from the vehicle. The soldier in charge, a captain by his insignia, followed her wherever she went. When Mother Nature called, the girl had to insist on being given some privacy. This opportunity was just what she had been waiting for. After making sure she knew where the witch was and that she was unobserved, the princess quickly examined the contents of the small package. It contained a fine, white powder. She was careful not to touch it lest it affect her as well. A tiny spoon was affixed to the outside. Carefully extending her senses, the young woman got a feel for the substance's vibration. She would now be able to detect it in anything offered to her. The princess felt it was a good idea to be prepared just in case the sorceress had plans to deprive her of her abilities!

On the way back to camp with her watchdog in tow, she looked around. Her father's people were nowhere to be seen. The captain was keeping a very close eye on her and was never far from her side. The man had red hair and a friendly, open face. He came across as a very nice and pleasant person and appeared much more amicable than the rest. She had found herself alone with him several times already with no one else within earshot. A perfect opportunity to strike up a conversation.

Arianna immediately suspected a trap. A lonely and bewildered princess would naturally turn to the one approachable person in the bunch, hoping to receive some help. King Vargos was known to be devious, and most innocent maidens would have fallen for this kind of trick. The real nature of the wily monarch she was trying to outmaneuver was starting to dawn on Arianna. Her escape would be hard won indeed and require all the knowledge and craftiness she had learned over the years. The situation with the officer, however, she could play to her advantage. Forewarned was, after all, forearmed.

~

The guards had started a small fire for her and the witch in a sheltered cove. This gave them some privacy from the rest of the soldiers which were arranged all around. Their campfires formed a large circle with this one making up the center. Getting in or out would be an enormous challenge, these guys knew what they were doing. Arianna returned to the fire once she had taken care of business. After a surreptitious look around, she sat down on a log and let her shoulders slump dejectedly. Sure enough, the friendly captain came over and reassuringly patted her arm. "It will be alright, Miss, just you wait. You will love your new home, and I am sure our king is eagerly awaiting you," he told her soothingly.

Arianna gave him a grateful smile. Time to put on a bit of a show and see what information she could gain. "Thank you. I just really miss my family, this is my first time away from home. Do you think my husband will like me? And what is he like? I have heard such terrible things about him, is he really like that?" she asked. The princess looked up at the man. The look on her face portrayed innocence as well as insecurity and fear. This was not very hard since she was feeling a bit out of her depth as it was. "I do not know what you have heard, but I have always found him to be a fair and honest man, and he will surely like you. You are a lovely young woman," the soldier replied. "I am Angus, if there is anything you need, just let me know."

The young lady gave the soldier a grateful smile. "Thank you, Angus. Please, can you tell me who the woman is I am traveling with? She scares me!" she asked innocently, adding just a touch of trembling to her soft voice. "She is Odessa, housekeeper of Darkmor. The Lord sent her along as your chaperone. You are right to be afraid of her, and if I were you, miss, I would do as she bids you. She is used to being obeyed without question," the captain replied. "But I am a princess! I am used to maids and such! How am I to get along without one?" she asked the officer wide-eyed. "I am sorry, princess, but I think you better learn and learn fast." Lowering his voice, Angus continued. "Do not anger that woman, she would like nothing better than to bury you somewhere along the way!"

Arianna, playing the role of the helpless princess, shivered. Given the situation, that was not very hard. The man's words had stunned her, but she had to be careful and not overdo the act. She had to assume that King Vargos's spies had reported that she had learned other things besides how to be a proper princess. She could only hope that they did not know just how far she had come in those pursuits. It all depended on who had spied on her and how much they had learned. A feeling of trepidation spread through her like a tidal wave.

The housekeeper came striding up. She looked down her shapely aquiline nose at the apprehensive young woman.

"You, girl, get up! Go make me some tea!" Arianna looked up at her and widened her eyes. She needed to come up with some token resistance to avoid suspicion, but without giving away that the compulsion was no longer working on her. She was, after all, well known for being stubborn and willful. The princess stood up and raised herself to her full height. Behind the malicious witch, she could see Angus shaking his head in warning. "I am not used to making tea. I am a princess and not some servant!" she calmly confronted the imperious woman.

The such challenged housekeeper's face turned white with fury. With one stride she reached the girl. Her hand wiped out and slapped the princess across the face. "I am Odessa, and my word is law at Darkmor Castle!" she spat. Brutally she grabbed the young woman by the hair and pulled Arianna's face close to her own. The sorceress's eyes were huge, and the girl could have sworn that she saw flames in their inky depth. "You will do as I tell you, princess or not, and you will do well to remember this! Do I make myself clear?" the witch continued indignantly.

Pretending to cower in fear was easy at this point. Obediently, Arianna nodded her head. When the nasty woman gave her one last shake, she involuntarily let out a terrified squeak. No adult had ever hit her before or treated her with such cruelty. When the furious Odessa finally released the princess's hair, it did not take much for the girl to shrink away from the evil that was emanating from this worshipper of the Dark Gods.

Most of the qualms about using the Witchbane on this nasty enchantress disappeared at this moment. The young lady realized she would have to be very circumspect. As she set about making the pot of tea, she considered, for a brief moment, adding a small amount of the powder to the fragrant brew. A feeling of wrongness rose up inside her, and she decided to heed it. Somehow, this just did not feel like the right time.

Angus was watching every movement she was making like a hawk. Being the officer in charge, he was responsible for the safety of all. The captain seemed to take his duty very seriously. Earlier he had tried hard to come across as her ally, but from what Arianna had observed, he was taking his orders straight from the sorceress. She would have to be patient. Deep down she felt sure the right opportunity to administer the Witchbane would come. To successfully escape, the princess would have to continue assessing her situation and eventually come up with a good plan. To start with, she needed more information. What was that evil woman up to? Arianna considered some of the things she would do if she were in the other's shoes. Extending a tendril of powers, she checked the pot. It was just that, deliciously smelling and comfortingly hot tea.

The mistrustful Odessa was also keeping a very close eye on the girl during the tea preparation. This gave Arianna an idea. Maybe she should give the sorceress something to be alarmed about? After filling a cup from the kettle, the princess made sure that the mug was out of sight of the suspicious woman for just a few seconds. That should be long enough to make the witch believe that something could have been added to the fragrant drink.

Arianna silently walked over and handed the sorceress the cup. Odessa studied her angrily with glittering, fathomless eyes. "You drink it!" the witch commanded, handing the tea back. Glad to have followed her instinct as well as for the hot beverage, Arianna took a careful sip. "Drink!" screeched the detestable woman. "I am sorry, I am trying! It is hot," Arianna replied with her voice quaking. She wanted to make sure to appear as terrified as most princesses in her place would have been. That was not hard, something about this lady made her deeply afraid. Acting intimidated and fearful was getting easier all the time.

"I had heard you had more spunk than this! Funny what happens when you meet real life, isn't it? All nice and good playing the brave princess when daddy is there to make sure nothing happens to you! Get over there, out of my sight, you useless wretch!" the irritated witch spat with a look of utter disdain on her haughty face. It seemed to Arianna that she had succeeded in her ploy. She had been dismissed as just another helpless princess, but she would have to be careful and make sure to keep up the pretense.

To get to the place she had been banned to, she had to walk past the captain. The officer handed her a threadbare blanket. She thanked him for this small kindness, having any cover was better than none. Making herself as comfortable as she could at the spot far off on the other side of the fire, she surreptitiously continued to watch the sorceress. The woman had been dipping into the powder every few hours or so all day. It should be just about time for her next dose. Sure enough, the princess saw her bring the bundle out again.

Just as the witch opened up the small package and was getting ready to dig out some of the powder, the envoy walked up. It did not take long for a heated argument to erupt between the two. Occasional glances in her direction told the princess that their quarrel had something to do with her. If she could only hear what was being said! The lowered, furious voices carried faintly across the fire but were not distinct enough to overhear. Try as she might, Arianna was not able to make out the words. It would be so easy if she could only use her magic, but that could give her away.

Taking such a risk to eavesdrop on their conversation was not worth it.

Listening in was not an option, but what about adding to that powder in the woman's possession? This could be her chance! The witch was suitably distracted, and the open packet of Dragon's Blood was still on her lap in plain sight. Arianna, acting quickly, concentrated on the content of the pack of Witchbane in her pocket. Using just a tiny fraction of her powers, she transferred a small amount of the substance to the sorceress's stash. The girl did not think that it would take much to have a devastating effect. Now, that she had the feel for that pouch, she would be able to add more Witchbane to it anytime she pleased and whenever it seemed safe. That had been almost too easy!

~

The small act of magic reminded the princess of her years growing up and her home. Since her training had begun at such an early age, transferring compounds from one place to another was child's play for her. After all, she had been doing this kind of exercise since she was four. Arianna could now accomplish the feat with optimal control and while remaining shielded. Baladazar had made it a fun game for the little girl to steal candy from him without his detecting the use of her powers. By the time the princess was five, nothing in the castle had been safe from her. Some of the servants had begun whispering that a poltergeist had taken up residence in the fortress.

The old wizard had, at times, come to regret teaching her so well and so early. Using his rather significant powers of persuasion, he did finally manage to make the youngster understand that her abilities had to remain a secret. Only the two of them, her mother, and the loyal nurse could know. Baladazar told her that she had to be more careful and needed to stop moving things around the castle. Knowing that she needed some place to practice, he had given her permission to exercise her powers in his room. As she got older, the magician had to get more and more inventive to keep the mischievous child out of the things he did not wish her to explore just yet.

His playful apprentice had moved items around his chamber just because she could. For years, the exasperated wizard never knew what he would find when he returned to his rooms. When the princess learned how to use her magic to successfully hide his belongings from him, he had enough. One day, when the girl had infuriated him to the point that he had lost his temper, he discovered the ultimate weapon against the talented youngster, the threat of discontinuing her training. From that day forth, none of his possessions were ever bothered again, and things in the castle remained quiet as well.

~

Arianna forced her mind back to the present and continued to watch the quarreling pair. Finally, the argument between Odessa and Sebastian seemed to draw to a close. The fuming envoy stalked off in a huff. It appeared the witch had maintained the upper hand in the dispute, but the signs of the sorceress's fury could not be mistaken even from way across the fire where the princess was sitting. Right now was definitely not the time to draw the evil woman's attention! Making herself as small and as invisible as possible, Arianna watched as the irate witch dug her spoon into the compound and placed the powder in her mouth. The princess almost felt sorry for her. The loss of powers for a gifted person was a terrible thing. It was sort of like being suddenly deaf, dumb, and blind, cut-off from one's most important senses.

The princess slowly sipped her tea, the only nourishment of any kind she had so far received from her surly escorts. Pulling out one of the waybiscuits, she carefully dunked it into the brew. She was hungry and thirsty, and this small meal did little to ease her. There was no way she was going to ask for anything right now, not with that woman being in such a vile mood. She was supposed to become their next queen, and this was a strange way of treating the bride of their king. It seemed that no one really cared how she fared. The girl was fairly certain that this night no other food or comfort of any kind would be coming her way.

Figuring that it was best to stay as inconspicuous as possible, Arianna rolled herself into the thin blanket she had been given and pretended to go to sleep. Her face, where the witch's hand had connected with her soft skin, still burned like fire. How dare that wretched woman treat her in such a way! Fury rose up within her, and the princess had to push down the deep, churning anger at the cruel treatment she had experienced at the hands of that enchantress. For a moment, it threatened to overwhelm her better senses. Such dark feelings were very unlike her, and she realized that they would affect her shields if she did not get them under control.

Some primal part of her just wanted to reach out and strike the other dead. It would not even be that hard. She had been forced to still a heart before in a poor horse which had been too severely injured for her to heal. She had hated the feeling of the life-force ebbing away even if it did end the poor animal's suffering. Taking a life was something she never wanted to have to do again, especially not a human one. Remembering the incident brought her back to her senses and she finally calmed. She had to keep her emotions from overpowering her reasoning. It would not do to give away the extent of her own powers since she was not prepared to do battle with the sorceress or slip past all those soldiers.

The threadbare blanket she had been given smelled of horse which comforted her. It was old and had several holes allowing the cold night air to penetrate through the flimsy fabric. This worn cover had seen better days. She would make do with what she was given, but it seemed the nasty enchantress was going out of her way to make Arianna as miserable as possible. The girl figured that asking for another blanket would do no good and would only lead to another confrontation. That would be a really bad idea considering the witch's present mood.

Now that she was calm once again, she could more objectively evaluate her situation. Even if she had acted more like herself and had used her powers, going up against the sorceress without adequate preparations would have been difficult if not downright foolish. As a practitioner of the Dark Arts, that woman was prepared to do anything to win. The amount of power Arianna had detected were such that the witch's knowledge of black magic had to be substantial. She had never even met nor dealt with someone like this before. Challenging that kind of a person to a sorcerous battle was not something the princess was ready for.

The girl felt sure that her best course of action was for the enchantress and her cohorts to think her suitable intimidated and cowed. The typical royal young lady would have probably been in tears and hysterics by now after receiving this kind of harsh treatment. Arianna could not see herself acting that way and figured it would only cause the witch to become suspicious. It seemed that her escorts did not know all that much about her, only the general tidbits any citizen of the castle would have known. But, even from that, they would have gathered that she was usually calm and competent and not given to fits of temper. Arianna was more than a little thankful for all the effort which had been made to keep the actual extent of her training a secret.

~~~

Chapter Four

Know Thy Enemy

*I*n her training with Anders, he had always stressed how important it was to ascertain as much about your opponent as possible. It was time to gather additional information. Tightly rolled into her thin blanket, Arianna closed her eyes. Very carefully she extended just a tiny tendril of her senses. The princess allowed this minute ribbon of power to waft about as if without purpose, all the while steering it just ever so slightly in the directions which interested her. She needed to know as much as she could about the people surrounding her. There was some risk in this action, but even if the witch did notice this tiny filament of undisciplined appearing magic, she would most likely dismiss it as wild power. Many a talented but untrained person gave off such in their sleep. Even if detected, it should not arouse undue suspicion.

Where the enchantress sat on the other side of the fire, Arianna perceived a dull red, angry glow interlaced with flashes of black. Moving out further, she realized that the soldiers had given her and Odessa a wide berth. She was surprised to sense abject fear from these men. The princess had to change her initial assessment of them. Many of the guards seemed to be decent men forced to serve in the army of their demanding lord. There were a few among them who were cruel and full of darkness, but to the princess's surprise, these were a tiny minority.

It was not hard to find the envoy, Sebastian. His furious anger, self-pity, and fear stood out like a fiery beacon as did his hatred for the witch. The argument the princess had observed between him and Odessa had not gone well for the pathetic emissary. Ugly resentment smoldered in the vile man's heart. To Arianna's surprise, some of it was also directed at her. What had she ever done to this horrid little fellow? Not wanting to be anywhere near the objects of his blazing rage, the emissary had chosen to make his bed as far away from the witch and the girl as he could and still be within the guards' protection.

Letting the tiny spark of her awareness drift along, she came to the outskirts of the camp. Her father's guards had chosen a spot a little separate from the rest. Now the princess was glad that they were far enough away not to have been witness to the earlier scene. It would not do for Gunther and his men to feel that they needed to come to her rescue against the much larger force of the witch's soldiers. Retreating back into herself, the princess mulled over what she had learned.

Arianna had confirmed that the sorceress was the real source of power in this camp and that all feared her. She would have to be very careful and hope that the Witchbane would do its terrible job. The princess had only a little bit of knowledge of that particular herb. She was not sure how combining it with Dragon's Blood would affect its workings. Would this unusual mixture still bring about the desired result? She needed it to lower the sorceress's perceptions and hopefully her abilities as well, and soon so she could make good her escape.

After reinforcing her shields to ensure that they would not slip while she slept, the princess tried to calm her racing mind. She was still upset about the earlier incidents. Never in her life had she been treated this cruelly and with such haughty disdain. She was being made to feel more like a prisoner or a servant than a princess. That woman actually seemed to carry a grudge against her. What had she ever done to her? She needed more information about what was going on here, and she would have to be extremely careful how she acquired it.

Being treated in such a disrespectful way was putting the life of her servants into a whole new light. The princess now regretted any moments of impatience she had ever shown with any of them. In spite of her allowing the abuse to happen to hide her own powers, it was still very unsettling, and it was exhausting her emotionally. She was physically uncomfortable as well. The old blanket was providing little warmth. She was freezing, and her feet felt like ice. Being too cold to be able to sleep, she decided to do one more quick check on the witch. Was it her imagination or was the sorceress's angry aura just a little less vibrant? Only time would tell, but she would most likely know by morning. It was a long while before Arianna finally drifted off into a restless sleep.

~

As soon as she began to dream, she was pulled into her winged friend's world, and Kyrill came to join her. He immediately wrapped his arms around her. A deep feeling of peace came over her. "Are you ok, sweetheart? I could tell how upset you have been all day. Please tell me, what is going on?" he inquired.

Once they had made themselves comfortable at the table in the hut, the princess related the day's events. The young man's striking face grew serious. He looked at her with great concern and tightly grasped her hands. "My love, have faith that it will all work out. Stay strong and stick to your father's plan. I will send someone to find you!" he told her urgently. His words made Arianna feel better. Maybe she was not as alone as she had thought.

~

In the meantime, Castle Maridar was buzzing with activity. King Roderic was in his element. Messengers were being dispatched to the other sovereigns describing the situation and asking for the formation of an allegiance of kingdoms. The monarch knew that together they could defeat Vargos with ease. He was aware that his fellow kings were terrified of the self-declared overlord and, therefore, no one had ever even dared to propose such an alliance. They all had been cowering before the malicious ruler, and this had given him more and more power. Roderic felt it was time to put a stop to this tyranny once and for all.

In the town and castle, several people had been identified as having been sneaking about and listening in on conversations. Some of these incidents might have been entirely innocent but just to make sure, all the perpetrators had been placed in the dungeon for safe-keeping and were now well guarded. Of one person's guilt, there had been no doubt. The traitor had been caught in the middle of penning a message detailing the activities in the castle.

The spy had not been with them for long. He had been hired only a few weeks ago to help with the stores. Some of the man's activities had already caused several people to become suspicious, even before the evil king's force appeared. He had been seen acting very furtive and was always sneaking about. When the guards had knocked and then entered his chamber, they had found him so intent on his letter that he never even heard them. News of the content of this message had spread through the fortress with lightning speed and had incited the fury of the inhabitants of Maridar. A mob had formed, and the guards had been hard pressed in their efforts to protect the rascal and keep the traitor from being lynched right there on the spot.

After this incident, alarm spread through the castle and city. Suspicion of any person who had not lived among them for years and who could not be vouched for by at least several people grew way out of proportion. The wariness spread and the once friendly populace regarded each other with distrust. Any incident, no matter how minor, was being investigated. Baladazar had been called and asked to use his magic to check the storerooms and stores for tampering and possible poisoning. The wizard could find no trace of trouble even after an exhaustive examination of the supplies.

Provisions had been brought in from the countryside all day, and it seemed that the treacherous man had not had the opportunity to cause any mischief with all the comings and goings. The master of stores and his helpers had checked every bag and had kept a sharp eye on things as it was. Just to be on the safe side, guards were placed in the storerooms. For additional security, the master, along with most of his helpers, made their beds right there among the goods.

King Roderic sent out riders to warn the outlying farms and to spread the word of what had happened. He wanted his people to be aware of what could be heading their way. All were asked to remain calm and told that their ruler was doing his best to deal with this dire situation. Knowing how far the alarming reputation of the evil monarch had spread, Roderic still feared that disquiet might ensue. For some reason, the stories of the appalling fate of the kingdom of King Vargos's first wife seemed to have been passed along more than most other tales of such atrocities. King Roderic suspected the devious tyrant of having had a hand in this matter.

The vivid stories had seeded dread in people's minds. Roderic and the other oppressed kings were aware that the population of any of the kingdoms might, knowing this history, actually force their ruler into obedience to the tyrant's whims. In the past, any effort to stand up to the oppressor from any of the sovereigns had caused absolute panic among the people. This scheme had worked superbly for years now to keep the Eleven Kingdoms under King Vargos increasing control.

None of the monarchs had seriously considered standing up against the tyrant until now. Through intimidation, that monster had made himself their de-facto ruler. His cruelty had affected all the kingdoms. Roderic felt that they had lived in fear long enough, it was time to take a stand. He bitterly regretted not taking this step when his friend, King Darian, was forced to turn his daughter over to that despot. His own dear daughter was now paying the price for his lack of resolve and bravery.

~

Sometime after midnight, when things had calmed down in the castle and most people were deeply asleep, a small door opened in the great northeastern tower. This entryway was cleverly hidden and virtually undetectable from the outside. Seven figures slipped out quietly and headed for a nearby gully where nine horses had been stashed out of sight of the fortress by the cunning Anders. Each horse had sacks tied around their hooves to dampen the sound. Carefully staying out of sight of the castle's guards, the seven dark-cloaked individuals worked their way away from the stronghold. Captain Caleb himself was up on the northern rampart this night to make sure no one discovered the party's departure. He was telling a rousing tale to the other guards who had gathered in a group around him and were hanging on his every word.

It was a good night for slinking about. The diffuse light of the waxing moon was frequently obscured by the thick dark clouds racing overhead. The captain's respect for Anders grew with each passing moment for no sign of the group's passing was detectable even by his eagle eyes and from this lofty height. The agreed upon flash of light finally told him that the travelers had reached a safe distance, and the talented captain brought his enthralling story to a spectacular end.

Having the men so thoroughly sidetracked had served the fleeing family well but could not be tolerated in a time such as this. Therefore, Captain Caleb gave his guards a stern lecture on being preoccupied with other things while on duty. They should consider the kingdom as being at war and behave accordingly. He pointed out that the enemy could take advantage of just such a diversion. That he had provided this distraction himself seemed to have completely slipped his mind. Sheepishly his men returned to their posts to take up their vigils. His lesson had hit home, and the captain was very sure that it would be much harder to sneak anyone else out under the noses of the now highly alert guards.

~~~

Chapter Five

Surprising Success

he princess came awake to a sharp pain in her ribs caused by the kick of a pointy toed shoe. She had been dreaming and talking to her friend Kyrill. They had been comfortably sitting on a bench together in front of the hut in the high mountains. The girl hated being ripped away from him to return to the cruel reality of life with these unpleasant people. Not fully awake yet, she almost let slip her shields to unleash her powers on the unsuspecting witch. At the last moment, the young woman remembered where she was and pulled the magic back deep into herself. 'That was close!' Arianna thought to herself, 'I have to be more careful!'

"Get up and get ready, you lazy bum!" the impatient enchantress ordered her rudely. Quickly getting up, the girl was about to bend down and fold her blanket but stopped herself at the last moment. A spoiled young princess would never even consider such a thing. She had to remember to behave like a helpless noblewoman. These people did not need to realize that she was an experienced huntress.

Looking around, she saw guards packing up and getting ready to ride. All the fires had been extinguished. It seemed in her emotional exhaustion she had slept right through the morning meal.

"Is there no breakfast? May I have something to eat, please? I am hungry!" she then asked the sorceress in a plaintive voice. The nasty woman burst out laughing. "Her highness wants breakfast! What would you like, breakfast in bed? You want us to serve you hand over foot? You think you are so much better than us! Get in the carriage, you stupid, useless wretch!" Odessa spat at her through clenched teeth. Arianna shrank back from the pure hatred she saw in the witch's face. What had she ever done to this lady for her to dislike her this much?

The princess just stood there, stunned. When she did not move instantly, the sorceress grabbed her roughly by the arm and propelled her towards the carriage and up its stairs. Once again, she was cruelly shoved inside the vehicle. Arianna managed to keep from hitting her head by twisting her body at the last minute, but could not avoid painfully bumping her shoulder. Usually, she would have been silent, but remembering the helpless princess role, she cried out.

Tears of fury were running down her face as she sat there rubbing the bruise. "Oh look at that! The little baby is crying! She hurt her little bitty shoulder! Poor little princess!" the witch cackled. Seeing the girl cry and thinking them tears of pain and weakness seemed to have made the evil woman's day. She was contently smirking to herself while watching the secretly fuming princess. The thought that this harpy was in charge of her and this entire convoy was disconcerting.

In a way, Arianna was glad that she had been the one who had been chosen to be placed into the evil enchantress's power. She was much better equipped to handle this situation than any of her friends. Most of them were delicate and spoiled and would have been quickly broken by this kind of abuse. The girl gave heartfelt thanks that she had been allowed to have the training she did for it had prepared her well to survive whatever was to come.

Suddenly, a terrible truth occurred to her. What would happen once she escaped? Would another girl immediately take her place? It seemed very likely. Did that king even care who the next wife was? Arianna's gut instincts told her that it did not matter much to him just as long as his intended was a princess. Something had to be done before any other young women followed the first three wives to the grave. From her father's words she had deduced that he had an idea. Sacrificing herself to save another young lady the horrid fate of becoming the evil monarch's bride might jeopardize her dad's plans as well as the entire kingdom. She knew her sire depended on her to extract herself from this situation and that she needed to avoid getting recaptured at all cost.

~

The carriage rattled on over the rough road for hour after hour. The princess noticed that Odessa was indulging in the powder more and more often and in larger and larger doses. A quick check assured Arianna that the evil sorceress's powers were fluctuating wildly, but waning overall and rapidly so. It appeared the combination of the two herbs made the Witchbane's effect even stronger and faster, but also more capricious. About mid-morning, the malicious woman took out the package to examine it for tampering. She sniffed at the powder and tasted it. As far as Arianna recalled, Witchbane was totally undetectable except if you were familiar with its vibration. But, even this would be hard to do at this point since she had added only a minuscule amount and it was by now well mixed in with the other herb.

The witch was shooting suspicious glares at the princess while she carefully inspected the bundle once more. It seemed that the woman was very puzzled by the effect she was experiencing. Odessa, finding no evidence of foul play, started mumbling to herself. From the snippets the princess managed to understand, she was able to gather that the other had concluded that this unpleasant up and down of her magic she was suffering could be the natural result of the herb losing its potency. The sorceress seemed to think that she would be okay once she made a new batch of the compound. Until then, she would just have to take more. The enchantress determinedly took another dose, this one much larger than the previous ones.

For a few minutes, the mixture had the desired result. Then, all of a sudden, the power began to drain from the witch along with much of her color. Her mood, however, was getting rapidly worse. When Odessa caught Arianna shooting a furtive glance at her, she screamed at her to mind her own business. The woman's rage had grown such that the girl feared she would attack her. Shrinking back and drawing into herself, the princess made herself as small as possible. Yes, she could protect herself, but that would mean giving herself away. This unscrupulous lot would deal with her accordingly, and there would go any hope of escape. Until she was sure the Witchbane had reduced the sorceress's powers consistently, she would just have to do whatever was necessary to avoid a confrontation.

Determinedly, Arianna stared out the window and tried to ignore the witch. She only risked an occasional glance out of the corner of her eye. The princess could not help but notice that by noon, Odessa started looking positively ill. Much of the vigor and dark radiance she had extruded at the outset of their journey had faded away leaving her looking wan, tired and old. She had even stopped glaring at Arianna about an hour before. A worried frown had replaced the perpetual scowl on the delicate face, and the sorceress's hands were shaking like leaves.

"Stop the carriage!" the woman finally shouted at the driver when they were passing through a pleasant river valley. She slowly disembarked the vehicle and, in a low voice, ordered Arianna out as well. When the envoy rode up to inquire into the cause of the delay, Odessa informed him imperiously that she had decided they would stop for lunch. Sebastian's protest was silenced by an angry glare from the piercing black eyes. The guards were ordered to start a fire and to drag a log up for the witch to sit on. Once she was comfortably seated, the impatient lady ordered her trunk to be taken down from the back of the carriage and brought to her immediately.

The princess watched as the witch made a desperate effort to hide her growing weakness from the soldiers. Once the chest had been placed by her feet, the woman started to frantically dig in the good sized trunk looking for who knows what. Her face relaxed visibly when she triumphantly came up with a small package. Looking around, Odessa spotted the princess. The young woman had been trying in vain to blend in amongst the guards. "You there, stupid, make me some tea!" she screamed at the girl. Arianna hurried to obey.

After setting the tea things out, the princess went to get water. Angus, as usual, was shadowing her. The river was further back in the meadow, a little way from the camp. The two crossed the field in silence. After filling the kettle with the sweet, clear water, the princess turned to her guard. "Please, tell me, why does she hate me so?" the princess asked the jovial appearing man. Arianna was sure that they were far enough away from camp not to be overheard, but in any case, the sound of the water would cover any conversation they had.

Angus looked around nervously to make sure that there was no one within earshot. The princess was taken aback. Even the captain was afraid of that wicked woman. "She is not just the housekeeper, lady," he told Arianna. Seeing the girl's blank look and remembering that this was, after all, a princess, he elaborated. "She is the king's mistress, child. She does everything for the king but gets no respect. Matter of fact, the king treats her with contempt. There are some rumors that she is the real power behind the throne. Our illustrious ruler has left the running of the kingdom more and more in her hands while his majesty hunts, feasts, or entertains himself otherwise," the officer divulged.

The soldier wisely did not mention that the 'otherwise' was the monarch's pursuit of the castle's servant girls. Some things you just did not share with a princess. The facts that her future husband was a wastrel and had a mistress were bad enough. "I heard that even General Darius, the head of our army, does her bidding. There is only one thing she has not yet achieved. She is not queen and, legally, the power not hers. The king is not a kind man. He never lets her forget that she is just his servant to do with as he pleases. You are a threat to her, are in her way, just like all the other princesses!" He whispered to the stunned girl and then prodded her back towards the camp.

Now, things were starting to make a little more sense! Arianna had a lot to think about while they were walking back across the meadow. She was surprised that the captain had shared this information with her. Why this sudden honesty when he had so glibly lied to her before? Had he come to realize that she would not give him away?

~

As much as the princess disliked the witch, she could not help but feel compassion for the unhappy woman as well. She now understood why Odessa hated her so. Arianna had read enough to have a basic knowledge of court intrigue. The girl realized that she was the enchantress's rival for the place in the king's bed. If she married Vargos, she would have the position the witch so desperately craved. Was this why the other princesses had ended up dead? The sorceress must have hated them just as much! What must it be like to be the actual ruler of the kingdom but be forced to bow down to the queens and do their bidding? On top of this, have that heartless monarch constantly remind you that you are not good enough to be in their place? It had to be almost unbearable for the enchantress and must have infuriated her to no end.

These new insights allowed the princess to comprehend the witch's anger. To be so cruelly treated and watch helplessly as another was set above her time after time would anger any woman, but especially one with all the dark powers this one was able to wield. It sounded like Odessa did all the work of ruling the realm, but was forever the mistress. From Angus's words, the girl gathered that the cruel monarch treated the sorceress more like a servant than the head of state she actually was. The princess could understand how this kind of treatment would offend and anger the enchantress deeply and that she would be out for revenge. Odessa was ruthless and would get what she desired in the end, no matter how the despicable tyrant felt about it. The woman wanted power, all the power she could get. Any queen would be in the way of this ambition. Could the witch have been responsible for the death of King Vargos's previous three wives? The girl started to think that this was a good possibility.

Angus had been shooting the princess anxious sideways glances while they were walking back to the encampment. He urgently whispered to her: "Do not anger her, please, princess, for your own good!" Arianna gave him an almost imperceptible nod. Nothing was to be gained by irritating this despicable woman any more than she already was.

~

Once Arianna got back to the fire, she immediately started preparing the tea. Odessa watched her intently the entire time. The princess was mindful to keep the cup in full sight of the witch at all times. Carefully balancing the steaming cup on its saucer, Arianna took the tea to the glaring enchantress. She silently handed her the fragrant brew. "Not so high and mighty now, are we?" cackled the woman. Just as the princess was about to turn away, a claw-like hand shot out and cruelly grabbed the girl's arm. "Here, you try it first!" Odessa ordered. Silently Arianna took the cup and brought it to her lips. Using just a tiny tendril of her powers, the girl quickly verified that nothing had been added to the drink by the witch. The princess carefully took a sip only to have the cup ripped out of her hand. "Give me that tea! And get away from me, you miserable brat!" the angry sorceress spat.

Returning to the other side of the fire, the princess found a pleasant spot under a nearby tree. Arianna took a waybiscuit out of her pocket and silently began to eat. As Angus walked past to tend the horses, he quickly slipped her a small flask of water and a couple slices of bread with ham in between. He had been careful to ensure that his act of kindness went unobserved by Odessa. The princess gave him a grateful smile. She did not much care for the meat but at this point, anything was better than nothing.

So far the soldier had been very pleasant to her, but she still did not trust him. The girl checked the content of the bottle and to her great relief confirmed that it was just water. Facing away from the fire, she brought the flask to her mouth and took a long drink. The princess carefully slid the flagon in one of her pockets and, turning her back to the sorceress, ate the delicious tasting bread. What a relief to have water and food! She would just have to find a way to keep the canteen with her. It would be a great asset once she was off on her own. She needed to make sure that there was no opportunity to return it to the thoughtful soldier.

~

Odessa seemed to be too preoccupied to pay Arianna much attention. The princess watched her take a large dose of the new powder and saw the witch visibly brighten. A triumphant look of relief crossed the woman's face. The girl recalled that Witchbane kept on working for a while once it had been administered. Would the Dragon's Blood counteract the effect? She could not take that chance and would have to add some of the terrible powder to the woman's new stash as well at the earliest opportunity.

Very soon, however, life began to drain from the sorceress's face once more. It seemed that the invigorating effect of the compound had only been temporary. Within a few minutes, even the woman's hair appeared to have lost some of its color. Her face had turned deathly white. Arianna could not help but feel sorry for her. She would have preferred not to inflict further harm on the sorceress, but she needed to make sure that the witch could not track and find her.

Leaning back against the tree, the princess carefully reached out and located the pouch of uncontaminated powder in the enchantress's pocket. Quickly, she withdrew. It was one thing to find the little bag, adding the Witchbane, however, was another. The amount of power needed was much greater and, therefore, easier to detect. The woman was already suspicious and, in spite of being so sick, highly alert. Arianna needed the sorceress distracted. She would have to watch and wait.

Odessa had sunk into herself and suddenly looked small and frail. Finding the girl's eyes on her, the witch glared at the princess and would have probably found some way to torture her had not the envoy, Sebastian, shown up just at this moment. He seemed to sense that something was different, that there was a weakness in the sorceress that had not been there that morning. The princess was thrilled that the nasty emissary once again provided her with the perfect occasion for adding the Witchbane.

The opportunistic envoy pulled himself up to his full diminutive height and pushed out his fat chest. He reminded Arianna even more than ever of a blown up toad. Looking down his large and rather broad nose at the seated witch, he began to yell. "What is this? Are we putting down roots? We need to get going, woman! What do you want to do? Hang out here all day?" Odessa was furious. Pulling herself to her feet, she viciously grabbed the man by his coat. "Who do you think you are talking to? How dare you speak to me this way! We will leave when I am good and ready! Now be gone, you miserable snake!"

Even in her weakened state, the sorceress was still a formidable opponent, and the envoy slunk away. He was shooting hate filled looks over his shoulder at the enraged woman as he scooted back to his horse. As soon as he was out of sight, Odessa called for Angus and gave the order to pack up. She then scowled at Arianna. "Get over here, you useless thing!" she hissed. The young woman decided to obey immediately. Now was not the time for a confrontation.

The witch grabbed the girl's arm cruelly, digging in with her fingers. "Get over to that carriage!" she ordered.

Holding on to the princess's arm, the enchantress guided them towards the vehicle. What looked to all like Odessa dragging the girl was, in reality, the sorceress using her for support. Arianna was well aware of how weak her adversary must be to do this. For a moment, she felt sad and wished that there had been another way besides using this dreadful powder. Being such distracted, the princess stumbled. "Move it!" the witch hissed and dug in those long fingernails. With the sharp pain in her arm, any misgivings Arianna had harbored about using the Witchbane were drastically reduced.

The girl was relieved when they finally reached the carriage. "Help me in! And not a word to anyone or you will not see tomorrow! Is that clear?" the sorceress hissed at the princess. Arianna nodded her head and assisted the woman inside. Odessa was so weak that she had to aid her to her seat. She then slid on the bench across from the ashy looking witch. Angus climbed up the stairs to report that all was ready for travel.

"Good!" Odessa uttered. She then turned toward Arianna. "You, out! I am tired of your ugly face!" she spat. "Angus, take this wretch with you! I am sick of her company!" "Yes, mam!" the soldier responded and closed the carriage door once Arianna had disembarked. "Come along, girl, let's find you a horse," the captain ordered. Looking her up and down for a moment, he shook his head. "I have heard that you can ride. But how are you ever going to get on a horse in that skirt?"

The officer led Arianna over to the mounts. Going down the line, he stopped and checked out several of the animals. Giving each a friendly pat, he moved on until he finally reached a beautiful white mare. "I know this one well, she is very gentle, and a child could ride her. Her name is Queenie. Let me get you a saddle for her," Angus told the princess. "Thank you, Angus! She is beautiful!" Arianna replied. The soldier soon returned with a well-worn saddle and proceeded to get the horse ready for her. "I know this saddle does not look like much, but it is more comfortable than a newer one. I hope you do not mind, princess," he told her. "I am sure it is perfect and thank you again, Captain," the girl said smiling.

Now that they were out of earshot of the carriage, Angus was his usual polite self. He looked her up and down for a moment and then shook his head in disgust. "We do not have a sidesaddle, lady. There is no way you can ride in that gown! I can get you a shirt and some pants, princess, if you don't mind. They might not fit perfect or look as pretty as that dress, but at least, you won't break your neck falling off or trying to get on!"

Having secretly hoped for just such an offer, but being well aware that she must not appear too eager, the princess looked down at her skirt. Shrugging her shoulders with regret and carefully schooling her face into a mask of utter resignation, she nodded. Everything about her said that she was not happy with the turn of events, but was willing to make the best of things. "I will be right back, young lady!" Angus beamed at her with relief and rushed off to find something to wear for his royal charge. He soon returned with a stack of clothes as well as a blanket. "We do not have much time and no tent so I will hold the blanket around you. I will not peek, I promise! Can you get out of the dress on your own?"

The princess gave him a look as if genuinely scandalized and utterly horrified. She let her shoulders droop and finally gave the soldier a resigned nod. Angus made an improvised shelter around her and held out the clothes for her. Arianna unbuttoned the dress. After making sure Angus was keeping his word and not looking, she quickly removed the packet of Witchbane and slid it into her underclothes. Then, the girl slowly pulled off the dress and let it drop to the ground, making sure to take her time. There was no way she was going to give away just how fast she could get out of that garment.

She took the shirt from the soldier's hand and pulled it over her head. With relief, she realized that the top was long enough to cover any evidence of the leggings. The princess then grabbed the pants the captain was holding out to her. Sitting on her dress, she quickly removed her footwear. Thinking that the small pouch might show under her clothes, she slid it into her left shoe after pulling on the pants. The rest of her possessions she would move in plain sight so it would appear that she had nothing to hide.

Once she had retied her boots, the princess stood up, picked up her gown, and stepped out of the improvised shelter. Arianna started transferring the waybiscuits and other items to her shirt and pants pockets. The small flask of water she hung around her neck. She noticed that Angus was watching with great interest. The princess made sure he saw everything she relocated. There would be nothing out of the ordinary to report to his mistress.

"I am ready, Angus, thank you very much for your help and not peeking," the girl finally told him. "You are welcome, princess! Here let me have that dress, lady, I will put it into one of the trunks," the soldier replied, quickly snatching the gown. Not wanting to leave such a personal item in the hands of the witch who could possibly use it against her, Arianna quickly grabbed for the garment. "Please, Angus, I would feel so much better having it with me. Can't we put it somewhere on the horse?" she begged, giving him her most pleading look. "Alright, princess, if it means that much to you. I will fold it up and put it in your saddle bag," the officer replied after a moment.

The captain made a great show of folding the frock neatly and smoothing out the silky material. Finally, he had it reduced to a bundle small enough to fit into the bag. Arianna was well aware that this gesture, which on the surface appeared so innocent, had been used to thoroughly examine the dress and make sure there was nothing left hidden in its many pockets.

"May I keep the blanket as well, please?" Arianna asked the man as he helped her into the saddle of the horse. Angus nodded and turning to his men, barked a sharp order. The command to mount up had everyone scrambling for their steeds. Looking around to make sure no one was watching, the captain quickly stuffed the blanket into the opposite bag. The princess whispered. "Thank you, Angus, I will not forget your kindness!" The soldier blushed and quickly turned away. Once the officer had jumped on his horse and his men were lined up, the captain led his part of the column back on the road.

~~~

Chapter Six

A Plan Comes Together

It felt wonderful being on the back of a horse again and out of that frilly dress. Arianna was enjoying the ride immensely. She made sure, however, to appear at least somewhat sullen and unhappy about having been banned from the carriage and reduced to wearing men's clothing. Queenie was just as sweet and docile as Angus had told her and had a smooth and easy gait which made riding her a pleasure. The mare responded instantly to even the slightest touch and seemed to listen to everything the princess was telling her.

Arianna was really starting to like the horse and was beginning to think of possible ways to take the mount with her when she escaped. The one problem with this beautiful animal was its light coat. A horse that color would stand out in most landscapes. Queenie would be almost impossible to hide and would even show up brightly in the moonlight. This would unnecessarily complicate her getaway. She would have to come up with a way to get another horse before she became too attached to this one!

The highway was winding through serene forests and pleasant sunlit valleys. Arianna had traveled this way several times with her father and especially loved this stretch of road. About an hour after setting out, the column reached the beautiful Loera River Valley and soon the clattering of horses on the rock of the bridge filled the peaceful woods next to the tumbling water. The princess knew that this playful river was about a day's ride from the border. Tomorrow they would reach Lothrien. Arianna's heart was heavy knowing that she might never be able to return to her home. This could be the last time she saw this lovely place.

Soon after they had crossed the river, the exhausted witch looked out of the carriage and noticed the princess riding the beautiful pure white horse. Odessa's face contorted with fury, and she immediately called the column to a halt. Arianna watched as the enraged woman screamed out the window at the hapless Angus. The captain seemed to voice an occasional objection but to no avail. What was that all about? The chastised soldier finally nodded. Turning his steed, he rode back to the group of spare mounts.

Arianna watched as he checked several of the horses and finally settled on one. Taking the animal's lead, he headed towards the princess and dismounted beside her. "Please, lady, let me put you on the other horse. I should not have put you on Queenie. I thought you riding her would be alright and did not realize that Odessa had decided to lay claim to this horse as her own. She has gotten it in her head that she wants no one else to ride her. And, you look beautiful on this fine mare, like the young queen you will soon be. Seeing you like that angered her even further. This one here is Arabella. She is a bit more spirited and sometimes a little willful but also sweet and gentle. None of the horses except Queenie are used to women riders. This one here is the best of the rest, little lady. I hope you will like her. I am sorry about you having to switch, princess, this was my mistake. Can I please help you down?"

The man seemed genuinely troubled, and the princess felt pity for him. What must it be like to serve a woman like Odessa, to be subject to her every whim? "I am sure the horse will be just fine, Angus, thank you," she answered as she let the captain help her dismount. Arabella had wandered up and now regarded the princess with keen interest. The mare was a deep rich chestnut color and had bright, soulful eyes dancing with mirth. The princess knew horses pretty well and figured that this one could be a handful if she wanted to be! After a moment of careful inspection, the inquisitive steed started sniffing and nuzzling the princess.

Arianna reached out and gently petted the soft muzzle. She immediately liked her new mount. On contact, she sensed that there was something special about this horse. There seemed to be an instant connection between them. Queenie was beautiful, sweet, and a pleasure to ride but this mare appeared to have an interest in the world around her that appealed to the princess much more. The girl was actually quite amused that the irritable witch herself had been instrumental in providing her with the perfect steed.

Angus pulled Arabella up beside Queenie and quickly switched the saddle to her back. While he was getting her ready, Arianna was still getting to know her new mount. The mare was watching her with intense curiosity. The princess sensed an unbridled soul in this beautiful chestnut creature, very different from the docile, placid Queenie. This high-spirited replacement was full of fire and inquisitiveness, something which pleased her much more in a steed than total obedience. The girl felt that once she had won the intelligent horse's cooperation, they would make an excellent team.

And, she would blend in with her surroundings much better than any white animal ever could! Arianna was only too happy to let the possessive witch keep her lovely pale pet. Her new mount suited her needs much better. The princess felt so thrilled that it was hard not to let her delight at this opportune switch show.

Soon the officer helped her remount, and they were on their way once more. Later in the afternoon, clouds began to roll in, and it started to mist. Angus rode up and handed the princess a waterproof cloak which she gratefully accepted. He was gone before she could thank him. It was a brown oilskin cape with a generous hood and would help to keep off the worst of the elements. As the afternoon went on, the clouds grew darker and more threatening, and the weather deteriorated further. Soon rain was pouring down, and the road turned into muck. Horses and riders were a picture of pure misery. The longer it continued to rain, the worse the highway became. The unhappy animals moved along with heads hanging as they slogged through the ever increasing mud.

The more it rained, the slicker the road became. Much of the area was volcanic, and the soil, a fine, red clay, acquired a consistency resembling soap as soon as it got wet. It was also almost as slippery. Angus started to ride close to the princess to keep an eye on her. A particularly violent downpour left everyone huddled deeply in their cloaks. Arianna saw her chance to thank the friendly man without being overheard. "Thank you so much for the cape! Without it, I would be soaked to the skin by now!" Angus met her eyes for a moment and gave her a brief nod. He quickly looked away and shrugged further into his cape. It seemed that the captain was not in the mood for further conversation. The princess figured that if he were caught being too friendly with her, it would most likely cause trouble for him with the irritated witch. As peeved as that woman was already, nobody wanted to risk angering her further.

~

On and on they rode until darkness was starting to fall and the sorceress finally called a halt to their travels. After helping Arianna down from her horse, Angus went to tend to his mistress. To the princess's surprise, he soon came running back. "She wants you, lady! Not sure what for, but you better hurry!" he panted. "Be careful, little lady! She is in a terrible mood!" the captain warned her. Arianna hurried along with him to the carriage. "Leave us, Angus, and go set up my pavilion!" came an imperious voice from its interior. "And you, girl, get in here!" The princess quickly climbed into the vehicle.

The witch looked awful, her face was tight and drawn, and she looked almost deathly ill. Figuring she better wait until the nasty woman voiced her needs, Arianna regarded her silently. The witch glared back at her, but there was not much power left in that ugly stare. "I am sick and don't want them to see my weakness. You will help me get to the tent and into bed and make sure I am not disturbed. Tell them I am busy working on something and if they want better weather to leave me alone. And, you better make it look like I am dragging you. If you speak one word of this, I will know, and you will pay! Is that clear?" The princess obediently nodded her head. It seemed like the Witchbane and Dragon's Blood combination was really taking its toll on the sorceress and she felt pity for the suffering woman in spite of the treatment she was receiving at the other's hand.

It took only a few minutes for the tent to be erected, a fire started in front of it, and the bed and furnishings to be set up. A heater, burning the dry wood they carried for this, was warming up the inside. Once Angus reported that all was in readiness, Arianna helped the much-weakened sorceress out of the carriage and to her pleasantly warm and dry tent. A soft, comfortable looking bed piled high with pillows and blankets occupied the right side of the pavilion, a table and two chairs the opposite wall, and a dresser with a wash basin and towels was placed across from the entrance. Beside it was a serving table laden with fruit, cheese, bread, and even a bottle of wine.

Somehow Arianna had the suspicion that this tent had been originally meant for her, the king's bride, but that Odessa had decided to claim it for her own. No one would dare argue with the witch about her taking over this luxurious abode. The ruthless housekeeper's reign of terror was absolute, and few seemed to even dare to stand up to her. The princess could not help but admire the envoy for his occasional attempts of taking control. The man had to be either stupid or incredibly brave to do so. Or maybe, there was someone he was even more afraid of? Arianna pitied anyone who was forced to exist under the rule of that woman and King Vargos.

The pavilion was relatively luxurious. A carpet had been spread over the grass to keep the damp out, and a lantern suspended from a pole. Its soft yellow light gently illuminated the inside and chased the shadows far into the darkest corners. The witch, appearing to drag a reluctant princess along with her, slid into one of the chairs. The woman was slender but was leaning heavily on the girl to whom Odessa sure seemed to weigh a lot. Arianna was glad to be free of the extra weight. The sorceress dispatched Angus to take care of his soldiers and the horses after making sure that everything she might possibly need had been brought in.

Just as soon as the man left the tent, the witch began to visibly deflate. The woman had used up all her reserves to keep up appearances. What must it be like to never be able to show any weakness? To immediately have her authority challenged by the likes of the envoy whenever he even suspected a problem? Arianna realized that the sorceress was so feared and hated that the people she was oppressing were just waiting for a chance to get the upper hand. It seemed that only abject terror kept the wolves at bay. That was not the kind of life the princess thought she ever wanted for herself.

With the soldier gone, the ill-tempered housekeeper eyed Arianna with tired and strangely lifeless eyes. "Help me to bed! I will eat there!" the enchantress ordered. Quickly, the princess got them both out of their cloaks which she hung up to dry. She then offered to help the woman undress and into the lacy nightgown the soldier had laid out for her, but the witch only faintly shook her head. The sorceress was so worn out and tired that the princess had to almost drag her to the bed. Once there, the witch exhaustedly sank onto the well-padded pallet. She was so weak that Arianna had to pull her into a sitting position and built a support of pillows behind the woman's back so that the listless sorceress could sit up enough to be able to eat.

Arianna was just preparing a plate of bread and cheese for Odessa when the captain called from the entrance. He knew better than to enter the pavilion uninvited. "Don't let him in!" the frail-looking sorceress mouthed at Arianna. The princess quickly rushed to the entry where a patient Angus was standing holding a steaming bowl of soup. "Thank you, Angus. It smells wonderful. I will take it to her," she told him. A knowing glance was shared between the soldier and the girl. They were both only too aware that if the sorceress had her way, the princess would not get any of the steaming dish. Once again, she would be forced to make a meager meal out of the waybiscuits she was hoarding.

The young woman carefully carried the hot food to the witch who did not even have the strength left to eat by herself. Arianna had to spoon-feed her the stew. She had to hold the bread and cheese for Odessa so that she could take a bite. The girl had not expected the Witchbane to affect the sorceress this brutally. In spite of the awful way the enchantress had been treating her, the princess was starting to feel pretty guilty about having caused this severe a malaise in the other.

The witch's next words, however, wiped this out once again. "Get out and sleep in front of the pavilion! No one enters! Remember, tell them I am busy working on the weather or something! Don't even think about wandering off into one of the tents! I want you close just in case I need you!" Arianna could not help but feel disappointed. Deep down the princess had hoped to be able to remain in the lovely tent and maybe get at least a piece of bread or cheese even if that meant playing servant to the enchantress.

That, however, did not suit the ailing Odessa. The woman felt that having a witness to just how sick she was would never do. Now that the princess had seen her in such a state of weakness, she would have to make sure that the girl did not live to tell about it. The sorceress vowed that just as soon as she felt even a little bit better, that royal nuisance had seen her very last day. Not that she had ever harbored any real intent of letting the interloper reach her destination alive in the first place. Now the enchantress had an additional reason to make sure the girl did not arrive. Word of her temporary infirmity must never get around.

The princess could feel Odessa's hate filled stare on her back while she was donning her still dripping cloak. What could be going on in that evil woman's mind? Arianna was just grateful to be a little bit warmer and drier by now. Without a word, she stepped outside into the dark and stormy night. There was no shelter out here for her, but she did not want to irritate the already ill-tempered sorceress further by wandering away from the tent. Was she expected to sleep out here in the rain without any kind of a cover like an ill-treated dog? It sure seemed like this was the witch's intent. Resignedly, she pulled the cape around herself and settled down in the soaking wet grass as close to the side of the pavilion as she could.

~

Angus, having seen to the rest of the camp, came striding up. Seeing the girl huddled in the rain close to the pavilion entrance, a worried look crossed his face. "Princess! What are you doing out here?" he asked frowning. "It seems I am to sleep out here," the princess whispered back. It came out rather more pitiful than she intended. "Out here? You will catch your death! I will set you up a tent over there, close to the fire," the soldier said. "Thank you, Angus, that is so sweet of you, but I cannot leave here. She has ordered me to stay close to the entry just in case she needs me and to make sure she is not disturbed," Arianna told him in a low voice. She was cold and wet and the idea of spending the night right there without any shelter made her feel pretty miserable.

"I don't care what she says, but you will not be sleeping in the rain in front of her pavilion while she lounges in there in luxury!" came the soldier's angry reply. He was so enraged that his usually friendly face had turned a bright shade of red that was plainly visible even in the low light. "I will rig a shelter for you right here, young lady! Did you get anything

107

to eat?" When the princess shook her head, the scowl on the captain's face deepened. It seemed that his patience with the cruel sorceress was wearing thin. Angus shot a furious look in the direction where he thought the witch to be and stalked off.

Being true to his word, the officer returned after only a few minutes. He ordered two of his men to very quietly set up a small tent right beside the entrance to the pavilion. "This is not perfect but it will keep you dry, and you can make sure no one enters. I have an oilskin for you to put down underneath your blanket so it will not get soaked through. Here is your blanket and an extra one. I have taken care of Arabella. Sleep well, princess, I will wake you early so we can take the tent down and keep us both out of trouble. There is no sense in irritating her further. She is angry enough as it is!" Angus had whispered before he melted away into the darkness. Was this rebellion against the witch's wishes an act or had the so kindly seeming soldier had enough of the nasty woman's cruelty? Arianna was not sure and decided that it was best to keep up her guard.

The shelter was small but very welcome. The nearby fire kept the area well-lit. The exhausted princess had just gotten comfortable when she saw the toad-like envoy approach. With a sigh, she pulled the cloak back around herself. The tired girl slipped out of the tent and stepped in front of the entrance barring the emissary's way. "What is the meaning of this? And why are you sleeping out here?" hissed the pompous little man. "Obviously not out of choice! She is busy! I have strict orders not to let anyone disturb her!" Arianna whispered. "This time of night? Get out of my way, girl!" the unpleasant gent scoffed. His rudeness made the young lady even more determined to deny Sebastian his request.

The princess drew herself up taller and stood her ground against the annoyed envoy. "Are you willing to brave Odessa's anger? She would be furious about being disturbed! And, do you really wish to continue riding in this kind of weather?" she sweetly asked the scowling ambassador. Sebastian was visibly taken aback. If the sorceress was working magic, it would be the worst time ever to interrupt her. Who knows what the evil witch would do to him! A shiver of fear ran down the cowardly man's spine, and it took him a moment to respond. "Fine! Have it your way! I will deal with you both tomorrow!" the incensed emissary finally growled. Giving the girl a contemptuous look, the arrogant toady turned and stalked off into the night.

Shaking her head in disgust, Arianna returned to her tent. She once again rolled into her blankets and pulled the cape over herself for additional warmth. With a sigh, the princess realized that this was the most comfortable she had been at night since setting out. The girl was grateful for the oilskin pad keeping the wet and cold of the ground away from her. Leaning up on one elbow, she took out a waybiscuit and the canteen and began to consume her meager meal.

~

Tomorrow, they would cross the border. It was time to come up with an escape plan for that night. The girl started by reviewing all the information she had gained about the soldiers, how they set up camp, and their routines. The sorceress was too weak at this point and no longer presented much of a threat. Still, the princess intended to slip away without using her powers. Arianna began to evaluate the strength and weaknesses of different possibilities and finally started to formulate a plan which would allow her to escape with minimum effort.

"Princess?" came a sudden low voice from the back of her tent, startling the girl out of her thoughts. "Yes?" she whispered back parting the flap. She had recognized the voice as belonging to the captain. "Here, lady, something warm for you to eat. After a day like today, you need it," the soldier said pushing a bowl of steaming soup and a spoon into the young woman's hands. It smelled delicious! "Thank you, Angus, thank you! You don't know how much I appreciate this!" a grateful Arianna whispered. "Don't let her see it!" the embarrassed officer whispered and was gone.

The soup was the first hot food Arianna had received from her escorts since they had left her father's castle. It smelled delicious and made her taste buds tingle. She had just about put the spoon in her mouth when good sense reasserted itself. She was so hungry that she had almost forgotten to check for any foreign substances. To her great relief, the girl found that all the bowl contained were wonderfully smelling nutritious vegetables and meat in a savory sauce. Her gratefulness that it was just that, good, warm food, was enormous. She had not realized that she was that famished.

The girl relished every bite but all too soon the meal was gone. Her thoughts wandered to the sorceress. The woman was incredibly ambitious and full of anger. From what she had learned about the enchantress, the princess figured that Odessa would stop at nothing to achieve her goals. That witch was a terrible enemy to have. She must have made the lives of the other brides' pure hell! But, even knowing that, Arianna felt a little guilty about causing the enchantress to become this ill by administering the Witchbane. Yes, she probably deserved it, but still!

Listening to the heavy deluge pounding on her small shelter, the young woman ardently hoped that the rain would let up by morning. Riding in that kind of weather had been less than pleasant, and she was not looking forward to a repeat of that slog through the muck. The constant worry about the horse slipping and being thrown made for a tense ride.

The princess sent a prayer to her Goddess asking for more favorable conditions and for protection for her family. Was it raining this hard where her sisters and aunt were as well? In order to get away unobserved, they would not be able to travel by coach this time. Arianna was worried about them, none of them were used to such hardships. She could only hope that they were well cared for by whoever was guiding them to safety. Determinedly the girl wrenched her troubled thoughts away from the concerns for her family and to more pleasant memories of her home instead. After a while, she managed to fall asleep.

~

Kyrill, her dream friend, joined her just as he had the night before and every time she had been upset since that first dream when she was nine years old. She told him all which had transpired that day, and she could see the worry in his eyes. Together they discussed several options for an escape, and the princess was glad to have his valuable input. He turned out to be an astute tactician and asked some pointed questions which led her to look at the situation in a whole new light. It was not long before they had a solid plan which Arianna felt comfortable with. Their discussion moved on to more enjoyable subjects. Around the young man, she felt happy and relaxed. These tranquil nightly visits were helping to sustain her through these troubled days.

~~~

Chapter Seven

One Last Day

Arianna felt like she had only just fallen asleep when Angus shook her awake. The first rays of dawn were working their way over the horizon, and the darkness was beginning to recede. The rain was no longer coming down as hard which the princess noted with deep thankfulness. As she was getting up, she sent a quick prayer to her goddess pleading that the weather would stay that way or even improve further. The officer quickly folded up the blanket and pad and handed them to her. Next, he expertly took down the small shelter. The feat was accomplished in mere minutes, and Arianna followed him over to the horses and her saddle. Once her bedding was safely stowed in the packs, the princess hastily returned to her post at the entrance of the pavilion. It would not do to have the witch wake up and find her gone.

As it was, she had not been back for more than a few moments when a weak voice called from within. The princess quickly entered and was severely taken aback by the changed appearance of the enchantress. Had the woman been using magic to make herself appear more attractive and younger than she actually was? The princess had suspected as much yesterday, but now she was sure. The witch barely looked like the same person who had so terrorized her just a day ago!

Arianna could not help but feel deep pity for the other and a fair amount of guilt. Not even the knowledge that the sorceress's reign of terror might now come to an end could make her feel right about this. Yes, Odessa had been beyond nasty, but what kind of king would place someone this obviously cruel and heartless in charge of his kingdom? Only a depraved one and not one she wanted anything to do with or meet!

"I am so tired," the stricken sorceress whispered. "Bring me my bag!" The princess quickly jumped to obey. "Help me sit up!" the witch ordered. Arianna helped the listless woman into a sitting position and stuffed pillows behind her. The enchantress feverishly dug around in her bag and finally located what she had been searching for. "Water, I need water," she croaked. There was a pitcher of water and a goblet on the table across the tent, and princess rushed to fetch her a cup. The witch poured a liberal amount of powder into the vessel and stirred it before drinking it down. Arianna watched as color flooded back into the exhausted woman's face and some energy returned to her body.

Odessa's voice was a tiny bit stronger as she ordered the princess to help her change clothes. Soon she was regally ensconced in a chair ready to eat breakfast. She seemed much healthier once more. The princess thought it best to mention that the envoy had come by the night before. But, how should she address the woman? The girl figured if she called her 'Odessa' it would be too familiar. Calling her 'housekeeper' was factual but might be like poking a stick into a hornet's nest. The other names which came to the girl's mind were even less useful. The princess concluded that it might be best to use no title at all to avoid infuriating the touchy witch. "The envoy wanted to speak with you last night," she finally said. The sorceress gave her a sharp look. "Yes, I heard. Nasty little toad, isn't he? I am sure we will see him this morning."

Before the princess could reply, Angus appeared at the entrance. Once he received permission to enter, he set out a sumptuous meal for breakfast. Arianna began to realize that they must have a cook along especially for the royal guest and that the witch had taken this privilege for her own as well. The soldier brought in eggs, bread, fruit, and hot scones which smelled delicious. Arianna's mouth watered. Seeing the yearning looks the princess was given the well-laden table, the witch looked her up and down speculatively. "Getting a bit thin, aren't you? Sit, girl, and eat! But don't bother me with your stupid chatter!" the enchantress ordered.

This kindness was completely unexpected, and Arianna was only too happy to obey. This was a real treat! The princess ate ravenously. It seemed the bowl of wonderful stew the kind captain had provided her with the night before had only left her more hungry than ever before. The princess figured that there was enough food here that she could safely take a few extra pieces for later without it being noticed. If only she were wearing her dress with all the multitude of storage spaces Greta had sewn in for her! The riding pants and shirt did not have large enough pockets and were too tight to squirrel away much. A visible bulge would have been an instant giveaway.

All too soon, the soldier reappeared to clean up and get them on the way. Strange that the commander of the entire column would take it upon himself to serve the witch in this fashion. "Angus, I want to get going quickly today and get as far as we can. I want minimal breaks and my horses to be switched around noon so we can keep going," the sorceress ordered. "Do I make myself clear?" the enchantress inquired. "Yes, mam!" the officer replied giving the woman a curious look. It seemed Odessa was suddenly in a great hurry to get back to Darkmoor Castle. The princess figured that the enchantress believed that something there would help her condition or allow her to determine what was causing her illness. Arianna thought it might be best to remove the Witchbane from the Dragon's Blood compound before she escaped.

Once again the color had begun to drain from the sorceress's face, and her strength appeared to be declining fast. "Help me to the carriage," the witch ordered harshly. Arianna did as she was asked and had barely settled the woman into her seat when the envoy approached. Seeing how wasted the enchantress looked, he climbed into the carriage unbidden and made himself comfortable on the bench opposite the ailing woman. Arianna was not surprised that the revolting emissary would try to take advantage of the situation. He struck her as a typical bully. Mean on the outside, but a coward at heart. Definitely not her kind of person!

The princess watched as the witch drew herself up and sternly faced the emissary. "What do you want, Sebastian?" she spat at the obnoxious little person. The man eyed her for a moment and seeing her paleness and thinking her too weak to defend herself; a contemptuous smile spread over his face. "I wanted to speak to you last night, but that one there would not let me enter!" the envoy barked, pointing at Arianna. "Tell me, woman, why is she not sleeping in the tent meant for her? Are you even feeding her? She is looking a bit pale and thin!" he continued getting angrier and louder as he went along. "I am charged to get her back to the castle safely, and you know the master! My life is done for if I fail in this because of you!" he screamed at the enchantress. "I am taking over the care of the princess, you incompetent cow!"

The sorceress's face had turned red with fury during the envoy's words. Arianna could sense that the woman was desperately searching for some source of power she could tap into. Having the emissary looking after her did not fit into the princess's plan. To maintain the status quo, the enchantress needed to regain the upper hand over that vile man. The girl had heard that some dark witches could draw power from others. Could Odessa? Arianna thought about the evil surrounding the enchantress. Did she want that woman touching her magic and drawing on her powers? Not only could that be very dangerous since the sorceress might figure out how much there truly was but to allow that evil to touch her without shields? No way!

Was there a way to give Odessa a quick little boost without her noticing? Probably not. But, maybe she could supply the witch with a convenient outside source. Deciding that the last alternative was the best, Arianna waited for just the right moment. As the enchantress cast around frantically for some source of power, the princess hastily brushed up against Sebastian and imbued him with a slight amount of magical energy.

Odessa quickly detected that force in the envoy. The sorceress reached out and placed her slender left hand on the fat one of the ugly man for a brief instant. The emissary flinched and turned pale. It took a moment, but then color flooded into the witch's face, and her eyes took on a dangerous glint. The ambassador, who had just regained a little of his color, blanched perceptibly. A glowing sphere of power suddenly appeared in the enchantress's hand, and she pointed the orb in the direction of the now completely terrified man. The envoy was backing up rapidly and as far as the cushions of the carriage would allow. He was watching the sorceress with bulging eyes. At this moment, he reminded Arianna more than ever of an oversized toad.

"So you think I am done for, do you now, Sebastian? Well, think again! I am just suffering from a bit of indigestion, you pathetic sycophant, nothing more! Now get out of my carriage, you fat little toad, before I actually change you into one!" the witch hissed sending a spark of power at the visibly shrinking man. Fury was contorting the woman's face, and even the princess shrank back from the unbridled evil emanating from the enraged sorceress.

With an undignified whimper, the castigated envoy shot out the door and took off running. The triumphant enchantress's cruel laughter followed behind him, spurring him on to yet greater speed. The look he shot back towards them was one of pure hatred. The ugly little man had once again lost his play for power against the witch, but Arianna was sure he would try again, given half a chance. She could not wait to be gone from this nest of vipers! Today they would reach the border and tonight she would make her getaway. The princess was looking forward to the solitude of being out in nature. Being all alone out there in the wild would not be easy, but then again, anything was better than company like this!

A sigh which was close to a sob drew the girl's eyes away from the fleeing envoy. The expenditure of power had cost the sorceress dearly. Her face had become even more deathly white than before, and she appeared to be unable to remain erect. Arianna watched as the evil woman started to sag against the side of the carriage and rushed to assist her. A few well-placed pillows helped keep the lady upright. The girl could not help but feel compassion for the stricken witch, she had not intended to cause her this kind of harm. She was puzzled by this severe reaction. From what the princess remembered reading about Witchbane, it seemed strange that the powder had taken effect that quickly and to this extent. Was the combination with the Dragon's Blood to blame?

With a mental shrug, the girl tried to push away her pity. After all, how much compassion had this wicked woman shown her or the other princesses? Seeing the hatred the sorceress had for her, she was seriously wondering about the mysterious death of the young queens. Had the witch been the one instrumental in the young ladies' death? As strange and as cruel as the passing of each of these unfortunate girls had been, that was a possibility Arianna could no longer discount. The more she learned of the woman, the more she thought that the evil Odessa had found opportune ways to dispose of her rivals and had made it notable to discourage any future brides.

~

The sorceress being this weak and powerless was good for her plans but having inflicted this kind of injury on another human being almost made the princess physically ill. The girl hoped that she would never have to do something like this again. At least, there was no way that the witch would be able to track her magically once she was away. The enchantress appeared to have barely enough strength left to stay coherent. To be this weak now, she must have been using a tremendous amount of power on a daily basis. From the changed appearance it was obvious that the woman had even used it to make herself more appealing. She must have been doing this for years. Where had she been getting that much magic?

Arianna was surprised that the enchantress's energy had been depleted this completely and this fast. It really baffled her. Witchbane took away the ability to connect to one's source of power, but only a relatively large amount of the herb should cause such an extreme effect. The minute quantity the princess had added to the packages should not have produced this detrimental an outcome. It was almost as if Odessa was getting more of that compound from another source. As sick and as weak as the sorceress was, she might need a long time to get back to her former self. The more she tried to use what power she had left, the longer it would take her to recover and the greater the chance became of burning out the source of her abilities for good.

The idea of possibly having impaired the woman for life horrified Arianna. If the sorceress totally lost her powers, it would feel like being deaf, dumb, and blind. A truly horrendous fate for anyone used to tapping into the magic of their world. It would leave an emptiness inside the witch that few others had survived. The princess fervently wished that there had been another option.

The girl knew that her father was counting on her to stick to his plan. She was only too aware that Odessa had been the biggest obstacle to getting away and fooling the soldiers into believing her dead. That threat was now eliminated but at what cost? The princess still felt guilty even with everything she had learned these last couple days. That the witch had intended to make sure that Arianna never reached King Vargos alive only made her feel a little better. She realized that her very life had depended on putting this truly evil woman out of commission. The ploy had succeeded beyond her expectations, but the princess felt sad that she had been forced to resort to such a cruel device.

None of the other options she had considered had seemed viable. Yes, she could have taken on the witch. They would have dueled, but she probably would have been killed. The princess was fairly convinced that her personal powers were stronger than those of the sorceress. But could she have won against her? Most likely not, not even one on one. The older woman was far more experienced and would have used spells against her that the princess had never even heard of or would have ever considered using.

And, there were the soldiers who were too afraid to be anything but fiercely loyal to the cruel sorceress. Angus would have been there in an instant to do the woman's bidding. Taking them all on would have been foolish at best. They would have overwhelmed her, and the best outcome after that would have been that she made it to the Darkmoor Castle alive. Somehow, however, Arianna doubted that she would have been allowed to live. Openly displaying the actual extent of her powers would have provided the witch with the perfect excuse, as well as a convenient opportunity, to permanently dispose of her newest rival.

Her death would have accomplished nothing as long as the sorceress was still able to practice her evil craft. Arianna would have been replaced by the next princess. Her family was making sacrifices of their own at this very minute, and all would have been in vain. Even if she had survived the battle, displaying her abilities would have gotten her shunned for life, if not hunted and killed out of fear. Such had been the fate of one of her distant aunts. The unlucky lady had used her magic to defend herself against a hostile king. Her people had grown so afraid of her that they had hired an assassin to put an end to their queen. She had died by the man's slow blade, persecuted and alone, in one of the mountain passes leading to the family's last refuge, the Hidden Castle. No, Arianna did not intend to share her powerful relative's sad destiny.

The Witchbane had been the best and most viable approach, the only alternative available to her. Countless people in Lothrien as well as in the other kingdoms had suffered under the brutal rule of the sorceress. In a way, the woman was getting a dose of her own medicine. How many had been helpless before her?

The princess was a kindhearted person and even telling herself all this only made her feel only a tiny bit better. She had caused harm and would have to live with the consequences of her actions even if it was done for the greater good of not just herself but many others as well. From what she had observed, the sorceress rule of terror had netted her plenty of enemies. The envoy was just waiting for his chance to take over. Their latest exchange had ended in his deep humiliation yet once again, and he hated the woman with a passion.

What kind of vicious degradations had Odessa heaped on the emissary over the years to make him feel that way? Sebastian struck Arianna as a nasty and sneaky little man, a real opportunist, but that kind of deep-seated loathing seemed extreme, even for him. Once he realized the exact condition of his reviled adversary, he would jump at the chance to avenge himself for all the mortifications he had suffered over the years. The princess feared it might not turn out too well for the witch. She only hoped that she was long gone by then!

~

A sound drew the princess's thoughtful gaze away from the open door and back to the stricken witch. "Get my bag,"

Odessa whispered. The princess hurried back to the spot where the pavilion had been. Angus and his soldiers had taken it down already, and the sorceress's possessions were sitting in a neat pile ready to be stowed on the carriage. Arianna quickly grabbed the satchel and headed back to the vehicle. She placed it on the woman's lap who reached in and brought out the now familiar packet of powder.

The sorceress was so intent on getting the spoon full of the restorative in her mouth she never even noticed the small amount of powder trickling to the floor nor the brief use of power as Arianna removed the Witchbane from the rest of the compound. The princess wanted this to be the last dose of the horrible stuff the stricken witch would receive from her hands. Using the other parcels familiar vibrations, the girl quickly located the package in the sorceress's skirt pocket. Why had Odessa sent her for the bag? Could the enchantress have forgotten about the pack she had on her? Or had there been some other reason? Arianna mentally shrugged off these questions. She had no way of answering them at this time. With just a thought, she translocated the herb from the second batch of Dragon's Blood as well.

Odessa perked up a little after ingesting the compound. But, once again, the result was short lived. Arianna had noticed that the effect of the herbs wore off faster each time and left the sorceress even more depleted. The woman was barely coherent now and the brief use of power to cow the envoy had made her condition worse than ever. "I want to be alone, go ride with Angus, girl. Tell him to get a move on it!" the woman muttered wearily.

That was the nicest the sorceress had ever talked to her and made the princess realize just how awful the woman felt. Climbing out of the carriage, she shut the door. The girl was only too happy to be out in the open and ride the beautiful horse. For a moment, Arianna had been afraid that the witch might want her to stay in the coach just in case she needed help. The thought of being shut up in that contrivance all day long with the ill-tempered woman made the princess cringe.

~~~

Chapter Eight

A Long Days Ride

*R*iding her elation about being allowed to ride, the princess headed towards the horses. She watched the pavilion and its contents being quickly stowed in the wagons. It seemed Angus knew his mistress well and had picked up on the witch's impatience. The soldier was in the process of saddling Arabella when Arianna walked up. "She wants us to get going as soon as possible," the girl told him. Shooting an unreadable look towards the carriage, the officer looked at the princess. "That is what I figured, and we are almost ready. You are to ride with us again?" "Yes, and thank you for saddling Arabella, and thank you for choosing her for me. She is an excellent horse!" Arianna replied. Once the mare was saddled, the captain helped the princess to mount. In just a few minutes the long column set out on the day's journey.

It was still drizzling just a little bit on and off, but nothing like the day before. Arianna started out riding a short distance behind the carriage. She was still upset and needed a bit of solitude to bring herself back into the present.

Observing the beauty of the world around her often helped with that. The woods were dripping with moisture from the rain the day before, and a fine mist was hanging in the trees. It was beautiful but gave the whole world a dreamlike quality. The princess wished that she could wake up and that the last few days had just been a horrifying dream.

As the morning went on, she dropped back a little and joined Angus and his men. The soldiers, feeling braver due to the absence of the sharp eyes of their intimidating mistress, actually exchanged almost friendly nods with the girl. Arianna was glad when the world around them began to brighten, and the mist started to burn off. Finally, the sun broke through the clouds and sunshine lit up the woods on more and more frequent occasions. The warmth felt wonderful and soon they were riding in a cloud of steam from the wet horses and cloaks.

Around noon, Arianna could tell that the carriage horses were getting tired but still Odessa had not given the signal to stop. They were moving at a relatively fast pace, and it was taking a toll on the poor animals. Angus was starting to scrutinize the tired horses with concern, and he finally rode up beside the coach. The princess watched as he called out to the witch within and saw him receive a weak wave in return. The captain immediately called for a halt and ordered the steeds to be exchanged. One of his men helped the princess dismount, and the soldiers bustled about getting ready to set up for lunch. Angus, seeing their activity, gave a sharp order to pack back up and to get ready to remount. The expression on his face told Arianna how displeased the captain was at having to deprive his men and the animals of a well-earned rest.

Just as soon as fresh horses were in the coach's harnesses, they were back on their way. After some initial grumbling, the men took out lunches from their packs. It seemed they were all well prepared for just such an occasion but like it, they did not. Seeing the princess chew on her meager ration of waybread, one of the men offered her a part of his meal. When the girl gratefully accepted, others started sharing their food. It soon became a game who could provide her the choicest pieces. Laughter echoed among the group, and it was only Angus's warning glance which finally subdued the merriment. Arianna was happy. The ice had been broken, the reticent soldiers were talking to her!

As the princess was eating the morsels the men had shared with her, the captain came up beside her and steered her a little way from the others. "Make sure you put some of that in your pack, young lady. It might come in handy later," he told her with a wink. Arianna was so shocked she turned pale. Did he know she was going to escape? And would he try to stop her or tell the witch? Seeing her face, the commander laughed. "Don't look so worried, princess! It will all work out! Just put as much food back as you can, we still have a long ride ahead of us!" The girl was aghast. Had she just given herself away? She concernedly watched the observant officer as he rode ahead once more.

When the afternoon wore on and the princess was still holding up without complaint, the respect of the men around her grew and with it the way they addressed her. 'Hey girl' turned into 'Lady' and finally 'Princess.' Arianna was happy to have their company; it kept her from mulling over all the things which could go wrong during her planned escape. The soldiers asked about her home and she about theirs. The impression she gained from their stories was of an unhappy place run by a tyrant who used fear to maintain control.

The contrast to Maridanmar was stark, and the girl was only too happy to tell the men about her beautiful home and its people. She was aware that she needed to be careful. The less they knew about the castle, the better. She soon switched to telling tales of people's silly exploits. The princess had a talent for storytelling and muffled laughter was her reward for this most welcome entertainment. Whenever the merriment became too loud, fearful glances were shot at the silent Angus and the nearby carriage. Arianna noticed with amusement that the distance between their group and the coach had grown as the afternoon wore on.

A couple of times Arianna had overheard whisperings among the troops. Odessa had not been able to hide her deteriorating condition. The witch's weakness had been noticed, and there seemed to be a rumor of her imminent demise. The news appeared to fill most of the fighters with glee and more than a little relief. The princess watched as a soldier traveled from group to group. The whispering would start wherever he went, and mirthless smiles broke out on many faces. The mood in the convoy began to lighten visibly, and Arianna had never seen her escort this relaxed. It seemed the sorceress had few friends if any but a fair number of people wishing her ill. The girl was glad that she had removed the Witchbane from the pouch. Hopefully, this would give the woman a small fighting chance once Arianna had made good her escape.

Later that afternoon, they finally reached the border. Captain Gunther and some of his fighters rode up. The Lothrien guards were waiting for the command from their captain to intercept King Roderic's soldiers. After a brief glance at the princess, Angus shook his head. Her escort relaxed and even respectfully moved back a little to allow Arianna some privacy with her people. Gunther and his men were happy to see her.

Pulling up his horse beside the girl, her father's trusted soldier gave her a respectful salute and then eyed her carefully. His face darkened as he noticed the bruises the witch's hand had left on her cheek. Arianna had seen them in the woman's mirror that morning and Gunther's sharp eyes missed little. They took in the disheveled hair, the smudges under the girl's eyes from lack of food and sleep, and how thin she had become in the last two days.

The princess knew the man well and could tell how angry he was from the jumping of the veins at his temples. On the practice yard, this had often been a warning for an explosion to come. Arianna silently shook her head at him and gave him a pleading look. There was nothing anyone could do to help her right now. Causing a scene would only make her position more precarious. "Good-bye, my Princess, and may the Gods be with you! You will be missed! We wish you all the best!" the captain sadly told a teary-eyed Arianna. "Please tell my father and family that I love them and not to worry. I am sure everything will work out. And my love to you and my people!" she replied bravely.

Gunther and his men saluted their princess one last time and then took their leave. They would return to the beloved home she most likely would never see again. The girl watched them ride away for a moment until Angus gave the command to continue. They needed to catch up with the coach. Arianna was well aware that the news of the treatment she was receiving from King Vargos's people would greatly upset her father, but there was nothing she could do about that. It was not as if any of them had been given a choice in the matter.

It was almost evening but still, on and on they rode. The horses were now walking along with their heads hanging. The exhaustion of the day's ride showed plainly on both mounts and riders. It was almost entirely dark before Odessa finally consented to let the captain look for a campsite for the night. Arianna had watched Angus ask the witch several times over the last couple hours only to be told to keep going. Anger and concern were written plainly all over the officer's face, and she saw his sigh of relief when they were finally allowed to stop. The captain sent a few of his men scouting ahead for a good location, and it was not long before they returned.

The seasoned soldier rode ahead to check out the spot and, finding that it served their needs, had the company move a little way off the road into the woods. He ordered camp to be set up in a pleasant glade. A small creek was tumbling along happily at the far end. The pavilion was erected first, and Arianna once again helped the ailing witch to her tent. The sorceress sank gratefully into a chair, and the princess helped her sip a cup of tea. Soon the woman took out the package containing her restorative and after ingesting a huge dose, a minute trace of color returned to her ashen cheeks.

When Angus brought in dinner, he eyed the enchantress with concern. The woman pulled herself up. "It is only a bit of a sour stomach, I will be fine soon. Be careful how you behave, my man, and tell that to your soldiers! I heard your laughter! I will remember how all of you acted when you thought I was down. Don't think I will ever forget this! I will make all of you pay for your insolence and disrespect! I am still in charge, and you will do well to remember that next time you question my decisions!"

Angus had visibly paled at Odessa's words, but Arianna knew him well enough by now to sense his suppressed fury. He saluted the woman smartly and turning on his heel, left the pavilion. The sorceress ruled by fear alone. What would happen when the people she terrorized realized that she had no powers left? Would any of them show her even the slightest bit of mercy? Somehow the princess was starting to doubt that.

"You, help me to bed!" The words startled the girl out of her reverie. "Hurry up! What are you doing just standing there like some idiot?" the witch spat at her furiously. Her voice dripped with venom. Her usual bad temper had returned with a vengeance now that she was feeling a tiny bit better.

Arianna hurried to obey. The woman appeared a little stronger than she had been that morning but now feeling this sick was making her more irate and nasty than ever. The girl had not thought that was possible and could not help feeling a bit of incredulity. "Get me some food and be quick about it, you stupid wretch!" Odessa hissed. The princess fixed her a plate of bread, meat, and cheese and brought her a bowl of fresh venison stew. It smelled delicious and was making Arianna's stomach growl with hunger.

The witch was still too weak to eat on her own, and the young woman had to feed her once again. When all the delicious food was gone, Odessa was still not satisfied. "Go get my candies from over there! Hurry up!" The princess fed the insatiable lady several of the artfully decorated chocolates. Finally, it seemed the other had eaten enough. "Wipe my face and then get my brushes!" the sorceress demanded after she finished the last of the sweet treats. Arianna silently fetched the two brushes which had been laid out. She held them out to the nasty woman. "Don't just stand there! Brush my hair! And you better not pull it either! And no, not that one! This brush! Give me the other one, you fool!" Odessa snarled crossly.

After complying with the rude command, the girl started undoing the witch's long black braid. She gently and carefully brushed the tangled locks. Stroke after stroke brought out a little of the hair's former shine, but it was still a far cry from its once brilliant luster. Odessa seemed to be genuinely enjoying herself. Whenever the princess accidently pulled some of the strands even the slightest bit, the malicious sorceress would turn and aim a vicious blow at her arm with the other brush.

The princess made sure to flinch every time she was struck. The woman was very weak, but the smacks still had enough power to hurt. This nasty person was treating her more and more like a maidservant instead of the princess she was! And now that they were into Lothrien, the witch seemed to be getting meaner than ever! The girl worked hard on not letting anger get the better of her. It would be a waste of her energy to give in to such negative emotions and would do more harm than good.

After a while, Arianna's arm felt like it was going to fall off. The skin was red from all the hits she had received. Finally, the witch allowed her to stop. "Enough! Now, help me lay down and cover me up, you useless brat!" growled the sorceress. While she was assisting the witch with getting comfortable, the princess realized just how frail the woman had become. Removing the Witchbane had barely improved the sorceress awful condition. Instead, feeling even a tiny bit better appeared to have fueled her ill temper.

"Now get out and if you say one word to anyone about all this, you are dead! You are not that different from those other royal brats! Don't even think about standing up against me or you will share their fate sooner than later! I got rid of them, I can get rid of you!" the sorceress jeered at the girl. Arianna could not believe it! The despicable woman had just admitted to killing the king's previous wives! Not only that, but the enchantress had also confirmed the princess's suspicion that the witch had never intended to let her reach Darkmoor Castle alive!

The wicked woman glared at the girl. "I know you are making friends with the soldiers, don't think I did not see you today! You better be real careful what you say, tell them I will be just fine. That I am just temporarily indisposed. Do you understand me?" growled the weakened sorceress. Arianna nodded and left the pavilion. As she closed the flaps to the tent, she could not get the witch's words out of her mind. For a moment, a small part of her was glad that she had added the Witchbane to the sorceress's powder. Shame almost immediately flooded her heart.

How could she possibly feel this way? She was a gentle and kind person and helped people. She was of the light! This dark part of herself was something that she had always suppressed. She had done her best to avoid harming anyone for most of her life. But, in this case, there had been little choice. Not adding that dreadful powder would have ended up being detrimental to herself. Arianna realized that she was capable of bringing out the buried warrior inside of herself when she had to. She was on her own in this situation. If she did not take care of herself, who would? How could she help others if she did not protect herself? The girl realized that she was not prepared to sacrifice her life for someone as evil as this witch and that she was willing to do what must be done to gain her freedom.

Arianna had always held herself to very high standards. This had been so easy back at her home. Now came the understanding that she was human and was being pushed to her limits. She was fighting back the best way she could. For a very brief moment, she had almost regretted removing the rest of the herbs, but her heart told her it had been the right thing to do. Having compassion and love was what made her different from that evil sorceress. To kill three innocent women just to further one's own ambitions! How could the king not see what was going on in his own castle? Or was he aware of the things this horrible woman had done and just did not care?

~

Once the princess had left the pavilion, the witch took stock of her situation. She felt terribly tired and had little magical power left. The tiny bit she had been forced to use on the envoy seemed to have drained most of her energy. She had never felt this helpless before, and it severely frightened her. Something was very wrong with her, and she was not sure how much longer she would be able to hide this. She feared that she was already losing control over the soldiers.

Good thing that royal brat was so easily cowed! It had been fun to treat that silly thing like her personal maidservant! Too bad she could not keep her, she had enjoyed hitting the defenseless twit! The witch smiled smugly and felt a deep sense of satisfaction. She had shown that stupid little git who was superior, who was really in charge! If only the men were so easily intimidated!

As her thoughts lit onto the soldiers who seemed to have taken a liking to the girl, a simmering rage filled the debilitated woman. It was burning through her veins leaving more weakness in its wake. Odessa was too furious to notice. The enchantress was relishing the notion of dealing with them all just as soon as she was stronger! How dare they laugh and make merry while she was feeling this bad? And why was she this ill? Before the sorceress could follow this line of thought any further, exhaustion overwhelmed her, and she fell deeply asleep.

~

After she had securely closed the tent flaps behind her, Arianna wandered over to the fire where Angus and his men were having dinner. It seemed they had placed a log for her to sit on where she would be close enough to the flames to be comfortably warm. One of the soldiers gallantly waved her to it. She smiled at the man gratefully. Without a word, one of the other fighters pushed a bowl of stew and a large chunk of bread into her hands. The soup smelled delicious. After checking the food for anything which might hurt her, Arianna ate hungrily. No one seemed to dare to speak above a whisper. They were within earshot of the tent, and it seemed Angus had delivered the evil witch's warning.

Still, the mood around the fire was much brighter than it had been on their entire trip. The troops usually had beer with their dinner but tonight the keg was considerably larger than the previous days. Angus might have allowed this indulgence to offset the hard day's travel as well as the sorceress's threats. The soldiers were being very pleasant to the princess and were treating her almost like a little sister. Arianna genuinely appreciated the men's friendliness. She felt more than a little guilty as she used her magic to transfer a fair amount of the sleeping powder from the packet in her pouch to their large barrel of beer.

To the princess, it seemed that discipline had been relaxed now that her escorts were back in their own kingdom. An overwhelming feeling of relief permeated the camp. Even being this large a force, they must have feared an attack by her father the entire time. Being back on home soil, they seemed to feel safe once more. The atmosphere among the men was almost festive in spite of them being tired after the hard ride of the day. The soldiers knew that they would be home soon. This mission had gone much smoother than any of them had expected, they had been treated with more respect and courtesy by Maridanmar's king and people than they were used to.

Arianna noticed that fighters from the two other companies were wandering in to share in the beer. While the rest of the camp was much more animated, the atmosphere around their fire was surreal. No one dared to talk out loud, and if any of them forgot and spoke a little above a whisper, he was immediately shushed by the others. Frequent fearful glances were shot at the not so distant pavilion. None of them wanted to anger the infuriated witch any further.

After a while, the soldiers decided that being this quiet and staying this close to the irritable sorceress was no fun. With the captain's permission, they took the keg and moved further away. This left the officer and the princess alone at the fire. Arianna was glad to see them go. The more of the doctored beer was shared with the rest of the camp, the easier her escape would be.

Angus had been sitting across the fire from her and somewhat apart from his men. He was staring into the flames and seemed to be deep in thought. She had noticed that he was drinking much less than the others and from a small keg at his side. Sensing her watching him, the soldier looked up and met Arianna's eyes. "Let's go check on your horse, princess!" he told her. His request startled her and caused a brief moment of fear to grip her heart. What was the man up to now?

The captain led the way over to her mount. Arianna petted the mare who was very happy with this unexpected nightly visit. "Princess, your saddle is right here, and I have added more food, a knife, a spare canteen, and an extra blanket and pad to the pack as well as four rags and some pieces of rope. I assume you know what those are for?" Angus addressed her.

136

The princess was stunned. What was this all about? Was he helping her escape or trying to feel her out for the witch? For a moment, Arianna was so taken aback by his comment that she could only gape at him. She finally mumbled. "Thank you. You are most kind!" The soldier gave her a knowing smile. "Maybe it is time you went to bed, young lady? Get some rest? I put your tent a little further away from her highness this night so that you won't disturb her. I hear a commotion over there, and better go check on my soldiers. Have a pleasant evening, princess, and be safe!"

The young woman stared perplexedly at the officer's retreating back. She was absent-mindedly stroking the delighted horse who was nuzzling her shoulder in return. What had just happened? Was he setting her up or making sure she got away? She would have to be extra careful. Maybe she should move Arabella to a different location? That, however, would be a dead giveaway that she was up to no good. If she only knew if she could trust that man!

Giving the affectionate mare a final pat, the princess headed over to her tent, deeply in thought. There was nothing she could do now but wait and hope all would go well and that Angus would not betray her. After brushing her hair, Arianna laid down and rolled herself in her blankets. For a moment, she appreciated the pad underneath her and the warmth of the two covers. Such a change from that first night! Taking several deep breaths, she centered herself and reached out to her goddess. She had done everything she could, but a little divine help could never hurt.

~

Far away to the north lay the home of the winged shapeshifters, Eagle's Nest Aerie. It was well concealed in the high mountains. A day's flight further north was the Hidden Castle, the almost impenetrable refuge of last resort for the royal family of Re'adeen. In return for sanctuary, the winged people had promised to assist the rulers in times of need. The Eagle tribes appreciated being able to live in peace, without persecution. As people often fear that which they do not understand, the humans in most kingdoms had been terrified of the flying folk. That fear had turned into hatred in Lothrien and any eagle seen there, shapeshifter or other, had been hunted down and killed mercilessly.

Once, long ago, the Eagles had contently lived all over the Eleven Kingdoms and beyond. Eventually, the regular humans had turned on them and had driven them further and further to the north. Only in Re'adeen and Maridanmar had the winged ones been treated with tolerance and kindness. Three hundred years ago, a long dead king of Re'adeen had welcomed the refugees from all the other realms. The monarch was a shrewd man and saw the shapeshifters as powerful allies, especially if he could keep them hidden from the rest of the world. His new friends would be the kingdom's secret weapon, one he hoped would never need to be deployed.

Re'adeen was to a large part a mountain realm, and there were plenty of places for the eagle-folk to live since they preferred the high peaks to any flatland home. A treaty had been signed between the so very diverse societies, and the uninhabited heights became the home of the winged tribes. In return, the King of the Eagles agreed to act as an advisor when needed and to help protect the kingdom. Stories of hauntings and ghosts kept regular people away from the region around the Aerie. The winged ones just wanted to be left in peace and avoided contact with humans. Over the years, the shapeshifters were all but forgotten. Only the royal family of Re'adeen was aware of their existence, and the knowledge was passed down from ruler to ruler.

To the Eagles, it had been a great shock when their young prince, Kyrill, had been drawn into the dreams of the Princess of Maridanmar. That she had the blood of the kings of Re'adeen running in her veins, only partially explained this unusual event. An even greater surprise, however, had been the young man's declaration that the girl was his lifemate. The attraction he felt for her could not be mistaken. Such a thing had never happened before. Until that day, the shapeshifters had always found their mates among their own kind. There was usually only one such partner and the bond between the pair came into being at birth.

The Aerie's seers had been consulted, and they had confirmed the boy's claim. The contact with the young lady had been sanctioned. Since the princess seemed to travel to their realm in her dreams, a hut on the side of a mountain a safe distance away from their sanctuary had been cleaned and furnished for these meetings. A charged crystal of light blue Bergquartz helped draw her there. No full human had ever seen the Eagle's home, and they preferred to keep it that way.

Over the years, the young woman had met others of their tribe, and she and the prince had become more than just friends. Great care had been taken to make sure that the princess could never be completely certain of their existence. The Elders felt that it was best if the girl believed that it was all just a dream.

Kyrill had disagreed but had been overruled. This had frustrated him endlessly. How was he ever going to claim this girl if she did not even know that he was real? She was his one and only love, his soulmate, and he was being kept away from her! The young man felt that if he had been allowed to properly court Arianna, this entire debacle might have been avoided. Now she was in a truly dangerous situation, and he and his people were unable to help.

~

The prince was pacing. He was too anxious to sit still. Concern for his mate had him completely on edge. Their bond had deepened to the point where he was able to pick up on the princess's emotions. All day long he had gotten snippets of feelings from Arianna. What he had sensed had not been pleasant and had increased his apprehension. If he could only be there to help! She had to escape this very night or she would be too far into Lothrien to be able to evade King Vargos's soldiers. He desperately wanted to know what had happened, to talk to her, to hold her but knew he would not see her anytime soon. Since this was the night she had to get away from her escorts, she would not be able to risk going to sleep.

The young prince was seething with frustration. If there was only something he could do! He loved Arianna with every fiber of his being and hated that she was in such terrible danger. But, he was a member of the royal family and had responsibilities towards his people. Kyrill had been forbidden to endanger himself by going too close to the humans, especially in Lothrien. His father had sent scouts out to assist the girl just as soon as she crossed the border to Larandar. The treaty with the Kingdom of Re'adeen made it their obligation to help the princess, but nothing could be done until she left that dreaded realm.

Part of him wanted to rush out and save her this very minute, she was his mate, his life. His father, knowing the power of a lifebond, had placed him under guard to ensure his compliance. The prince knew that in time he would find a way to slip away. Once his love was safely away from King Vargos's column and into Larandar, no force or responsibility would hold him back from going to her. For now, however, he needed to organize her rescue from here. Kyrill had sent several of his own warriors out towards the border of that unfriendly kingdom. They had strict orders not to cross into those hostile lands. All he could do was wait, and the inactivity was driving him crazy.

~~~

Chapter Nine

Surprise In The Night

Slowly the sounds around the princess's tent were dying away as more and more soldiers rolled themselves in their blankets and fell deeply asleep. She would have to wait until all was quiet and figured sometimes after the middle of the night would probably be best. Carefully extending a tendril of her senses, she began to explore her surroundings. First, she checked the pavilion. The girl was relieved to note that the witch was so deeply asleep that not much would wake her. Next, she let the wisp of her consciousness drift across the rest of the camp. Only here and there did Arianna detect a sentinel on duty.

Those soldiers on guard would be the ones she would have to watch out for since they had avoided the tainted beer. The girl knew that the captain did not tolerate drinking before or on duty. She had been unfortunate enough to witness the punishment of one of these men who dared to imbibe in a very small cup of beer with his meal. The whip had cruelly bitten into the man's back, and she had winced with every lash. It had shown her another side of the usually so jovial

143

soldier. He was a fair commander, but his rules were not to be broken.

~

Sometimes after the middle of the night, just as she was about to make her move, Arianna's senses suddenly went on high alert. Carefully sending out her awareness, she searched for the cause of this alarm. There, close to the perimeter of their camp! Someone was sneaking in! Could this be Gunther and his men coming to her aid? No, this did not feel like anyone she knew, none of her people would have so cold-bloodedly slit a man's throat when tying him up and gagging him would do! Whoever it was, they seemed to be heading this way! Coming to a decision, the princess quickly slid out of her tent dragging the blankets and pad along with her. She bundled them up and grabbed her things, never realizing that she was leaving her brush behind. Arianna started crawling towards her horse, all the while staying to the shadows as much as she could.

She was still able to see the pavilion from the place the horses had been picketed. So far nothing moved and so she carefully set about saddling her mare. The blanket and pad were quickly tied to the saddle, she would roll them up properly later. Her instincts warned her that the focus of the intruders was the pavilion and that they had formed a large circle around it. Unfortunately, they now had her surrounded as well.

From what she had sensed, she concluded that these men were vicious. Riding through their line might easily get her killed. Arianna cowered down among a nearby clump of bushes. From here she had a good view of the witch's tent. She watched as dark figures entered stealthily. Soon they emerged dragging the woman along. The sorceress was unceremoniously dumped on the ground in the faint light of the dying fire. The intruders formed a circle around her. "Where is the princess, you old hag? What have you done with her?" a rough voice demanded.

Several logs were tossed on the fire, and the light brightened. Arianna could now make out that the voice belonged to a tall man who appeared to be in charge. He cruelly grabbed Odessa by the hair and pulled her up to his face. The princess shivered, and she sent a silent 'thank you' to the captive enchantress. The woman's mean-spirited refusal to allow the girl to remain in the tent had saved her from sharing the sorceress's fate.

The witch was tied, and a rag had been shoved in her mouth. She seemed to be still half asleep. She was visibly trying to pull herself together and looked around desperately for help. "Ah, are you hoping for someone to come to your assistance? Poor old thing, those who are left alive are all sound asleep! We added enough sleeping powder to their beer that I would be surprised if they wake up before noon tomorrow! And, are you sure they would even come to your aid? Fear does not engender loyalty, hag! So where is the young lady? You won't tell me? You don't know how happy that makes me! Hand me the flask with the Witchbane!" the man ordered.

Arianna could hear the sorceress's terrified whimper. "Pull the gag out and open her mouth!" ordered the harsh voice. The witch spluttered and coughed as the fluid was poured down her throat. "Just so that you know, you have been dosing yourself for days! Did you enjoy the sweets the king sent along for the princess? It is amazing what a knife to the throat and the threat to one's family will do to get an honest merchant to add just a little something!" the man smirked and then continued. "Oh, and there is enough Witchbane in this flask to kill your magic powers forever.

One less of you nasty lot in this world! And, it will burn you all the way down. Will kill your voice, most likely! I am sure your old friend the envoy will be so thrilled!"

The cruel laughter of several of the men echoed through the night. It seemed they knew the witch and were enjoying taunting her. Arianna had never seen anyone being treated this brutally and could only feel sorry for the woman, murderess or not. These men were beyond malicious. It appeared that whoever these intruders were, they were looking for her! What did they want? Were they friend or foe? One thing was certain, they sure disliked witches. Would they see her in a similar light if they knew? The princess was glad that she had not tried to escape using her magic. She might have received the same treatment as the witch if they had figured out that she had powers as well!

After hearing the man's words, it suddenly made sense to Arianna how the minor amount of the herbs she had added to the restorative had produced such an overwhelming effect. She had not been the only one to drug the woman! And it was as she had suspected, all that delicious food, the pleasant pavilion, and the other little luxuries had been for the king's new bride. The witch had condemned herself to this fate when she appropriated what was meant for the princess. These men had figured that Odessa would take all the benefits sent along for the new queen for herself and had prepared accordingly. Whoever this bunch was, they appeared to know the sorceress well.

The awful scene around the fire held the girl spellbound. "Got no powers left now, do you, hag?" the man taunted the defenseless enchantress. Arianna never even sensed anyone approach, but suddenly a hand covered her mouth. She had been so intent on the spectacle that she had not paid attention to her surroundings. She was roughly pulled up and drug over to the group. "Look what I found hiding by the horses! Now who might this be? Could this be our lost princess? She sure doesn't look like much in those clothes!" her captor smirked.

The man in charge was still holding the witch up by the hair. Now that Arianna was closer, she could make out details even her sharp eyes had missed in the low light. This guy was too much! He was dressed like one would imagine a fairytale bandit to be dressed and was just getting ready to pour more of the Witchbane down the sorceress's throat. The woman was gasping for air and sobbing desperately. When the leader noticed his man dragging Arianna into the light of the fire, he released his hold on Odessa's long hair and callously let her drop to the ground.

After eyeing the captive princess up and down, he greeted her with a polite bow. "Ah! I see we found the little bird! Welcome, your highness, to our little court. May I present the jury," the man stated grandly waving his hand at his men. "I am the judge and the executioner, and she has been found guilty by all!" Heads nodded in agreement all around the circle. "Excuse us please, my Lady, while we continue with the sentence," the flamboyant man went on politely and with a bow. All Arianna could think was that this guy was wrong in so many ways. Not just his dress but also his manners. Her instincts told her that she would have to be very careful around this strange person.

The intruder once again brutally picked up the defenseless witch by the hair. Gone was the suave gentleman. The princess was shocked to witness the complete change in his personality. She wondered if the man's features changed as drastically but the flashy bandit was wearing a mask, as were his men. All she could see of his face was his mouth which had now turned down into a thin, cruel line. His dress made him stand out from the rest of the outlaws like a peacock from a flock of peahens. His clothes were much more expensive and colorful than those of the other thugs and somehow more fit for the theater than invading an armed camp.

The whole scene would have been almost comical had not their hatred for the sorceress been palatable in the air. What must she have done to them to loathe her this much? Once again the man viciously shoved the flask deep into the witch's throat and squeezed the remainder of the fluid from the leather flagon. The sorceress flopped lifelessly to the ground when the bandit finally released her. That seemed to infuriate him even further. Grabbing the woman by the neck, he pulled her up and shook her until a shivering breath issued from the enchantress's throat. "Good! I want you to live and suffer like you made so many around you suffer!" the enraged man snarled into Odessa's face before throwing her away from himself like something one truly reviled.

Turning, the flashy man once again focused his attention on Arianna, who was still being firmly held by her sly captor. "So, my princess, how are you? We came to rescue you, for a price that is. At least, that way you will reach your future husband alive. And with that hag powerless, you might actually remain that way," the bandit stated pompously, pointing at the witch. When he turned back towards the girl, he seemed to notice for the first time that she was still being held. "Get your hands off her, man!" the outlaw barked. "Do you have a name, your Highness?" he then addressed her with a gallant little bow.

Arianna stood there with her mouth open. She was stunned and felt like she had been dragged into some bizarre play or was having a wild nightmare with characters too strange to believe. Who was this guy? If she understood him correctly, he and his group of bandits intended holding her for ransom. Her rebuked captor had released her on the flashy man's orders, but she was definitely their prisoner. Had she left just a little earlier, she might have gotten away! Instead, she had fallen into the hands of this lot. The princess saw few options and figured it was best to play along with this peculiar charade for now.

Taking her cue from his courtly demeanor, the girl gave the showy bandit a deep curtsy. "I am Princess Arianna of Maridanmar and who do I have the honor of addressing?" she asked politely. "I am Alandor, King of the Bandits! Known and feared by all in this lovely Kingdom of Lothrien and you, my princess, are my honored guest. Do not worry, we will not harm you and will deliver you to his Highness, the King, in due time once he has paid our ransom. It is a pleasure making your acquaintance!" the flashy man answered with a deep bow and the grandiose gesture of sweeping off his hat. His courtly manners might have looked slightly less ridiculous to Arianna had he actually been wearing something on his head.

Alandor the Bandit King! Even the princess had heard of this man. Tales of his exploits were all the rage at the castle. He was supposed to be very good looking, and Arianna had heard many a maid sigh at the mention of his name. He was known to be fiendishly clever and had been a thorn in King Vargos's side for many a year now. No one knew where his hideout was; he was said to be like a ghost, strike and be gone. No amount of bounty for his delivery, dead or alive, had netted results.

And now she was his 'guest'! The princess was less than thrilled. This poppycock showing up had just messed up her escape. Since the location of the outlaw's hideout was a complete mystery, it could be anywhere. Arianna figured that it was best to assume that the lair was close by. She needed to find a way to get away from this bunch quickly. Their leader was way too shrewd and most likely there would be little to no chance of escaping once she reached his stronghold. He might play the fool and come across as crazy as a loon, but his reputation proved him to be a hard and brilliant man.

Turning away, the man gave several orders in a voice too quiet for her to hear. Arianna was horrified to see a bloody Angus and one of his soldiers being drug into the firelight. The friendly officer looked more dead than alive. His man was in much better shape and conscious. The captain came to once he was doused with a bucket of cold water. For a moment he hung there, sputtering, then he burst into action. Angus was desperately trying to break free from the grip of the two large outlaws holding him on either side. "Stop that nonsense, man!" Alandor ordered. He walked over and slapped the captain hard across the face. "Do I have your attention, my dear fellow?" the bandit calmly asked the infuriated man.

The captive officer glared at him and continued to struggle for a moment, then finally nodded. "I know you are Angus, the captain of the guard, but who might this young fellow be?" the cocky man asked the young soldier while pulling his head up by the chin. "I am Aaron, sir," replied the young man who was little more than a boy. "Well hello, dear Aaron, a pleasure making your acquaintance!" the bandit thrilled looking the young man up and down like something he would like to acquire. "Pretty, aren't you? Would you like to play with me?" he asked patting an appalled Aaron's arm seductively. Alandor had placed himself very cleverly in such a way that his gesture was blocked from the princess's sight.

The young soldier paled and recoiled visibly. "Don't worry, boy, no time for a dalliance now," the brigand laughed. "Lucky for you I need you here, or I might have taken you along for a little fun later on! I am sure you would get to like my attentions after a while!" the lecherous cad said in a voice low enough to ensure that he could not be overheard by Arianna. He gave the alarmed soldier a knowing wink. His men were laughing uproariously at the lad's horrified expression. The bandit king seemed to finally take pity on the young man. "Had you going there, now didn't I? Don't look so shocked, dear boy! But just between us, I do prefer the ladies!" he pronounced. His bandits laughed just the harder seeing the soldier's relieved expression.

Turing his attention back to Angus, all playfulness disappeared from the rogue's demeanor. "Now to business!" he continued with a sigh. "The princess is my hostage and you, dear man, and you, you delicious boy, will let the king know the price he will pay for the return of his lovely bride! We want 5000 pieces of gold, a mere snippet for our good lord!" the flashy bandit stated grandly. "Oh and thank you for taking such good care of the lovely lady for us," he continued smirking sarcastically. "I thought that Vargos send the pavilion and the cook for the princess and not that insufferable hag? Whose man are you anyhow? Well, your foul mistress is done for, my odious friend, you better quickly reconsider your allegiance!"

A couple of the bandits stepped aside and for the first time, Angus caught sight of his mistress. "What have you done to her?" he asked in horror. "Given her a wee bit of Witchbane, my loathsome comrade!" The bandit answered with an affected wave towards the stricken witch. Puffing himself up like the peacock he resembled, he continued.

"Well, maybe more than a wee bit, she will never use her evil magic against anyone ever again! Her appalling reign of terror has come to a well-deserved end. The only reason you two live, my pungent friend, is that I require a messenger and your soldier as a witness. Please give the king greetings from Alandor the Great and congratulate him on the sagacious choice of a fine-looking new wife! I bid you both a most delightful night!" The colorful bandit ended his flowery speech with a deep bow. "Tie them up and gag them! Let's ride before any of this lot wakes up! I can do without the pleasure of killing any more of this incompetent lot!" he ordered with a laugh, giving Aaron a swat on the rear as he walked past.

With a grandiose gesture, the bandit took the princess's hand and started to parade her away from the fire towards their horses. Unfortunately, he was also leading her away from her mount as well as her possessions. The girl pulled his hand until the rogue came to a stop. "Wait, please, good sir, my horse is already saddled and loaded with some of my things. Would it not be better to return me to my future husband in one of my dresses instead of a soldier's garb?" Arianna asked the flashy outlaw with a hopeful smile.

"And, it would indeed warm my heart if I was allowed to have the company of my beautiful mount for the upcoming journey. Oh, and maybe we could take Queenie as well? She is a very sweet mare, and the witch claims her as her own. I think she deserves a better master! " the princess continued once she had the man's undivided attention. Alandor gave her an indulgent look. "After what you have been through, anything you want, my poppet!" he answered, bowing grandly. This man was just too much, but as long as she was able to keep Arabella, playing his silly little game was well worth it. "Come then, my princess, let us retrieve your fair mounts!"

With another one of his expansive gestures, the flamboyant bandit let Arianna lead him back to her horse. He ordered one of his men to get the beautiful white mare. Alandor carefully checked Arabella over and gave the animal, who was enthusiastically nuzzling Arianna, an affectionate pat. "She looks like a good horse, my pretty. You rode her yesterday, did you not, my sweet, and you traveled for many arduous hours?" he asked. The princess could only nod.

"We will bring her with us for your pleasure, but would her ladyship consent to riding one of my fine horses until this one is quite recovered? My horses are fresh while this one has yet to recuperate from all that exertion she has done in the last few days. My man there will make sure she is well taken care off, and as long as she keeps up, we will bring her along. Does this meet with her highness's approval?" he finished with an extravagant bow. "Yes, kind sir and I thank you!" Arianna replied and going along with his courtly manners, gave him a deep curtsy. As much as she would love to ride her own horse, she could not argue with the flashy bandit's logic.

The order was quickly given. The princess and her gallantly behaving escort were once more heading for the intruder's horses. "Oh, and my precious? Do not get it into your pretty little head to leave signs for the king's soldiers to follow. If you do not know this by now, this lot are not your friends, we are. Pardon me for stating the obvious, my cherished pet, but I do hope you know that your precious days were numbered? That ghastly hag would have never allowed you to reach that gloomy castle alive, my sweetest. I and my trusty men will take the best of care of you from now on so do not be afraid, my little blossom!" Alandor told her, smiling down at her. Did this guy always talk like this or was this some kind of game?

Arianna was introduced to her new mount, a beautiful black mare. When she asked what the horse was called, her question was met with a blank stare. It appeared the bandits did not name their animals. Turning to Alandor, she looked up at him beseechingly. "May I give her a name then, kind sir? I have always named my horses, it would just make me feel so much better having something to call her!" she pleaded with the gaudy man smiling up at him innocently. "It is but a small thing, you sweet natured creature! Name away!" and with another imposing gesture of his hand, Alandor granted the princess her wish. "I will call her Azariel then, and I am most grateful for your kindness, good sir!" The girl thanked him with a bob.

Soon, she was securely mounted on her new horse. They set out single file, the bandit king leading the way. The princess watched the man behind her pull Arabella along. She spotted Queenie further down the line. The king's soldiers had camped in a glade a little way off the road, and the outlaws were now retracing their way back through the camp towards the wide forest path leading to the highway. She was riding directly behind Alandor as he guided her and his thugs through the silent camp.

The woods were utterly quiet, the night seemed to be holding its breath. The only sounds to be heard were an occasional snore from one of the heavily drugged soldiers. The untended fires were slowly going out, and darkness was descending on the hushed glade. With the steadily reducing firelight, it was getting harder and harder to see. Riding through the forest in the dark of night would make for slow going. To speed things up, the sly bandit took the exact path the soldiers had taken and quickly guided them back to the road.

The trees had been cut back in a wide swath from the highway, and the moon was now illuminating their way. Not a word had been spoken since they had left the camp. It seemed that the showy bandit's troops were well trained. With a sweeping gesture, he gave the command for all but six of his men to ride south. Arianna realized that this would leave an easy trail for the soldiers to follow. The larger group was also taking the highly visible Queenie along.

The resourceful villain then had the rest of them and the princess spread out across the road facing towards the south. He had them back up their mounts for a stretch of about 40 feet. At his command, everyone stopped. Rags were tied over the horses' hoofs. Once they were all set, they turned their steeds and headed north toward Maridanmar. Their tracks would be less visible and blend in with those of the company of soldiers from the previous day. Any pursuit should follow the other group south.

The princess was greatly relieved that they had left behind live witnesses. Not only did she detest violence and had been horrified by the murders of the sentries and the brutal treatment of the witch and Angus, but it also helped her people. This way, the hateful ruler would learn that her own kingdom had nothing to do with the escape. King Vargos was said to be a nasty and vindictive monarch. From what Arianna had heard from his own men, she believed his reputation to be well deserved. Who else would give one such as that horrible witch free reign?

Worshippers of the Dark Arts had a reputation for abject cruelty. The princess was sure now that the enchantress belonged to this malicious sect. Anyone who knowingly associated with one such as Odessa, and who turned that kind of an individual lose on his own people, had to be just as evil as the sorceress. There was no way she ever wanted to make this man's acquaintance let alone become his wife. She had heard that to him, life was cheap. Would he even pay the exorbitant fee for his bride? The princess had no intention of sticking around these sneaky bandits long enough to find out.

At a rapid clip, Alandor had them move north on the moonlit road. There was just enough light to see by. Being well familiar with how to track and how to hide the traces of one's passing, the princess could only admire the bandit leader's shrewdness. Riding backward a short distance to blend in their trail and then covering the hooves to hide their imprints had been brilliant. He still kept them spread out. Arianna figured that, to the untrained observer, their tracks would be almost invisible since it was not unusual to have movement back and forth along a column of soldiers.

When they came to a meadow with a wide shallow creek meandering close to the road, Alandor gave the signal to stop. The ground had been churned up close to the water, and the princess figured that some of the men had allowed their horses to drink here the previous day. The bandit king waved for the princess to follow him and carefully rode his horse into the sleepily murmuring stream. The water appeared deceptively smooth, but the current was incredibly strong. It should wash away any signs of their passing.

Fighting against the flow, her valiant horse followed that of the ostentatious bandit upstream. They were now moving south, back into the direction they had just come from. Arianna was glad when the bandit king guided his mount onto a pebble-strewn beach. Her mare, with her hooves covered, had slipped several times on some of the slimy stones of the riverbed. The princess had worried about

Azariel getting hurt. She was only too aware that Alandor would show no mercy to a lame horse. Also, the idea of ending up in the cold water was less than appealing.

Riding in a streambed to lose one's pursuers was a trick well-known to the princess. The rocky creek bed and the rapid current would leave few traces to be found of their passing, even for the best tracker. Alandor's reputation for moving like a ghost was well deserved. The girl's heart was sinking, escaping from this bunch could turn out to be even harder than from the soldiers. Their showy leader was way too shrewd for her liking! If the man could track as well as he could misdirect, she would be hard pressed to keep from being recaptured.

The bandit king rode a little way into the trees and away from the creek. He called for Arianna to join him. Side by side they waited for the rest of the outlaws. No words were exchanged. The others followed their path and had soon reached them. Alandor led them further into the woods. Arianna watched with interest while the last of the men used branches to carefully wipe out all traces of their passing on the soft forest floor.

These guys were good! The princess was not thrilled with the depth of their skills but glad that she knew just how well trained they were before making her getaway. She would have to think of something a bit different here. The girl figured that she did have one advantage. These men had no reason to suspect her of having this kind of knowledge, and she would make sure to keep it that way.

The pretentious scoundrel slowly led them down a game trail in the gloomy, silent woods. It was truly dark now that they were back in the forest. The bright light of the moon only managed to penetrate the thick leafy cover here and there leaving the rest in deep, dark shadow. Riding while constantly trying to penetrate the murky blackness was exhausting. Arianna was getting very fatigued. She was greatly relieved when they finally made camp in a well-hidden glade. No fire was lit, and the bandits just got off their horses, unrolled their bedrolls, and went to sleep. Voices were kept to a little above a whisper and guards were set. Alandor pointed to a comfortable pad and blanket next to his own. After checking on her horses, the princess gratefully slipped into this makeshift bed. It was softer and warmer than anything she had slept in since leaving her home.

Arianna was so very tired but desperately needed to know if any of the men around her had any kind of magical ability. Shielding herself heavily, she sent out the tiniest of tendrils. Carefully checking each mind, she was soon reassured. None of them had any abilities beyond what was usually found in the general population and not even their leader had much more power than the rest. She did notice that he scratched at his chest when her probing mind briefly touched his. Interesting! She would have to explore this further tomorrow. Exhaustion overwhelmed her, and she was quickly asleep.

~

As soon as she began to dream, Kyrill was there. He had been waiting impatiently and was greatly relieved to be finally able to talk to her. The princess told him what had happened that day and her impression of the bandits. Arianna also mentioned the effect her probe had elicited on the canny Alandor. The prince was instantly concerned. He warned the girl to be extra careful while using her powers. The man could be wearing some sort of a talisman, and she needed to make figuring out what the outlaw had around his neck a high priority. Good thing the bandit king had been so deeply asleep that her light touch had not awoken him!

The young couple came up with several scenarios which might allow her to escape but none felt quite right. Arianna would have to play the situation by ear. For now, she was just content to be safely cuddled in Kyrill's arms, even if it was just a dream.

~~~

Chapter Ten

Disaster Reigns

*B*ack at the camp, Angus was desperately trying to free himself. From where he lay, he could hear the witch gagging and fighting to breathe. The captain felt little pity for her. The sorceress had used his family as hostages to make sure he would do everything she bid him do. His primary concern was actually for the princess. He had set things up so that the young woman could escape. What horrible luck that this had played right into the hands of Alandor and that she was now a prisoner of that poppycock bandit.

From his dealings with the man in the past, Angus knew that the outlaw was only marginally better than the sorceress. That cad would sell his own mother if there were profit to be had. He hid his real personality behind courtly and gallant manners but was, in all actuality, crazy as a loon. Clever as a fox as well. It was not just a persistent rumor that the bandit had been impossible to track. The captain figured he would need help retrieving the princess. He knew just who could aid him with that. But, to get the assistance he required, he would have to contact his king.

Angus wiggled his way close to the dying fire. He managed to set ablaze the trailing ends of the rope binding his hands. Gritting his teeth against the pain, the captain held still until the bonds had burned enough to finally loosen ever so slightly. That was the moment he had been waiting for, and he used his considerable strength to pull the cords apart. Once his hands were free, he set about untying his legs and removing their gags. "Are you alright?" he asked his soldier as he cut the bindings around the man's wrists and ankles.

"Yes, sir, I am well and really glad to be alive! I think they killed everyone else who was awake. I saw so many bodies as they hauled me here!" the young man answered with a shudder. "Aaron, I am sorry, but I need you to pull yourself together. You are all I have, and I need you. Go check the camp and try to wake any you can. And, see if you can find the pigeons!" Angus ordered. Seeing the boy visibly pale, he reassuringly patted his shoulder. "I have confidence in you. I know you can you handle this," the captain soothingly told the young man. Arron swallowed and visibly steeled himself. He looked up and met his superior's eyes. "Yes, sir, consider it done!" the youngster answered bravely.

The captain hated sending the young soldier on this dreaded errand, but he needed some time with the witch. As soon as the boy was off, Angus strode over to the sorceress. He felt like kicking her but was too decent a man to take his anger out on any helpless being. Instead, the officer picked up the unconscious woman and carried her to the pavilion. There, he sat her none too gently on her bed and propped her up with some pillows. If she was to live, he needed to make it easier for her to breathe. Getting a wet cloth, he wiped her face. Just as he was done, Odessa regained awareness. She started grabbing for her neck and tried to speak. When no sound would emerge from her tortured throat, she looked up at the captain with such anguish that he could not help but feel pity for the malicious enchantress.

The officer did not know much about Witchbane except that all magic users feared it. Whatever the brigands had given her, it had severely burned the woman's esophagus. Seeing that the water carafe and goblets were still in place, he filled a cup and tried to hand it to the trembling sorceress. He realized that she was shaking too much and was too weak to hold on to it. The witch was in bad shape, there was little life left in her. She was having a terrible time breathing and could barely hold up her head.

The captain, like most others in their kingdom, had severely suffered at the hands of this wicked woman. He undoubtedly did not feel very charitable towards her but was too kind a man to deny her solace. Supporting the sorceress's head, he set the cup against her lips. Slowly he let some water trickle into her parched mouth. He was appalled at the expression of pure agony on the witch's face when she tried to swallow the life-giving fluid. The pain was such that she again fell into deep unconsciousness. Angus covered her up and then left to take care of the camp and his men.

~

The night was cold and dark under the trees and getting the campfires going to give his sleeping men some warmth became an immediate priority. The officer started going from fire to fire and placing more logs on the still hot coals. As he went, he took stock of the dead. The captain was relieved to see that he had not lost as many men as he had at first feared. Some of the sentries must have imbibed in the tainted beer as well. They had fallen asleep at their posts which had most likely saved their lives.

What it would not spare them, however, was their superior's punishment. Angus would deal with them once the camp was awake and things settled down a bit. For now, he had more important things to do. The captain moved quickly and with purpose and soon caught up with Aaron. "They killed most of the sentries, sir, and I have not found anyone I can wake. But I did find some of the pigeons!" the young man stated proudly displaying the cage.

"Keep checking and let me have those birds!" Angus ordered. Taking the crate, he set off back into the direction of the pavilion. Placing the pigeons on the table, he fed and watered them. They would have a long way to fly come morning. Using the witch's pen and paper, he carefully wrote a note requesting aid. The birds could not carry much and the message, therefore, had to be brief: 'Princess kidnapped by Alandor, Odessa disabled, need help, send Tristan! Captain Angus Tremaine.' Making several copies, he precisely folded up the notes. Taking out one bird at a time, the captain gently inserted the papers into the small tubes tied to the pigeons' legs. He would send all but one to increase the chance of his plea for help reaching its desired destination.

The birds could not fly until it was light enough for them to see so, for now, they would remain in their shelter. Angus placed a cloth over the cage to calm them and to encourage them to sleep for a while. He needed the little messengers in top form so that they could cover the distance as quickly as possible. Before leaving the tent, the captain once more checked on the sorceress. The woman still appeared completely unconscious, but he did not trust her. The witch would not want word of this disaster to reach the castle. Looking back at the table and the covered crate, he made up his mind. Taking the cage with him, he headed back out to deal with the situation in the camp.

Just as Angus had placed yet another log on the fire, Aaron showed up with a sleepy-eyed and very guilty looking soldier in tow. "This one is sort of awake, sir, he is one of the sentries and only drank just a little," he reported. "Good, I want you two to start making some kahve! Aaron, make sure your buddy here drinks several cups! Let's see if we can't wake up a few more! And wake the envoy up, I do not care how! We need to go after the princess just as soon as it gets light!" "Yes sir!" both his men responded and dashed off. Angus went to check on the horses. To his great relief, Arabella was gone. But why had they also taken Queenie?

What was that girl up to now? Angus had long since figured out that the princess was far more resourceful and cunning than she let on. For a royal young lady, she was much too comfortable in men's clothing, and she rode like a boy. No noblewoman he had ever known would have been able to stay in the saddle all day without getting some serious blisters. This one, however, seemed to actually enjoy it and had suffered no ill effects whatsoever. The captain was reasonably sure that there was much which had been hidden from them by this young woman.

The calmness and composure she had shown while enduring the abuse by the hag spoke of great poise. She had never actually complained or cried like her predecessors. No, this one was cut from a very different cloth than the rest! The captain, knowing people well, had felt that the helplessness the princess did display was just an act. The more he had gotten to know her, the greater his respect and admiration for the young girl had become.

He had once had the pleasure of meeting her mother, Queen Anna, and had been most impressed. There was a woman who was confident in herself, calm, and exceedingly kind. Angus had instantly liked her and had never forgotten her compassion towards him. She had saved him from being brutally punished for something the then Prince Vargos's had done. The queen had handled the situation with great diplomacy and had expertly manipulated the irate king of Lothrien into forgetting all about the chastisement he was just about to dole out.

The captain had never had an opportunity to thank the lady. Helping her daughter escape had been his way of paying back the debt which he felt he had incurred so many years ago. He had tried to do this in such a way that it did not put his family in more danger and thought he had succeeded quite well. The girl should have been off on her own by now, free to go where she pleased. Why did fate have to intervene by sending that rotten crook?

~

The hours crept by and to the impatient Angus it felt like the night would never end. He wandered from fire to fire checking on his men, making sure none rolled to close to the flames in their drugged sleep. Aaron and his buddy kept supplying him with kahve. They did manage to pour some of the reviving liquid down a few of the more awake soldiers. The rest were still in deep slumber, and the sound of snoring around the place appeared almost deafening to the officer's ears. The envoy was spoon-fed kahve, and his throat massaged to make him swallow but had not yet awoken. At least, they had a few men out as sentries now and would be alerted if any more surprises showed up. Defending themselves, on the other hand, would be a different story.

Finally, the first light of dawn began to slowly tinge the velvet night sky. Angus released the pigeons, but it appeared the little messengers had a mind of their own. They seemed to think that it was still too dark to fly so instead of heading for the castle, the five drowsy birds flew up into the nearest tree, put their heads under their wings, and went back to sleep. The captain watched in frustration for a moment then called for Aaron. "Soldier, make sure those things gets on their way as soon as it is a little lighter!" he ordered pointing at the peacefully slumbering birds. "Yes, sir, I sure will!" came the prompt reply.

The young man was nervously stepping from foot to foot. "Sir, you said you do not care how we wake up the envoy. Did you mean this?" the apprehensive soldier asked, giving his captain a hopeful look. The officer knew most of them hated the arrogant little toad, himself included, but he was still a powerful man who had the ear of the king. "Within reason, Aaron, within reason! But I do need him awake! What did you have in mind?" Angus replied with a grin. "We thought the cold water of the creek might wake him, sir!" the young man replied with a broad smile. His captain could not help himself and let out a laugh. Well, this was, after all, an emergency, and the end justified the means. "Do it!" he ordered. "Oh and Aaron? I hereby grant you the rank of lieutenant. Congratulations!" The newly promoted man let out of whoop and dashed off to do his worst to awaken the comatose Sebastian.

~

The commander gathered three of the more awake soldiers together as well as a couple of his scouts. Angus was finalizing preparations to chase after the bandits when the envoy came stumbling up. He was dripping wet, and his face was red with fury. "Are you responsible for this? How dare you let them throw me into the creek?" the nasty little fellow screamed at the officer. "I demand to know immediately what is going on here! Did SHE authorize this?" he sputtered. The commander looked at him calmly. "Come with me, please," he told the enraged emissary.

The captain turned and strode towards the witch's pavilion. Sebastian had to almost run to keep up with the much taller man. By the change of his face from red to purple, it was evident that this incensed him further. Angus motioned him into the tent and pointed to the unconscious sorceress who was still gasping for air.

"What is wrong with her?" the envoy demanded. "Alandor, the Bandit King, poured Witchbane down her, and it was strong enough to burn her throat. He also made off with the princess," the captain answered. "Witchbane? What does it do?" questioned the instantly hopeful Sebastian. Maybe he would finally have the upper hand after all! The part about the princess's abduction had completely escaped him. "I guess it takes their powers and, according to the bandits, given in large enough doses, burns out their magical abilities forever," Angus replied. "You mean she is powerless? Can't do anything anymore to any of us?" the envoy asked with unsuppressed glee. "It seems so, and right now she is barely surviving as it is. I am sure you want to keep her alive to face the justice of our 'kindhearted' king," the captain told him. The elated emissary immediately dashed to the entrance of the tent and shouted for soldiers.

Two sleepy looking men responded to his call and Sebastian waved them into the tent impatiently. "Tie her up and move her out of here, I want the princess to have her tent back!" he commanded pompously. Seeing the fear of the men as they approached the sorceress, the fat little envoy ambled over and cruelly grabbed the woman by the hair and shook her head. "She is done for, see? Can't do a thing to you, not anymore! Now get her out of here!" he bellowed. "Where would you like us to put her?" the now maliciously grinning soldiers inquired. "I do not care but let's get her to the castle alive, alright?" Sebastian replied with a malevolent smirk of his own. He knew that turning the hated witch over to the soldiers did not bode well for her. The evil woman had terrorized them all, and few would show her mercy now that her powers were gone.

The soldiers roughly tied up the unconscious sorceress. When they started to shove a rag in the gasping woman's mouth, Angus objected. "We want to get her to the castle to stand trial! If you cover her mouth, you make it harder for her to breathe, and she could die!" the officer protested. The envoy overruled him. Sebastian was not prepared to take any chances where that witch was concerned. She had terrorized and humiliated him for too long.

"Now let's get the princess moved in here!" the envoy ordered after the tied and gagged sorceress had been roughly carried out of the pavilion. "Sir, did you not hear me? The princess has been kidnapped! The bandits carried her off with them last night! They doused the witch so she would not be able to follow them!" the captain impatiently told the obnoxious little man. Once these words finally sunk in, the emissary turned deathly pale.

Sebastian knew he was done for. Conveying the princess safely to the castle had been the job the king had assigned him. His sovereign was not tolerant where failure was concerned. "Kidnapped? You mean they took her?" he squeaked. "Yes, sir, and I need to get going to try to bring her back. I have sent for help from the castle," he told the much-shrunken man. "Bring her back? Yes, yes, by all means! Why are you still standing there? Go find her! Please find her!" the envoy begged, sinking on the bed so recently occupied by the witch.

The captain watched for a moment as the devastated emissary placed his head in his hands in despair and started to sob. He knew that the toady was not really worried about the princess, just his own hide. Sebastian began to rock back and forth and to repeat over and over again. "What am I going to do?" The nasty little man was substantially deflated. He was only too aware that if the princess was not found and delivered to the castle unharmed, his life was forfeit. The envoy's despondent cries followed Angus out of the pavilion as he strode back over to the horses where his men were waiting. They were ready to ride.

~~~

Chapter Eleven

A Desperate Pursuit

*L*eaving a freshly promoted Aaron in charge, Captain Angus Tremaine led his men along the path. Each soldier was pulling along an extra horse. This would allow them to ride faster and further and would give them a better chance of catching up with the bandits. The new lieutenant, anticipating his commander's needs, had ordered several of his soldiers to look for traces of the brigands while his captain dealt with the envoy. And, he had made sure the sleepy birds went on their way. The scouts had found no hint of a second trail leading away from the camp. That left them with the conclusion that the kidnappers had ridden out the same way they had brought their horses in, on the main track leading directly back to the road.

The bandit king had been troubling the realm for many years, and the captain had made it his business to learn as much as he could about the outlaw. The man was said to move like a ghost. He would strike and then disappear without a trace. Angus feared that attempting to follow the criminal might be a waste of time but still, he had to try for

171

Arianna's sake. The officer did not want to see the sweet princess married to his hateful sovereign. What he had learned about Alandor, however, made him believe that she was in worse hands right now. That this bright young woman should be at the mercy of either man did not sit well with him in the first place. He was determined that, if it were at all possible, he would find a way for her to escape and take charge of her own life.

Once the group of soldiers reached the road, their best scout dismounted to look for tracks. "It seems they have gone south, captain, or, at least, most of them!" he reported to his superior after a careful search of the area. "Just as I expected! A diversion to send us in the wrong direction! That is what I would do, and take the princess the opposite way instead," Angus replied. The shrewd captain decided to follow his instincts and head toward the north. Aid from the castle should arrive within a couple days, and the officer knew that he needed to leave signs for the troops to follow. After clearly marking the turn-off, the soldiers kicked the horses into a fast trot.

At first, there was no evidence at all that any of the bandits had gone this way until here and there a smudged hoof print drew their attention. "Using rags, were they?" the scouts said with amusement. Now that they knew what to look for, it made the trail easier to follow. The covered hooves left a faint but noticeable trace. And, they had confirmation that they were heading in the right direction. Keeping a careful eye on the tracks on the road, the company moved north as fast as they could.

Suspecting some trick from the crafty criminal, Angus was prepared when the smudged hoof prints they had been following suddenly stopped. Turning around, he and his scouts carefully checked the sides of the road. There were hoof prints all over from his large group passing the day before. In one spot a couple of his men had ridden on the side of the highway. They had left a distinct trail. What drew the captain's attention was an indent in this track leading away from the road. The cloth-covered hooves had actually wiped out his soldiers' prints. It had been much too dark for the bandits to realize that they had left a clear path for the captain to follow. Angus traced the trail with his eyes and took notice of the creek. Oldest trick in the book! He immediately figured that the outlaws had ridden up or down in the river to try to throw off pursuit.

Sending his scouts in both directions, he had them carefully check the banks of the merry little stream. And, once again they got lucky! One single hoof print gave away the place where the group had exited the creek the night before. Carefully, with his best guide in the lead, the group followed the trail. At first, there was evidence of care having been taken by the outlaws to hide their tracks, but the further the soldiers got away from the river, the more apparent their path became. It seemed the bandits were getting careless and thought they had successfully shaken off all followers.

~

After some hard riding, the determined captain and his men reached the glade where the robbers had made camp for a few hours. There was no evidence of fires, but the horse dung left behind still had more than just a little hint of warmth to it. The bandits must have slept for quite a while, feeling overconfident that their tricks had thrown off any pursuit by the soldiers. The men were thrilled. They were not too far behind, and if they hurried, they might be able to catch up with the fleeing outlaws before too much longer.

Encouraged by the closeness of their quarry, the group of soldiers spurred their horses on to even greater speed.

There was a chance after all that they might be able to overtake that mangy lot and rescue the kidnapped princess. Angus was leaving signs every chance he got. The reinforcements would follow his marks just as soon as they arrived from the castle. Aaron would make certain of that. The captain was glad to have such a competent fellow in charge of the debilitated camp. The young man had ably risen to the occasion and sure deserved his promotion.

They had been riding almost due west for a while when around midday the tracks they had been following were joined by two more horses. Angus figured that these were the bandit leader's scouts who had been checking behind the villains for pursuit. The captain hoped that he and his men had been far enough behind to have gone unnoticed. He was glad that he had followed his intuition instead of chasing after the larger company of the rascals heading south. The officer was sure they would have led him on a merry chase. There was no telling where that lot intended to meet back up with their illustrious leader.

Two additional horses could mean two more outlaws or two scouts returning. It was hard to tell exactly how many mounts had been moving along the forest path, but it seemed to be at least nine. The determined commander was not happy that he and his men were outnumbered. A feeling of unease began to settle in his gut. This trail was just too easily followed and from what he had heard about Alandor, that man was a terribly cunning fellow. Were he and his soldiers being lured into a trap? What had happened to the brigands' uncanny ability to just disappear? "Be alert for anything!" the officer ordered his companions as they rode through the serene woods.

All of them were aware to one degree or another of the bandit leader's reputation. As they silently trotted through the thick forest, the soldiers kept looking around nervously. There was no evidence of trouble. The only sounds were from their horses, and all appeared peaceful. The birdsong echoing among the sunlit trees would cease at their passage and then quickly resume. The buzz of insects was loud enough to be heard even over the pounding of the hooves. To the captain and his men, all seemed as it should. Angus, however, being a prudent man and lifelong soldier, was only too aware that appearances could be deceiving.

~

It would take time for the pigeons to reach the castle and more time for their elven scout to arrive at the camp. The officer realized that it was up to him and his men to rescue the captured princess. And, if he could lay his hands on Alandor in the process, even better. That outlaw had been a thorn in the side of the king for many years now. Angus would have loved nothing better than to put a stop to the rascal's thieving and terrorizing. Bringing in the bandit leader might even make up a little for losing the princess. The chances of success were slim, however. The captain was a realistic man. In the past, even the best trackers had lost the trail of the brigands every time.

No one had ever been able to locate the flamboyant Alandor's hideout, not even the king's best scout. Angus was only too aware of this. That he and his men had made it this far, had been pure luck and a bit of cunning on his part. Think like the enemy! Had it not been for that they might be chasing shadows down the road somewhere. But, the pursuit being this easy had him severely concerned. Was this a false trail as well? The path they were following was meandering through the peaceful woods, and the traces of the bandit's passage were so obvious that they could have been followed by anyone. If the rogues kept going in the same direction, they would soon reach the rocky foothills which extended west all the way to the mountains.

The captain knew that only the most skilled tracker could follow prints across rocky terrain. Neither he nor his men had that kind of talent. They had to get to the princess before then. Once they caught up with the thugs, how could they overcome them? They would be facing a superior number of well-trained fighters.

Add to this that he and his men were not in the best shape at the moment. Angus was hurting all over from the beating he had received. His companions were still recovering from the after-effects of the sleeping draft after having been drugged the night before. The officer would have to be cunning and find some advantage to even the odds. If they were going to help the princess, they needed to get her away from her captors and soon.

Sending the two scouts ahead, he spurred his men on to even greater speed. They fairly flew along the path weaving its way through the woods in the desperate hope that they would catch up with the kidnappers in time.

~~~

Chapter Twelve

A Clever Switch

It was well past dawn when the bandit leader shook Arianna awake. "Good morning, your radiant highness! Time to get up! I hope you slept well, my dearest dove?" he gallantly addressed her. The man bowed to her deeply as soon as she sat up and grabbed her hand. Before she knew what happened, he had placed a faint kiss on her palm. Yuck! On the back of the hand would have been bad enough but on the palm? That gesture had been way too intimate for her liking!

Feeling disoriented for a moment, the princess shook her head. Could this be some sort of a nightmare? Memories of the night before flooded in. No, this was real, even if it did feel like a bad dream. The girl focused on the flamboyant man. Now that she saw him in the daylight, he very much reminded her of a peacock. The brilliant colors of his garments encouraged that resemblance further. He was still wearing a mask, as were all his men, but while theirs were more utilitarian, his was a beautiful dark purple and ornately stitched.

What a bizarre scene! But, as long as she was this poppycock's prisoner, she would have to play along. Getting back into the spirit of his courtly manners, she answered. "Thank you, good sir, I slept very well and most comfortably. But do pray, would you please tell me where I might take care of my morning ablutions?" Following his directions, she set out to do just that. One of his men was trailing behind. After a pleading look, the outlaw even gave her a modicum of privacy to conduct her business. How much she was starting to miss indoor toilets! A bathtub would have been pure heaven!

When the princess returned to the camp, one of the men handed her some bread, meat, and cheese for breakfast. She started eating ravenously; she was always hungry of late. All that fresh air and the lack of food for the first couple days appeared to have left her half-starved. By the time she was done, Azariel and Arabella were already saddled and ready. She watched two of the bandits heading out. Arianna figured they were sent back to keep an eye out for possible pursuit. It was just a moment before Alandor gave the order to saddle up.

One of the bandits brought over more food wrapped in a cloth and handed it up to her once she was mounted on Azariel. She thanked him effusively for his kindness; he must have seen how famished she was. He also handed her a flask with water. The princess accepted it gratefully and gave the man a sweet smile. These bandits were treating her so much better than her royal escort had done! But then again, she was worth a lot of money to them. The tidy sum of 5000 gold pieces was enough to live on for a very long time or to buy a small kingdom.

"Is there anything else you require, fair maiden?" Alandor inquired. "Not at this time and thank you for your kind regard," Arianna answered. "If you are still hungry, you may eat while we ride, my beautiful lady, but please, no leaving a trail of breadcrumbs for those nasty soldiers to follow!" the bandit joked. The princess laughed. "Now why would I want them to find me, good sir? To drag me back and be subjected to that toady envoy and that horrid witch once more? No, dear sir, I prefer the present company!" she assured him.

Could she possibly make a deal with this man? The payoff was terribly high, and the princess knew her father and aunt together would be hard pressed to come up with even half that amount. She had heard that King Vargos had more money than most of the other monarchs, but that hefty a sum should even hurt his coiffeurs and leave the realm depleted. This once again brought up the question in the girl's mind. Would the malicious monarch be willing to pay that kind of money for his reluctant bride?

Pondering this subject further while following Alandor along the peaceful forest trail, Arianna hit on a disturbing notion. What if the bandit did not intend to turn her over at all and therefore set the ransom so high that not even the richest of the kings could pay it? The thought suddenly terrified her and felt somehow right. What could he really have in mind for her? Something felt off, but the princess was not sure about the source of her apprehension. Whatever it was, she had no desire to find out. She needed to get away from these bandits and soon! 'My Lady, please help me! Give me a sign! Tell me what I should do!' She ardently prayed. Opening her senses just a little, she waited for an answer.

Since she was relatively unobserved, this was also a good time to check each man once more to make sure that her own magic would go unnoticed. Remembering the bandit leader scratching his chest and Kyrill's warning, she started with Alandor. If he had something warning him of magic, she would have one shot at this. She very carefully used the tiniest tendril of awareness to check the man's neck and chest area. As her senses slid over him, she found a crystal hidden under his clothes. A magic detector! It would heat up in the presence of power and alert its bearer. The princess could feel it starting to warm just a little now at her probing. She quickly placed a shield around the pendant and then scanned the rest of the men for any magical items. She almost sighed with relief that this was the only crystal of its kind in the outlaws' possession.

Now that the talisman was dealt with, she carefully examined the bandit king for any trace of arcane abilities. She confirmed that he was just as non-magic as she had found him to be the night before, as were the rest of his men. Just to make sure, Arianna let her senses drift through all their packs. She felt a whole lot better when nothing else which could threaten her turned up. She would still be extra careful, but it was time to turn her attention back to the crystal. What to do about it? She had come to severely dislike the pompous bandit and regarded him as a real danger to herself and others. Leaving the powerful jewel in his possession just did not strike her as a wise idea.

Carefully reaching out with her mind, she examined it closer. It was just a regular crystal; there seemed to be no special markings on the pendant at all. It would be indistinguishable from any other amulet of its kind, and its shape was fairly regular as well. That gave her a delightfully wicked idea. Kyrill had mentioned that his warriors had seen a dragon over this area. He assumed that the creature's den was somewhere in the mountains not far from here. The scaled beasts were notoriously attached to their hoard. Even the theft of a minor thing, such as a small crystal, would be seen as unforgivable and the trinket retrieved at all cost. Arianna remembered the rumors of how this obnoxious brigand had given the slip to all the trackers sent after him. Let him try that with a very determined dragon!

Since there was no room for mistakes, the princess decided to go over the crystal once more. And, a good thing she did! This time, she noticed something she had totally missed before. There was just one little notch there, but she instantly felt that it had some significance to the outlaw. She would have to make sure to duplicate this on the copy. Firmly holding the image of the crystal in mind, she let a small part of her consciousness travel towards the mountains. Soon she found traces of magic which led her straight to the dragon's den.

What a fantastic place! There was so much treasure here, it completely amazed her. Looking for a twin to the crystal would be like looking for a needle in a haystack! And, she had to be very cautious. If she used too much power, she would awaken the dragon. Remembering that the Lady had insisted that she call on her in times of need, Arianna sent a quick prayer for help to her Goddess. Suddenly, she felt a slight tug to the left. She followed it all the while casting about for just the right stone. The girl was careful to just use a minute tendril of her awareness, but she still had to beware of the dragon. Leaving even a trace of her passing would lead it to her and not the bandit as she intended.

The insistent pulling guided her to a far corner of the cave. It seemed this was the area the huge creature kept its less valuable hoard. The princess soon located a crystal identical to the one belonging to the outlaw. After making sure that it was just a plain stone and completely inert, she transported the gem into her hand. Sending it this far a distance had been no problem for her. It was time to make sure Alandor would get the attention he deserved. Should she wake up the dragon? From what she knew of the reptilian firebreathers, it might stir soon, or it could be weeks. She needed the great beast to deal with the scoundrel now and not some time in the distant future.

Dropping a crystal on the pile with a loud ping woke the huge monster. It voiced its displeasure with an earthshaking roar. Now, to give it some direction. Disguising her magic, Arianna used the tiniest amount of power possible. She sent a fleeting image of Alandor rolling in gold and gems inside a cave to the vast mind. Time to go! The princess willed the tendril back to herself and slammed shut her shields. No human might have been able to find the brigands' fortress, but she was sure the dragon would. And, the idea of treasure to be gained should keep the giant being from attacking while they were still on their way. The princess hoped to be long gone before the large creature came calling.

Before she could swap them, she needed to make this jewel look exactly like the other one. Opening her shields a minute bit, she reached out with her magic. The girl gently nudged the crystal's matrix just a little to add the tiny notch. Satisfied that the gem was now an exact copy of the one worn by the bandit leader, Arianna prepared to make the switch. Holding the crystal in her hand, she envisioned it replacing the magic seeker and voila! It was done. The harmless gem took its potent twin's place in the wire cage designed to allow it to be worn close to the outlaw's chest. During the exchange, the man never flinched or showed any other signs of alarm. It seemed her deed had gone unnoticed, but the princess decided that it would still be prudent to remain extra vigilant.

Keeping the gem shielded, the princess transferred it to the medicine bag she wore around her neck. As an extra precaution, she placed a spell of aversion on the talisman in addition to the incantations already protecting the pouch. So far nobody had searched her, and she was glad that her shirt was loose enough to hide the small lump. She had worn the little sack for years and had placed enchantments around it every few months to make sure it was always concealed from prying eyes. Unless someone knew it was there, they would never see or feel it. Not even her maid had known of the satchel's existence.

The day had started out feeling a bit like a nightmare but was getting better. Having averted the danger of her magic use being detected, Arianna let out a sigh of relief. Looking around she became aware of the lush forest and that the foggy morning had turned into a beautiful, bright day. They had been riding for some time, and the sun was standing almost directly overhead in the sky. The woods were lit up brilliantly, and only an occasional cloud caused shadows to slink through the magnificent trees. The air smelled fresh and was full of the scent of conifers and the occasional flower. Arianna would have really enjoyed this journey had she been on her own as planned. Being kidnapped by this lot had upset all her well-laid plans. The princess was not unduly worried, however. She believed that everything happened for a reason and that something good would come out of this as well. She just had to wait and see and, at the right time, all would become clear.

They were moving along at a fast trot, and her gut told her that they had a long way yet to go. It would have been nice to have more information but, oh well! A while later, the two scouts Alandor had sent out earlier that morning caught up with them. They must have brought good news.

The flashy bandit visibly relaxed after taking their report. If there was any pursuit, it must be far behind by now. In a quick prayer, she thanked her Lady for her help and, grudgingly, asked for further assistance. She actually felt lighter after this brief contact with her divine benefactor. The girl looked around herself with renewed confidence. The woods were glorious, and the contrast of the dark, tall trees against the vibrantly blue sky filled her with warm appreciation. The princess decided she might as well enjoy herself and have faith that some sort of help would turn up.

~~~

Chapter Thirteen

New Friends

lowly the soft forest floor was changing to rocky soil. The dense trees were giving way to more open spaces, allowing bushes and other low vegetation to reach up high towards the sky. Sunlight was filtering down in some areas onto the mossy ground. Where before they had been able to see a good distance among the tall trees, bushes were now crowding in on them on both sides of the path for long stretches. They were still following the game trail. Arianna guessed it was used by deer and other ruminants. Suddenly, the picture of an elk flashed into the princess's awareness followed by one of a stampede. Searching carefully with her mind, she located a herd of the large animals not far away.

So this was the Goddess's suggestion! To use a stampeding herd of elk to make good her escape! The princess loved the idea but thought a little help from some of the local fairies might go a long way toward making the endeavor a success. She had adored the many fey forest dwellers in the woods around the castle since she was a small child and had always gotten along well with them. With time, a deep bond had been forged, and the princess had gladly accepted the small moon symbol on her left wrist marking her as one of their own. There should be elementals here in these woods as well. Maybe they would be willing to help her.

The fairies were often shy, and any contact had to be initiated carefully. The princess decided to delicately reach out with her mind and search for any wood spirits who might be able to assist her. Putting the intent forward of finding someone prepared to help, she let a tiny band of consciousness flow out and wander where it was drawn. Just then, Alandor turned to check on her. The girl gave him a bright smile. Reassured, the bandit gave her a friendly wave and turned to the front once more. Good thing Baladazar had trained her so well. She had learned to compartmentalize. Arianna would be alert to her surroundings while part of her mind turned inward and worked her magic. She had perfected this years ago and using her powers was as natural to her as breathing.

~

The princess had displayed feats of magic almost from birth. Her mother, Queen Anna, had immediately sent for her own trusted and completely loyal nanny, Ruth. The king had dispatched his fastest team of horses to Re'adeen, but it had still taken several long days before the nurse had arrived. Until the woman reached the castle, only the queen had cared for the infant. All the servants, except one faithful chambermaid, had been banned from her chambers with the excuse that mother and child were ill and needed to rest.

The elderly lady had her own magical abilities and was well equipped to deal with gifted children. She handled the talented infant with patience and love and managed to hide most of the minor incidences which happened on a daily basis. The ones she could not hide, she blamed on spirits. The queen had insisted that Arianna's teaching was begun as early as possible and kept entirely secret. She did not want her daughter to have to deal with the same prejudices she had been forced to endure.

Even for the two adept ladies, dealing with a small child with magic that strong had proved to be a challenge. They had needed someone with more extensive training than they had been privileged to. The king had asked his friend and advisor, Baladazar, for help. The magician had moved into the castle under the pretext of becoming the court wizard.

At times, Baladazar, a very powerful sorcerer, Queen Anna, and the nanny had almost despaired. Dealing with a toddler with that kind of power was challenging at best. Punishment for any bad behavior would have been dangerous had the child not been so good natured. The three feared that they would eventually run out of excuses for the odd and often childish occurrences around the castle. They needed to get the little princess to see reason.

The wizard had always made the lessons fun for the child. She was extremely bright and loved learning about magic and the world around her. The adults had finally seen themselves forced to use this against the exuberant toddler. After being told her lessons would come to an end if she did not stop the mischief, the small girl had mostly behaved herself.

~

Sometimes, however, the princess had felt strongly that someone needed to be taught a lesson. Especially when dealing with the situation in a conventional way had not yielded the desired result. One such case had been the groom she caught beating her pony. The man's cruel behavior toward her beloved pet had deeply upset her. The girl hated seeing anyone mistreat any defenseless animal, but this had hit too close to her heart. The first time she had given him a stern warning and informed the stable master. Just to be sure, she had also set wards on her pony so she would know the instant it happened again. It was a good thing she did.

The man had been furious about the talking to he received from the then eight-year-old princess as well as the stable master. He had intended to take his anger out on the defenseless animal. When he had reached out to strike the first blow, to his immense surprise, his left arm had taken on a life of its own. The whip had started furiously beating him about his face and head, the same places he had aimed for on the unfortunate pony. Time after time the whip had come down and hit the stunned man. He had ended up getting a dose of his own medicine. The groom had tried to get his arm under control but to no avail. He had attempted to imprison the offending appendage in a hay manger, but that did not work out too well either. Finally, he had gone running for the barn door all the while screaming for help.

It had been quite the spectacle when the terrified man had come racing into the courtyard beating himself, all the while screaming to make it stop. And, would you not know it, the stable master had been there to see the display. The panicked groom had never even noticed it when the blows stopped. He had kept on running around screaming for help.

Two of the other stable hands finally had to get a hold of him. They had pinned him to the ground until he calmed. The master had loomed over the cad and had inquired what he had been doing and why he had been beating himself. At first, the groom had refused to answer, but then the frightened man had admitted to having gone to beat the pony and that somehow his own arm had turned against him.

The stable master, who like most others did not like the man to start with, saw little humor in the situation. Abusing any animal was severely frowned on in the castle. Most figured the vicious stable hand had gotten what he deserved and that his own shriveled up consciousness had finally gotten the better of him. The man was escorted to the gates that very hour and sent off to a job herding cattle far, far to the north. Life and the people there were rough, and the letter warned his new master of the groom's violent tendencies and unstable disposition. No, life would not be pleasant for him there.

No one except Baladazar and the queen had ever suspected that their princess might have had something to do with this strange affair. After all, she had been in the kitchen talking to the maids during the entire incident.

~

Most feats of magic were easy for Arianna, including finding whatever she needed or desired. The tiny ribbon of consciousness she sent out was drawn here and there. It moved about a bit indecisively at first. Suddenly, it streaked off in a straight line. It had located a group of forest sprites. The fairies were surreptitiously watching the passing riders. The princess could feel their anger as they observed the outlaws from a nearby knoll. The little ones appeared extremely wary and on high alert. Approaching them might be a challenge.

The reaction to her mind's careful contact was one of alarm and far from welcoming. It sent the sprites into a panic. She ended up raising her arm and brushing some hair out of her face to cover the gesture of displaying her wrist. Only after they had seen the mark identifying her as a friend did the fairies calm down just enough to listen. The girl had to assure them over and over again that she was not with the bandits by choice but their prisoner. She repeatedly asked to be allowed to speak to their queen but to no avail. They were still afraid of her.

The group of elementals was so rattled that it took the appearance of their queen to finally settle them down. To have a strange human mind make contact with them so unexpectedly had never happened to them before. The little monarch took over the conversation. Arianna had to explain her situation yet once again, and she repeated her request for help. The queen, Liza, was hesitant at first. The tiny ruler insisted that the princess allow her full access to her memories which the girl was a bit apprehensive about granting. Having no other options, she finally consented. Seeing the truth in the young woman's mind, the small regent's mistrust faded.

Negotiations between the two parties began. The queen related to the princess that they had also suffered at the bandits' hands. She and her people were eager for revenge. They would be happy to help the girl get away if this fouled up things for the outlaws. Arianna could not make out from the queen's thoughts exactly what had happened, but it seemed that whatever it was had injured several of the sprites and had damaged their homes. One thing, however, came through loud and clear. The fairies felt that the injury which had been done to them had been done out of pure spite and malice. And, in their opinion, such acts were typical of most human beings.

Whatever it was the bandits had done and whether it had been done on purpose or not, their action had sparked these capricious beings ire. The little fairies had been waiting for an opportunity to get back at these callous men. The sprites told Arianna that they had been thinking of different ways to get even with the cruel humans. Their biggest problem had been that they had too many brilliant ideas. Each elemental had felt that their idea was best, and so they had not been able to settle on one. Their queen had tried to keep the peace, but the discussions had gotten rather heated at times ending with bloody noses, scratched faces, or worse.

Now that they had accepted the princess, they saw her almost as one of their own. That the sweet young woman their queen was communicating with was the prisoner of these beastly men infuriated the vengeful beings even further. They were happy to hear that the girl had a plan. That was even better than trying to come up with one of their own! The mischievous little creatures were all prepared to vote for their new friend's idea since this did not give status to one of the others. Getting revenge and helping a maiden in distress? Perfect!

The princess carefully outlined her strategy and asked the queen if she knew a good spot to execute their ploy. The tiny monarch sure did, and a picture of the area flowed into Arianna's mind. It was a small clearing with a wide game path intersecting the one she and the bandits were on. It would do nicely for what they had planned. The queen explained the plot to her people, and the prospect of what was about to come the bandits' way left the sprites cackling with glee. They immediately began 'improving' on the plan.

The girl was not sure how she felt about this. From her years of interactions with fairies, the princess was only too aware that they could be willful and that they could not always be trusted. There had been several groups of wood sprites around her home and Arianna had gotten to know them well.

This group, however, was different. They were much less friendly to humans and very, very vengeful. She had noticed that there was more of a conversation going on than she was privileged to and inquired carefully if there was some sort of a problem. The petite queen assured the young woman that everything was under control. She and her sprites would make sure that the girl got safely away with her horses.

Feeling the concern Arianna had for the steeds sat well with the nature-loving fairies. They had promised that they would make sure that Azariel came along as well. The girl had been unwilling to leave the beautiful mare behind. Liza insisted that there was no need to worry. She, the Queen of the Fairies, would personally make sure the princess escaped from these awful men. The little sprite told Arianna to be ready to flee and that they would cover her tracks and prevent any pursuit. No one would be able to follow her as long as the fairies were with her. In spite of all these assurances, the young woman suspected that her idea had been hijacked. Nagging misgiving left her with an uncomfortable feeling in the pit of her stomach.

~

The capricious elementals did have a couple 'requests' in return for their assistance. The tiny queen enlightened the princess that some of her people wanted to accompany the young woman. They were bored and looking for entertainment and felt that traveling along with the girl was sure to prove full of surprises. Liza told Arianna that this would benefit them all. The fairies would get their adventure and in return, they would warn their new friend and help her avoid most dangers. The queen stated that it would be a win-win situation for both parties.

Arianna loved most nature spirits but especially sprites. She found them adorable and their antics delightful even if they were rather naughty at times. The girl was only too happy to agree to let some of them come along. She figured it was a small price to pay for an effective escape and having company for the long journey ahead would be nice as well.

The princess was less thrilled about providing consent to allow the fairies free reign in dealing with these ignoble men. Whatever the outlaws had done, they had certainly succeeded in thoroughly angering the little ones. The sprites were buzzing with anticipation of the upcoming revenge. They seemed to be really looking forward to getting even with these unpleasant rascals. Arianna had heard that elementals could be exceedingly cruel. She could only hope that the well-armed bandits were up to the challenge. They were grown men, after all, and should be able to take care of themselves. In any case, what other options did she have? This might be her only and best chance to escape.

Hurting anyone was very much against the princess's nature. Yes, she was the prisoner of these lawless men, but so far they had treated her with courtesy and respect. It was their leader she had the biggest problem with. The girl could feel deep in her heart that the fate Alandor had planned for her was not a pleasant one. When she did pass this on to the Queen, Liza was thoughtful for a moment. The diminutive monarch assured the princess that she would do what she could to make sure none of the brigands got hurt too badly. Somehow those words did not come across as very sincere. Arianna let out a resigned sigh. It seemed that was the best she could do for the scoundrels.

As soon as they had reached an agreement, the sprites raced for the elk and took control of the herd. They started to move the animals in the direction of the bandits' path. The princess was informed by Liza that the outlaws came through here often and always went the same way. The woods in this area were not as dense, and the glade coming up was perfectly suited for their purpose. The queen sent a general picture of where and how much further to Arianna's mind but the princess figured that it might be best to get her own understanding of the lay of the land. She would have to find an opportunity once they got closer to the place. A soaring raptor might be willing to let her share its vision, and the bird's eye view would help put distances in perspective.

~

To make sure that there was no chance of losing the rest of her meager possessions, Arianna needed to change horses and quickly. The kidnapping had destroyed any opportunity of retrieving the stash which had been left for her near the border. All her other belongings were still with the soldiers. How could she get Alandor to let her ride Arabella? It only took the princess a moment to come up with a solution. Making contact with her gentle steed's mind, she began to carefully persuade Azariel that she needed help. Could the mare act like her hoof hurt from stepping on a stone? The princess detected a willingness to help but also fear of the bandits. Patiently explaining a simplified version of the plan and assuring the mare that she would be coming along, finally convinced her reticent mount. A feeling of love and deep thankfulness told the young woman much about the animal's life with the bandits, and she felt deep pity for the sensitive creature.

As soon as the girl gave the signal, the clever steed started throwing its head and neighing loudly. Azariel was favoring her left front leg and acting as if she was in severe pain. The smart mare was putting on a pretty good show. She began to limp and slow down more and more and finally came to a full stop. The princess pretended to try to get her to move, but the horse refused to take another step. Had the girl not known better, she would have thought something was seriously wrong with it.

Arianna acted greatly concerned and was caressing the mare's neck as if trying to calm her. Azariel turned her head and gave her a look and then neighed again loudly, pawing the ground as if trying to dislodge something from her hoof. It seemed the eager steed was improvising a bit, and the princess sent it a quick warning not to overdo the performance.

What a day! It seemed no one wanted to stick to any plan she came up with! If they were not careful, this could turn out badly. The bandits might decide to put the injured mount down right there on the spot. The mare seemed to understand her concern and allowed herself to be visibly calmed by her rider's touch. What a good girl! Sliding off Azariel's back with the help of one of the bandits, she petted the animal gratefully.

The robber riding behind Arianna had called out to Alandor just as soon as he noticed that her horse was having trouble. The bandit king was riding back towards them. The princess's obliging steed was standing there looking miserable, favoring the limb. Alandor quickly dismounted and began checking its hoof and leg. "Is she alright? What is wrong with her?" Arianna asked making sure to sound appropriately anxious. "Nothing noticeable, just a bit of soreness, my adorable swan. The poor thing must have stepped on a rock or something, my little turtle dove. Do not worry your pretty little head. I am sure your valiant mount will be right as rain, but I fear it will not be able to carry a rider, light of my life. Your own horse should be recovered enough by now, my adorable kitten," the pompous thief assured her.

Turning away from her, his entire demeanor changed. "Bring the lady's horse!" his harsh command rang out and was instantly followed. Facing the princess again, he once more modulated his voice into the syrupy sweetness she by now had come to utterly detest. The more time she spent with this guy, the more uncomfortable she felt in his presence. "May I assist you into the saddle of your good horse, my precious one?" the showy man inquired with an elegant bow. His overly chivalrous behavior and flowery speech were completely out of place in these wild woods. Had his demeanor not nauseated the princess so much she would have thought it absolutely hilarious. As it was, she had to bite the inside of her cheek to keep from laughing out loud.

Soon she was astride Arabella, and they were ready to set out once more. The bandit king guided his steed next to hers. "What will you do with the poor horse?" she asked Alandor, pointing at her so obviously injured mount. "One of my men will lead it, but if your fair mount cannot keep up, the animal will have to find its own way home, my radiant butterfly!" the gaudy bandit answered. "Azariel and I get along well, and she might do better for me. May I lead the mare, please? I will make sure she keeps up! She is such a sweet thing, and I just hate the idea of her being out here all alone! Please, dear sir?" the princess pleaded. She looked at the showy man with eyes huge with concern.

Alandor smiled at her indulgently and reached for her hand. "If it means that much to you, my sweet little goddess, by all means! But please, my jewel, be careful! If she pulls too hard, my bright sun, just let go of the reins. I do not want to see you take a fall, my precious. It would break my heart to see you hurt, light of my life!" the flashy outlaw stated grandly before gallantly placing an intimate kiss in the center of her palm. His touch made the princess flinch, a fact not lost on the man. Did he think that her reaction was one of pleasure or did he realize it was from utter revulsion? Arianna

196

could barely resist the impulse of immediately wiping the offending spot on her pants to remove his unwelcome caress.

To the girl's immense relief, the path soon became too narrow for two horses to walk abreast. Alandor took the lead once more. He kept looking back and checking on her, and the princess would give him a reassuring smile each time. Was he suspecting something?

Every few minutes Arianna connected to the Queen of the Sprites. The tiny monarch assured her each time that their plan was progressing beautifully. Why then did she continue to have such grave misgivings? Maybe now was the time to take a look at the glade.

Spotting a red-tailed hawk flying overhead, the princess used just a tiny part of her consciousness to reach out to the raptor. It was willing to let her see through its eyes and she soon got a bird's eye view of the area. There! That must be the open space the queen had shown her just ahead! The spot was perfect for the stampede.

Everything appeared to be going as intended but the closer they got to the glade, the more the princess's apprehension continued to grow. Her gut instinct was telling her that the fairies were up to no-good. If her need had not been so great, she would have called the entire thing off. The girl decided that it was time to get her mounts prepared for the chaos she was sure would result from the 'improvements' to her escape plan.

Making contact with Arabella's mind, she imparted a brief version of what to expect. She assured the mare that the fairies were their friends and that there was no reason to be afraid. The horse began to quiver with excitement. The spirited animal was actually looking forward to the mayhem and to an all-out run. Azariel was equally eager, and, having done all that she could on her end, Arianna checked with Queen Liza one last time.

"Do not worry, child, all will be well and go according to plan! We will guide and protect you, little one! No harm will come to you!" The princess somehow was not at all reassured by the queen's words. There had been too much-suppressed merriment about the upcoming rout in the petite fairy's mind. And who was Liza to call her little one? The tiny sprite did not even reach to her knees!

Reaching out one last time to contact Azariel, she asked the wily horse to please just follow Arabella and not to come to any sudden stops. Just in case, Arianna loosened her grip on the mares lead. It would not do to have the horse pull her out of the saddle. She was as prepared as possible. Now, all she could do was wait.

~

Alandor seemed to have assured himself that she was capable of leading the injured horse. He was no longer keeping such a close eye on her but continued to turn around in the saddle every few minutes and make eye contact with her. The smarmy smile he gave her each time made her skin crawl. The obsequious bandit was truly giving her the creeps. The next time he faced her, he blew her a kiss. She could not believe it! Was this guy starting to openly flirt with her? His words and now actions seemed to be escalating in a direction she had no desire to go.

Just the idea made her feel like throwing up. From what she could see of the man's face below the mask, he was not unattractive. His reputation as being extremely handsome could be well deserved. His personality and his manners, on the other hand, were a different thing altogether. The overly saccharine behavior he had been displaying towards her would have turned her stomach from any man. Add to that the cruelty she had seen him show to others and that was enough to make her want to be as far away from the disingenuous man as she could possibly get and as soon as she could get there.

The princess had come to realize that Alandor regarded himself as a law unto himself with no regard for anyone else. From what she remembered of his reputation, he was said to be utterly untrustworthy. After having the misfortune of meeting him, Arianna could well believe that. She had no idea what this rogue had in mind for her but was sure that she would not like it.

Could the ransom just be a rouse meant to mislead his own men? Had that scoundrel ever even intended to collect it? Could his goal have been to keep her for his own all along? What a horrible thought! In any case, she was not going to stick around to find out. She could only hope that whatever the fairies had in mind would not go too badly for the outlaw's unfortunate men.

~~~

Chapter Fourteen

A Good Plan Gone Awry

*T*he group of bandits was quietly moving along the meandering path through the tranquil forest. The peaceful woods were filled with birdsong and the buzz of insects which continued in spite of their passing. The air smelled of pine needles and early spring days. The warm sun and pleasing surroundings, along with the lack of sleep, had several of the men dozing on their mounts.

Arianna was still riding a short distance behind the bandit king. He had finally given up trying to flirt with her and also seemed to be half asleep. She knew they were nearing the clearing where the ambush was planned. Being the only one on the alert, she noticed how suddenly a hush descended upon the serene woods. Oh, oh! That was not good! Just a herd of elk would not have caused this pervasive a silence. What were the little ones up to? Whatever it was, there was nothing she could do about it now. A quick thought to her horses let them know that the time for their escape was near. "Be ready, child!" the sweet voice of the fairy queen sounded in her mind.

Before the bandits were even aware of any danger, the herd of elk came tearing down the intersecting forest trail. Arianna and her mounts were immediately surrounded, and the two horses were racing along at breakneck speed with the stampeding animals. In but a moment they had charged across the sunny clearing and then were heading down the broad path into the woods. The queen of the sprites, Liza, winked into appearance in front of the princess and took over guiding her horse. Arianna turned to take a look back, but the glade and the bandits had already been left far behind. All she could see were more of the large animals thundering down the forest trail.

"Go ahead, cast your mind back to the clearing! I have got you," the little queen invited her. The laughter in her voice filled the princess with a profound feeling of unease and trepidation. What had her little friends done? Did she really want to see what was happening to the men? The girl felt partially responsible for the outlaws' fate and decided that she needed to face the consequences of her actions. No matter what had happened, she would have to deal with it. Arianna perceived not doing so as cowardly and completely unacceptable.

It was safer to use an animal or other being for such observations than casting part of her awareness back towards the glade while trying to stay on the galloping horse. One of the sprites immediately volunteered to let her watch through its eyes. It took a moment for Arianna to fine-tune her vision and hearing. When she had finally managed to adjust her senses and was able to observe what was happening to the bandits, she gasped and quickly withdrew. The fairy queen happily filled her in on what was transpiring and projected the pictures of the carnage gleefully into the horrified girl's mind.

It seemed the elk had been followed by three of the largest bears the princess had ever seen. The bandits and their steeds had been sleepily plodding along. Both horses and riders had been in a bit of a daze. When the stampeding herd hit the clearing and ran into the group, confusion ensued.

The frightened mounts spooked just as soon as they smelled the predators and the outlaws suddenly found themselves on foot and in the midst of a churning mass of animals. Alandor had been unhorsed as well and was now separated from his men by the panicked ruminants. Most of the herd had continued down the trail, and the left behind elk soon enough got themselves sorted out and raced after the rest. The bandit's horses were running right along with them. The poor beasts had been treated so callously by the brigands that they felt not even the slightest bit of loyalty towards their masters. The much-abused mounts were only too happy to escape into freedom.

The voracious bears, poked awake from their winter slumber by the sprites and accordingly enraged, had initially been pursuing the elk. Once the herd raced on, they became aware of much easier prey. Men on foot were no match for these immense predators. After only a moment's hesitation, the three ravenous carnivores started to pursue the unlucky outlaws. The bandit leader, finding himself on the opposite side of the clearing, was now separated from his men by the huge and very hungry bears.

With nothing on mind but his own survival, Alandor went running down the path in the direction they had been traveling in as fast as his legs would carry him, a salivating bear in hot pursuit. The two remaining beasts went after the rest of the brigands. Every time one of the men tried to separate from the others and save himself by climbing a tree, he would run into some sort of a barrier and actually lose ground. The princess realized that the terrified bandits were systematically being herded down the path in front of the lumbering animals by the vengeful fairies.

These men were used to riding and running was definitely not their forte. Soon their breaths were coming in desperate gasps, and their strength was flagging. The bears were steadily gaining on them. The merciless sprites were purposely holding the large creatures back; they wanted to prolong the men's terror and desperate flight. Arianna recoiled in horror when the first of the bandits went down from a single swipe of deadly claws. Tears were running down her face as she watched one after the other of the bandits fall prey to the huge carnivores. When the last man had been killed, the sprites left the bears to do as they pleased. The fairies figured that the voracious beasts had earned their meal.

Now the queen shifted her attention to Alandor, who in the meantime had been frantically running for his life. For some reason the outlaw could not understand, the bear was not gaining on him but staying at the same distance behind him. This gave him the faint hope that somehow he might yet get out of this fiasco alive. Terror was lending the man endurance and speed. The dandy had probably never moved this fast or far on his own two feet in his entire life. Even though Arianna disliked the crook intensely, she could not help but feel compassion for his plight.

Whatever had been done to the sprites, the bandit king was the one they held responsible. He was the one they hated the most. It was plain that the unfortunate man was terrified out of his wits and that the little ones intended to keep him that way as long as possible. How the mighty had fallen! Gone was all that bravado and swagger. While he was running, the rogue was crying and blubbering in despair. The mocking laughter of the watching elementals was filling the forest around him. This was scaring the already panicked villain even more and spurring him on in his desperate flight.

The woods around the fleeing bandit were filled with sprites. There were many more of the little fairies in addition to the ones belonging to the small group Arianna had contacted. Liza told the princess that they had not been the only ones the outlaws had wronged. Elementals from far and wide had come to watch the demise of these hated men.

Alandor was the last left alive. The bandit leader might have been in a bit better shape than his men, but even his strength was starting to fail. The drooling carnivore was allowed to slowly gain on the doomed outlaw. The bear was just a couple feet behind the flagging man now. Alandor could already feel the beast's hot and rancid breath on his neck. Suddenly, a deafening roar came from the sky. A tongue of fire shot out at the hungry bear who reared back in terror.

The ravenous beast, crazed with bloodlust, hated to give up its prey. It had been so close! For just one brief moment it considered taking a stand. That was until a loud voice screamed into every mind and almost knocked the bear of its feet. "He is mine! Go take your sport elsewhere or I will set your forest on fire!" The affronted predator had by this time spotted his adversary. One look was enough to send him fleeing in the opposite direction as fast as his paws would carry him. Dealing with this kind of enemy for one puny human meal was not on his agenda. There had been more game back in the clearing, and he knew his brothers would share.

The large carnivore was not the only one to flee. The gleeful laughter had died away and quick as lightning most of the sprites had melted into the trees. This dragon was one being none of them dared to take on. They were not happy about letting this most hated of all their enemies get away, but at least they had gotten even with the rest of his men. One thing none of the fairies could understand. What interest could that immense firebreather possibly have in this human?

~

Alandor had felt the heat singing his back. He had heard the roar of some large being. None of this made any sense to him and at this moment, he really did not care. All he knew was that he needed to get away. He was more stumbling than running now but still he kept going. All his focus was on the ground ahead of him. When he had just about reached the limits of his endurance and felt that he could go no further, he glanced up. Hope filled him when he realized that he was moving through a copse of dense, tall trees. Looking around desperately, he picked the tallest one and raced towards it. With one last massive expenditure of energy, he began to climb. Higher and higher he worked his way up the tree until he finally felt safe.

Here the once so self-assured bandit king sat shaking with fright and reaction to the horror he had just survived. Tears of terror and exhaustion were running down his face. Making himself as small as possible, he tried to still his breath which was still coming in painful gasps. Looking down on the trail, he searched for the pursuing bear. Alandor was greatly surprised to find the path as well as the woods surrounding the tree, deserted. The outlaw was thoroughly confused. What had happened back there? Was he safe up here? He knew some bears were able to climb trees and from the look of the huge animal which had been chasing him, getting to him up here would not be overly difficult for it.

The man finally relaxed when after a while birdsong and the buzz of insects returned to the up to then silent forest.

So here the brigand sat in the gently swaying tree and considered his options. He had no intentions of going back for his men or the princess. Losing the young woman he regretted the most. She would have been such a lovely thing cleaned and fattened up a bit, a welcome addition to his small harem. The villain had purposely set the ransom unreasonably high. He had wanted to make sure that King Vargos would never even consider paying the exorbitant sum.

Alandor had really looked forward to having another royal playmate. This one had spirit and would have provided him with many entertaining hours trying to break her. She might have even lasted longer than her predecessors, but eventually, she would have learned to obey. Just like all the other high and mighty ladies had. Who knows, he might have even been able to fall in love with this one! But then again, he had thought this before. There had been something different about this princess, however. Maybe she would have been more trouble than she was worth and he was better off without her.

The callous rascal finally decided that he needed a nap. Running for his very life had left him completely drained. Moving around until he was settled in as safely and comfortably as possible on the branches of the magnificent tree, he closed his eyes and quickly fell into exhausted slumber. When he began snoring after a few minutes and appeared to be deeply asleep, as if by magic, the buckles holding his spurs on started to come undone. Ever so slowly the straps loosened and began to slip off his boots. The cruel spikes went sailing off into the woods. The man never even heard them hit.

~

Alandor had been asleep for just a few minutes when he was suddenly awoken by the sound of a horse heading down the path. He was thrilled, his luck was holding, as always! "Help, help!" He yelled down from his lofty post. He leaned out as far as he safely could to see who was coming down the trail. The hope of turning this entire situation to his advantage, at last, flared brightly in the man's shriveled heart. Whoever it was, this would not be their lucky day. The cowardly bandit had every intention of rewarding his unsuspecting rescuer with a blade to the ribs.

Try as he might, the rascal could not get a glimpse at his savior. It seemed that he was standing directly under the tree. The only answer to the bandit king's cries for help was a neighing. He had to reposition himself to be able to peek down between the branches of the tree to the forest floor. All he could see was a horse. Where was the rider? That had him a little concerned, but the rascal was confident that he could handle most adversaries. The good news was that if the horse was here and acting this calmly, then the bear was most likely nowhere near.

Alandor started to work his way down the tree all the while keeping a wary eye out for the missing horseman. Stopping just above the lowest branches but still high enough to have the advantage over anyone attacking from below, he took another careful look around. To his complete surprise, all he saw was one of his own mounts happily grazing below. The outlaw was ecstatic. How much luck could one man have?

After dropping down carefully so he would not scare the animal, he grabbed for the reins. Once the rogue had them safely in his hand, his feeling of elation was so great that he almost started to sing. Pulling the steed along, he headed back to the path. He quickly mounted, all the while keeping a careful eye out for the bear. It just would not do to be caught out in the open by that huge creature. As soon as he was securely seated in the saddle, he kicked the horse into a fast canter and shortly after, into a run. He wanted to get away from this area as quickly as he could.

As he was cruelly digging his heels into the horse's side to get it to go even faster, he paused. Something did not feel right! Perplexed, Alandor looked down at his left boot. His spurs were missing! He checked his right side and discovered those gone as well. He must have lost them while running from the bear! In any case, there was no way he was sticking around here to look for them. That beast had come awfully close to having him as a snack once; he was not about to give it a second chance!

Remembering that narrow escape made him shudder. He had feared that he was a goner. What had singed his back and made that deafening roar? He had never encountered any animal which made a sound like that. It seemed to have come from above. Looking up into the sky, the obnoxious bandit king saw nothing but a bird flying high above. Well, whatever it had been, it had saved him. It seemed to be gone now, so he was not going to worry about it any longer. Alandor happily headed for home. The fate of his loyal men or the captured princess were of little importance to him. He never even spared them a second thought.

~ ~ ~

Chapter Fifteen

The Dragon

*T*he stampeding herd of elk and the horses among them had slowed when the animals began to tire. They had finally come to a stop in a pleasant meadow. Now that the danger was passed, they were all grazing peacefully. Both Arianna and the fairy queen had witnessed from afar the dragon saving the loathsome bandit leader. Liza was furious to have been deprived of her revenge against this most hated of foes. Why had that giant menace taken an interest in that despicable human? And, what had lured that creature to her forest? Seeing the guilty look on the princess's face, the tiny monarch scrutinized the girl with narrowed eyes.

"What brought that thing here and why did it save him?" the little queen hissed through clenched teeth. Arianna figured it was best to stick to the truth. She told the little fairy about the crystal she had stolen from the dragon's hoard and exchanged for the horrible man's powerful pendant. And of the picture of treasure she had used to awaken the dragon. To help Liza understand why she had done this, the girl conveyed some of the many stories she had heard about the brigand. She patiently relayed to the queen how no human or any other tracker had ever been able to find the hideout of this most cunning outlaw. A dragon seeking treasure and revenge, however, might just be able to do so.

Many of the sprites had joined them while she was sharing this information. They were listening with great interest. The princess ended her explanation by pointing out that if they had followed her plan, the dragon would not have felt it needed to interfere. It was only when the man's life was threatened that it intervened. At first, there was stony silence. Then, abruptly, the tiny queen laughed. "That, dear child, was truly wicked of you! To involve a dragon, however, is never a good idea. They are fickle and greedy and a danger to any woods," she explained.

Liza sighed. "I would have liked to have my own revenge on that man but having the dragon go after him is a close second. I guess it will have to do. I am just glad that great brute did not cause a fire in my forest!" she continued. For a moment, the tiny queen seemed far away in her thoughts. Arianna figured that she was checking on her people and the situation. The princess was very thankful that the petite ruler had forgiven her for having been instrumental in derailing the fairy's revenge.

"That ghastly man is hiding up a tree, sound asleep. I don't think he will dare to come down for a while without a good reason. I want him and that flame throwing monster far away from my trees. As much as I hate to do it, we will have to provide that dreadful man with an expedient way to continue his journey. In a bit, I will have a couple of my sprites take him a horse. They will shadow him and bring back the news of his final demise when that scaly menace finds what it wants!" the Queen informed the relieved girl. At least Alandor's death would be one she would only indirectly be responsible for.

Suddenly cries echoed through the clearing. "The dragon, the dragon comes!" Within seconds, Arianna and her two mounts found themselves alone in the glade. Elk, horses, and sprites had vanished like magic. "Don't even try to flee, little thief, I will speak with you!" boomed a voice in her head. With a sigh, the princess resigned herself to the confrontation. "May I take my horses back into the woods a little so that they will not panic?" she asked. The girl was not sure how to properly address a dragon and so decided that it was best to avoid an address of any form rather than angering the great beast. "Yes, but be quick about it or I will eat you and them!" came the thunderous reply.

Arianna directed her mares to the edge of the forest where she quickly dismounted. Tying their reins securely to the saddles, she told the two to head for the safety of the woods. At first, she thought her loyal steeds would refuse, but when she expressed the urgency of her command they obeyed. Bravely the princess walked back into the glade. The horses were barely out of sight when the dragon landed just a few feet in front of the girl. The scaly beast angrily puffed itself up to its full size. The creature was glorious and absolutely enormous as it stood there towering over the slender young woman.

The princess was aware that fleeing was not an option. There was no place around here where she would be able to hide from this magnificent hunter. And, it was not her way to avoid taking responsibility for her actions. The girl figured that the only choice she had which would not hurt the sprites or the forest, was to face her adversary with courage. "I am Arianna, Princess of Maridanmar. Who do I have the honor of addressing?" she, therefore, inquired politely.

The irritated dragon was taken aback for a moment by this bold but respectful greeting. Having the puny human stand up to it must not have been what it expected. The massive creature eyed the young woman speculatively. "I am Galata the Dragon, and you stole from me," the scaled being grumbled indignantly, punctuating her words with a menacing twitch of her barbed tail. Then, as Arianna's words sank in, a thoughtful expression crossed the huge face. "A princess? Out here? How?" the gigantic lady asked inquisitively.

Before Arianna could answer, Galata continued. "What are you, some type of sorceress? What kind of a fancy trick did you use to divert my attention away from you and onto that man?" the dragon questioned in a softer voice. "It was very well done and left only the smallest of traces. I would not have found you had it not been for the sprites. What are you, a human, doing with these obnoxious little creatures anyhow?"

Curiosity seemed to be getting the better of the annoyed beast. "Tell me your story!" demanded the inquisitive dragon as she settled herself in comfortably. "And you, sprites, I mean you no harm. You can come out now, I know you are there!" Slowly the little fairies winked into existence around them. "A story? We love stories!" they whispered excitedly. Soon many of the small elementals were clustered in a circle around the princess and the dragon. Even the two horses had found their way back into the clearing.

Storytelling had been something Arianna had always loved. She began by relating to them the events of the day the envoy had come demanding her hand in marriage. Her audience was soon spellbound. When she described the treatment she had received from the malicious witch, gasps and angry mutters broke out. Wicked little smiles showed how much the tiny ones appreciated the effect the Witchbane had on the evil sorceress. Then she told them of the night the bandits took over the camp and kidnapped her and of the enormous ransom the bandit king had demanded for her safe return.

This part especially interested Galata, and she asked many questions about the riches of King Vargos. Arianna told her that all she knew was that the evil monarch had amassed a much larger fortune than the rest of the realms. The dragon grumbled a bit at not getting more details but finally relented, and the princess finished her story. Galata then inquired about Alandor. Arianna searched her memories and related all the rumors she could remember to her curious listeners.

The tale about the bandit king keeping his female hostages as his personal prisoners incensed the scaled creature. It also profoundly affected the fairy queen who turned white with fury. At that moment, a bond formed between the two so very different females. A silent discussion between queen and dragon ensued. It seemed that not even the rest of the sprites were privileged to this exchange. The princess felt chills when the two so dissimilar beings beamed at each other and nodded. From the looks of those toothy smiles, someone was in deep trouble, and some sort of a bargain had been struck.

Galata once again turned her attention to the princess. "I appreciate that the theft of my jewel was done out of real need, and I see that the treasure you took from that horrible man might help you on your way. But, it is mine by right, and I want it in return for the one you took from me. Give it to me!" she demanded. Arianna had expected as much and had already transferred the gem from the secret pouch to her pocket. Without argument, she presented the jewel to the acquisitive dragon who took it and examined it carefully. "A kind of plain thing that but still, full of power! You did right liberating this gem from that evil man! I have many more just like it, come to think of it. Thank you for giving it to me and for your interesting story. Let this little jewel be my gift to you and may it serve you well!" Galata declared grandly. "Thank you!" the princess stammered, surprised. She had not expected this generosity from one who loved jewels above all else. Could the aversion spell have had anything to do with this?

Soon the dragon said its good-byes to the group assembled in the meadow and set out to follow Alandor once more. Galata would make sure that the bandit king reached his home alive. She was greedy for riches, and the picture of the villain and his treasure seemed to have firmly stuck in her mind. Arianna had not missed a second silent exchange between the queen and the dragon just before the giant beast took off into the sky. Something was going on here, but what?

The massive creature was soon no more than a small birdlike speck high among the clouds, and the horses and elk were once again grazing calmly in the peaceful clearing. The princess and Liza wistfully watched the dragon fly off into the distance. Arianna loved the giant flyer's grace and power and could not help but admire the great beast. The girl was also wondering how it would feel to soar like that, to have the air slip by under one's wings. The closest to that feeling she had ever come had been during the times when she had shared bodies with a willing raptor. Turning into a bird was easy but flying was not.

~

A rustling drew the princess's attention back to the present. "Child, do you really think that horrible man keeps women imprisoned in his hideout?" the Queen of the Sprites asked apprehensively. "I do not know, Queen Liza, but he was definitely giving me an awful feeling. He was calling me all these endearments. My precious, my turtledove, and so many more, it was actually making me feel sick. If he does have women imprisoned, I pity them! I think he is a very cruel man who tries to hide his true nature under all that extravagant behavior," replied Arianna. "Why do you ask, your highness?" she inquired curiously.

"The dragon and I do not like to see any defenseless female in the power of one such as him. We will not even send him a mare! Galata will send word when she finds that nasty man's lair and my sprites and I will help her gain entry. If any women are kept prisoner there, we will free them. We want you well on the way before then, child! You need to concentrate on getting as far from here as you can. We are sure the soldiers will try to recapture you, and from what the dragon has heard, that evil king has an excellent scout!" the queen answered.

Arianna was both pleased and astonished. So that was what the two had discussed! "I would be honored to assist you, my Queen!" the princess volunteered. "Oh no, my child, we want to see you safe! My sprites and Galata will be enough to deal with those wicked men!" The dainty queen suddenly tilted her beautiful head. An expression of concern crossed the delicate features. "You need to leave now! More men are entering our forest. Do not worry, we will not let them find you! My sprites will guide you, and there will be no trace of your passing for even the keenest eyes to find!" the little monarch reassured the startled girl. Liza gave a shrill trill, and several sprites appeared with little sacks on their shoulders, ready to travel. "Good-bye, my child, and safe travels! Now hurry!" she told the girl.

For a moment, the princess felt the touch of tiny lips on her cheeks and with that the fairies were gone. Only she, her new companions, and the animals remained in the sunlit glade. Arianna whistled for her horses and mounted. Seven of the tiny sprites joined her, and as soon as everyone was comfortably settled, the princess set off yet once again.

She was more than ready to continue her journey and to put as much distance as she could between herself and the carnage back on the path. As they were riding out of the glade, the princess turned in the saddle. "Good-bye, your Highness, and thank you!" she shouted. Her only answer was a sudden rustling of the trees, but she was sure the little queen had heard her.

To the girl's surprise, three more horses were following along. Being able to switch mounts frequently would allow her to travel much faster and cover a greater distance in a shorter period of time. The sprites quickly took the extra mounts in hand, and they set out along the trail in a rapid canter.

~~~

Chapter Sixteen

A Gruesome Discovery

It was not much later that Angus and his soldiers reached the scene of the massacre. The two scouts the captain had sent ahead had returned white as ghosts. They reported that they had come around a bend in the path and almost run into the first of the bears. That the brute was well sated was the only thing which saved them. The beast was ready for a nap and did not feel like chasing down these new arrivals. So, instead of attacking, he gave the men a warning roar and then ambled off to find a pleasant spot for a nice long nap.

Both men had been unseated by their rearing mounts. Their first priority had been to catch their spooked horses, but that took them a while. Being stuck in this forest on foot with a large carnivore like that was not something they even wanted to contemplate. When they were finally back in the saddle and had a chance to look around, they were aghast by the carnage. The soldiers lost any food and drink left in their stomachs right there. In one area the entire path and the bushes bordering it were drenched in blood. Apart from some chewed bones, a partially eaten head, and some shredded clothes, not much remained of the unlucky man. The scouts decided that is was time to return to the rest of the group.

The two soldiers told their captain that the animal they had almost run into was the largest bear they had ever seen. Angus took this with a grain of salt; he figured that any predator seemed big to a frightened man. The officer felt it would be best to keep the nervous horses as well as most of his men away from the grizzly scene. Having made this decision, he looked around for a place which might give his small company at least some protection.

Locating a marginally defensible copse of trees within walking distance of the carnage, he led his men into the meager shelter. He commanded his soldiers to dismount and put the horses in the middle. This would help to keep them calm and protect them. The captain had his men collect wood and start small fires in a circle around their position to repel any wild animals. The fires might even deter the bear but if not the flaming brands they had prepared would. He gave the order for all four of them to stay on high alert and to keep a close eye on their mounts. The animals would warn them if any danger approached.

Taking only the oldest of the men with him, a well-seasoned sergeant, Angus carefully proceeded down the path on foot. The captain was not the greatest of trackers. It had been many years since he had needed this skill. Still, he was reasonably sure now that they were following nine horses. The clever princess had somehow managed to talk the brigands into taking her mount along. Knowing as much about the bandit king as Angus did, the soldier figured that the crafty thief had put the girl on one of his own horses. An outlaw was most likely pulling Arabella along by the reins.

That would leave eight riders - seven bandits and one kidnapped princess.

Coming up to the grizzly scene, the commander shuddered at the expression of horror and pain imprinted on what remained of the face of the severed head. This man died a terrible death, and Angus could not help but feel compassion for him. His sergeant gave him a questioning look and made a digging motion, but the captain shook his head. It was best not to disturb the prize of the huge carnivore. As long as there were some remains left for the bear, it might leave him and his men alone. That could be their only chance to get safely through the voracious predator's domain.

Leading the way, the officer cautiously crept along the path in the direction the outlaw had come from. From the tracks left in the soft soil, he figured that the man had been running for his life. Soon they reached a second pile of mostly eaten remains. The remnants were definitely from one of the brigands. Angus almost sighed with relief that it was not the princess. He knew that the men would have been able to easily outrun the girl and feared that she had been the first to get caught by the ferocious beast. Moving further along the path, they started to hear snoring. Proceeding as quietly as possible, they soon discovered the source.

Angus was taken aback. His scouts were right, this beast was huge! Was this the same one his men had run into earlier or were there more than one of the large animals? Most male bears hunted alone, so that would be rather unusual. From the paw prints left on the trail, the captain feared that they were dealing with at least two of the humongous creatures. Could there be more of these immense predators? This snoring behemoth had fallen sound asleep right there in the middle of the bloody carnage. Two partially eaten corpses were strewn around it. Carefully the captain and his man worked their way nearer. Finally, they dared go no closer. Enough remained of the two bodies that the officer could tell that neither belonged to the princess.

Backtracking a little, the sergeant found a small side path between the bushes. The two soldiers moved along it stealthily, all the while listening for any sound of the large hunters. The head high hedges on each side left them feeling on edge. The bushes were so dense that a bear could stand within a foot of them, and they would never even know it. This thick vegetation was prime territory for an ambush. The two men would have been much happier if they had been able to see what was going on around them. Angus could not help but sigh with relief when the narrow track once again rejoined the much wider path. Here, at least, they might have a little more warning.

The wind had shifted direction and carried the smell of the next victim to them before they ever reached it. Proceeding with utmost caution, they crept closer. To their relief, no bear remained, only what was left off yet another ripped apart corpse. Angus ascertained that these remains had also belonged to a bandit. He exchanged a sickened glance with the sergeant. Out of the party of eight, only three remained.

None of the scraps of clothes had looked like the fancy things Alandor had worn, so he, one of his men, and the princess were left to find. Judging from what they had seen so far, the group must have been surprised by the huge meat-eaters and unhorsed. The captain was starting to doubt that any had survived the vicious attacks. Both men fully expected to find the rest of the bodies a little further along the path. With a heavy heart, Angus led the way down the trail. He was dreading what he was sure he would find. In the soft forest soil, deep indents of booted feet and the largest paws either man had ever seen told a story which chilled both men to the bone.

It was not long before they discovered the last of Alandor's men. This scene was much less gruesome than the others. The man had been brutally killed by a swipe of sharp talons but was mostly uneaten. It seemed the bear had stopped for the kill and to take a quick bite but had then decided to chase after the rest. Sure they would find the body of the princess next, Angus and his sergeant proceeded cautiously. The trail continued to be torn up by the imprints of boots and the large paws of at least two of the predators. It was almost as if the men had been herded along by the massive beasts. There were plenty of trees about, why had none of them climbed one?

When the two soldiers finally reached a clearing traversed by a second game trail, they realized that they had found the scene where it had all begun. A herd of large hoofed animals had crossed through the clearing. Angus figured they might have been elk and that they had most likely been stampeded by the voracious bears. What puzzled him was why the big carnivores were awake in the first place. It was still kind of early in the spring for the hefty beasts to be out of their dens. Having their rest cut short would make them even grumpier than usual. What had disturbed the bears' winter sleep? To the seasoned officer, something felt wrong.

From the signs on the forest floor, the captain gathered that the predators had run into the group of riders while pursuing the herd. The sudden appearance of the ravenous carnivores must have spooked the horses. The men had been thrown and had consequently been chased by the bears who considered them easier prey than the fleet-footed elk. The glade was peaceful now and utterly deserted. Angus was puzzled that they had found no trace of the princess or the bandit king so far. The officer decided to continue further down their original path. Within a few feet, the sergeant discovered deep imprints of one single set of shoed feet.

The soldiers realized immediately that the boots were too large to belong to the princess. These tracks had to have been made by Alandor. The two men decided to follow the trail to ascertain the fate of the flamboyant bandit. It would be nice to be able to report the outlaw's death to the king, it might just earn them the long overdue promotion. The large prints of a giant bear obliterated some of the booted impressions. Alandor had been running for his life with the huge predator right on his heels. Further down the path, deep claw marks in the soft soil showed where the bear had come to a dead stop and then turned around sharply. Its tracks led off into the woods. What had happened here? Had the hungry beast seen easier prey? And what was up with the scorch marks a few feet from where the pursuing carnivore had turned around?

The brigand had continued running down the trail until he reached a large fir. The captain could tell from the broken branches that the scamp must have climbed the tree like death was right behind him. The imprints of a lone horse showed the rest of the story. One of the mounts must have found its way there and Alandor had coaxed it over. The callous man had fled without ever going back to look for his men or the princess. No decent leader would behave in such a cowardly fashion! Angus would make sure that that bit of information found its way into the bandit king's lore. It might not be so easy for him to recruit men after that.

The only one left unaccounted for now was Arianna. Could the princess have been riding the horse? After some debate, neither man thought so. The hoof imprints were just not deep enough for the steed to have been carrying two riders. So where then was the girl? Did she meet up with this scoundrel further ahead? Did it make any sense following Alandor? The captain figured that given half a chance, Arianna would be well on her way. Just to be sure, the two soldiers proceeded down the path for a short distance. Within a few minutes, it became apparent that no second horse had joined up with the rapidly fleeing bandit leader. From the deep hoof prints left by Alandor's unfortunate mount, it was evident that the brigand was cruelly pushing the horse and would not get far if he continued at that speed.

Not wanting to get caught in the domain of these massive predators in the dark, Angus decided that they better make their way back to the rest of his group. The two men circled the clearing where it had all started looking for clues but found nothing. They also made a quick detour down the second trail in the direction the stampeding herd had been racing. Once again they came up with no evidence to help them in their quest. Hoof prints showed that some of the outlaws' horses had been running along with the fleeing herd. The two soldiers figured it unlikely that the princess would have been able to remain in the saddle when men who made their living riding had all been thrown. How could she disappear without a trace? What had happened to her? With a heavy heart, Angus decided to abandon their search. He had done all he could for the girl. Maybe Tristan could find her.

On their way, they almost ran into one of the huge bears. Its snuffling sounds had carried just far enough in the quiet forest to give them a much-appreciated warning. Quickly climbing a large tree, the two men watched the hefty beast wander along the path underneath them. They figured that it was on its way to the yet uneaten man. Seeing the creature in its full glory, the captain wished that his scouts had been exaggerating. This gigantic carnivore truly was the biggest animal of its kind he had ever seen! Making sure the enormous male was well on the way, the soldiers quietly climbed down the tree and continued on the path. Their senses were on high alert. The stench of the victims warned them ahead of times of each gory scene. The afternoon sun had done its putrid work on the sparse remains of the unlucky bandits. The smell was almost overwhelming in places. Angus and the sergeant were tremendously thankful when they left the grizzly scenes behind.

~

Reaching the copse where he had left his men, the captain was extremely relieved to find all was well. He immediately gave the order to saddle up. Angus wanted to get as far away from this gruesome place as quickly as possible. He led his men back towards the main camp at a fast canter. The large predators were almost out of food and the more distance he could put between his group and those bears before nightfall, the safer he would feel. It was best not to be anywhere around here when those vicious brutes went hunting again.

It was late afternoon by now, and there was no way the officer and his men could make it back to the camp before full dark. When the horses were getting winded, the captain gave the order to switch mounts. Being trained soldiers, they could do this with ease as long as the path was wide enough. Slowing down just a little to make the switch, they were soon on their way again at full speed. None of them had felt like stopping since the scouts had shared the gruesome details of their bloody discovery with the other two lads. All the men were more than a little nervous about the bears.

After some hard riding, the scenery around them began to change. They had once again reached the comparative safety of the deep woods. The underbrush here consisted mostly of ferns. Gone were the huge bushes bordering the trail. The six men sighed with relief. They could now see more of their surroundings. This made them all feel a little safer especially since the day had moved on towards evening and the light was beginning to fail. It was time to find a place for the night. Angus finally spotted a knoll which would provide them with a small extent of a tactical advantage. Without being told, his men collected a large quantity of wood for the fire. The horses were tied at the far end of their camp, and a roaring blaze started between themselves and the trail. Large sticks were set on fire and then extinguished. They would serve as torches in case of an attack by the bears.

After they had set up camp and their defenses as best they could, it was time to get some rest. The soldiers were supposed to be taking shifts sleeping, but every crashing sound in the quiet night forest brought the entire group to instant alertness. The captain could not blame them, what they had seen or been told off that day would have been enough to put the most experienced fighter on edge. The officer thought that they were far enough away to avoid any further encounter with the voracious beasts. His mind returned to the princess. What had happened to her? She was barely more than a girl, a noblewoman at that. How could she possibly survive out there in the wild? His only remaining hope was that Tristan would find her before it was too late.

~~~

Chapter Seventeen

What On Earth Is Going On?

*A*landor was galloping along the forest path at breakneck speed. All he could think of was to get as far away as possible from the bear and whatever else had been there. The second creature had saved his life. The outlaw was not sure if this had been done intentionally. In any case, that thing might change its mind and come after him after all. It had sounded big, and the scoundrel had no desire to meet his inadvertent rescuer.

The bandit king, as are many bullies, was actually a coward at heart. He had always bluffed his way through most situations. The man had no love or understanding for others. His own life was the only thing important to him, and he had little regard for anyone or anything else. Animals, even horses, counted for nothing. There was always another if you rode one to its limits. To him, the poor steed which was carrying him further and further away from the threat in an all-out gallop was just an expedient way to escape from danger.

The three sprites who had brought the bandit leader his horse were riding along with him unnoticed. Invisibility was such a useful trait! So far they had been strictly following their queen's orders, but they had begun to be alarmed about the man's treatment of the by now frothing animal. The ruthless bandit, in his abject fear, kept spurring his ill-fated mount on to greater and greater speed. If this kept up, the poor creature would soon drop dead. Finally, the little elementals could take it no more and decided enough was enough. Their first idea was to use their nimble little fingers to loosen the saddle strap and let the bandit slide to the ground and break his ugly neck. Their monarch would not be happy with this and neither would that big obnoxious dragon. With much regret, they discarded that plan.

By now, their hatred of the outlaw had grown to such proportions that the sprites would have loved nothing more than to watch him die right there on the path. But, they had strict orders to make sure the man reached his home. Having to keep this most hated of all the bandits alive went against everything they believed in. They knew better than to disobey, however. And, they were on a rescue mission of sorts. That filled all three of the little fairies with great pride. If they succeeded, they would gain great standing among their peers.

Unfortunately, the only way they could complete this important assignment was if the wretched man led them to his keep. Therefore, whether they liked it or not, the bandit king had to stay alive. After discarding several more plans which would have grievously injured the heartless villain, they finally hit on a winner. Alandor suddenly slid off the back of his horse in something resembling slow motion and only hit his head, rear, and back instead of breaking his neck.

There he sat on the trail in bewilderment and watched his ride disappear in the distance.

Recovering from the shock of suddenly finding himself in the dirt instead of on the back of the horse, the bewildered brigand remembered the bear. Holding his aching rear, the man got to his feet. He could have sworn he heard some low snickering, but could see no one around. Slowly and painfully, the bandit leader began to walk. He kept going over his sudden unsaddling in his mind but try as he might; he had no understanding of what had just happened. One minute he was happily riding along, the next he hit the ground. Almost like magic but that was impossible. His talisman would have warned him.

It was a long way yet to his hideout. On foot, it would take him several days to reach the place where the rest of the bandits should be waiting. That was if they decided to hang around. Who knew for sure with a bunch of cutthroats like that?

Trudging along disconsolately for about a quarter of a league, Alandor became seriously thirsty. He was not used to walking or running, and he had been forced to do both this very day. It was taking a lot out of the flamboyant outlaw. His clothes were in ruin, his men and the princess most likely dead, and he was all alone out here in these woods filled with all kinds of nasty creatures. Now his horse was gone too. Feeling very sorry for himself, the crook began to mutter unhappily under his breath. He would be limping into the camp with nothing to show for their expedition. That would not go over well. He better come up with an excellent story.

What could he possibly tell his men that would cover up his fleeing and leaving the rest to their fate? They were attacked by a dragon, and only he escaped by the skin of his teeth? No, too outlandish. And who would ever believe the truth? That a stampeding herd of elk and a bear were responsible for his current despondent state? As the bandit was talking to himself, he could have sworn he once again heard gleeful chuckles. He looked around suspiciously but, as before, no one was to be seen.

Finally, Alandor could take it no more. Sinking down into the grass on the side of the trail, the bandit bitterly lamented his unfair lot. Here he was, having survived that horrible bear attack, only to be dying of thirst! Had fate ever been more cruel to any man? Soon he was sobbing in deepest despair. The two sprites, who had so efficiently slid the ruthless man of his horse, shook their heads in disgust. Their brother had no idea how lucky he was! He, at least, did not have to listen to this self-pitying drivel! They had to keep this man alive, but how? There was a creek just a few feet away, and if this pathetic human would ever stop sniveling and feeling sorry for himself, he would see it!

Tapping their tiny feet, the sprites waited for the overwhelmed man to compose himself but his wailing was getting louder and more desperate all the time. The sound of his pitiful bawling was now echoing through the woods and would soon attract unwelcome attention. This guy was too much!

After a whispered discussion, the two brothers decided that they had to do something before trouble found them. Combining their powers, they soon had the despondent man sailing through the air and plopping into the stream with a great splash. The water was just a little deeper at the spot where he landed than they had anticipated. Before they knew it, the bandit appeared to be drowning.

The fairies looked at each other in utter disbelief. The water was not that deep! The foolish human was flailing about as if death was imminent any second now! When would this idiot think of standing up? They were just about to interfere when Alandor was washed into a slightly shallower spot by the gentle current. Bumping his rear seemed to bring him to his senses. The bandit sat up sputtering. For the first time, it dawned on him where he was. How did he suddenly get in this creek? There had to be spirits at work here! That could be the only explanation for his sudden dunking. The bandit king looked around in fear but except the very faint sound of barely suppressed laughter, there was nothing out of the ordinary to be seen or heard.

After quenching his thirst, the brigand made his way back to the path and started walking once more. Every once in a while, he caught sight of two foxes which seemed to follow him. Curious that! He had been trying to fathom why these animals behaved so strangely when he hit upon a terrible thought. Maybe they were waiting for him to die and wanted to eat him? This very notion brought on a new bout of feeling very sorry for himself. Alandor started muttering once more, and large tears were rolling down his dusty cheeks.

How could fate do this to him? He was usually so very lucky. How could this situation possibly get worse? The light was failing, and he was all alone in the woods. With those terrible bears around here and now these scavenging foxes, there was no way he was sleeping on the ground. It suddenly dawned on him that what he needed was a very tall tree. Finding fault with tree after tree, he shuffled along.

Just as the last of the light was about to disappear behind the horizon, the picky man finally spotted the perfect specimen, a proud and tall fir with plenty of climbable limbs. He was soon happily ensconced in a fork in its tall branches.

His improved mood, however, did not last very long. He had not eaten for hours and now that he had settled in, hunger was asserting itself. His stomach started growling, and this gave rise to a whole new tirade of bitter complaining about how unfair life was treating him.

The two sprites were comfortably resting in a large bird's nest in a nearby tree. They finally could take it no longer. In despair, they stuck their fingers in their ears trying to shut out the incessant whining. Something had to be done here. A helpful owl took the urgent plea to their brother to hurry up and return with that horse. If the man was left to walk all the way to his home, he would never make it alive. They would have to either kill him just to stop his complaining, or something would hear him and do it for them!

The brothers were greatly relieved when the once so proud bandit king finally fell into a restless sleep. Silence at last! Was increased status really worth all this? The two sprites were starting to have serious doubts about that.

~~~

Chapter Eighteen

And Chaos Reigns

The new lieutenant Aaron had his hands full. The camp was in complete disarray, and it seemed a thousand things needed his attention all at once. He was starting to feel a little overwhelmed, but there was nothing to be done about that. The envoy had fallen back to sleep right there on the witch's bed. Their efforts to wake him were in vain; the man did not even twitch. He was dead to the world and most likely would be that way for many, many more hours. No help organizing the stricken camp was coming from that source anytime soon.

The commander of the rear unit had been one of the men killed by the bandits. The second in command was still out cold. When some of the troops began waking up, there was no one to tell them what they should be doing. The conditions they found themselves in were far from usual and not having a person in charge further confused the half-awake soldiers. Therefore, Aaron saw himself forced to promote one of the slightly more awake sergeants to the position of temporary commander.

The young lieutenant was doing the best he could, but there were a lot of decisions to be made, and he had never really been in charge before. Especially not of the entire column. He appreciated his captain's confidence in him, but this was more than he had bargained for. Most of the soldiers were still sound asleep and snoring loudly. The few who were awake enough to be useful had been put to the task of going around the camp and checking on the men. They had to keep moving the sleepers. Some had rolled too close to the newly stoked fires and needed to be pulled further away from the flames. Unfortunately, for several this help had come too late. And then, there was the sorceress. No, this being in charge was definitely not fun.

The new officer found himself in the position where he had to protect that wretched woman. He had just barely prevented one of his men from taking advantage of the unconscious witch. It would bring the envoy's displeasure down upon his head, but Aaron had seen no other option but to move her back into the tent Odessa had once occupied and where Sebastian now slept. They had made a bed for her on the floor and leaned her up against a saddle. The enchantress was having a terrible time breathing and was so deeply unconscious and in such sorry state that he could only pity her. Feeling that she was no longer a danger to anyone, the young lieutenant had removed her gag.

More pressing matters had required Aaron to leave her. Thinking the woman safe enough where she was, he had headed out to tend to all the things which seemed to crop up constantly and needed his attention. Some of his men must have watched him leave and took advantage of his absence. The soldiers were a superstitious lot, and they had been deathly afraid of the powerful witch. Having no understanding of her weakened state and that the sorceress might not even survive, the cads had taken it upon themselves to make sure that the enchantress would never utter another spell.

The next time the fledgling commander had a minute to check on Odessa, he was shocked to find her choking on her own blood. Opening her mouth, the young man saw with horror that someone had cut out her tongue. He had seen fear lead people to do all kinds of things before which they would usually never even consider, but this act of cruelty had been so pointless. It was beyond Aaron's understanding how anyone could do something so despicable to another human being. This sick and defenseless woman was no longer a threat to anyone. She was just barely alive. If he could not stop the bleeding, she would die before long.

Furious, the lieutenant, stalked over to the closest fire. He thrust his blade into the flames and waited for it to become white-hot. Ordering two of his reluctant men to get over to the witch and to hold her, he pried open her mouth. One of his men had to help keep it open. Using the glowing blade, the young lieutenant cauterized the bleeding stump. Soon the stench of burnt human flesh filled the air and made them all gag.

Aaron could barely keep from throwing up and not only because of the smell. He had been charged with Odessa's well-being and had been told to make sure this woman stayed alive. Having such an odious act happen on his watch was terrible, he had let his captain down. This woman was his responsibility. He would do whatever it took to make sure that she would live until Angus returned. After making sure the sorceress was settled in as comfortable as possible, he set two of his trusted friends to watch over her.

~

It was around noon when most of the sleepers started to stir. Many awoke feeling terribly ill. Nausea, headaches, and blurred vision were some of the milder symptoms. Aaron had his helpers go around and pass out cups of water and kahve. The cook finally started to wake up as well but had to be plied with several cups of the brew before he became even marginally coherent. Once he was somewhat functional, he began preparing a large pot of oats. It seemed that was all the man felt capable of doing at the moment. Still, the warm meal helped settle upset stomachs and made the soldiers feel a little better. The commander of the front unit finally woke up as well and groggily took over command of his troops relieving the harried lieutenant of some of his many responsibilities.

It was late afternoon by the time the envoy woke up again. Aaron was glad that he had had the foresight to have his men erect an additional tent and move the barely alive sorceress to it. Sebastian would have been furious to find the reviled witch in his tent. As it was, the man was even more unbearable than usual. Aaron assigned a couple of his soldiers to the toad-like gentleman to make sure he was fed and taken care off. He had noticed blood on one of these men's sleeves and suspected that he was responsible for the mutilation of the enchantress. The other one was his buddy and had most likely helped.

Having to deal with the insufferable lackey was a fit punishment for the time being in his mind. He watched with amusement as the two unhappy soldiers raced around trying to please Sebastian. He was not surprised when they approached him and begged him to release them from serving the horrid little man. The two were so desperate that when Aaron refused, they went as far as confessing to their mutilation of the helpless Odessa in the hope to get out of that disagreeable duty. Come to find out, cutting out the sorceress's tongue had not been the only vile act they had perpetrated on the defenseless woman. It seemed they would rather face punishment for their crimes than be subjected to the wiles of the emissary. The lieutenant promptly had them both arrested and bound.

~

Dealing with the cantankerous envoy and protecting the witch were not the only problems the new officer was facing. Being in charge of the entire camp was a tremendous responsibility. Before the captain left, he had decided to task the sentries with helping with the fires. That left the site totally defenseless and wide open to attack, but as it was now daytime, they were more needed in the camp. As more and more soldiers awoke, Aaron had put the most able-bodied on guard duty. No one stood watch alone; this would have left the still somewhat dazed men in too vulnerable a position. Aaron figured better fewer guard posts than risking more of his charges. Not knowing where the bandits were and if they were coming back or if there was someone else out there just waiting to take advantage of the disabled camp had made the young man fairly nervous.

Also, there were the dead to deal with. The ruthless brigands had killed every single man on duty and all others whom they found awake in the camp. Burying the bodies would have to wait. Right now they needed to take care of the living and get things up and running again. It seemed that whatever the outlaws had added to the beer had been pretty nasty stuff. What the new officer did not know was that the princess had also added a sleeping powder and that the combination of the two different compounds was responsible for making those who imbibed the most so severely ill.

A good third of the men were so sick when they woke up that they could barely lift their heads. Aaron finally saw himself forced to create a hospital area next to the pavilion to care more efficiently for the worst afflicted. He assigned several soldiers to nursing duty. Others he had go around the camp and collect all those still sleeping so that they could be watched over. Once they had done what they could for the living and more of the soldiers were functional, the young commander sent some of the men to locate all the dead and lay them out in rows outside the camp.

It was early evening before the lieutenant had enough able bodied men to start digging the graves. They had set out as three units of 30 men each plus a cook and the commanders of each unit and their sergeants, all in all, a troop of over 100 men. Now, barely seventy remained and of these six were off chasing after the bandits and 15 were still too sick for duty. The column had felt safe being on their home turf. Due to the large number of men they had been spread out more than they should have been. Guards had been minimal. Who after all would attack a force their size in their own kingdom?

One of the first things the young lieutenant had wanted to do was tighten the perimeter. He intended to move everybody in closer to the pavilion and abandon the outlying areas. That would make the camp easier to protect. Not having enough able-bodied men had forced him to wait until the afternoon. Once the size of their site had been significantly decreased, Aaron felt much better about their ability to guard and defend themselves.

The sun was going down before some normalcy returned to the stricken camp. The new commander could finally sit down for a breather. His men had been less of a problem then the personages they were meant to protect. The envoy was one of the ones feeling extremely sick. The pathetic toady was alternating between being difficult and pitiful. The lieutenant had assigned one of his most stoic soldiers to look after the demanding emissary and the unconscious witch. It did not take long before the nasty little sycophant was getting to even this usually unflappable warrior.

Shifts had been assigned for guard duty, plenty of firewood collected, and all was in readiness for the night. None of the soldiers complained about not getting their usual ration of beer. The young officer suspected that some of them would happily do without their usual tankard for several more days. There had been no way of knowing which casks had been contaminated with the sleeping powder, and so Aaron had ordered them all dumped to avoid any temptation.

The woods were filled with all the regular sounds and peaceful. The sleeping area had been drastically reduced and was arranged close to the pavilion and tent. The soldiers usually liked to be a much further apart from each other. This night, however, the men seemed to find comfort in the nearness of their neighbors. Most of the inhabitants of the camp were still very much on edge, and only the self-centered envoy got a decent night's rest.

None of the soldiers were able to completely relax their vigilance. Any sound from the pitch black woods would have them sit up alertly on their bedrolls. The previous night's attack had not just cost their comrades their life but had also been a devastating blow to their pride. They would not be surprised again.

When the first light of dawn started to slowly drive the darkness from underneath the towering trees, Aaron and his men were greatly relieved. They had survived the night without incidents and would soon be on their way back to the castle and safety.

~~~

Chapter Nineteen

Out On Her Own

Wanting to get out of the cursed kingdom of Lothrien as quickly as possible, Arianna had considered heading due north and into Larandar. She discarded this option rather quickly. If anyone was tracking her, this would be the direction they would expect her to go and then back to her own kingdom from there. That course of action could spell doom for her people, and that was not a chance the young woman was ready to take. Heading south would take her further into Lothrien and away from where she wanted to go. It would also increase the distance from possible help by Kyrill's people. That was assuming that the winged shapeshifters were actually real and not just a figment of her imagination.

South was also the direction the large party of outlaws had gone. The princess figured that their lair was somewhere to the northwest in the foothills or mountains. That had been the general direction their small group had been traveling in before the stampede. From what she had overheard, the rest of the bandits would also be heading back to their home after laying a false trail. To reach the hills, they would eventually have to swing west and then due north. If she headed south, it would be unexpected. The danger of running into those rascals, however, made it not a good option. Meeting that lot again was something she preferred to avoid at all costs.

If she was to get to Re'adeen, she would need to head northwest. She would have to travel very carefully and keep alert at all times to prevent being recaptured. And, as far as she knew, Alandor was alive as well and somewhere out there. That creepy man was one person she absolutely did not intend to cross path with ever again. Considering all her options, Arianna decided that heading due west, for the time being, would be the safest way for her to go. Yes, it kept her away from Kyrill's people and in King Vargos's kingdom for a longer amount of time but it would also be a direction they might not expect her to go. And, it should keep her out of the path of the bandits.

The princess followed the game trail north. She was looking for a track taking her in the desired direction. When she passed an intersecting path leading due west, a plan popped into her mind. Instead of turning west, Arianna continued to travel north for a while longer. When she reached a nice open clearing a good distance from the turnoff, she instantly felt that this place was perfect for what she needed. Bringing her horses to a stop, the young woman started to unsaddle four of the five mounts. After checking all the saddlebags for anything useful and adding that to her own packs, she carried the saddles to the side of the small meadow. The girl covered them with leaves and branches. She allowed them to show just a little. An observant scout riding past should spot them rather quickly.

The fairies were going to hide her trail but just in case the soldiers somehow got past them, a little misdirection would not hurt. Arianna set out to make it look like she had spent the night in the glade or had at least taken a long rest there. Loving her animals, she would have naturally relieved them of their burdens. Arianna hoped that her pursuers figured that she, being a princess and not used to such chores, had found it too tiresome to saddle all the horses back up. If she had left the gear out in the open, it would have been way too obvious.

Angus, who would most likely be leading the pursuit, would have been instantly suspicious. Thinking of the captain, Arianna threw a few more branches on the pile and set about blending it in just a little bit better. Finally, she was satisfied. She knew that she had done the job well enough that it would fool even that perceptive man. They would find the saddles, but not easily. Hopefully, the men would assume that she had been trying to hide her trail and had continued heading north toward the next kingdom. It would not fool them for long but might help cover her tracks.

One of the saddles the girl kept for carrying supplies and her blankets and such. She had always disliked the feeling of the stiff leather against her legs and was much more comfortable riding bareback. To get to Re'adeen, she had a long way to go. The princess needed to minimize the stress on her body and on the horses. Saddling five horses each morning would not only have been tedious but would have slowed her down and increased the chance of being recaptured. There was no way she could relax her guard even a little while she was within the borders of King Vargos's kingdom. Arianna wanted to put as much distance between herself and the men following her as she possibly could.

~

Remembering Alandor's trick, she explained to the fairies what she wanted to do. The little ones thought that fooling the humans would be great fun and had no trouble convincing the horses to walk backward the way they had come. Their antics soon had the princess laughing. Both horses and sprites seemed to be having a delightful time. Once they reached the path leading west, Arianna decided that it might be a good idea to back down this trail for a bit as well. Cheers greeted her plan. There was a grumbling of disappointment when the girl suggested after a while that they could turn back around. Stopping the horses, she patiently explained to her new friends that they needed to get as far away as possible from here, and that was better done facing the way they were moving.

The little ones brightened considerably when the princess proposed that instead, they might want to get some of the local wildlife to trample their tracks. That should confuse the humans even more. Five of the fairies immediately set out to see what could be done. It was not long before they returned and gleefully reported that several cooperative deer and a herd of wild pigs had been only too happy to help with the ploy and were now enthusiastically racing up and down both trails. In return, the sprites had unearthed some special treats for the animals.

"Thank you, my wonderful little friends! That was so clever of you and truly amazing! It should keep those nasty men busy for a long while!" Arianna continued to praise their efforts effusively. She could tell by the slight pink of their faces how pleased they were. "Since you guys are so superb at confusing those humans, would it be possible to erase all evidence of our passing from now on? Leave them no trail to follow?" she asked them curiously. "Oh yes, Lady, we can do that. That is very easy. Watch please," one of the fairies told her.

The princess gave the command to move out. When she looked back, she exclaimed in amazement. Every hoof print behind them started to disappear, wiped out as if it had never existed. It would be very hard for anyone to follow their trail now! The little fairies were delighted with her reaction, and all earlier discontent was entirely forgotten. The little ones were especially pleased when the girl told them how happy she was to have them for company and how incredibly helpful they were being. It seemed flattery and gratefulness were the way to these tiny beings hearts.

Frequently switching horses they were covering ground at a good pace. By late afternoon, the small group had gotten much closer to the foothills. The forest was less dense here which made traveling so much easier. If she had been a bandit, this would have been where she would have preferred to ride. This thought left Arianna feeling a little anxious. What she needed were eyes in the sky. She turned to the fairies. The sprites near her home had often ridden on some of the large birds and had tremendously enjoyed the feeling of flying. She told this to her new friends and asked if one of them would be willing to give this mode of transport a try.

One of the little ones was fairly bouncing with enthusiasm. "What is your name?" the princess asked her gently. "I am Blossom, your majesty. Can I ride into the sky? Please? I will be your eyes! I have very sharp eyes, will tell you all that I see! Please? Please?" the tiny fairy begged. The little one was so cute in her excitement that Arianna could not help but feel a deep wave of love for this sweet being. She was so lucky to have these delightful little people along for company on what would otherwise be a long, arduous, and lonely journey. "If that is your wish so be it," the princess told the eager sprite.

Casting out with her mind, Arianna soon found a hawk willing to carry the tiny girl. She and the fairy would stay in constant contact, and Blossom would alert her if she saw anything out of the ordinary. With her mind put at ease, traveling became a lot more pleasant. She struck up a conversation with the rest of the fairies and learned much about their everyday lives. The young woman had been friends with sprites for many years, but listening to these little ones gave her an entirely new understanding of their feelings and thoughts, something which until now she had been denied.

As the shadows were getting longer and longer, the princess's energy began to wane. She had not slept much the nights before. That and all the horror she had witnessed this day had exhausted her. She asked her willing helpers if they had knowledge of a safe place to spend the night. The little ones immediately spread out to look for some sort of shelter. Several locations presented a valid option for the sprites but not so for the princess. Crawling into a bramble bush or hiding in a hole in the ground had just not appealed to her very much. Arianna explained what kind of place she had in mind. This left one spot which seemed perfect. They would stop for the night on a hill with a tall tree peeking out above the rest of the forest.

Arianna unsaddled the pack horse and spread out her bedroll and blankets under the large tree. She asked the fairies to wake her when it was fully dark and almost instantly fell into an exhausted sleep. As the light paled, the young woman slumbered peacefully surrounded by the grazing horses and guarded by her new friends. Birdsong died away, and the creatures in the woods settled down to rest. The tranquil evening turned into night as the light dimmed ever so slowly. After the sun had dropped well below the horizon, darkness fell all at once. The last of the warmth faded away, and the nocturnal chill of early spring descended upon the land.

The sprites let the girl rest until the black of night had fully settled over the hills before rousing her gently. The princess sat up yawning, and it took her a moment to remember why she had asked them to wake her. "Since you can see in the dark much better than I, could you help me climb that tree?" she asked the fairies. The little ones reacted confused. "There is no danger here. Why would you want to do such a silly thing in the middle of the night, Lady? If you really wanted to climb that there tree, can it not wait until morning?" Blossom finally inquired.

"No, my little friends, I need to do this now. Only at night can I see the fires of the evil men and we will know where they are," the girl explained to them. "But Lady, why not see through my eyes? I can fly up there quick as can be," the sprite responded. "That is an excellent idea, Blossom, but your vision is different from mine. I would not be able to judge the distance accurately, and I do need to know how far away from us they are. I don't like it much either but up I must go," she explained. Now that they understood why she needed to do this, her concerned friends readily agreed to help. With the fairies guiding her hands and feet, Arianna carefully worked her way up the immense tree. Higher and higher she climbed until finally, she could see all across the land.

The princess had chosen this spot for just this purpose. The tall tree on the little knoll towered over the rest of the forest. Looking first to the east, she spotted the fires of the witch's camp. She could barely make them out. The place, as well as the sorceress, had been in pretty bad shape when the bandits had abducted her. For a moment, she wondered how the woman was doing. Odessa had been in terrible condition when she had last seen her, just barely alive. Arianna could not help but feel pity for her and also some guilt in having contributed to the doom of the enchantress. In spite of the cruel and disrespectful treatment she had received from the wicked housekeeper, there was no anger left in her heart towards the lady. After seeing the way Alandor had treated the defenseless witch, all that remained was compassion

Losing one's magic was a terrible thing, especially when one had been as powerful as the sorceress had been. Arianna could only hope she would learn to adjust. She understood instinctively just how hard it would be for Odessa. The enchantress had relied on her craft for even the most basic things. Reaching out, she let her mind travel towards the camp until she found the unlucky woman. Ever so gently, she touched the still unconscious mind and recoiled. Tears started rolling down the princess's face for she had grasped the horror of what had happened to the witch that day in this one brief contact. No one, regardless of what they had done, deserved such a fate!

Her thoughts turned to her Goddess, and she sent a silent prayer asking for healing for the stricken sorceress. Warmth filled her and a profound feeling of being comforted. Arianna's heart filled with gratitude and deep love for her kindhearted deity who would help even this devoted disciple of the Dark Arts. "Thank you, my Lady," the girl whispered with a voice still choked with tears.

Resolutely, the princess tore her eyes away from the distant camp and searched the dark forest between herself and the distant fires for any evidence of pursuit. It did not take her long to find it. It looked like one single fire, but it sure was big. It seemed that King Vargos's people had come after her even with the chaos reigning in the afflicted camp. The girl figured that Angus was most likely leading them. The soldiers were much closer than she would have liked. In the morning, she would have to get going at first light and ride as long and far as she could if she wanted to make sure that they would not catch up with her.

Now to find the rest of the outlaws. Calming herself, she searched the woods to the south. There, a long way off and a little bit to the southeast was the faint flickering radiance of more campfires. That must be the main force of the bandits. She felt a profound sense of relief that they were too far away to be an immediate threat, unlike the soldiers. Just to be sure, Arianna searched the rest of the woods, but no other fires were sending their glimmering sparks up into the velvety night sky. Her reconnaissance had yielded the location of three of the groups presenting a danger to her. This left just one. Where was Alandor?

A brisk spring wind was blowing through the trees chilling her a little, but the swaying of the huge tree was somehow soothing and almost hypnotic. Her eyes were starting to close, and she shook herself awake. Realizing that remaining on her lofty perch would not solve the puzzle of the missing bandit and only get her hurt, the princess carefully descended the tree. The sprites were again guiding her hands and feet.

It felt good to stand on the solid forest floor once more. Arianna thanked the fairies for their valuable assistance. She had come to realize how much they liked being treated in a kindly and almost gallant fashion. They would have genuinely appreciated the flowery speech Alandor had used whenever he had spoken to her. Wishing her seven little friends a good night, the princess crawled back into her bed.

Knowing that she was safe and well-guarded, it was not long before she was deeply asleep once more.

~

Kyrill was pacing restlessly in the small mountain hut. He had been extremely concerned when he felt the princess fall asleep but could not reach her. He had no way of knowing what had happened to her this day and feared that she might be unconscious or possibly drugged. He kept monitoring her and was surprised when she woke up after a while. What was going on with her?

Being stuck here and not being able to come to her aid was driving the young man to distraction. The king, knowing his son well, was having him guarded. His sire was prepared to stop him, by force if necessary, if he even thought about heading into Lothrien. As long as she was in that cursed kingdom, there was nothing he could do to help. The waiting was about to make him lose patience with all the restrictions his elders kept placing on him.

The prince realized that Arianna was still not entirely certain that he actually existed and that their love was real. As long as she had been in Maridanmar, their interactions had to be kept dreamlike. He had hated that but had been given no choice. Now, that things had changed, it was taking time to convince her. The princess loved and relied on him and was starting to believe in their bond more every day but was still holding back.

To Kyrill, on the other hand, she was everything and had been from the day he had first met her. The Eagles, as his people referred to themselves, mated for life and usually had a strong soulbond to their prospective partner from a very young age. The prince loved Arianna with all his heart, his soul, his being. Any threat to her that he could not rush out and vanquish was torture for him.

The young Eagle's connection to his mate had grown so strong over the last few days that he shared everything she felt. Experiencing all those strong emotions right along with his love had been hard on him. All he wanted to do is rescue her, shelter her in his arms, and bring her home to his people's mountain hideaway. Kyrill could not wait to start their life together. He was very tired of being told to stay put and knew he could not do so much longer.

His knees went weak, so great was his relief when he felt Arianna slide into sleep again and was able to join her in her dreams. Within seconds, the prince was holding her in his arms and was checking the amused girl over to make sure she was ok. After a gentle kiss, she began to relay to him the events of the day. It was not long before he began to understand the reasons for his love's earlier fatigue. What a day she had had! When she told Kyrill about the horrible fate of the bandits, tears started to roll down her face. The princess ended up sobbing in his arms until she was able to compose herself once more. The young woman was emotionally and physically exhausted. No wonder she had been too deeply asleep for him to reach her!

After Arianna had laid out the entire situation, she told the prince that she planned on riding toward the west to avoid the bandits as well as the soldiers. Kyrill agreed that for the time being that was the best option but counseled her to start turning just a little to the north around noon. He reminded her that he could not help her as long as she was in that wretched kingdom. The young man would have preferred it had she headed straight to the north along the edge of the foothills, but with the outlaw's lair somewhere in that vicinity, that was not a safe option.

The prince decided that first thing in the morning he would send out some of his men to look for Alandor's lair. If he wanted to keep his lady safe and be able to properly advise her on which way she should travel, he needed all the information he could get. The game trails were slow going and at this pace, it would take her more than two days to reach the foothills and even longer before she would cross into Larandar. If everything went according to plan, she should cross the border on the third day. Then, all they had to do was find her!

~~~

Chapter Twenty

A New Day Dawns

The gently spreading light of the early dawn saw Angus and his men getting ready to ride. None of them had liked spending the night this close to the bears' domain. They had been only too happy to get up early and be on their way as soon as possible. It did not take them long to break camp and get mounted up. The captain led the way and decided to keep the horses to a fast walk. They had a way to go, and he did not want to unduly exhaust the poor beasts. Animals and humans alike were still feeling the effects of the terror of the day before.

To save their mounts, the riders changed horses every couple leagues, wherever they could do so without stopping. The sun was high in the sky when they reached the road. Knowing that they would be back with the rest of the men soon was a relief for them all. Switching horses once more, the small company set off at a fast trot. It was much easier and safer moving along the highway than on the game trails in the woods. They were making good time now.

It was not long before they reached the clearing. Angus immediately took in the reduction of the perimeter of the camp. The pavilion and a tent were still standing, but otherwise, things were ready for travel. He was extremely pleased and proud of his new lieutenant. The man had done well in his absence. It was early afternoon by this time, and the sensible Aaron had figured this could be about the time his captain would return. The sentries had seen the large fire the night before, and the young commander had guessed that the search party was on its way back. The circumspect officer wanted to have things ready so that they could get going at a moment's notice.

After a brief rest and a steaming cup of kahve, the captain gave the command to move out. The tent and the pavilion had been taken down and stowed in the meantime, and all was ready for travel. Aaron was glad to have his captain there to deal with Sebastian. The ailing envoy refused point blank to have the still unconscious witch placed in the carriage with him. Angus finally relented and had the sorceress put in one of the wagons. That presented him with a problem, however. The woman was still too sick to be left untended. The cook eventually volunteered to look after her, and the commander thanked him for his kind offer.

The seasoned officer was only too well aware of how much the enchantress had been hated. He realized that most of his men would feel much better if she was securely guarded. Angus assigned a couple of trusted soldiers to ride at the sides of the wagon to keep an eye on the situation. He hoped this would keep the still unconscious witch from being harmed further as well as prevent her from causing trouble when she woke up.

The mood of the column was subdued. They had lost over a third of their comrades, and their hearts were heavy.

Even knowing that they were heading home and back to the castle did little for the three companies' spirits. As they rode through peaceful woods brilliantly lit by the late afternoon sun, the usual light-hearted banter was missing. Their numbers were significantly diminished, and the majority of the bandits had come this way. There was no way of knowing how many men they could be dealing with, and this had them all on high alert.

The captain had been this way many times before and knew of a protected valley up ahead where they could spend the night in comparative safety. He felt that this would be the best place for them to camp. He kept his men moving in spite of Sebastian's vociferous complaints. Let the envoy take it up with the king, the protection of the column was Angus's prime responsibility. He would do what he must to keep them as safe as possible now that the witch was no longer calling the shots.

It was near dark by the time they finally reached the sheltered spot the commander had chosen for the night. The vale was located just a short distance off the road. The soldiers began immediately to set up camp. Angus had given orders to once again put the pavilion and the tent for the witch in the middle. The men were told to bed down in a tight circle around them. After the experience with the bandits, his troops were only too happy to obey.

The gorge itself was horseshoe shaped and enclosed by steep cliffs. This made it easy to guard the entrance but still left the possibility of an enemy sliding down a rope or rolling down rocks from above. The captain figured that as long as they stayed in the center of the valley, they should be safe enough. This spot was far better than being out in the woods where an enemy could sneak up on them through the trees.

The officer decided that they would set enough guards to make sure that any attempts to reach the valley floor would be instantly detected. The cliff was rather crumbly, and falling rocks would alert the sentries. His men were aware of such ploys and would be watching sharply. Lighting the rope on fire would take care of the rest. Angus figured that the outlaws were long gone but preferred to play it safe. The horses were tied opposite the valley opening, behind the camp, and were soon contently cropping the juicy grass. The two supply wagons were used to block the entrance and to give the men a sheltered position in case of an attack.

Angus had several of his men collect firewood along the way and soon the cook had a nice little fire going close to the pavilion. It was not long before the smell of a savory stew drifted through the campsite. Even the envoy had ceased some of his complainings. He was not a soldier, but smart enough to see the benefit of a sheltered space such as this.

The witch was starting to regain consciousness for short periods, and the officer had her brought out to the fire. Since none of his men were comfortable dealing with the sorceress, the captain himself tried to feed her some of the broth. Attempting to swallow caused the woman such pain that, after a while, some of his men winced every time she choked down a bit of the liquid. It seemed her throat was so burned that it would take a long while to heal. Angus did manage to get a little food and some water down her before she lapsed back into unconsciousness once more.

Most of the soldiers were still weary from their ordeal, and none of them had rested well the night before. Being in a place where they felt somewhat safe allowed them to relax for the first time since the attack. With the letdown came extreme tiredness and the sound of snoring soon filled the air. That was making it hard for the guards to stay awake.

Their captain had expected this and, to make sure the sentries were as alert as possible at all times, had ordered short shifts for this night. He had also doubled up the guards. Angus had no intention of a repeat of that vicious attack and wanted the camp to have ample warning of any intrusion.

~~~

Chapter Twenty One

Patience Is A Virtue

At first, Alandor slept quite comfortably in the fork of the large tree, but in his eagerness to go to sleep, he had forgotten to tie himself to the trunk. Soon he began to slip, and the much-tested sprites had to intervene to prevent him from dropping to the ground. They had to take action several more times during the night, and one of the little fairies had to be awake and close by instead of comfortably asleep in that thickly padded bird nest.

The pair was relieved when dawn appeared on the horizon. Their brother had received their message. He and the by now much-recovered horse were patiently waiting at the foot of the tree. The sprites had thought it best to make sure the man had food and water. They had lost all respect for the once so very self-assured bandit king. This guy was about as incompetent about surviving on his own as they had ever seen. The fairies were hoping that providing for some of the man's needs would reduce his endless complaining at least by a little. More than that they did not dare to expect.

The three sprites had not yet decided how they would deal with the situation if the outlaw once again brutally pushed the poor beast. Being elementals, they loved animals. Abuse of a defenseless being in any form terribly upset them and could just not be tolerated. They had felt bad enough about returning the unlucky creature to this cruel brigand. Unfortunately, they had not been able to come up with a better solution.

If the man had to walk, it would just take too long. The miserable wretch might not make it back to his hideout alive if they had to listen to him the entire time. In spite of the queen's commands, they were sure they would not be able to help themselves. An unfortunate accident would end up taking the pathetic man's life somehow, somewhere. They had seriously been considering doing him harm the day before and their journey with this monster had just begun.

~

The bandit king was thrilled to see his horse grazing beneath the tree when he awoke. Maybe his good luck had finally returned! After climbing down from his perch, he happily petted the mount. Such an act of niceness was unusual for him, but his heart was overflowing with relief. His loyal steed had found him again! What a smart and devoted animal! This thought led to a contemplation of the bond between horses and men. Maybe the little princess had been on to something with the naming of her mares.

Alandor figured that this horse with no name, which had returned to him twice now, had earned the privilege of being referred to with something other than 'hey horse!' But what to call this faithful beast? No mount of his had ever done anything like this before. All the others would have been long gone, running as fast as they could to put as much distance between themselves and him as possible. Only this one kept coming back to him, in spite of the cruel way he had treated the animal. The princess had made it appear so easy giving her horse a name, so why was it so hard for him to come up with something?

Discarding several names as entirely too ridiculous, the man finally settled on calling the animal 'Finder.' That was the only name which made perfect sense to him. After all, this trusty steed kept finding him. He almost felt something like gratitude in his heart. Having the horse would allow him to get to the meetup place in time after all. Alandor was whistling happily. Climbing into the saddle, he discovered that his water flask was still full and that there was even food left in the saddle bags. How had he missed this the day before? He must have still been in shock after meeting that bear. Kicking the horse into a walk, the bandit king guided it back to the trail. Once he was heading in the right direction, he set about eating breakfast. Life looked so much better already!

Alandor was much kinder to the horse this day. He was still puzzled by finding himself suddenly in the middle of the path instead of in the saddle. Something had happened, and he did not want to take a chance at it reoccurring. The animal seemed to like its new name and feeling rather lonesome; the bandit king started talking to the patient beast. He actually found that he enjoyed this one sided communication with Finder, who seemed to be listening intently. The outlaw even stopped at a creek to let his mount drink and graze for a bit. While the horse was enjoying the fragrant grass, the brigand made himself comfortable by reclining against a convenient tree. He continued telling his silent companion colorful tales.

The longer the scoundrel spoke, the more personal his stories became. It was almost as if the floodgates had opened and out poured all that he had been holding in for so many years. After a while, the chatty man started divulging some of his most intimate feelings. He was happier than he had been in a long time. 'What an excellent audience this loyal horse makes! It listens but never talks back, and all my secrets are safe with it' Alandor contently thought to himself. At times, the smart creature would even turn its head to regard him with those soulful eyes. 'Seriously? That was very ingenious of you!' he could almost hear it say. The outlaw smiled at the notion and feeling encouraged, continued on with his monolog.

~

Had the bandit king known that other ears were listening intently, he would have been a little more careful with his tales. The fairies were thrilled. One of the invisible brothers was sitting between the ears of the horse encouraging it every once in a while to give the man an interested look. The other two were lounging on its rump. As it was, the elated sprites were starting to get a fairly good idea about the location of the hideout from the outlaw's description. For a while, they thought that they might be able to find the fortress by themselves with all the information they had overheard.

All those high hopes were dashed when the talkative chap started chatting about the many traps he had designed to make approaching his hideout near impossible. The poor little guys' spirits sank as they realized that they would have a very hard time reaching the sanctuary alive. They had hoped that they could finally get rid of this imbecile! The three brothers continued to listen glumly as the bandit prattled on about his aggrandized feats of ingenuity.

~

Alandor kept looking around warily as he rode through the sunlit forest. The woods consisted once more of tall trees but with little understory due to the rocky ground. The absence of big bushes made for much better visibility. The villain had concluded that spirits had something to do with his fall from the horse the previous day. He was determined to catch a glimpse of them. That his antagonists could be sharing the horse with him, never even occurred to the man. When the outlaw started to reflect on the morning's events, he remembered the water bottle and the food in his saddlebags. Thinking back to the day before, he was fairly sure that there had been none of the life-giving fluid left. The food could have been there, he had been in a terrible hurry after all and could have missed it quite easily, but the water? No way.

Something seemed to be intervening on his behalf. Who could it possibly be, way out here in these woods? And, why were they helping him? His relationship with the fey had been adversarial at best. They had never assisted him before, no, rather the opposite. Forest spirits were well known for playing mischievous pranks on unsuspecting travelers. He and his men had experienced this on many occasions. They had grown very tired of burrs under their sleeping blankets, missing horses, fouled water, or other mischiefs down that line. So when they had come across an opportunity for revenge on the tiresome creatures, they had been only too happy to do their worst.

One day, the outlaw and his gang had stumbled on something that looked like a toy village in a sheltered glade deep in the forest. Alandor had immediately seen his chance. He had left one man behind to keep an eye on the tiny dwellings from a safe distance while he and the rest of the bandits collected branches and twigs. They had then sneaked up on the miniature houses, surrounded them, and quickly thrown the firewood over the top of the buildings. Then they had set the branches ablaze. Alandor and his thugs had taken great delight in watching the little village burn and were prepared to kill anything trying to escape. They had hoped this would put an end to whatever was bothering them on their passages through the forest.

Their callous act, however, had only made things worse. The 'miserable little beasts' were now out for revenge of their own. Every time the outlaws came through that part of the forest, their lives became pure misery. Things had soon gotten so out of hand that several of the men ended up getting hurt, some seriously. Only luck had prevented these incidents from getting them all killed. After a few truly dangerous and malicious pranks had been played on him and his lads, Alandor had decided to change their route and to avoid that section of the woods altogether.

The incident with the fey had happened over a year ago and yesterday had been the first time in a long time that Alandor and his thugs had been anywhere near that area. Could those wicked little beings have expanded their territory? Could they have recognized him and his men and started the stampede? Set that bear on him to finally get their long overdue revenge? Now that was a disturbing thought, and it made Alandor shudder.

If that had been the case, who then was helping him now? Was he being set up for something worse? Looking around anxiously, the bandit king decided he would be extra careful from now on. Alandor searched his brain for information about forest spirits. He remembered hearing that these beings hated humans who were unkind to animals. That could explain why he had so suddenly sailed out of the saddle and been roughly deposited on the path! But why then had they allowed the horse to come back? And, why had his talisman not warned him? None of this made any sense to him. Just to err on the side of caution, however, he would be nicer to his mount than he had ever been to any being in his whole life.

The day went on, and Alandor let the horse set its own pace as long as it kept moving faster than he could walk. He stopped every couple hours to give the animal a break and let it graze. And he was talking to it and even petting it, something he had never even considered doing before until this day. In the past, he had been more prone to dig his spurs into the horse's side than to give it a reassuring pat.

Thinking of his beloved spurs made him reflect on their unexplained disappearance. Maybe he had not lost them during his desperate run from the bear after all but during his nap in the tree! The fey hated iron, and they would have especially hated those sharp metal wheels. Anyhow, gone was gone, and he might as well resign himself that he would never find them again. He would have a new and nicer pair made when he arrived back at his home. The horse seemed to be moving just fine without being forced on, but he missed them. They had been genuinely good spurs, very toothy for maximum effect, and had left plenty a horse's side bloody in the past. Most nature spirits would abhor such treatment of any living being. As long as they were helping him get back to his men, that loss was a small price to pay.

On and on the path wound its way through the wooded hills. It was much slower going on the uneven game trail than on the road. Alandor had been silent while contemplating the subject of the spirits. Now he started talking to the horse once again. "Finder, we have a long way left to go. Do you think we could move just a little faster?" the bandit king politely asked his patient mount. The horse turned its head for a moment to look at him and whinnied. Then it increased its speed to a fast walk. The man was stunned! The dumb beast had understood him! How could that be? And, it had done as he asked without spurs or anything!

The outlaw started reflecting on his observations of the princess and her horses. He had seen how easily the young woman had dealt with her mounts and how eager the animals had been to please her. They seemed to genuinely love the girl. The man had thought that the young woman had a special knack with horses. Now he wondered. Could it be that just treating the animals with respect got the job done for which he had been using whip and spurs? That notion stunned Alandor for a moment. If he had been mistaken about that, what else had he been wrong about? Could his trying to force his imprisoned ladies to love him have made them hate him worse? Would treating them with respect and kindness have worked better? Could he have been handling them and his men wrong all along?

This very idea rocked the outlaw's view of the world and was too much for the self-centered brigand's ego to take. It decided that that kind of deranged thinking was insanity and should be discarded that very minute. Shutters slammed down in his mind with incredible force. All the valuable insights the rogue had just gained were locked away instantly and hidden deep in the dark crevices of his self-absorbed brain. Old patterns began to reassert themselves.

No, Alandor decided, he had always done things a certain way, and it had brought him resounding success. Why should he change now? He was richer than many a king. He had not just one but several beautiful women he called his own. Most monarchs had to put up with the whims of their females but not him. His ladies were there for the taking. They were at his beck and call anytime he pleased, and he could do with them whatever he wanted.

He, the mighty, the elusive Alandor had trained his ladies well. He had broken their spirits and made them his own. They were happy with anything he gave them, sweet and compliant. Each and every one of them had learned that the dungeon was a very unpleasant place to be. And, they all feared his whip and his temper. He had never shown them even the slightest bit of mercy, and they might not love him, but they would do anything to stay in his favor.

The bandit king was a cruel man and severely punished anyone who displeased him. To him, it made no difference if the offender was a beast, a lady, or even one of his men. Having this kind of power gave the outlaw great pleasure. He liked beating those weaker than himself; it made him feel strong and all powerful. The horse responding so readily had to have been just a fluke. But, to be on the safe side, he would treat the beast nicely until he reached his men. Then, with other mounts at his disposal, the miserable brute would pay for putting him through the indignities he was having to suffer. Throwing him off the way it had! "Just wait until we reach my men, you stupid wretch! You will pay bitterly for all the delays and for unhorsing me for no good reason at all! My whip will show you who the master is!" he mumbled under his breath.

The cruel brigand's angry words sent cold chills down the fairies' spines. Treating the horse kindly was all an act to achieve his objective of meeting up with the rest of the thugs! This man was truly rotten to the core. For a moment, the fairies had thought that this foul mortal had a heart after all. Hearing his whispered words, however, wiped out any last doubt that the man deserved what was coming to him. Their anger was so palatable in the air that even the insensitive Alandor felt it like an icy breeze. The rogue looked around nervously but could not find the source of his unease.

~

The bandit king traveled until the sun had almost completely set. The twilight was causing strange shadows to appear in the ever darkening woods. This was putting the scoundrel more on edge by the minute, and fear was beginning to assert itself. The outlaw assumed that the bear was far behind him by now, but there could be other dangers. The frightened brigand decided that he would feel much safer off the ground.

In the last of the light, the rogue spotted a magnificent tree, tall and straight. He loosely tied the horse to some close to the ground branches so it could graze and began his climb. It was almost entirely dark now, and the man was climbing more by touch than sight. When he reached a suitable height, he started feeling around for a fork to sleep in. He finally located what he was looking for. It would have to do but would not be as comfortable as the one he slept in the night before. Alandor realized he would have to be very careful not to roll off in his sleep and secured himself to the branches to make sure he would not fall.

~

The sprites, brothers named Twig, Leaf, and Bork, made sure the bandit was safely tied in and sound asleep before gliding down the tree. A quick check confirmed that the horse was doing fine and off they raced to a nearby tree to have a discussion. Perching on a couple of low branches, they eyed each other in disbelief. "Did you hear? Did you hear? Him intends to beat that there horse!" they chattered excitedly. "What to do? Dump him on his nasty head? Drown him in a river? Drop him down a cliff?" they asked each other time after time.

All three were terribly upset. That human was one of the worst kinds, and they were stuck with getting him back to his home alive! All they wanted to do was take the horse and leave the miserable wretch to his fate. They had just calmed a little when a new horror entered their tiny heads. They remembered what the bandit had told the horse about his imprisoned ladies and how he kept them nice and compliant and obedient to his every whim. Recalling those cruel words was just too much, and their fury rose even higher. They decided that they would do something truly awful to this man once the women were free and they would take great pleasure in contemplating his death until the time came.

Twig finally managed to calm his brothers. None of them felt like helping the outlaw any longer and from this day on they would take great pleasure in hearing him complain. Never again would they fill his bags with food or his flask with water as they had done that morning. That act of kindness might have already given away their existence to the horrid creature. They would be very careful from now on to hide their presence and take no more chances that could make the whole plan go awry! Let the nasty human fend for himself!

"Come to me!" a commanding voice suddenly interrupted their contemplations. The unexpected call blasting into their minds knocked all three sprites of their perches. The dragon! The fairies looked at each other warily. Had the nosy beast overheard their discussion? If she had, there was nothing to be done about it. With a resigned shrug of their small shoulders, they decided they better comply. The apprehensive brothers hurried to a nearby glade to obey the summons.

~

The dragon lady Galata eyed each one of the little sprites thoroughly. She could tell they were terribly upset. "Little ones, what has you so in an uproar?" she asked gently.

"Come, sit, and tell me!" she continued. With a welcoming gesture of one of her claws, she invited the sprites to make themselves comfortable on her thick tail which she curled in front of her nose.

The three started talking all at once, and Galata had to interrupt the onslaught of words. She mildly asked them to please speak one at a time. Once the sprites had begun their story, they did not seem to be able to stop themselves. It did not take long for the dragon to understand their ire. That man was a real monster! "Remember the mission, little ones! There are those who desperately need our help! Keep this in mind, please, no matter how much you would like to break that human animal's neck!" the dragon admonished them.

"I promise you, he will get his, and it will not be pleasant. Slow and excruciatingly painful, I think. Would you like to be part of this?" Galata went on. "Oh yes, lady! More than anything!" the fairies cried with gleeful anticipation. Forgotten were status and rewards by their queen. Nothing seemed as significant or sweet anymore as revenge on this malicious man.

The eager fairies told their massive new friend all they had learned that day. About the hideout, about the traps, everything they could think of which might be noteworthy. The dragon mulled this over for a while and then had the obliging brothers repeat everything they had learned about the location of the lair of the vicious bandit. Galata promised to go looking for the hideout this very night and if she found it, and if she thought she could get in or get them in to rescue the ladies, they would deal with this horrible mortal once and for all. But until such a time, the dragon emphasized, they needed to do their absolute best to keep him alive no matter how bothersome he became. With this urgent reminder, Galata sent the much calmer sprites on their way.

Glumly, but with more hope in their hearts, the brothers returned to the tree where the bandit was blissfully sleeping. They settled in to take turns to watch over man and horse. The night seemed to go on forever, and the brothers were relieved when the first light of dawn started sending red-tinged fingers along the shadowy forest floor. Birds began to sing and the smell of pine needles in the crisp morning air gave the place such a peaceful feel that they almost forgot about the outlaw still deeply asleep above them.

The minute the depraved man awoke, however, it seemed as if a cloud of darkness descended upon the pleasant woods. To their horror, the fairies realized that his resolute rejection of his finer thoughts and feelings the day before had further allowed the evil in his heart and soul to grow.

~~~

Chapter Twenty Two

A Mostly Pleasant Day

he early morning light swept across the dark woods and started to illuminate the small hills and valleys around the little knoll Arianna was peacefully sleeping on. An explorative sunbeam tickled her nose, and the girl woke up with a sneeze. Looking around, the princess heart filled with joy and deep peace. She took in the incredible beauty of the early morning forest. To her, the sound of birdsong was the loveliest music she had ever heard; no orchestra had ever seemed quite so sweet.

This was her first morning alone. It had been days since she had felt such a deep sense of contentment. How wonderful it was to be away from all those horrible people! Having Kyrill there to talk to and advise her at night was also a great comfort. She had come to truly value his counsel and him! If only he were real! She loved this dream prince so much that she was not sure she would ever be able to open her heart to a real one. All the young noblemen she had met had left little impression and faded to nothingness when likened to her dream friend. They were just not him, could not even begin to compare to this amazing winged man.

~

Being a princess and having been taught at least some of the 'proper' decorum from a young age on, she would have never felt comfortable kissing one of her admirers. Yes, she was a lot more unconventional than most, but that kind of contact with the opposite sex was not acceptable. She had also never even wanted to. Arianna was polite to the young men and treated them with kindness and respect but also made sure that they did not cross her boundaries. Most of them understood rather quickly that she had no interest in them, none, not even a smidgen.

The girl's indifference towards her suitors had left her aunt in despair. How could the lady ever find a husband for her oldest niece if she turned down all the eligible men? The more the young woman had balked, the more functions she had ended up attending. She loved to dance, but most of the get-togethers had been downright boring. Being a princess, she was supposed to be chaperoned at all times at any public event. Arianna was rather inventive, however, and had usually managed to slip away from her guardian. There were much better things to do than being fawned over by a bunch of simpering boys. Her preferred sanctuary had been the library. Most castles had one, and she had really enjoyed perusing the different types of books.

At first, the princess had been unaware that her escapes had been noticed by some of her admirers. Then, she had begun to unexpectedly meet some of the young men in the hallways of the castles. The young lady had soon come to realize that her routine had been found out. Arianna firmly believed in doing no harm, but after a while, obnoxious boys had become the exception. When the accidental run-ins had begun to happen way too often, Arianna had decided to find out what was behind all this foolishness. One of the rascals finally divulged that she had become the object of a bet among the young nobles- kiss the Ice-Princess.

Arianna was well known for being sweet and kind but unapproachable when it came to anything romantic. Unfortunately, this also presented the mischievous princes with a most welcome challenge. The young men saw it as great fun to attempt to steal a kiss from any of the well-bred young ladies, but especially from her. Those who had tried, and there had been more than a few, had been left with their checks tingling from the sharp slap of a small hand. If that did not deter them, a quick jab with her knee had left them gasping for air. The boys had become more inventive over the months and she more devious in misleading and discouraging them. If she was completely honest, she had enjoyed the game almost as much as they did.

The princess was reserved and standoffish towards men in real life, but she felt entitled to do as she pleased in her dreams. None of those restrictive conventions and rules applied here. She was permitted to follow her heart. Arianna and the dream prince had practically grown up together. They had spent a lot of time together. She had joined him at the hut sometimes several times a week. Their relationship had evolved over time from being close friends to being in love. With Kyrill, there was no shyness, no holding back. His kisses and hugs left her tingling and longing for more. She had a good idea what that more was but, even in dreams, she was not willing to go there without being wed.

~

With a sigh, the princess put her reminiscence aside. Now it was time to get up and start the day. The fairies were happy to see her rise, and she cheerfully greeted her friends.

They had been eagerly waiting for her to wake up but had wanted to let her sleep as long as she would. The little ones even rolled up the bedroll and blankets the second Arianna turned her back to check on the horses. This was the first time she had a good chance to examine the three extra mounts. One of them was not doing well; it seemed yesterday's exertion had exhausted it badly. The girl gently laid her hands against the poor beast's neck and sent strength and healing energy into the gelding. The fairies joined her and started assisting as well. Arianna was thrilled to see some of the dullness leave the sickly steed's eyes.

From the scars on his rump and on his sides it looked like the gelding had been treated badly for a long time. "Blossom, do you want to fly again today or may I entrust this beautiful being into your hands?" she asked the little sprite who was hovering by her side and appeared to be the spokesperson for the seven little fairies. A shrill whistle erupted, and Arianna instinctively covered her ears. What looked like a boy fairy quickly appeared. "This is Roots. He will fly this day. I will care for the horse," the dainty sprite declared regally. The princess looked at her carefully. This little one was more than she seemed, she had an unmistaken air of royalty about her. Could this be Queen Liza's own precious daughter?

"I think it is sad to have nothing to call him. Would you please think of a name for him, and the others as well?" the girl asked her tiny companion. A thoughtful expression came over the fairy's face. "Would you like to be called Chestnut? It is a beautiful name for a beautiful horse," the little one addressed the mount. The horse visibly brightened, it seemed kindness and love were doing their healing magic already. Of the other two mounts, the mare was a bit nervous and tended to shy. She ended up being named Squirrel, the gelding Copper due to his lovely bright red color.

"Oh, and Blossom? One more thing. We did not have time for proper introductions yesterday. May I please know your names since we will be traveling together?" Arianna asked. The tiny fairy's face lit up with pleasure. This young woman was one human who knew how to treat them with the courtesy they deserved! "This here is Petal, the lovely one there is Rosebud, and these fine fellows are Silver and Ash. That quiet one over there is called River. Roots you have already met," the sprite said pointing at each one of her friends. Each fairy bowed as their name was called.

The princess earnestly and in a very courteous fashion greeted each of the little people in turn. "Thank you for all your help and for being my companions on this journey. It would be very lonesome indeed without you," the princess told them sincerely. She actually was glad for their company, and she was also more than thrilled to have the opportunity to get to know these fey little creatures better. She was indeed becoming fairy kin.

After saddling Copper, the girl securely fastened her bedroll and blankets to the packs. She had been very lucky to have located enough supplies in the other saddlebags to sustain her for several days. Her new friends had some food in their bundles but had told her that they usually relied pretty heavily on what they could find in the world around them. Spring had barely begun, and the forest was just starting to awake from its winter sleep. There were no berries to be had, and any nuts were usually hoarded by an industrious squirrel. Since Arianna had plenty of provisions of her own, the princess invited the sprites to share her breakfast. As soon as they were done and things put away, it was time to get on their way. Arianna mounted Azariel and headed back to the trail.

~

Riding along through the early morning woods, the princess's thoughts drifted back to the last few days. The events she had witnessed and participated in weight heavily on her very soul. She was not sure if there was anything she could have done better. That, however, did not help much with her feelings of guilt. Would things have turned out differently if she had not meddled? Might some of the soldiers still be alive? And Odessa? The witch's brutal treatment had genuinely upset Arianna. She felt a deep sense of responsibility for contributing to the sorceress's current state. The woman had been totally defenseless and still those men had been deathly afraid. Could this be her own fate if people ever found out about the true extent of her powers?

Her escape from the bandits had also turned into a disaster. The princess had not expected the sprites to go as far as setting the men up to be killed. The fairies around the castle had always been so sweet and friendly. She had never encountered their dark side but had been aware that it was there. What she had not known was what kind of violence the elementals were capable of. She had been naïve in her dealings with the enraged sprites and wished she had made more of an effort to find out what the little ones had planned. She might have been able to do something to prevent the slaughter of the outlaws. Yes, they had not been the best of men, but they did not deserve to die in such a grizzly manner.

For a moment, the feeling that all the deaths of the last days would not have happened had it not been for her overwhelmed the princess. Shaking her head, the girl decided that no good would come from allowing those thoughts to take hold in her heart and soul. She had done the best she could and knew how. Things always happened the way they should even when it did turn out bad. Now was not the time to let all this guilt and sadness come forth. The time for grieving would come later.

Resolutely, Arianna lifted her head and took in the beauty around her. As always, this lightened her mood. It was still early in the day. Here and there thick mist was hanging in the moss covered trees giving them a look of unreality. In places, fog was drifting through the forest diffusing the bright light of the sun. The whole scene reminded the girl of a painting she had seen of an enchanted forest. The princess felt like she was riding along in some mystical world.

As the sun rose higher in the sky and the haze burned off, the beauty of the dark green trees against the vibrantly blue sky broke through all the sadness. It filled the girl's heart with such love and pure joy that it helped to erase some of the shadows which had crept into her soul in the last few days. The princess understood that no one could have gone through what she had without some emotional scars. She would have to deal with those later. Right now she needed to concentrate solely on her survival and on reaching her still so very far off destination.

~

It was time to switch mounts. Arabella was happy to see her and as usual, nuzzled her shoulder. Up she went, and within seconds, Arianna was happily ensconced on the mare's shining back. Off they went once more. When the sun reached the highest point in the sky, the princess started looking around for a place to rest the steaming horses. As luck would have it, they soon reached a meadow bordering a clear, lively stream. She and the sprites shared a meal and then watched the contented animals crop the sweet new grass. This place was so peaceful and the sound of the burbling stream so soothing that the girl became drowsy and started to fall asleep.

When Arianna started slumping over, it woke her abruptly. This would not do! There were men behind her and others heading this way. They had to keep moving to stay ahead of the pursuit. As long as they lingered, they were all in danger. She was tired from the last few days but now was not the time to sleep. They needed to get a long way away from here before this day was done. Regretfully, the princess called over Azariel and mounted up. She headed her group back on the path. The girl was grateful to the sprites for handling the rest of the horses.

~

The sun was blazing and the day started to feel uncharacteristically warm. They were further south, but this was still just the very beginning of spring. Temperatures should not be this high. Soon it became so hot that it reminded the princess more of the sweltering heat of late summer. It felt like they were riding through a furnace. Arianna was sweating as were the horses. Even the sprites began to look a bit wilted, and their beautiful wings were drooping.

The forest was much more open here and allowed for plenty of sunshine to reach the dusty trail. The uncommon heat kept building as the afternoon wore on. It was sapping their strength. The wind had gone to sleep, and no welcoming breeze was wafting across the land to refresh them. Soon their pace had slowed down to a sluggish walk. It was not until almost evening that the temperature finally started to drop. Arianna was glad to see shadows begin to predominate in the tranquil woods. Welcome coolness was washing over the exhausted group and reviving them as the day moved on to dusk.

It was time to find a safe place to spend the night. The princess and the sprites started looking around. They wanted to stay close to the path but not right next to it. Best would be a small clearing or a hill which they could defend if they had to. Soon they spotted the perfect place. Ahead was a mound with a pleasant grove of trees. The girl felt a strange draw towards this welcoming site. Something about it seemed to call to her and the closer she rode, the stronger it got. The princess instantly became wary and brought her horse to a stop. There was no way she was setting foot in there without knowing more about it.

"Do you feel drawn to that copse of trees, Blossom?" she inquired. "Yes, Lady, all of us do, even the horses," came the sprite's prompt reply. "Is this some sort of a trap? Why is it calling us? Do you have any idea?" she questioned Blossom. "I do not know, Lady, should we go see?" "No, Blossom, wait. Let me," the princess responded. Strengthening her shields and stretching out just a tiny tendril of her powers she explored the stand of trees.

There was an altar at one side of the grove, but it seemed to have been abandoned long ago. The princess could detect no power resonating within its ancient stones. Arianna examined the stand of trees very carefully. It was an old place, so very welcoming and peaceful. She could detect no threat of any kind; all seemed well. It appeared to be an ideal spot to spend the night and even had water for the horses. Why then did she feel so on edge?

~~~

Chapter Twenty Three

Coming Into Her Own

𝕿he girl had not been able to find the slightest evidence of anything untoward in the glade but just to be sure, she asked the sprites to look as well. Blossom checked thoroughly but was unable to detect even a hint of danger. Being tired from the day's ride, Arianna decided to disregard her misgivings. They seemed to be wholly unfounded. Resolutely she led the way into the copse. Soon the horses were comfortably grazing, and the girl and the sprites were sharing the evening meal.

After spreading out her bedroll, the princess gratefully slid into her bed and was quickly sound asleep. Stealthily, a slight mist started to rise from the altar and waft across the clearing towards them. One by one the sprites sank down around her. Soon all of the fairies were just as insensible as the girl. The animals were also affected. The horses appeared dazed and kept shaking their heads as if to free themselves of something unpleasant which was trying to ensnare them.

~

Kyrill could feel the princess fall into slumber and prepared to join her in her dreams. As his spirit reached for Arianna's sleeping form and had almost touched her, he was suddenly and painfully repelled. It felt like running into an invisible wall, and the impact left him dazed for a moment. Cautiously, he tried again. Something or someone was blocking him from getting to his love. Stretching out his mind, he carefully examined the barrier and recoiled. There was an evil at work here, ancient and cruel, and his mate was caught in its web!

The young man knew instantly that his princess was in terrible danger. Whatever was blocking him had felt too malicious to have good intentions. He needed to wake her, but how? That barrier was too powerful for him to get through. If Arianna was going to survive this, she needed to leave there and quickly. Before the trap she had inadvertently stepped into overwhelmed her. It had been sprung and time was of the essence. He might not be able to help her, but he knew someone who could. Changing to his winged form, Kyrill sped back to the Aerie faster than he had ever flown before and raced to the home of his people's most powerful witch, Cassandra.

One look at the young prince's face told the perceptive old sorceress all she needed to know. His mate had to be in terrible trouble for this usually so composed man to be in such a desperate state. Fleet-footed, even for her advanced years, the enchantress raced to her door and sounded the alarm. Next, she questioned Kyrill and had him describe in detail what he had felt. His answers gave her the information she needed. Cassandra began setting out incense, potions, and candles. She knew it would be best to have the help of some of her people just to be safe. Soon, the others arrived and, at her command, quickly arranged in a circle around them.

Downing the content of the flask in front of her, the witch grabbed Kyrill's hands. "Take me there!" she commanded. The prince was only too happy to oblige. Once again he was being daunted by something which felt cold, slimy, and disturbing on so many levels. This time, however, he was not alone. He opened himself up fully and the immense power of the sorceress, bolstered by the life-force and magic of his people, rushed through him and pierced a whole through the greasy veil. Without a second thought for his own safety, the young man dove through the opening and catapulted into his love's enchanted dream. "Wake, wake now! You must leave before it's too late!" he screamed into her sedated mind.

~

Arianna jumped up like she had been doused with cold water. Seeing her friends asleep around her and no one left on guard told her that something was terribly wrong. Even the horses were fighting to stay awake. Looking around and seeing the fog near the altar, she instantly grasped that they were in deep trouble. The princess felt something slimy brushing up against her mind, trying to overtake her again, and shoved back hard. Her resistance must have taken it by surprise because she managed to push back the stupor which threatened to engulf her.

The mist was now starting to coalescence into distinct figures. Wraiths! That was bad news indeed. Good thing Arianna and the fairies had chosen to sleep this far away from that altar! Had they been closer, they might have stood no chance at all. As it was, they needed to get out of here and fast! Quickly grabbing the sprites and placing them on her bedroll, the young woman started to fight her way out of the glade, pulling her bed along. A whistle to the horses helped shake them out of their daze, and they began to follow.

Every step the princess took felt like walking in quicksand. It seemed to take forever to move just a few paces. Lifting her feet appeared to get harder and harder the closer she got to the grove's edge. The bedding was getting heavier as well. Something was definitely fighting to keep her. When she looked back, she noticed what looked like fine netting made out of some type of luminous threads. To her horror, she spotted a shimmering figure caught within, struggling to get free. It took her only a second to comprehend that this was the essence of Kyrill, her love. He was not a dream, he was real, and he was fighting for his very existence! Arianna realized that it must have been his desperate shout which had awoken her just a few minutes ago.

Seeing her sweetheart being attacked and pieces of his spirit body being carried away by the horrible wraiths was too much for Arianna. Tears were streaming down her face as she sank to the grassy floor. She could feel her very life-force ebbing, and her resolve disappear. "Go!" Kyrill shouted at her. How could she leave him to be torn apart in here? What could she do? Those disembodied beings were getting more and more solid. They would surely kill him. She knew in her heart if she did not do something right now, they would all perish. In desperation, she called on her Goddess and help arrived almost instantly.

A bright, angry light flared across the clearing distracting the shadowy evil just long enough to allow the girl to make good her escape. Arianna suddenly felt like a weight was being lifted off her and with one enormous last effort she rolled herself over the border of that vicious trap. She pulled the bedroll after herself. The sprites let out small moans as they tumbled into the grass but, at least, they were alive.

Now that she was safe, wrath rose up within her. Whatever these things were, they were killing her mate! All the barriers she had built to keep her powers in check were suddenly blown to pieces. Raw force and rage infused her. Fury, like she had never known in her life, gave her power beyond what she had ever imagined she could possibly wield. Grabbing her knife off the bed, she determinedly ran back into the copse. She rushed to Kyrill's side and started cutting the luminous threads, systematically working on setting him free.

He was deeply unconscious by the time she had managed to remove the last of the filaments from his spirit body. The creatures kept attacking and had continued to rip out pieces of his very being. They had taken these parts of her love for their own and would use them to feed on and increase their dark powers. Arianna knew that if she did not retrieve these bits, this amazing man whom she loved so deeply would die. She needed to get back all that had been stolen.

For a moment, she stood quietly and centered herself. Then, she pushed her awareness deep into the earth. She searched until she found a powerful ley line and, in spite of knowing the danger to herself, reached out for it. Seizing it, she allowed this vast power to flow through her. She knew if it was too much, she might never be able to do magic again, that it could burn out her gift for good. To her, however, saving her mate was worth any risk.

Her long silken hair rose up and begun flaring around her. Each strand was outlined with a warm, golden light and sparks shot out all around her. Lightning was crackling on her fingertips. For a moment, Arianna could only look at her hands in amazement. Like an avenging angel or a goddess, she stood there, outlined by a blazing radiance which sizzled with power.

Pointing her hands, the girl released beams of pure light in all directions. Wherever she could sense part of him, her power would flow. The princess found and retrieved each little piece of the essence of her deeply unconscious love. As soon as she had collected enough parts, she started to weave them together. When she had ascertained that there was nothing left behind, she gently returned the glowing orb to his spirit self.

Something caught her attention. She had been sure she had collected all of him, but suddenly she was no longer so certain. Wait, there! There was something! She could feel it now that it had come to her notice. Quick as lightning, a tendril of her power shot out and grabbed one of the vaporous beings. All the creature's intents were laid bare to her by this one touch. Outrage flared brightly, and her eyes narrowed. This thing had a tiny kernel of him, had hidden it deep inside of itself. It had thought it could make off with that piece of his soul and use it against him.

The wraith was going to overpower Kyrill and take control of his actions. It had been so gleeful that it was the only one left with a fragment of his essence. That would have given it a distinct advantage over its brethren. It would have been able to control all of him now that the princess had put her mate back together again. Without a second's hesitation, the girl tore into the misty corpse and ripped out that small piece of her love. Then, almost like an afterthought, with a flick of that tendril, she wiped out the shade as if it had never existed.

Kyrill's eyes were open when she returned her attention to him. He was looking at her in awe. For a moment, she was afraid that he would reject her, fear her, as so many of her people would have. When she hesitantly met his eyes, he smiled. She could hear his gentle words and they warmed her heart. "You are magnificent, and I love you. Embrace who you are, my Princess. This night you have come into your own."

Wonder filled her. For the first time, she knew beyond a shadow of a doubt that he was her true mate, that their love was real. Carefully, she held out the tiny piece of his soul towards him so he could take back that which was his. But instead, he only shook his head and pointed towards her. Reaching out an ethereal hand, he took the piece and placed it over her heart, and she allowed it within.

The moment she accepted this tiny fragment inside her very soul, their bond grew even stronger. All of a sudden, he appeared to become much more substantial. Smiling she blew him a kiss. "Go back now, my love, and thank you! You risked your life to save mine. I will never forget that! Go now so I can deal with this dreadful trap. I cannot leave it for some unwary traveler to stumble upon," she told him gently.

"I would if I could, my beautiful lady, but it seems I am stuck," came his amused reply. The princess glanced up and saw that the hole in the dome-shaped barrier that he had descended through had closed tightly behind him, squeezing the lifeline connecting him to his body. There was no way he could fit through to return to his people. As Arianna was considering options, she noticed a pulsing begin around the thin, luminous cord.

Someone was trying to tear a new opening in the gelatinous fabric, and she immediately added her power to enlarge it. An old woman's face looked back at her with deep reverence for a moment. The lady smiled and sent Arianna a salute before grasping Kyrill and pulling him back through the veil. "I will see you soon, my Princess," his faint voice echoed. The hole closed behind him, and she knew he was safe.

Now that he was gone it was time to deal with this terrible place and its ghastly inhabitants once and for all. Making sure all the sprites and horses were safe, the girl used a tendril of her incredible power to throw the rest of her possessions clear of the copse. Connecting to her Goddess, she opened herself up to channeling the Lady's additional force. Arianna knew she would need all the magic she could handle to take care of this menace. Her eyes began to gleam with pure power. She focused on one after the other of the spirit beings, and they perished in the blaze of her fury.

When the princess was sure that she had gotten them all, she turned her attention toward that dread altar. It had been the source of the wraiths, and they had been cleverly hidden. With one single thought directed its way, the powerful relic burst into ferocious flames burning so hot that even the rock was consumed and turned into ash. The place where it had stood for many a century was seared clean of the ancient taint. Once this was accomplished, the air around the girl seemed to lighten, and she could breathe freely again. She could feel her fury begin to drain away and total exhaustion taking its place.

~

The sprites, who had awoken as soon as they were out of the influence of the oppressing force, had seen all that had transpired. They had watched the princess embrace her inner warrior when the wraiths threatened the life of her mate. An intense wildness had glimmered in their eyes as they witnessed the gentle girl's transformation from helpless victim to powerful warrior goddess. Her entire being had been outlined by golden fire, and bright sparks had crackled in her hair. She had been magnificent! She would be their lady from this day forward, and they would love her forever.

The little fairies, being well familiar with magic, had expected their princess to experience a crash after using this much power. She would need to sleep, and quickly. Therefore, they had spread out the bedroll a safe distance away from the grove. They kept encouraging Arianna as the now totally drained girl stumbled towards them. All the young woman's strength gave out just as she reached her bed and she was asleep almost before her face hit the mat.

The sprites gently pushed the exhausted sorceress, for that was what she had truly become this night, the rest of the way onto the bedroll and covered her with the blankets. Each one placed a tiny hand on her check and infused her with just a little bit of their power. It was not much but would have to do until they could get some food into her in the morning.

The princess would need fish, and eggs if they could find them. As soon as it grew light, they would go searching. Settling around Arianna, they excitedly chattered about what they had seen. The princess could have easily just saved herself but, instead, had quickly placed each one of them on the mat and pulled them all clear. She had also managed to motivate the horses to come along.

Without the man, however, she would not have woken. The man had saved them all. Without him, they and even the horses would now be dead. He had risked his own life and almost lost it to warn them. They owed him and one day, they vowed, they would find a way to repay the gift of life he and their lady had so unselfishly presented them with.

~~~

Chapter Twenty Four

The Envoy's Escape

*T*he night passed peacefully, and a glorious dawn greeted the sleeping camp. All were eager to get going. If they covered enough distance this day, they would reach the castle before nightfall on the next. Breakfast, therefore, was a pretty hurried affair and soon they were back on the road. Since it had not rained here in the last few days and traffic was minimal this far away from the castle, the tracks of the bandits' horses were still visible in the dirt. Realizing that these men might be somewhere ahead of them, possibly planning an ambush, filled many of the soldiers with apprehension.

The sun had almost reached its highest point in the sky when the outlaws' trail diverged from their own. The captain sent two of his best scouts out after them. The pair would have a better chance going unnoticed than a larger force. He hoped that his men might be able to find Alandor's hideout so that they could avenge the theft of the princess and put a stop to the criminals.

Each man carried a couple homing pigeons which would allow them to report the location of the brigands' lair directly back to the castle. Angus was sure the king would want to deal with that lot once and for all after the violent attack on the monarch's soldiers and the theft of his bride. Why he had tolerated the thieving as long as he did in the first place was a mystery to the captain to start with.

It was just a little past noon when his forward scouts reported that a large group was coming their way. Could Alandor's thugs have cut further south and were now coming back towards them? The men did not believe so. They had watched the column for a while just to make sure. The travelers looked more like a military unit and were riding in a well-disciplined formation.

The way to the castle was south and then east at the turnoff. This group was coming from the right direction. Angus knew the pigeons should have reached the castle the day before. If the troops had set out almost immediately and had ridden part of the night, they could have gotten this far. Were these their own people coming out to meet them? That would be a welcome respite. The captain would be more than happy to have reinforcement since his weakened unit would not do overly well in a fight. He only hoped that the king had sent the elven scout along.

~

No one paid much attention to the envoy who turned white as a ghost when he heard the news of the riders. The man was only too well aware of what fate awaited him at the hands of his sovereign's guards. He suspected that he would be taken back to the castle in chains, like a common criminal. The idea of having all his friends and acquaintances see him such mortified the vain little man. He regarded himself as a very important person and being publicly perceived to have fallen from grace would just be too much.

In Sebastian's eyes, only the king and his sorceress were above him. He severely envied her for having achieved this superior position. The little sycophant had never been able to stand up to the enchantress which made him hate her as well. And, she frightened him terribly. Especially since the day he had dared to play a prank on the witch. He had never expected her to find out that it was him who had replaced her fancy wine with the cheap stuff used in the kitchen.

Odessa had seen nothing amusing about the entire affair and to his absolute horror, she had cornered him in the garden. Next thing he knew, the envoy had suddenly found himself turned into the giant toad he so resembled. To this day, he could still hear her cruel laughter ringing in his ears. Sebastian's humiliation had known no bounds when the king came upon them on his evening walk. The heartless monarch had seen the entire incident as incredibly amusing. When the callous ruler finally managed to stifle his laughter, he ordered the enchantress to turn the 'toady' back into a man. From that day on, the emissary had avoided her as much as he could.

The witch had never let the envoy forget the power she held over him. He was terrified of both her and his king. Sebastian had dreaded this assignment and resented the young woman he was meant to protect. Having to stand up to the sorceress for the princess's sake had been one of the hardest things he had ever had to do, but he was only too well aware of the punishment he faced if he did not. His tyrannical ruler had told him that if he let anything happen to the princess, it would cost him his head. Feeling like he was between a rock and a hard place, it had taken all the courage he could muster to question Odessa's treatment of the young lady.

Each time the petrified emissary had seen himself forced to confront the malevolent witch, his knees had been shaking. His stomach had hurt, and he had felt like he would throw up. He had ended up soaked in sweat. Sebastian had been only too thrilled with the enchantress's total loss of power but was aware that his sovereign would blame him for not bringing the princess safely to Darkmoor. That she had been stolen from them would not matter. These extenuating circumstances would make no difference to his stern monarch. The envoy, knowing the king as well as he did, was aware that excuses were in vain.

~

Long before the incident with the witch, Sebastian had been thinking that it might be time to find a quiet little place, far removed from any court, in one of the other kingdoms. At the time, he had even considered taking his family along. The run-in with the hateful sorceress had become the deciding factor. The emissary had set out to find a haven for himself. The search needed to be done without anyone knowing. Since his leaving and looking for such a refuge would have been too obvious, he had set this task to one of his men.

The envoy had two servants he trusted implicitly. Both filled multiple roles in his household which consisted of just him and his men ever since his spiteful wife had banned him to a separate part of the mansion. His valet, Gilbert, doubled as his secretary, confidant, and advisor. Flanders, his huntsman, was his groom as well as his spy. Sebastian felt very lucky to have them. If his greedy and self-centered wife could have had her way, he would have had no retainers at all. His lady, however, was all about comfort and her staff was quite large. It seemed that she needed a different maid or man for every little thing.

The emissary had shared his intentions with his loyal servants. He had sent Flanders out to find them a refuge. The huntsman had been ideal for the job. It had not taken the sly man long to find a place, a small mountain chalet with large grounds. The little castle was perfect since it was occupied by a reclusive man, a Squire Tom Buchanan, who few in the area had ever seen. As fate would have it, this nobleman also shared the residence with his two servants. Flanders had decided to acquire the dwelling.

After finding out everything he could about the castle and its inhabitants, the huntsman had shown up at the lord's doorstep dripping blood from an injury he supposedly sustained during his travels. The aristocrat had taken pity on him and had allowed him into the mansion. Flanders had used his time at the residence to find out all he could about the squire. The man reminded him a little of his master, just thinner and much, much kinder. Even their facial features were similar enough; they could have been related! The hunter had tried to purchase the chalet and grounds, but the squire would not hear of it. The solitary man had liked where he was. It was remote and very peaceful, and he had few people to deal with the majority of the time.

Flanders had tried several times to convince the stubborn aristocrat that selling was in his best interest. When the lord of the castle finally had enough, he had told the huntsman to be gone the next morning. That night, Sebastian's servant had taken things into his own hands and smothered Squire Tom in his sleep. When the retainers found their master dead the next morning, they were distraught. They had loved their lord and had served him faithfully for many years. The pair was glad when the huntsman offered to help dig the grave.

They would have the burial right after the customary three-night wake.

After two days, when the initial grief had worn off, the retainers had started talking excitedly about their plans for the estate. The hunter had once again offered to buy the castle, but the servants rebuffed his proposal. Flanders had had enough at this point, and when the three of them set out to bury the squire, he had very efficiently slit both the men's throats. Being out on the grounds had saved him from having to clean up a mess and made it easier to dispose of the bodies.

Equally as competently, the huntsman had then found a nice couple to take care of the chalet until he could return with his master. Sebastian had slid seamlessly into the unfortunate lord's life and property. Being told how alike he and the squire had looked but that the man had been somewhat thinner, the envoy had decided to start shedding some of the weight. He was determined to become Squire Tom, in mannerisms as well as looks, even if he had little time he could spend at the castle for the time being.

~

The assignment of fetching the princess had been bad, but worse still had been the news that the housekeeper was going to accompany them. Sebastian had instantly known that he was in big trouble. What was the king thinking? The emissary suspected the witch of the deaths of the three unfortunate queens but had never been able to prove it. A new bride would not be to the power-hungry enchantress's liking.

The nasty woman had used the time since the death of the last spouse to her advantage. She had expanded and further solidified her power. The head of the army, General Darius, was well under her control and the witch had made herself the secret ruler of the realm. All she lacked was the official seal of approval she would have as King Vargos's queen. This she was being denied yet once again. Maybe the monarch suspected that his days would be numbered if he ever did make the sorceress his wife.

When she was told about the new bride, the woman had hidden her feelings well in front of the king. But, once out of the throne room, her eyes had glittered dangerously, and her mouth had set in a grim, determined line. Sebastian could just tell that she was up to no good.

The toady had decided to push down his fear since his life might well depend on knowing what the housekeeper was up to. He had followed the infuriated enchantress. Sebastian had been hiding behind a column above her when the enraged sorceress ran into her one confidante, her second in command Teresa. This woman was almost as despicable as her mistress. Odessa, thinking that there was no one about or just not caring, had freely vented her ire. She had made no bones about the depth of her hatred for this newest usurper of her position and had told her friend about her plans for this latest intended wife.

The envoy had realized right then that the princess would never reach the castle alive. He had also been only too aware that he would be the one taking the blame for her death. Sebastian had always looked out for himself first, and he could be diabolically sneaky. He hated Odessa. There was no way he would take the fall for the enchantress's removal of her latest rival. He had decided at that very moment that it was time to leave this dreadful place.

~

The little man had figured out long ago that he would never be allowed to leave peacefully. Therefore, his exit had been prepared in complete secrecy. He and his trusted servants had devised a method of getting his property out of town without causing undue attention or alerting his always suspicious wife. There had been so much art in the house that it had been easy to squirrel away what he wanted. He had merely looked for a painting similar in size and subject and then switched it for the one he desired.

The envoy traveled a lot, something he was immensely grateful for. It got him out of the house and away from the contempt of his family. His new sanctuary was half a day's travel off the main road in the Galandrien Mountains, very private, and far away from any neighbors. Sebastian had been sent on several missions to Noridea in the last few years. Every time he went in the right direction, some of his assets would go with him and find their way to the little chalet.

He and his men had devised a backup plan for the occasions when the emissary was unable to get away from his escort. A rented barn close to the main road had been used to keep a carriage identical to the one his valet was driving. They had used brown horses very similar in looks for both vehicles. The huntsman, who was well known for coming and going all the time anyhow, would travel ahead and get their horses from a nearby farm. There was a convenient grove of trees, perfect for hiding the horses and wagon, at the turnoff leading into the mountains. Flanders would wait there and keep an eye out for the caravan. Gilbert would fall behind with the coach and just as soon as the soldiers were out of sight, they would make the switch.

Since the team was fresh, the valet would have no problem catching back up to the column of soldiers, and no one was ever any wiser. The hunter would head off into the mountains with the coach. The couple they had hired to look after the chalet would help him unload and switch the horses. Just as soon as the last item was out of the carriage, Flanders was on his way back to the barn. After the horses had been dropped off at the farm and his own mount retrieved, the wily hunter would set out to catch up with his master. Usually, when he arrived back at the caravan, his mount was loaded down with game. The cooks just loved him.

~

After overhearing Odessa, the emissary had raced home as fast as his fat little legs would carry him. He had immediately prepared for his permanent departure and had quietly ordered Gilbert to pack up what was left of his most prized possessions. At this point, his conscious had started to niggle at him ever so slightly. What about his family? His daughters were his own flesh and blood after all. Once the king realized that Sebastian had escaped his clutches, the cruel monarch would take his fury out on the fugitive's wife and daughters. Was it fair to leave them behind? But, did he really want to take them along?

For many years now the relationship between the envoy and his wife had been more than a little acrimonious. Had the emissary told his wife, Esme, that he was in trouble and needed to leave, she would have laughed at him and called him a failure. She would have told all her friends destroying any chance of escape. There was no love left between the two of them and had not been for a long time.

Both of them had become plump over the years, but each thought they deserved a lot better than they had gotten in the other. Esme had taken control of the house and children years ago. She made sure he knew just how much she reviled him and that she despised the very sight of him. The only use Sebastian's wife had for her downtrodden husband was as the provider for their luxurious lifestyle.

The envoy had inherited the mansion and more money than he could ever manage to spend. He was handsomely paid for his job as the king's emissary. Unfortunately, he did not get to enjoy what should have been rightfully his. His wife had banned him to the east wing. That section of the house was in some disrepair and shabby compared to the rest of the manor. Sebastian was afraid of Esme's temper and could not bring himself to stand up to her. He had lost more and more ground with each passing year. Recently, he and his servants had been forbidden to set foot in the rest of the house. There was a small kitchen in his wing of the home, and his valet had started preparing their meals there.

Once, long ago, Sebastian had loved his wife more than anything in the world. The toad-like diplomat had met her at Castle Suzette in Wymara. He had thought Esme the most exquisite woman he had ever seen. Her father had held a high position at the court, and the smitten man had not realized just how spoiled and pampered the young lady had grown up. She had been so sweet and attentive, so well mannered and polite. The envoy had fallen head over heels in love with the delightful young woman.

Unfortunately, he had found out too late how well she had hidden her vile temper and nasty disposition behind those innocent smiles. As Esme got older, her personality had started to imprint on those delicate features destroying all the beauty which had once been there. She was discontent with her life and everything about it, but especially him. The lady disparaged his position at court, their luxurious and well-appointed house and grounds, and especially his looks. The only thing she loved were the children.

His two daughters, Ora and Valentine, Sebastian did have some fondness for, but their mother had turned them against him long ago. Still, he had not felt right about leaving them behind, and the sneaky man had tried to find a way to get the girls out of harm's way without giving away his intentions. He had finally decided that he would try to send them for a visit to his wife's parents in neighboring Wymara. They had not seen their grandparents in a number of years.

Mustering up his courage, the envoy had entered his family's part of the mansion. He had figured that he would find his spouse and children in the well-appointed salon at that time a day. Sebastian had greeted them cordially and had carefully presented the idea. He had not been prepared for the viciousness of his daughters' reply. They had scoffed at him and told him rudely that they had other plans and how dare he interfere in their lives? His wife had bluntly asked him why he was in the house in the first place. After he had wished them a polite and very formal good-bye, the chastised man had slunk out of the room like a dog with his tail between his legs.

Enough had been enough, and the browbeaten envoy had decided right there to leave his offspring to their fate. In the meantime, his trusted servants had quietly loaded up the carriage with the remainder of Sebastian's most beloved things. The next day, when they had left the house early in the morning, the envoy had been riding his favorite horse ahead of the carriage driven by the valet. Flanders, as usual, had been trailing behind. Nothing had looked out of the ordinary and as always, no one in the mansion had cared that they were leaving or had told them farewell.

There had been no time to send the huntsman ahead so the sly trio had come up with a different plan. They had waited until they were well past the turn-off to Noridea and all had settled in for the night. Then, Sebastian and Gilbert had staged a heated argument. Their voices had risen loud enough for most of the camp to hear. In a fit of temper, the envoy had ordered his servant to return to his home with the coach. The valet had been on his way the next morning. To all those watching, he had looked like an unlucky retainer who had earned his master's worst ire instead of a man taking his lord's possessions to freedom.

~

Sebastian was a shrewd man. He had believed that he was prepared for the reinforcements' arrival. He knew that Angus had sent a message to the castle before leaving to rescue the princess. The envoy figured that depending on how quickly the troops had set out, the king's guard should reach them late this night or early the next day. That morning, pretending to take pity on the witch, he had ordered the soldiers to put the still very weak woman in the carriage. He knew that this would not arouse too much suspicion since he had ridden every day until he had fallen so horribly ill from the poison the bandits had put in the beer.

Knowing the punishment he was facing, the emissary realized that he would most likely be arrested on sight. He had no intention of sticking around for that kind of humiliation. The toady was incredibly relieved that he was finally well enough to be able to ride. Escape in the carriage would have been impossible but on horseback, he and Flanders should be able to do it. They needed to be ready to leave and this day could be their last chance. He had hoped that the king's men would take their time and had not counted on them arriving as early as this.

When the anxious envoy heard of the column of men moving their way, he exchanged a surreptitious glance with the loyal Flanders. They had not expected reinforcements to reach them this soon and had intended to slip away later that afternoon. Now, this was no longer an option. They needed to take action right now while the captain was busy with the scouts.

~

Shortly after hearing the news, the huntsman started acting worried about his master's horse. The two started falling back towards the end of the column. Row upon row of unsuspecting soldiers passed by them. Finally, all who were left were the rear guards. "Do you have a problem? Can we help?" one of the men inquired. "I think my master's horse might be ailing. We are going to stop so that I can check it over but just in case it cannot be ridden, may we have one of your spare horses?" the wily Flanders answered, dismounting from his steed.

The soldiers intended to stay with the pair, but a few rude comments from Sebastian and some reassuring words from the huntsman soon had them on their way. They were only too happy to leave an extra horse behind just as long as they did not have to be around that awful little man. After all, this was not the first time they had left him and his servants behind and they had always turned back up in the past. That was the last any of them ever saw of the envoy.

~

The worried-looking groom had made a great show of checking his master's mount until the last of the rear guards were out of sight. Then, Sebastian and his loyal servant quickly made a dash for the game trail they had chosen as their escape route. Once they had ridden in far enough to be invisible from the road, the cunning Flanders went back and used a horse blanket to wipe out any signs of their passing. The man was aware that this would not deter a really good scout, but it would make it a little more difficult for the average soldier.

The huntsman was now in his element. Out here in the woods is where he loved to be. He and the envoy set out on their horses in a fast walk towards the mountains. There was a little-known pass which would lead them across into

Noridea and towards their new home. Thanks to the kindness of the soldiers, they now had five mounts. The two they were riding, the two packhorses the retainer had been leading, and the extra horse the soldiers had so generously supplied them with. Having an extra steed could come in handy on their trip across the peaks.

Flanders guided them unerringly down the game trails. He had no intention of letting anyone find them because his master's life would not be the only one forfeit if they did. His love for this much-despised man was such that Flanders was prepared to defend him with his dying breath. He would do anything to keep him safe.

Sebastian had protected him from Prince Vargos many years ago. They had been strangers then, and Flanders had never forgotten that kindness. He had begged the envoy to be allowed to serve him and had done so faithfully since. Losing the pursuit would not be hard for the hunter since he was one of the best woodsmen in the whole kingdom and only Tristan was better.

The fleeing envoy and his man had not gotten as far as they would have liked when the approaching dark forced them to camp. They would be hard to find even now, but the pair were hoping for rain to help further erase the signs of their passing. Working together, they unsaddled the horses and hobbled them so they could graze. Sebastian was a bit clumsy at first. Menial labor was not something he was used to, but he caught on quickly. The two fugitives shared a cold meal. They had decided that lighting a fire would be foolish. It could be seen from a long way away and act as a beacon for the king's scouts. The hunter took the first watch, and Sebastian rolled himself in his blanket.

The emissary knew that the trip ahead of him would not be easy but still he felt light and unburdened for the first time in many years. The man looked forward to the future with eagerness and a strange sense of delight. It was funny, but sleeping out here on the hard ground in the dark woods while running for his life, he felt peaceful. Almost immediately he fell into a deep, restful slumber.

~~~

Chapter Twenty Five

Reinforcement Arrives

*I*f Sebastian believed that his preparations to leave had gone unnoticed, he was wrong. Angus was only too well aware of the punishment awaiting the little sycophant over the loss of the princess. The captain had noticed some unusual activities at the man's tent late that previous evening. The officer had decided that he might need to unobtrusively keep an eye on things. He was sure that if the envoy returned to the castle, he would be sentenced to death by their harsh king. He had always thought the despicable gent a cowering fool but could not blame him for wanting to run.

When his soldiers reported that the emissary and his groom had not caught back up with the rest of the column, Angus was not surprised. He was secretly amused that the pair had managed to make off with an additional horse. Unfortunately, this put the captain in a bad spot. He had now lost the envoy as well as the princess. The king would not be pleased. The officer needed to make a considerable effort to retrieve the little traitor. Secretly he doubted that much of anything would convince his monarch to let him live anyhow.

311

But, there was always hope, and so Angus sent two of his scouts and ten of his men back to see if they could find the emissary and his servant.

Knowing the skills of the crafty Flanders, the captain was sure that the pair was long gone and that it would be incredibly hard to find even a trace of their passing. He was therefore not surprised when his soldiers returned and reported that there was no sign of the two men or the horses. They claimed that it was almost as if the ground had swallowed them up. The scouts had carefully searched the area where Sebastian and the hunter had last been seen. No trace of the envoy and Flanders even having been there remained. In an attempt to cover his back and to keep up appearances, the officer ordered the troops to go back and look once more.

~

As the distant travelers worked their way closer, Angus's scouts could finally make out the flag of their king. They reported that the reinforcements were really pushing their horses and would reach them before too long. The captain decided to set up camp in a clearing with a convenient small creek. They would have kahve and food waiting for the men. It was late afternoon by the time the group reached them. Not being sure what to expect, Angus anxiously greeted Captain Gordro and his lieutenant. When they returned his cordial greeting in a friendly manner and treated him with civility, the captain was greatly relieved. The ill-fated officer had been prepared to be arrested on sight as he was sure Sebastian would have been.

It took the commander just a few moments to spot the elf among the riders. They had sent him as he had requested! If anyone could find and save the princess, this tracker could. The man was the best scout in the land and went by the name of Tristan. He had been working for the king for years, but no one knew his elven name or much about him. The scout was a legend, and many claimed that his tracking abilities were supernatural. He always found his man or in this case, woman. After seeing the carnage caused by the bears, Angus feared that Arianna was out there somewhere and that she had been injured in the stampede or trying to escape. The girl might be in dire need of aid and the sooner they found her, the better.

The tracker immediately approached the captain and took him aside. "Tell me what happened and all that you know which might help me to find her," he demanded impatiently. Angus conveyed to him the events of the night of the attack and of his discoveries following after the bandits. He shared what they had found at the place of the stampeded. At times, the elf asked pointed questions. The scout was trying to get as clear a picture as possible of what had gone on. "You marked where they turned off?" Tristan asked when the officer finished his report. Angus nodded and described the symbols they had left behind. Finally, the tracker seemed satisfied that he had learned all that he could.

The scout was always no nonsense and this day even more so. It seemed the king was anxious for the return of his bride. "Do you have any items belonging to the princess that she was recently in contact with?" came the elf's next question. Having anticipated this request, Angus nodded to one of his soldiers who brought forward the ratty old horse blanket as well as a few small items left behind by the girl. "What is this?" Tristan inquired, fingering the cloth. "She slept in that," Angus replied.

The tracker shot the captain an incredulous look. "Are you serious? A princess? In this?" Shaking his head in disbelief, he examined each item, finally settling on a small brush. "I will take this," the elf stated and went to his horse. In one leap he was mounted and ready to ride. "Wait, don't you want to take some of the men with you?" Angus inquired. "No, they will only slow me down. I leave now, alone," came the curt reply as the famous hunter of men turned his horse to set off into the twilight. "Wait for me here!" rang out his imperious command before horse and rider melted away into the dusk.

~

The companies would have to remain where they were since no one disobeyed an order by the king's favorite scout. The man moved like a ghost, here one minute, gone the next. Angus thoughtfully stared at the place the elf had been only a moment ago. Once Tristan brought the princess back, there would be little the captain could do to prevent her upcoming marriage. The tracker was one of his friends, maybe he would have an idea. Still, being queen was better than dying out there all alone in the wild. Turning to his guests, Angus asked the captain of the reinforcement and his lieutenant to join him at the fire closest to the pavilion.

Aaron and the two commanders of the forward and rear guards were already waiting. At their captain's questioning look, they could only shake their heads. The envoy, his groom, and their horses had not been found. "So, Angus, first things first. Where is the witch? Is it true she is powerless now?" Gordro inquired, curiosity burning in his eyes. "I seriously doubt she will ever harm anyone again, my friend. The bandits poured an herb called Witchbane down her. The brew was so potent, it burned her throat, and it is agony for her to swallow. Then, some of the men took it upon themselves to make sure she would never speak again. We have had a hard time keeping her alive," Angus replied.

"Why, for all saint's sake, are you even keeping her alive? Let that miserable hag die!" the captain of the guard shouted with incredulity. Angus calmly replied "Because death is what she wants! Life for her without her powers is not worth living. She made all of us suffer for years! Let the king decide her fate. I am sure it won't be pleasant after he hears how she treated the princess!" The officer stared at him in disbelief for a moment, then let out a humorless laugh. "When you put it that way, I see your point! You are right, my friend, an easy death is too good for her!" Gordro replied with a cold smile. "May I see the once so high and mighty one?" he continued.

"Aaron, please have them bring the witch," Angus ordered. Soon Odessa was pulled into the light of the fire. The men handled her none too gently. Not even her pitiful state could completely erase the hatred they felt. The vile sorceress was only a shadow of her former glorious self. She was weak from dehydration and starvation. The witch was so utterly exhausted that she was unable to stand on her own. Her once lustrous hair was dull and scraggly. Blood and food stains discolored the front of the enchantress's dress. The thoroughly filthy garment no longer fit her and was hanging loosely on her now almost skeletal frame.

The sorceress had realized pretty quickly that her connection to the divine had been severed forever. Her dark magic had been everything to her since she was a young girl. Without it, she saw no reason for living. The captain, however, was determined that he would deliver the witch alive. Getting food and water into the enchantress had been one of his first priorities. Her throat was still not healed, and she was barely able to swallow. Getting any nourishment down her had been difficult at best. Especially, since Odessa was fighting him every step of the way. Cleaning her up had not been something the soldier had found the patience for especially since the woman herself did not seem to care.

"How the mighty have fallen! The way you look now, I don't think the king will find you quite as appealing!" Captain Gordro gloated while walking around the pathetic looking witch who was being held up by Aaron. He waved over his sergeant. "Take the hag into custody! Get her out of my sight!" The soldier sniffed and visibly gagged. "Take two men and give her a bath down at the creek and get her into some clean clothes! She stinks!" the officer ordered after seeing his man's reaction. A thoughtful expression crossed Gordro's features. "Oh and Sergeant? Make sure she stays alive to face the justice of the king!" came his growled command.

The young lieutenant was only too happy to hand over the witch. Aaron looked at his captain for permission and was relieved to see him nod his approval. Trying to keep the sorceress safe had been difficult since most of the soldiers could not be trusted with her. She had been too cruel and inspired so much fear and hatred in the men that they had been finding backhanded methods to torture the defenseless enchantress in small but malicious ways. Both Aaron and Angus had been at a loss how to treat any who harmed her. The two soldiers who had cut out her tongue were still being kept as prisoners but were celebrated as heroes by the rest of the camp.

"Now that we have gotten that out of the way, what about the princess? What happened that night? Did you find any trace of her?" asked Gordro's up to now silent lieutenant. Roland, being a half-breed, usually kept to himself. Lothrien was a place where prejudice abounded, and few of mixed race cared to live or were tolerated. To have reached lieutenant was almost a miracle of sorts. It would not have been possible without his captain who was his stalwart supporter. Roland was only too aware that he had never been fully accepted by King Vargos and most of the men. His only real friends over the years had been Gordro and Angus whom he was now watching expectantly.

The captain gave a detailed account of the search for the princess. He began with the aftermath of the attack by the bandits and then went on to tell the assembled group about their futile quest. His audience was spellbound. The officer was a decent storyteller and giant bears, as well as the mystery of why the rascals did not climb the large trees along the trail to escape the menace chasing them, made for a good yarn. What possible reason could they have had to keep running? None of the soldiers could understand this and felt that because of the outlaws' unwise choice they had ended up dead.

When Angus mentioned the scorch marks, both Gordro and Roland wanted to know more. Soon speculations were tossed back and forth, getting more fantastic by the minute. Possibilities were brought up and discarded. None of them, however, could come up with any viable explanation for the presence of burnt dirt on the trail. Next, the captain spoke of their tracking of Alandor and their search for any sign of the kidnapped princess. All the men felt that it was impossible that the girl could have stayed in the saddle when all those experienced riders were unhorsed. She was a lady, after all, a noblewoman. What could have possibly happened to her? Had she managed to climb a tree and escape?

"Angus, my old friend, what was it you were showing Tristan? Something she had been in contact with recently?" Roland inquired. "Only a few of her things and a blanket she used a few days ago. The bandits took the ones she had been using the last couple days with them," the captain replied handing the tattered horse blanket over. The lieutenant took the material and stared at it in disbelief. He poked his index finger through one of the holes. "Are you serious? You made a princess sleep in THAT?" the soldier asked, appalled.

"Not me, man!" Angus replied with indignation. "Her high and mightiness took over the tent, the cook, and, in the end, the carriage as well. I did manage to slip the girl some better bedding after a bit but the first night that wretched hag was watching her like a hawk! And you know what she was like when you crossed her!" he continued. All heads nodded in sympathy. At one time or another, all of them had suffered the wrath of the malicious witch.

"That elf took something of hers and is tracking her then. I would sure like to know how he does it and what he does with the things. It is truly uncanny how that fairy finds people. I just hope he is never sent after me," Gordro stated, making the sign against evil behind his back. None of them had ever been allowed to witness how Tristan used personal items to chase down his targets. Unless the king commanded otherwise, the tracker usually hunted the fugitives on his own.

The scout was feared throughout Lothrien. His reputation actually kept many citizens from trying to flee the realm. It was common knowledge that whoever the king sent him after, the tracker would find. He would promptly deliver the escapee back to their unforgiving ruler. The elf's integrity was beyond reproach, and no amount of money would work as a bribe.

The only one who had ever gotten away with his crimes was Alandor. Somehow the ruthless man managed to strike and escape without leaving a trace. No personal possessions of the merciless outlaw and his rogues had ever been found. This had made it impossible for Tristan to work his magic.

And, the bandits had always struck right after the tracker had been sent out on a mission. By the time the scout returned, the king usually had another person he had needed hunting down and so had never even bothered to send the elf after the brigands. Keeping the kingdom safe was not that high a priority for the self-involved monarch.

"You told us of the princess but not about the attack itself. What happened?" Roland inquired. The atmosphere around the fire became subdued when Angus recounted the earlier events of that night. Captain Gordro and his lieutenant were shocked at how many men had been killed. The king's soldiers and guards were a tight knit group, and all had lost friends at the vicious bandits' hands. There was a lot of anger in the air, and many of the men were eager to avenge their fallen brethren. Too bad that the princess was no longer with the brigands. Tristan could have led them right to their lair. It would have been the perfect chance to put an end to the menace of these thugs once and for all. The roads and small towns of the kingdom would have been much safer once more.

Since Gordro would be reporting directly to the king, he started to ask questions about the way the princess had been treated. The newcomers were aghast at the cruelty Odessa had heaped upon the young woman and Sebastian's failure to protect her. "So, Angus, where is our nasty little friend, the envoy? We have orders to arrest him, but I have not seen his ugly face anywhere around here," Roland inquired. "We are looking for him, but it seems that he and his retainer have decided to make themselves scares," the captain replied. "I have men out searching for them as we speak!"

Angry muttering greeted the officer's words. Sebastian was almost as hated as the witch. The soldiers had looked forward to taking the pompous little man down a peg or two, or, maybe even three. Most of them had been unlucky enough to accompany the emissary on one of his many missions over the years. The toady had given himself airs for too long. He had always treated his armed escorts with utter contempt. The men had relished the news of his downfall.

The foul little bootlicker had been responsible for the princess's well-being. He had failed miserably, and the king wanted him brought back in chains. The soldiers had had high hopes of getting even for all the humiliations the envoy had heaped on them for so long and were bitterly disappointed that the man had escaped before getting his just deserts.

~~~

Chapter Twenty Six

The Morning After

*G*entle but persistent tugging awoke Arianna. She could barely open her eyes. Her entire body was a mass of pain. She tried to sit up but discovered that she did not have the strength. Seeing her so weak upset her little fairy friends greatly, and they decided something had to be done. The sprites convinced Arabella and Azariel to help them drag the saddle over and push it next to the bedroll. With much encouragement, they got the princess to scoot up enough so she could use it to lean on. That task accomplished, the exhausted girl's eyes closed and she fell deeply asleep once more.

A little while later, a delicious aroma started to tease its way into the young woman's consciousness. It took a bit for the smell to register fully, but when it did, she suddenly realized just how hungry she was and opened her eyes. Deep gratefulness filled her heart. The little ones had gotten a fire going and were frying up fish. In an iron skillet at that! Arianna knew that fairies were allergic to the metal and that it could injure them grievously. She could only hope none of them had gotten burned by it. Good thing that the pan had a handle covered with wood.

Her mouth was watering by the time the sprites brought her a piece of the fish wrapped in leaves. She ate ravenously and decided that no meal had ever tasted this good. She had no clue what they had done, but somehow the flavor of the meat seasoned with herbs was so much more intense than anything she had eaten before. Could it be that embracing her powers had enhanced her senses? In any case, these guys were amazing cooks! Once the last piece of the fish was gone, they brought her some eggs. Arianna was so hungry she consumed every morsel plus two waybiscuits and could have eaten more. The sprites also pushed her to drink plenty of water and slowly she could feel the weakness recede.

By the time the sun was at its highest point in the sky, the princess finally felt recovered enough to continue her journey. It took all the girl's strength to saddle Arabella who waited patiently for her mistress to get the job done. The intelligent horse even knelt down to allow the completely exhausted girl easier access to the saddle. It had taken a while before they were finally ready to set out. Arianna was so weak from the exertion of getting the horses ready that she barely managed to stay in the saddle. She would have liked nothing better than to sleep all day but they needed to get away from this place.

The lingering memory of the evil they had encountered made them all uncomfortable to be near that glade, even in the bright sunshine. And, what if someone had seen last night's light show and decided to come and investigate? She was being hunted, after all, any distance she managed to put between herself and this horrible place was good.

Also, there was the prince. Now that she was certain that he was real, Arianna could not wait to finally meet the real-life Kyrill. As long as they were moving, she was getting closer to him. He had not come into her dreams again that night, and she was more than a little concerned. His spirit had appeared to be healed, and she had done what she could but how had all that affected his body? Could this have seriously harmed him? Until he came to her again in her dreams, there was no way to know.

The further they traveled away from the glade, the faster the princess's energy began to replenish. It seemed that the terrible place had not lost all its power. This made the girl wonder if maybe she had not managed to destroy all the evil present in that copse. She had done what she could and saved herself, Kyrill, and the sprites. Whatever had remained had been well hidden, and she could only hope that no other human stumbled into the trap which so nearly had cost them all their lives.

Arianna was getting stronger but was far from being her usual self. Travel this day was slow, and they took frequent breaks so that she could eat. She could not remember ever haven eaten this much in one day in her entire life. The sprites kept pushing food on her even while they were moving. When they did stop, Arianna did not like the idea of a fire, but the little ones insisted. It was that or eating the fish raw which at first did not truly appeal to the girl.

All that cooking, however, was severely slowing them down and by mid-afternoon, the young woman decided to eat the fish raw rather than losing more time. It was not really that bad and actually seemed to nourish her more. The deciding factor had been when she had seen what was left after the fairies attempted to hide the signs of their fire. Try as they might, a dead circle remained. Any scout would have no problem finding the places they had stopped at.

When the shadows began to lengthen and the day turned into evening, the princess felt that it was time to locate a place to rest until morning. She asked her little friends to please find them a place for the night. Soon Blossom came zipping back. "Lady, we need to move just a bit further and faster. We found a really nice cave and went to explore. We were so excited about our great discovery that we did not notice the bear. It seems we accidently woke it up with our chatter. We tried to talk to it, but it would not listen. It is very angry, and some of the others are leading it away," the out of breath fairy reported.

Usually, the princess could appease just about any wild beast but in her weakened state, this might not be a sure thing. At her command, Arabella immediately picked up the pace. Arianna was very relieved when the rest of the sprites joined them, and all were unharmed. The girl had become very fond of her little friends and could not stand the thought of any of them being injured. When they had moved on far enough to be out of the grumpy bear's reach, the little ones went looking for a shelter once more.

The fairies spread out and soon managed to find an adequate place. They were not too happy with this one, however. The refuge, created by a large rock overhang, provided enough space for themselves, the princess, and the horses. In their eyes, it was nowhere near as good as that wonderful cave had been, but it would have to do. A fine mist had started to fill the air, and they were barely settled in when it began to pour. Arianna was glad for the rain; it would erase more of the traces of their fires and make her so much harder to find.

Unrolling her bedroll and covers next to the back wall of their shelter, the girl gratefully slipped under her blankets. Once again, her stomach started to grumble. How could she possibly still be hungry? She had been eating all day! And well, thanks to her friends. She had discovered that the little fairies were great fishermen when they wanted to be. And clever as well. They had woven a basket and within minutes had managed to lure several fish into their trap. The princess had watched them in amazement. "How did you catch the fish so quickly?" she inquired curiously.

The sprites looked at each other. How could they best explain this to a human? "We told them of your need. They came to us willingly to provide you with their life-force. You are fairy friend and all that we have and our forest supplies, is there for you. We will do all that we can to get you safely away from this place and those evil men," Blossom replied. Arianna felt humbled at the little one's words and was especially glad now that she had given thanks before eating each piece of the fish. Just thinking of food made her stomach growl loudly and the little ones started laughing.

By the time the princess had eaten yet another raw fish and two more biscuits, she was barely able to keep her eyes open. After she had rinsed her fingers clean in the falling rain, she slid back under her blankets and settled in for the night. She was so tired that it did not take her long to fall into a deep sleep.

~

Within minutes, she was with Kyrill. Arianna had worried about him for a good part of the day until it had occurred to her that she would have sensed it if he had been hurt. Now that she knew that their love was not just a beautiful dream, the princess had become aware of the bond they shared. It was so intense that she would have felt it if he had been seriously injured. That realization had given her some modicum of peace. Still, the girl had been anxious to see him and talk to him about the events of the previous night. His total acceptance of her powers and complete lack of fear had made her love him so much more and made it easier for the princess to embrace all of herself.

Her handsome prince had saved her life, in the process risking his own. Seeing him trapped and fighting for his life had shocked Arianna. It had awoken a protectiveness toward him which had completely surprised her. To save him, she had embraced a part of herself which she had feared and shied away from in the past. Until that moment, the princess had chosen to be gentle and kind. The warrior part of her was anything but and had frightened her deeply. What truly amazed the girl was that she felt whole for the first time in many years. Part of her had been missing and embracing it had made her stronger. She had finally come into her own.

The amount of force Arianna had channeled to save Kyrill and destroy the evil in the glade was beyond anything she would have ever thought possible. It could have burned out all her abilities and in a way she was surprised that it had not. She had checked and had been greatly relieved to discover that her powers were weak but intact.

If anything, she was more open than ever, almost as if some sort of a barrier had been removed between her and her magic and she wondered about that. Had she been blocking her own powers by only embracing the part of her which was good?

When the prince entered her dream, it was as if a weight lifted off her. He was pale but well and when he enclosed her in his arms the feeling of coming home was unbelievable. "Are you alright?" she asked him anxiously. "Yes, thanks to you and our healers. You were incredible!" he told her looking at her with such love and pride it made her heart skip a beat. Where her own people would have shunned her for life, this gorgeous man embraced all that she was. Not being able to go back to her home in Maridanmar was suddenly no longer so bad.

~~~

Chapter Twenty Seven

Tristan

The elf had been riding most of the night. Had he taken the humans along, they would have slowed him down significantly. Angus description of the distance to the spot where the bandits had left the road had been just as accurate as the scout had expected. He had stopped there for only a few short minutes while the night was darkest. Just as soon as the light of the moon filtered down through the trees into the shadowy forest, he had picked up the trail once again.

He and his horse, one of the few things he had been able to bring with him from his home, were used to moving through all kinds of terrain in the dark. As long as there was even the tiniest bit of light, their eyes were capable of amplifying it. This made it possible for them to see well enough in the dark to be able to travel when most others were forced to stop and rest. But that was not the only thing which was different about these two. The endurance of the scout and his horse was far superior to that of the humans as were most of their senses. He saw the people he reacquired for the king as prey and run as they might, he would always catch them. The more effort they put into losing him, the better he liked it. Tristan did love a challenge.

He had no feelings about any of the individuals he hunted down for his brutal monarch. Actually, he had no emotions at all. When his people and his love had turned on him, the pain had been so great that he had decided to discard that part of himself forever. All that once was good and decent in him had been locked away in the far recesses of his cold heart. Never again would he feel that kind of torment or let anyone close as he had her. Not only had he lost his home, his child, and his elves, but the one who had been the cause of it all had rejected him as well. That had been what had truly broken his heart.

Tristan had stopped caring about anyone or anything that very night so many years ago. Why then had he been so appalled when the captain showed him the blanket? What was wrong with him? Might it be because he usually did not chase women? What did it matter, anyhow? All he knew was that he would not give something in that kind of shape to a horse, let alone a human. What had been going on in that camp? He was confident that witch had been behind it all. Angus was a decent sort of man and would never treat anyone in such a harsh manner.

That sorceress had been trying to get complete control of the kingdom for years now. Tristan had watched her power grow almost daily. If she gained the throne, Lothrien would not be a place fit to live for anyone and least of all for an elf. The scout had warned the king on several occasions about the ambitions of his mistress. The monarch, who had been appearing as if in a daze of late, was convinced that everything was completely under control. Vargos, being a very arrogant man, had no doubt that he had the sorceress firmly in hand. The scout's well-meaning words had fallen on deaf ears. The malevolent ruler had been too blind to see that he was being played and had become nothing but a figurehead in his own kingdom.

Odessa had been the real power behind the throne for the last couple of years and had ruled Lothrien with an iron hand and abject cruelty. She had started to extend her influence out into the other realms. The witch wanted it all. Tristan believed that her ultimate goal had been to become empress of the Eleven Kingdoms. Maybe now that the enchantress was no longer a threat, things would get better for the monarchy's unhappy people. There was that slight hope, but the elf doubted it. As long as the depraved King Vargos was their ruler, little would change. He would just find another power-hungry fool to run the kingdom for him so he could play.

~

When it got too dark under the thick tree canopy to ride safely, Tristan dismounted and led the horse. The girl had a large head start, and if he wanted to catch up with her, he would have to keep going and move fast. The league-eating jog of his people soon brought him to a clearing where the silver light of the moon filtered down to the forest floor. The elf saw the markings Angus had left behind sparkling in the shimmering beams of the celestial orb. This had to be the camp where the bandits had spent the night. Lighting a torch, he took a brief look around. The scout found nothing of any significance. Time to move on.

When the sun was just starting to rise, and the shadows underneath the trees were beginning to lift, the tracker figured that he must be getting close to the area where the soldiers had encountered the bears. Extending his senses, he began to move with more caution. The smell hit his sensitive nose long before he reached the place where the last of

Alandor's men had died. There was not much left of the corpse, and he quickly moved on. The scene was similar at the next area where the bears had feasted. Since there was nothing left for them to eat here, the large carnivores would be out hunting again. Tristan had no intention of becoming their next meal.

Using his senses to check around, the tracker soon located the first of the bears. Angus had not over exaggerated! This beast was huge! The captain had mentioned that he had counted three of the brutes! The elf had seen some big bears in his long life, but if the other two were of equal size, they were definitely larger than any he had ever seen. He searched further until all three of the gigantic carnivores had been accounted for. One was too close to the trail for the scout's liking. It was time to shield himself and his horse. Hopefully, this would give them an advantage and allow them to slip past unnoticed.

Tristan and his mount moved silently and carefully through the dense undergrowth avoiding the trail. From the claw marks in the soil, he had figured that the bears used the path on a regular basis. He was soon glad he had taken this precaution. One of the huge beasts came ambling down the track. Had they been on the path, they would have run right into it. The elf froze and placed a calming hand on his horse's nose. The stallion was well trained and feared little, but the closeness of this kind of predator was enough to make even him nervous. The humans' horses must have been plain terrified. No wonder they had unseated their riders.

As soon as it was safe, the pair moved on. The scout recognized the area of the stampede from the captain's description and the deep imprints of split hooves in the soft forest soil. Taking out the princess's small brush, he placed it on his palm. A slight tug told him that the girl had turned onto the intersecting trail. Very interesting! Could she have been caught in the middle of the stampede and have been swept along with the charging herd? For now, it sure seemed that way.

The hunter followed the hoof prints further down the track leading north. He kept an eye out for any animal diverging from the rest. The elf used the princess's brush several more times to confirm the direction she had taken. The scout was fairly certain now that her horse must have been swept along with the herd. The path eventually led to a large clearing. Here, things really became confusing. Tristan was sure the young woman had entered along with the elk. But what was a dragon doing here? Judging from the size of those clawed feet, it had been a rather large one at that.

Had that scaled menace eaten the princess? There was no blood he could find anywhere around the glade. He did spot boot prints not far away from what must have been the front of the monster. What had that girl been doing, talking to the beast? Tristan was stunned. If that young woman had dared to stand there and face down such a creature, she must be braver than most. Angus had told him that this girl was different, but it seemed that the good captain did not even know the half of it. It sure looked like the man's worries about this young lady had been unfounded.

A verification of her travel direction told him that the princess had moved on from here and had continued to follow the path to the north. She was probably taking the shortest route home. His king would not be happy if he had to retrieve the young woman from her family in Maridanmar and the cruel monarch had inventive ways of punishing those who failed him. Tristan decided that he better keep moving as fast as he could to catch up with this girl. Soon horse and rider were racing down the path. The scout was in such a hurry that he almost missed the turnoff to the west. At first, he dismissed it, but his instincts kept telling him that something was up.

Turning around, he headed back to the place he had seen the small side trail. When he checked for the princess's route by using the brush, he was in for a surprise. First, it pointed weakly to the north, then it swung to point down the small path. Why would the girl be heading west? Her home was to the northeast! The scout carefully examined the forest floor. The prints had been heavily trampled by the local wildlife, but the horses seemed to have been traveling towards the trail to the north, not away from it. Something, however, did not appear quite right with these tracks. Had they been moving backward?

What a bright young woman! This hunt was turning out to be more fun than he had had in a long time. Who would have thought that a spoiled little princess would provide him with more sport than most men? He was rapidly following along the trail keeping an eye on the tracks when the horses' hoof prints suddenly disappeared into thin air. The elf felt happier than he had in many years and something resembling a smile played on his usually so somber features. Finally, someone was presenting him with an actual challenge! This girl was a worthy opponent. Too bad he would have to hand her over to his lecherous king.

Could a mere princess really be that resourceful? The more he pondered this, the less likely it seemed to Tristan. No woman should be able to do this well out here in the wild. The elf suddenly realized that the girl was not alone out here and that whoever was helping her was rather cunning. Following this young lady and whoever was helping her was unquestionably going to be enjoyable. The scout loved nothing more than a good hunt. His usual quarry was easily retrieved. Having to use all his considerable skills made him feel alive for the first time in a very long time. The tracker was looking forward to meeting this remarkable adversary, whoever it was. Was the magic the girl's or her companion's? He could not wait to find out!

The game trail meandered along among the trees and the scout verified the princess's direction of travel at every intersecting path. She kept going west, but why? Was she heading home or might she have a different destination in mind? He needed to figure this out and fast. First, he needed to establish her motives. King Vargos was a brute so why would she agree to marry him? Because she had no choice! What would happen if she returned home? None of the other kingdoms would stand up to the tyrant so the family would be on their own. Vargos would send for the princess again, and Maridanmar would have to hand her over or face war with Lothrien. Not very good options. So if she was not going home, where else might she head?

The scout went over every little detail he had amassed about his prey in the last day. Then he got it. Her mother had been Princess Anna of Re'adeen! That is where the princess must be heading and why she had started to travel due west! Angus had told him that the girl was very intelligent so she would also try to minimize her chances of meeting the bandits. Tristan was thrilled. This young lady and her associate might finally be opponents worthy of his significant skills. Whistling a merry tune, he hurried his horse along the path.

~

Had the elf not been so overconfident and looked around himself with his considerable abilities, he would have realized that he, the hunter, was himself being followed.

Bright little eyes observed all that he did. They did not miss how every time the scout brought out the brush, he suddenly moved along with greater certainty. And, that he took it out often. The small observers soon figured out that the item helped the tracker find the direction the girl had taken. They watched when Tristan found the knoll Arianna had spent the night on and examined the tree. Little brows wrinkled with concern. Their magic could not hide the princess from one such as him. They would need help if they were to keep her safe.

Silent as shadows they followed the scout. They needed to get a hold of that brush! The little ones realized that they would have to come up with a very good plan, and they would have to wait for just the right moment when the elf was distracted. What would work best? A squirrel, perhaps? They could not risk being seen or go near him. This man was heartless and would kill any of them without a second's hesitation. He could then find the rest. They would have to be very careful that he did not sense them and make sure that they always stayed out of his range. This hunter was very skilled and moved with an incredible speed; he was catching up fast with his prey. There was no way around it; they would have to do something before too much longer.

As close as the scout was getting, they needed to warn their friends and the princess. If all had gone well, the young lady and the sprites should still be a good two days ride ahead of the tracker. The girl and her companions would have to travel as fast as they could to stay in front of this monster until a way could be found to get Arianna out of harm's way. The small ones decided that the first thing to do was to send one of their number to tell the group about the menace following behind them and spur them on to much greater speed.

336

What they needed were fast transportation and one 'volunteer'. After a brief discussion, the one they had chosen was given his orders. They really did not care to fly, but this situation was calling for extraordinary measures. Soon a large hawk was seen streaking west with a tiny figure desperately clinging to its back. They had timed it perfect. The scout had been checking on the direction, and his sharp eyes were busy watching the brush.

~

Tristan was making excellent progress. Every time he touched the brush, he could feel that he was getting just a bit closer. His horse was sure footed and so much faster than any the humans were breeding. Happily, he petted his stallion's neck. This chase was going better than he had expected and no matter how good his adversaries were, they would soon be his. The tracker was enjoying this hunt so much, he almost did not want it to end. He had been surprised when suddenly every trace of the young lady's group disappeared. It was a pretty good feat to wipe out all evidence of the passing of five horses. There was not one single imprint of one single hoof to be found, and most other trackers would have been long since left behind. He, on the other hand, was getting closer to his target with every moment. Tristan was very proud of his ability to be able to follow his prey in spite of any and all efforts to shake him.

The scout was completely unprepared for what happened next. A moose came charging out of the forest and rammed into the side of his unsuspecting horse. The elf went flying, something which was rather unusual in itself. He had been so focused on what he was doing that he had been caught completely unawares. The scout had been using his magic to keep track of the princess's route. The brush, which had loosely rested on his open palm, flew off into the bushes.

The large animal raced on after giving the stallion a good kick in the chest. Mount and rider looked at each other in disbelief. What in Cer'ridwen's name had just happened?

He needed to find that brush and fast. The elf thought it had flown into the nearby shrubbery. Getting down on his hands and knees, he searched every bush, then all around the thickets but found no sign of the brush. He reached out with his mind and to his surprise, he could not even feel the small object's vibrations. How could it have just disappeared? Sitting down on the path, he centered himself and then opened himself to the world around him. He became one with the grass, the bushes, the trees, the very earth itself. In his vicinity, he could sense every animal racing across the forest soil, feel the birds in the trees, the rabbits in their burrows.

The one thing he did not locate was the brush. It had simply vanished. Had something or someone taken it? He could feel nothing close by except some squirrels and a small fox. Shaking himself, Tristan disconnected. So his direction finder was gone, but he had other senses he could use. From that small item and the golden hairs stuck in the bristles, the elf now had the princess's vibration. He should be close enough by now to be able to feel her as long as she was not shielded. Sending his mind out towards the west, it did not take him long to find what he was looking for.

The hunter was always careful, and anything unexplained immediately alerted his senses. He noticed as soon as he made contact with the girl's aura that her vibration had slightly changed. The young woman's energy was the same in most ways, but something was different. What had happened to her to cause this? He would have to keep a sharp eye out for clues. Maybe there was an explanation for this subtle alteration somewhere along the way. First, he needed to make sure he did not lose her, but that was easily done. Tristan attached a small filament of his soul to the princess's spirit body. This minute strand would allow him to follow her anywhere. She could hide wherever she pleased from now on, but he would always be able to find her.

Pulling back, he returned to his body. After stretching leisurely for a moment, he got to his feet. His stallion was grazing just a few feet away, and Tristan called him over. With one big leap, he bounded on his mount's back and off they went. He had the direction he needed to travel. The elf's valiant horse easily fell into a fast trot. The scout was annoyed about the time he had lost looking for the brush and was determined to make it up.

~

It was toward evening when the tracker started to feel a strange kind of unease. The further he went, the stronger it became. He finally identified a grove of trees as the source of this emanation. Tristan immediately became wary. What was this place? Looking around, he discovered horse tracks in the soft forest soil. This surprised him and increased his alarm. Here was clear evidence of the princess's passing as well as of her entering the clearing. The tracks told a strange tale and in fascination, he dismounted and followed them into the glade. He needed to know what had happened in there and if this was the source of the change he had sensed in the girl.

The second he stepped into the copse, he could feel the magic. It was as if he had crossed an invisible barrier. Tristan was one of the most powerful magic wielders of his people and was therefore only mildly concerned. He was more interested in the prints here which told a confusing story. One thing became apparent rather quickly. Someone or something had used an enormous amount of power in this clearing.

What he assumed might have once been an altar was now ash blowing in the wind. How could this be? The shrines in every sacred grove he had ever seen had been built of stone. It must have taken an incredible force to eradicate the slab of rock down to the very soil. The elf could still detect hints of magic, but there seemed to be no trace left of the elder gods whose temple this once had been. Something significant had happened, but Tristan was not sure what. Scorch marks in the grass radiating out from one spot puzzled him further. What had gone on in this glade?

What he could figure out was that the princess had apparently spent the night here, first within the circle and then without. Strange! Also, it appeared that this place had recently been cleansed of most of its ancient taint. To accomplish that would have taken an unbelievable amount of energy. Who had wielded that kind of force? Surely not that young girl!

The hunter could sense that more had happened here, but the tracks gave no clues. He was the best scout there was, and it bothered him that he could not figure out the sequence of events. That had never happened to him before! Looking up, he realized that he had lingered much longer than he should have and started to move out of the copse.

All at once, Tristan started to feel completely exhausted and beyond caring. Why was he suddenly so very tired? He should be setting out again immediately! The scout could barely keep his eyes open, and even the horse which had followed him in was growing progressively more drowsy. There was no way they could travel like this. Oh well, he would just have to make up for lost time the next day.

The elf stumbled over to his stallion and pulled free his bedroll and blanket. He did not even have the strength left to remove the saddle, and the horse seemed too tired to care. Dropping his bedding right there on the ground, he plummeted down and rolled himself in his blanket.

His last thoughts were of the princess. Who was this girl traveling with? He would have to approach her with caution because whoever was protecting her, had incredible power. That kind of magic was beyond even him. Soon he was deeply asleep, and the sounds of his snoring filled the copse of old trees. That night there was a great earthquake, but the scout was too deeply unconscious to take notice or care.

~~~

Chapter Twenty Eight

Arianna's Flight

While Tristan had been riding through the night, the princess had slept well and felt almost completely recovered. Knowing that Kyrill was unharmed and no longer needing to worry about him, had helped much. As soon as it started getting light, she was awake. "Good morning, dear ones!" she greeted the sprites cheerfully. The fairies were greatly relieved to see their companion feeling so much better and being so happy. This was much more like the girl they knew and loved!

After the friends had a quick breakfast, Arianna saddled Azariel, tied on her sleeping gear, and they were on their way. Switching horses frequently, they were making good time. The princess feared that she had lost a large part of her advantage by covering such a short distance the day before. She was determined to make up for some of it this day. About noon, the landscape begun to get increasingly more hilly. The girl decided that it was time to take a short break. After sharing a light meal with the sprites, they continued their ride.

The sun was sitting low on the horizon when the fairies cried out. A large hawk was zooming towards them. Arianna immediately steered her horse to intercept the approaching raptor and to protect her tiny friends. The big bird ended up landing on her arm which she had inadvertently raised to protect her eyes from its wings and sharp talons. A small worried face peeked around the feathered neck and two very bright eyes regarded her curiously. "Lady! Are you ok?" the slight being inquired apprehensively.

The princess looked into the golden eyes of the hawk and then smiled at the sprite. "I will be all right just as long as this one does not dig in his claws any more than he already has," she laughed. As if understanding her words, the raptor gently loosened the sharp talons gripping her vulnerable arm. Riding up beside Azariel, she placed the bird on the saddle. The girl gently helped the fairy, who seemed to have frozen in place, to relinquish his hold. "Now who would you be?" she asked softly. "I am Sky, my lady, and I am honored to make your acquaintance!" the little one said with a bow. "The honor is all mine, friend Sky," the princess replied and watched the sprite turn pink with pleasure.

The other fairies were still a bit weary of the hawk but were now peeking out from behind the princess. "Sky! What are you doing here? Tell me at once!" came the imperious command from the tiny Blossom. Arianna had no more doubt about who was in charge of her little friends. Remembering his mission, the little one turned pale. "A man, no elf! He follows! He is catching up and not far behind! You need to flee, move real fast!" he squeaked. Hearing those words, the princess turned white as a sheet. Could this be Tristan, the legendary elf scout? As far as she knew, no one had ever escaped him. Regardless of that, she would most certainly try. He was said to have powers, what kind she was not sure. The first thing she needed to do was shield them all!

While the girl was raising her shields, she noticed that something felt off. Knowing that she could trust her instincts, she stopped to check. A thin luminous thread had been attached to her! So that was how this hunter intended to find her! If she cut it, he would be instantly alerted. Who knew what other tricks this tracker had at his disposal! The next thing he sent her way might be impossible to lose. She would have to think about this and decide how to best deal with this unwelcome attachment. For now, they needed to try to get as far as they could before night overtook them.

The princess gave the word to her group, and they continued their journey. The horses were sensing the urgency of their flight and were soon racing along the narrow path. Arianna felt good about their progress, but it was not long before it got too dark to proceed. With that elf so close behind them, she realized they could not afford to sleep. They had been heading in a more northwesterly direction all day and should not be too far from the border. If she could get into Larandar, Kyrill and his men might be able to assist them.

Not sure how her little friends could help, she asked them if they had any ideas. The sprites did not take long to come up with a plan. They reminded her that they could see pretty well in the dark, and if she wanted, they could sit between the horses' ears and guide them along. Arianna was delighted and told them how very brilliant she thought the notion. It had taken only a few moments before all was set. The going was much slower than it had been but they were moving along in the direction she wanted to go, and this pleased her.

When it became too dark in the murky forest for even the sprites to see, they decided to rest in a small clearing. They would wait for the moon to rise and then continue their journey. Arianna was asleep as soon as she lay down on her bedroll.

~

Kyrill joined her, and she told him of all the things which had happened that day and 'about the scout who was following her trail. Together they came up with several ideas for the filament and how it might be used to mislead the hunter. The princess was so glad to have her love there to help develop a plan.

~

Suddenly, the friends were rudely awoken. The ground under them started to tremble. The horses were whinnying and the sprites crying out in fear. Then, the earth began rolling in great waves beneath them. The princess and her companions were terrified. The movement was so strong that she feared for the horses and shouted at them to lay down. Arianna was not sure if that was the best option, but she was afraid that they would break their legs if they were knocked down. With all the panic they did not seem to grasp what she wanted at first. Therefore, she quickly sent a picture into their minds. Arabella and Azariel understood immediately, but the others were slower to follow.

The last horse had just hit the ground when the movement intensified further. The earth was now bucking beneath them, and a sound like thunder hung in the air. The ferocious quaking went on and on and seemed to last for a very long time. Finally, the violent movement built to a crescendo and then began to slowly subside. Human, sprites, and animals lay there for a moment too stunned to move. Arianna was the first to recover and to get on her feet. She immediately checked on her friends. The sprites were badly shaken but uninjured. One of the horses had not been so lucky. Chestnut, being the weakest, had been the last one to follow her command and, on the way down, had hurt one of his legs.

The princess carefully examined the limb. She suspected it was broken. Extending her senses, she quickly confirmed those fears. The girl carefully checked along the break; it was clean and even. She had never healed such a break on a horse before but had mended other bones and was confident that she could fuse it. If it did not work, Chestnut had no chance at all. Asking her goddess for help, she ever so gently started working her way along the fracture encouraging cell growth. Pulling more power from the Earth, she strengthened the newly formed bone. The crack was healed, but the tissue was not as strong as it would be with time. There was no way this already weakened animal could continue the journey.

Gently, she encouraged Chestnut to get on his feet. At first, he did not want to. His leg had hurt badly, and he still remembered this. The fairies added their powers of persuasion and after a bit, they finally had the gelding on his, at first rather wobbly, legs. The horse was surprised for a moment that there was no pain. He instinctually realized that the princess had saved him and nuzzled her gratefully. Arianna's eyes were swimming with tears because she knew that she might have to let him go free. Could he survive out here all by himself? Should she ask the fairies to take him back to their home? The princess decided that she would bring up the option but leave the choice up to the little ones.

The sprites were elated that she had healed the injured steed but grew serious when she told them that they would not be able to take him along. They would have to ride hard to avoid the elf and Chestnut's leg was still too weak to keep up such a pace. "We will have to set him free unless one of you is willing to take him to safety," Arianna hesitantly stated. A discussion ensued among the fairies who hated the very idea of leaving their friend behind alone in the woods. As usual, Blossom took charge. "This is what we will do: Sky, River, and Silver, you three will go with the horse. Take it back to my mother, she will care for it there," she commanded.

Arianna hid her smile behind her hand. She had suspected correctly. The tiny sprite was Queen Liza's daughter! She felt honored that the monarch had entrusted her with the life of her child and was glad that so far she had managed to keep the little ones from harm. The princess had grown to like Sky and would miss him and the other two, but they all needed to be on their way. The moon had just risen, and it was time to move on. Rolling up her bedroll and blankets she tied them back to the saddle and got ready to ride. The fairies were saying tearful good-byes over and over again, and the princess soon realized that if she did not stop them, this could go on for a while.

"Good-bye, Sky, River, and Silver. Thank you for taking Chestnut to your home. Please give my thanks to your queen for all she has done! I wish you good travels and be safe. We will miss you!" Arianna told the three. The sprites kept hugging each other and seemed very reluctant to part. "My friends, we really, really need to go," she urged gently and after one last round of hugs, both parties were on their way. The three sprites would head south for half a day at the first opportunity before turning back to the east; this should ensure that they avoided the pursuing elf. The princess mounted Azariel, Blossom settled herself between the horse's ears, and they headed back onto the trail through the moonlit forest.

~

They had not gone far when the earth began to roll yet once again, but before the horses could lower themselves to the ground, the movement stopped. The princess let out her pent-up breath. That had not been too bad. It had grown dead silent in the forest for a moment, but now the insects continued their night song as the horses carefully picked their way along the dark trail. Their progress was interrupted several more times by the quaking of the ground beneath them. The sprites mentioned that it felt like the shaking originated from their right but they could not determine its source. Arianna had no idea what could be causing such a violent earthquake. It worried her as well as the fairies. Were they heading towards the root of this intense disturbance?

The moon had traveled a long way across the sky and was just about to set when the princess decided it was time for them to get a little more sleep. She told this to Blossom, who gave a sigh of relief. The earth was still shaking intensely at times, and the friends did not think it wise to camp too close to the trees. They moved on until they reached a good sized clearing. They could not sleep for long, and the girl decided to leave the saddle on her horse just in case they needed to flee. The princess quickly spread out her bedroll and blankets and gratefully slid into her bed. The weary sprites settled around her. They were all glad for the rest even if it would be brief.

Arianna said a prayer to her goddess thanking her for her help and protection. Remembering that the rule of free will kept the Lady from helping her unless she gave her consent, the princess tried to find a way around this. She wanted to make sure that assistance was always near and not just when she asked for it. What if she was in a position where she could not? The princess finally decided to give the Lady permission to interfere and save her anytime she pleased and told her that such actions would be more than welcome. The girl then bid her deity good night.

The young woman and most of the sprites were soon sound asleep. Roots, who was left to guard them, kept a close eye on things. He was tired but alert and with all his senses extended, no one would be able to sneak up on them, not even Tristan.

~

The prince had tried to reach Arianna, but her exhaustion was so great that she slept but did not dream. He could feel that she was well but that something had happened to her. His concern grew when the wise woman of his people came rushing into the hut. He instantly knew she was upset. Her hair was standing on end, and the always so polite seeress had not even knocked. "Kyrill! The Elder God! He has done something to keep the princess from reaching us! I cannot see what since he has placed a veil of mist over his creation. But, I can feel a long shadow running all the way along the border starting at that cursed grove! Come! We need to speak to your father!" urged Cassandra.

Pulling him along impatiently, the two took flight for the Aerie where they raced to his sire's quarters. Once again, the lady took no time for politeness but barged through the door. The prince realized that whatever was going on, it must be pretty serious since it had rattled her so. "The Elder God is going to kill her! You need to send your men out now to save her, and if they must, they need to be allowed to go into that cursed kingdom! The time for caution is over!" Cassandra had shouted at the surprised king before she collapsed to the floor. The wise woman was deeply unconscious, and all attempts to revive her were in vain. Her breathing was shallow and fast and her heart racing. "I am going to put a shield around her, father! Please get others to help!" shouted the prince.

Kyrill knelt beside the stricken woman and raised his shields around himself first. Then, he began to extend them around Cassandra. He could feel some resistance in the beginning, but as others joined in lending him power, they were able to push back the invisible force attacking the seeress and shelter the wise woman inside their combined shields.

Slowly, her breathing evened, and her heartbeat returned to normal. Finally, she opened her eyes. "It seems that evil has found a host to bring it into this world and can now reach us even here. All of us need to shield until it has been laid to rest. You need to get your men to the princess and fast, she is too precious to our people to lose!" she weakly told King Le'onard.

Giving his longtime friend and advisor a questioning look, an unspoken communication took place between the two. When the seeress nodded, the king sprang into action. Within minutes, several of his men were on their way. They had orders to rescue the princess no matter what it would take. It seemed that the young woman was not only important to his son but also vital to the survival of his people. Whatever needed to be done to save her was going to be done. Even if that meant taking all his men and retrieving her from the depths of Lothrien.

Kyrill desperately hoped that they would reach his mate in time. They had a large area to search. The princess and her horses were just one small group, and the woods would hide them well. The prince himself would head just over the border into Larandar to coordinate the search. He was only too aware that if he as part of the royal family set foot into Lothrien, the Dark God would see this as a declaration of war. It would allow him to break all the rules the other Gods had set down to restrain him. Nor'dur would love a chance to get even with the people who had once defied him. This would increase the peril Arianna already found herself in. It was best if the evil one never suspected to what extent the girl was associated with the Eagles he hated so much.

~~~

Chapter Twenty Nine

The Elder God

Slowly Tristan started to awake as the increasing brightness of the approaching dawn penetrated his eyelids. At first, he was dazed and confused. What had happened to him? Why was he asleep here in this grove and not following his prey? Had he continued on his way, he would have caught her by now! The elf was furious with himself. To give in to any kind of weakness was unacceptable.

The ground beneath him began to shake and buck, and the scout looked around in incomprehension. What was going on? The quaking stopped quickly enough, and Tristan got to his feet. His horse had gone back to grazing peacefully just a short distance away from him. There was something different about it; it's beautiful blue eyes seemed to shimmer with a reddish tint. Strange! The scout's mind still felt confused, and he was not sure all of a sudden if this gleam was new or had always been there. A voice in his mind told him that it did not matter, but that he should get going now. This jerked him out of his contemplations, and he headed for

353

his stallion. Why was he hanging around here? He needed to catch that witch and kill her! The elf came to a dead stop. Where had such a notion come from? Wasn't he trying to retrieve the princess for his king?

Before he could explore these notions further, they were abruptly cut off, and his eyes glazed over. Yes kill, he must kill. Jumping on the back of his horse, the elf guided it out of the grove. Soon they were galloping down the path in the direction he could feel the filament pull him. 'That had been such an ingenious idea,' a voice cackled with glee in his befuddled mind. Who was talking to him? Almost as soon as the thought arose, it was squashed. Riding out, he never even noticed that he left his bedroll and blankets behind.

~

Horse and rider raced down the forest path like a thing possessed which if truth be told, they were. The pair had been taken over by one who was pure evil. His name was Nor'dur, and he was the last of the Elder Gods. Once there had been many of them, but the people and other Gods had grown tired of their tyranny and had risen up against them. The Elders had been confined to Lothrien. When their worshippers turned their backs on them, his brethren had not been able to sustain themselves much longer. One after the other, they had faded away.

Now, only Nor'dur survived. The cruel God had found a way to permeate the very fiber of the realm. Nothing happened anywhere without his knowing. His evil influence was everywhere in the unlucky kingdom. He and his wraiths fed off the misery and cruelty their very existence was causing. When the princess had entered his lands, she had been like a bright beacon. She was draining him with her very presence. The God had felt the potential in the girl. He wanted her magic, it would sustain him for years. He had created the heat to slow her and bring her to the grove. She had fallen right into his trap and had almost been his.

Someone had dared to interfere and had woken her. Instead of draining the princess of her powers to add to his own, she had cleansed his sacred grove. When she had allowed her Goddess to work through her, Nor'dur had cowered in fear. Not even he could take on such as her. He had lost all his terrible wraiths that night, his companions of hundreds of years. They had helped him keep despair a bright flame in the land. Then, she had destroyed the altar which secured Nor'dur's very spirit to the land. This had set him adrift. He had been forced to dig deep into the soil of the grove to hide himself and to hold on. No one had ever treated him like this. The princess might be Brigit's disciple, but the ancient one's fury was such that he no longer cared. The girl had dealt him an intolerable injury. He would have his revenge no matter the cost.

The vengeful God had been thrilled when the elf and his stallion entered his copse. While they slept, Nor'dur became one with them both. This had anchored him firmly to Lothrien once more and had allowed him to work incredible magic. He had even been able to hit back at his old enemies, the Eagles. That would teach them to spy on his lands.

~

The pair Nor'dur now inhabited meant nothing to him, they were a means to an end. He drove them mercilessly. The elf and his horse raced along the narrow forest trails with reckless abandon, going just as fast as they possibly could. All the scout could think about was that he had to get to that girl before she escaped to that other land. He had to make her pay for what she had done to him and his children.

Never before had Tristan pushed his horse this brutally, this callously, and the valiant steed gave all that it had. When

355

its big heart was about to give out, Nor'dur finally took notice. It would not do to lose their mount. He started to feed dark energy into the failing body and began to sustain it. The stallion grew stronger, and new endurance flooded his veins. The more power it gained, the more its eyes changed. Overnight the orbs had turned from a light blue to almost lavender with the red hints Tristan had noticed. Now, however, they become more and more an eerie, glowing crimson.

Not even the occasional shaking of the ground beneath them got the two to slow down. The scout could feel that they were getting closer but that his victim was moving as well. While he laid sleeping, the wretched girl had found a way to travel during the night. But, it would do her no good. Deep down he knew she had no chance now; the trap was sprung, and she would soon be his.

That witch would never reach Larandar and safety alive; he had taken care of that. Let her try to escape, soon there would be no place left to run to. These thoughts filled him with a cold thrill and a bloodlust which would have been alien to him had he been in control of himself.

~

The princess and her friends had allowed themselves a brief nap to help regain some of their strength and head off the worst of their exhaustion. Except for the occasional shaking of the ground beneath them, the rest of the night had passed peacefully. The sprite on guard had orders to wake them just as soon as it became light and that he did. Arianna still felt pretty groggy from the day before, but time was of the essence. Breakfast would have to be eaten while they were on their way. They needed to get into Larandar and as quickly as they possibly could.

Crossing the border might not deter the elf, but at least, Kyrill's men would be able to assist them. The princess was aware that sending any soldiers into the lands of a hostile ruler without permission could be construed as an act of war. Arianna had learned over the years that the King of the Eagles, King Le'onard, was a peaceful man who avoided conflict as much as he could. Kyrill had told her that his father had given permission for his people to go right up to the border of the cursed kingdom. Being considered warriors of Re'adeen, the shapeshifters were allowed into Larandar, but they could not set foot on the ground of Lothrien.

Once she was across the border, she needed to find help fast and before that tracker caught up with her. The lands along the boundary were deserted, nobody wanted to live this close to the land of King Vargos. The vile hunter could easily sneak across, grab her, and take her back into Lothrien without anyone ever being the wiser. He could then deliver her to his wicked king at his leisure. From what she had heard of the elf, she seriously doubted that such a little thing as violating another sovereign's territory would stop him from getting his prize. And, even if his misdeed ever became known, who would have the courage to complain to the tyrant?

They had to keep ahead of the scout at all cost. The elf was a seasoned warrior, hunter, and kidnapper. If he got a hold of her, escape would be extremely difficult. He was wise to all kinds of tricks and was rumored to have very strong magic. His king sent him out all the time to retrieve people who thought they were better off elsewhere. Arianna had heard that the tracker brought back whoever he was sent after and no one had ever gotten away from him. Not that this would stop her from trying her best! In the princess's mind, avoiding the hunter in the first place was the best course of action.

The sprites had decided to continue guiding the horses, and they had them racing along as fast as they could. Since Arianna had found that filament attached to her by the elf, she had been using it to see how far he had come. She did not want him to notice so she kept each contact as brief as possible. When she had checked early that morning, Tristan had not moved, but now he was getting progressively closer and fast. When she passed that on to the fairies, they were greatly concerned and began making plans. There had to be a way to slow down that hunter! Soon, vines were crawling across the trail behind them, and bushes were spreading their branches as far as they could into the path.

The horses had been going almost all out for some time now. Arianna feared that the mounts would not be able to maintain this pace much longer. In spite of their speed, the tracker was catching up to them. The girl was so anxious that she did not realize for a while that something was different about the elf. Once she became aware of the change, however, it had her undivided attention. The princess examined the cord more carefully. There was a strange new vibration to the filament, angry and jarring, very unlike the day before when she had first discovered the thread. Arianna was even more alarmed. She had felt a similar vibration when she had battled with the wraiths in that grove. Had she missed something? And, had it now possessed this man who was chasing her to exact its revenge?

A bend in the trail was coming up, and the faithful mounts were going just as fast as they could. The turn seemed sharp and so the sprites had the animals slow down a little. That was what saved them. Something warned Arianna at the last minute that there was terrible danger ahead. "Stop!" she screamed and also send this as a mind command to all the horses. Arabella, who the princess was riding, felt the urgency in her mistress's command. The mare immediately tried to come to a dead stop, but this caused her to slide on the dusty path. She was still sliding when they reached the curve.

To the princess horror, the path just ended a short distance in front of them, and she and her mount were slipping right towards an abyss. Panic infused her. She would die just like her mother had! Complete terror flooded the girl and paralyzed her. The intelligent horse, on the other hand, took immediate action. She sat down on her rump and leaned herself as far backward as she possibly could. The second her frozen rider slid off, the mare threw herself sideways and finally came to a stop resting on her side with her legs dangling over the cliff.

The princess had been in the lead and the others a little behind. They had also barely managed to stop in time. Azariel had come close enough to almost push Arabella over the edge. Arianna was shaking like a leaf, but her beloved horse was in danger, and something had to be done and done quickly. The smart mare was laying very still. She seemed to understand that any movement might cause her to slip. The princess felt profound gratefulness. The loyal animal had saved them both with its quick thinking. Now it was up to her to return that momentous gift.

There was no way she could push or pull the horse back from the brink; she just did not have that kind of strength. Even if the sprites helped and they found a way to use the other horses, it would still take too long. That left only magic. With a quick prayer to her goddess, the young sorceress gathered her powers and started to slowly slide the anxious mare back from the edge. Arianna was still weak from her exertion in the Elder God's grove, and her strength was waning when the job was only halfway done. "Touch the tree," came a voice in her mind. Without a second thought, the princess reached out and placed her hand on the bark of a nearby elm. A welcome force flooded through her being infusing her with enough strength to give the horse the one necessary last tug.

The princess was still leaning against the tree, catching her breath from this magic exertion when a scream echoed through her mind. "Get away from there!!!" Instinctively, Arianna threw herself towards the path. Just in time! The elm she had been leaning on just a moment before had taken on a whole new form. It had turned ugly and deformed, and its bark was now pitch black. "Let's get out of here!" the young woman shouted to her companions who reacted immediately. Arabella had by then gotten to her feet. The princess grabbed the reins when she ran past the mare and followed the sprites back the way they had come hauling the horse along.

The friends stopped a little further on in a small clearing and Arianna mounted Azariel. She felt that Arabella was still too shaken to ride and pulled her along behind her instead. Now that they were heading back towards the east and the hunter, they needed to find a trail south fast so that they could avoid him.

This was a problem since none of them remembered seeing an intersecting path for a very long time. Their way to the west and north into Larandar was blocked. The princess had taken a good look at that vast chasm while she was leaning up against the tree. It extended as far to the west as she could see and was so wide that it could have easily swallowed her home in Maridanmar as well as the town. There was no way for them to get across.

Their only hope lay towards the east. It seemed that this gigantic crack in the earth was getting narrower in that direction. Maybe there was a place where they could go around it to reach Larandar. The hunter, however, was coming from there and heading directly towards them. If they did not manage to avoid him somehow, her chances of ever being free and getting to Kyrill were nil. So once again they were moving as fast as they could, only this time back in the direction they had just come from. They were racing into danger instead of away from it, right towards the possessed elf.

A shadow above them suddenly shut out the sun. Arianna looked up not knowing what to expect. All her senses were on high alert, and adrenaline was pumping through her body like mad. It was the dragon! "Stop in the clearing ahead!" came the imperious command. Another delay! The princess started to feel resigned to her fate. Unless they had missed a turn-off on their way, the one they all remembered was too far away, and they would never be able to reach it before running into the elf. There was no place left to run to so she might as well save her energy and wait for the scout!

The dragon had already landed in the clearing when they arrived. For the huge creature, it was a pretty tight fit. "Hurry!" Galata addressed the girl without preamble. "Grab your things! And drop that saddle on the ground, the sprites won't need it. Bring the reins, bags, and blankets. You are coming with me!" Arianna swiftly did as she was told and said a quick good-bye to the horses as well as to the sprites riding them. She would miss them all terribly. Without her to lead the scout to them, her friends could hide in the woods and let the hunter race past them. They might yet survive this!

A spirited discussion had broken out among the sprites. Finally, Blossom had enough. "Stop! You will take the horses to my mother! Rosebud and I are going with the princess! Now go hide!" she commanded. The princess, remembering the filament, realized that the hunter would most likely ride back to the east to go around, just as they had planned. "Wait! The elf will be coming back this way when he does not find us! Stay well-hidden until he has gone a long way back to the east. Remember, please, and be careful! Good-bye, my friends! I love you and thank you for everything!" the princess told them with tears in her eyes.

Time was of the essence; the hunter was now not far. The girl ran over to the dragon and proceeded to strap the horse blanket to the creature's back following Galata's instructions. She had to use the leads to help hold it. The saddle bags she was told to tie around the long sinuous neck. "Wrap your blankets around you and the sprites and hold on tight. Try to make yourself as flat as possible to minimize the chance of the hunter seeing you," ordered the large creature as she began beating her wings to lift off from the ground. Grabbing the saddle, the magnificent beast flew out over the abyss where she released it. No sense in giving hints to the elf.

Arianna was still settling in while they were already rising into the air. Once securely seated, she finally managed to look down to the ground. Of her friends and the horses, no signs remained. They should be well-hidden behind several clumps of dense, low trees by now. As she looked around, she took in the true immenseness of the gulch for the first time. That was no mere crevasse; this was a giant canyon. When the princess looked back at the spot where they had almost gone over, she noticed with concern that the blackness which had started with the tree appeared to be growing.

"Blossom?" she called softly. The sprite had been curled up against her watching the world below. Hearing her name, she stuck her head out further so that she could look up at Arianna with those beautiful, bright eyes. "Yes, Lady?" came the fairy's curious reply. "Can you still reach our friends?" "Let me try," came the immediate response and a look of deep concentration appeared on the tiny girl's face.

Blossom's brow began to wrinkle with alarm which soon turned into anger. "I cannot reach them, something is blocking me! Why do you ask?" the fairy inquired. "See that darkness? It is spreading! I do not think it would be good for them to be caught in it," Arianna told the sprite pointing out the dark blotch in the otherwise vibrantly green vegetation. A look of grave concern clouded the small elemental's delicate features.

Galata in the meantime had climbed higher and higher using the rising air of the thermals above the canyon. Then she streaked to the northwest. She planned to take the girl to the far mountains as the fairy queen had suggested. They figured that it would take that nasty elf time to go around the deep gulch. Once he reached Larandar and made his way through the foothills, the trails would become difficult for the horse. Riding in the steep mountains was hazardous at best. Eventually, the scout would have to abandon his mount. The extra time and a big head start would give the girl a much better chance to stay ahead of her pursuer.

~

The elf and his horse raced through the clearing the dragon had vacated just a few minutes earlier. The bushes and vines the sprites had encouraged to grow never even slowed their pursuers. Tristan was furious. The witch had almost been his! Instead of heading west, in fact, she had started moving towards him. Then, suddenly she was heading away from him and fast. None of the human horses should be able to run at that speed! What kind of magic was that wretched girl's companion using now?

Just a bit further ahead he spotted deep gouges in the soil. These marks were fresh and looked like the horses had desperately been trying to stop. Slowing way down, he leaned over his stallion's neck to examine the prints. He was so busy looking around that he had to grab for his mount's mane when the large steed suddenly came to a dead stop. Tearing his gaze away from the puzzle there in the soil, he looked ahead. The path was gone and in its place was the widest canyon he had ever seen.

Tristan had been this way many times before, and this deep crack in the earth was definitely new. Where had it come from and how? Then it dawned on him. The abrupt end of the trail was the reason for his quarry's sudden stop! From the looks of this, they had just barely made in time! So, where had they gone? He had not met them on the way. How could the horses and that witch disappear this completely?

The scout could feel the girl moving in a northwesterly direction, across the gulch. How could this be? It was almost as if she was flying across, but that would take more magic than any one human should possibly have! Tristan began to scan the skies and far off in the distance he noticed a speck of something.

Could that be the witch and her companion? Whatever or whoever it was, the distance was too great for his sharp eyes. Not even with Nor'dur enhancing his vision could he make it out clearly. Not that it mattered. If that girl was getting across, then he needed to do so as well. The scout carefully examined the canyon and noticed that it was getting much wider to the west but narrowed significantly in an easterly direction.

Now it made sense why the witch had been moving towards him! Having nowhere to go, she had turned back. She must have been looking for a way to go around this obstacle she so suddenly encountered. Did the girl realize he was hunting her? She was a sorceress, after all, so she must. Once she had to turn around, she should have been looking for a way to go south to avoid him. Instead, she was moving north. What kind of magic was this witch employing to get herself across this vast canyon?

That much power was way beyond the elf, and he wanted it, craved it. He decided that when he finally got his hands on the girl and whoever was helping her, he would take it all for his own. That these thoughts were completely alien to him never even occurred to the scout.

As he turned his stallion, he noticed the strange vegetation. It called out to him, and he hesitantly reached out his hand. The second he touched one of the leaves, his eyes rolled up in his head, and a current of raw power shot through his arm into him and his horse. It kept coming, and man and beast were convulsing with the force entering them. As the last of the blackness had drained from the tree, the flow abruptly stopped. Elf and mount stilled and his eyes rolled back into their sockets. Their color was now bright crimson and devoid of all life.

Without another moment's hesitation, horse and rider began racing back the way they had come. They fairly flew down the path with an unbelievable speed. They were going faster than any steed bred by the elves had ever gone before. All creatures whom they came close to felt the coldness of their passing and shivered as if someone had just walked over their grave.

~~~

Chapter Thirty

A Narrow Escape

The dragon had crossed the canyon and was flying high and fast towards the Northern Galandrien Mountains. She was aiming for the distant peaks close to the border with Re'adeen. It felt wonderful to be traveling this far and at this speed. She might just have to do this more often. The scaled lady was pulled out of her musings when the princess drew her attention. "Galata, we have been watching that dark spot over there by the canyon wall, and it is moving towards our friends. We encountered it earlier, and it is pure evil. Could you drop us right there on that mountain and please go back to warn them?" came Arianna's anxious request. The dragon, who had grown very fond of the capricious sprites, immediately agreed.

Quickly she spiraled down toward the closest mountain and, finding a large enough ledge, went in for a landing. Just as soon as the massive creature was settled down on the ground, the princess slid off and began to remove the horse blanket and pack. Galata watched her impatiently. Reaching out and giving the immense beast a brief hug, the princess dashed clear followed by the two little sprites. The dragon immediately began beating her vast wings forcing the three to duck down for cover. "Good-bye. Galata and well met! Thank you for everything!" her sensitive ears heard the princess shout. As soon as she was high enough, she was flying as fast as she could back to the south.

~

Without a passenger to worry about, the dragon could fly like the wind. She had been watching the spreading blackness with great concern since Arianna drew her attention to it. Galata realized that there was no time to lose. Giving it all she had, she fairly streaked across the sky. That tarnish was getting close to the clearing and fast. Her little friends were in terrible danger! The protective lady's anger helped stoke up her fire. After pumping her lungs like bellows a few times, she released a jet of flame on the offending vegetation to push it back from the glade. It resisted her at first, and she watched with great satisfaction when the unnatural foliage finally flared up and burned.

Landing in the clearing, the dragon called for the sprites who hesitantly came out of hiding. She told them of the danger heading their way. Since the elf had already passed them, horses and fairies were immediately on their way. Galata once more took to the sky and flew above them. She was keeping a sharp eye out for any possible danger. Her fire seemed to have slowed down the spread of that taint significantly, and they soon left it behind. Nothing was going to hurt the little ones if she had anything to say about it. If only this rescue had not increased the danger to the princess!

It was late afternoon when the small group reached the first turnoff to the south. Feeling much safer now from the terrible elf; they gladly headed that way. Petal, who Blossom had put in charge in her absence, made sure that no trace of their passage remained. On the spur of the moment, she also added a spell which would hide this path from most humans. She remembered the bandits only too well and figured it was best to be careful. When night fell, Galata bid them good-bye and flew off to her lair. She was exhausted and needed a good sleep after this day's exertions.

~

It was much colder up here in the mountains and Arianna was not dressed for this sudden change. The girl needed to find a way to stay warm and fast, she was already beginning to shiver. She did not have much, but it would have to do. The princess wrapped first one blanket around herself than the other but still felt the chill wind bite right through the cloth. Since the girl had no horse to ride, she no longer needed the horse blanket. Taking her knife, she made a slit in the middle and expanded it until it made a hole large enough to fit her head through. This blanket was much thicker and came down to her knees like a poncho. Tying the reins around her waist as a belt, she was finally starting to warm up.

The fairies were not used to this cold either and once again curled up close to Arianna. Her body heat would provide them with enough warmth to stay comfortable. Looking around to orient herself, the young woman decided that they needed to head to the north. Her best bet was to stay in the mountains even if this made for rough going. Suddenly, she remembered the filament. Following it should have drawn the hunter away from her friends and after her. If she was going to avoid capture, she needed to misdirect him. It was time to free herself of the thing.

Should she attach the thread to some agreeable creature and send the elf the wrong way like she and Kyrill had planned? She had not been shielding when the scout connected it the first time so it would be harder for him now that she was wise to this trick. There was no telling, however, what other wiles this monster had up his sleeve. She would have to be very careful. Finding an animal which was willing to take the strand might be her best option. Reaching out with her mind, she soon located two mountain goats. Gently, she coaxed them towards her. The pair was unused to humans and had no fear of her or the sprites.

Arianna slowly reached out her hand and gingerly patted their soft noses. It would have been so easy to pass the filament to them right then but in her mind, that was not how things were done. Slowly, and in pictures they could comprehend, she explained her need. They countered that they would be willing to mislead the man in return for some help.

The nanny had stepped on a sharp stone, and it had injured her hoof. Could the human ease her pain? The princess bent down and gently examined the wounded appendage. She could feel where the hurt was and started to draw it into herself. Then Arianna encouraged healing to seal the cut. As soon as she was done, the nanny bounced around her. There was no pain left; the damage to the hoof was completely gone.

Once the girl had completed her part of the bargain, the billy goat approached her with his head lowered to accept the cord. The princess overlaid her own vibrations over his before passing on the thread. Hopefully, this would be enough to fool the hunter. The nimble pair communicated that they would head west a bit and then up. With any luck, this trick would work and draw the elf after the goats. Arianna instructed her new friends on what to do to break the fine filament and asked them to please do so early the next day. She did not want either animal to get hurt but knew that she desperately needed as big a head start as she could possibly get.

Leading the scout astray should increase her lead. He had a long way to go to get around that canyon. The princess was still puzzled by that great gulch. She had never heard of a chasm here, and this one seemed to have formed overnight. Its creation must have been the source of those terrible earthquakes! The dragon flying her over the wide expanse together with the ruse with the filament should give her a bit more of a chance to avoid capture.

~

Picking up the saddle bags, Arianna started ascending the mountain. After some hard climbing, she finally spotted a game trail leading to the north. Pushing herself to the limit, the princess walked along as fast as she safely could on this steep, uneven path. Some stretches had sharp drop-offs to her right with cliffs plunging down hundreds of feet. The girl had to hug the rocks to traverse these. A fall from that height would have been deadly. The trail was way too narrow for a horse to travel and definitely more suited to mountain goats than to humans. At least the vigorous movement was keeping her warm. The sprites were making sure that they were leaving no trace behind for the elf to find.

There were few trees this high up. The ones who did grow up here were windswept and stunted. A cold current of air was blowing down from the mountain peak. When the day began to turn into evening, Arianna knew she needed to find shelter. As luck would have it, the path led them into a protected valley with a stream and a good sized stand of trees a short time later. The cliff on one side even had an inviting cave. The princess carefully approached the tempting shelter. She used her magic to search it. What the girl found, was a bear. She realized that she needed to come to some accommodation with this creature. She was grateful that this one was no longer in hibernation, it would make it easier to deal with. The fairies were terribly cold as well, and the temperature had started to plunge even further. If they were going to survive, they needed the warmth of this den.

After a whispered conversation, the three decided to try to make a deal with the bear. Arianna once again reached out with her mind and politely greeted the big creature. Its first reaction was one of fury, but the princess kept sending it love and after a while, the animal began to grow calmer. She talked to it softly, and finally, it consented that they could enter its home. Carefully, and making sure her hands were in plain sight at all times, the girl walked into the cave. The bear sniffed her and the sprites, and all held perfectly still. It seemed the large beast finally convinced itself that they were no threat and settled down on its bed of twigs, branches, and leaves.

Now that they had been accepted, Arianna and her two fairy friends found a spot for themselves as far into the cave as possible but not too close to the bear. None of them wanted to intrude into its space. The princess went back out into the valley and collected as many leaves and soft twigs as she could to make into a bed. Soon they had a somewhat comfortable little nest.

The bear, a large brown female, had been watching them and had grown curious. She wanted to know why they were up here in the mountains. The fairies were only too happy to share their story with her. When Arianna had Blossom inquire why their new friend was no longer asleep, they were told that a great shaking had awoken her. It had frightened the large creature so badly that she had fled her cave until the tremors subsided. The girl watched the large animal intently during this exchange. Could this great beast have a toothache? She had seen the poor beast flinch every time it moved it's big head.

Approaching their hostess respectfully, she asked what was ailing her. After some convincing, the bear agreed to let her take a look. Arianna visually inspected the area first; there was some redness between a pair of the lower teeth. Taking her hand and holding it over the inflamed region without touching gave her more information. After asking its permission, she took the bear's massive head in her hands. Closing her eyes, she sent her thoughts to the spot and examined it more carefully. It did not take her long to find the culprit. A bone splinter had jammed deep into the jaw. That would hurt to remove!

The princess explained to the bear what she had found and needed to do before she gingerly set out to dampen the pain receptors around the affected teeth as much as she could. Then, she started to force the splinter through the inflamed tissue. It slowly rose to the surface. The bear moaned with pain. When the small needle-like piece finally broke through to the surface, the princess carefully reached in and removed it. The creature roared with pain, but Arianna just stood there and waited for it to present her with its jaw once more. The wound was now bleeding freely, washing out the infection. After making sure it was clean, the girl healed the puncture and deadened the pain.

The sudden absence of that terrible ache in its jaw pleased the bear considerably. Since it had been so painful to eat, it would not have been able to put on weight after its winter hibernation, a death sentence of sorts. Without that extra padding, she would not have been able to survive the next cold season. The big female felt deep gratitude and even a stirring of love for this lost human cub. The girl was in danger. A sense of protectiveness surfaced in the bear.

Maybe she could help by taking this small person and her friends some distance towards wherever they were fleeing to.

It was dark in the cave, but she could sense how cold the girl was and also the sprites. Now that was one thing which could easily be taken care off and right then and there. Her own bed was far softer than theirs. "Come, join please," she sent and could feel the human's surprise. Soon Arianna, Blossom, and Rosebud were comfortably curled up between the bear's powerful legs. Sheltered from the wind and covered partially by big hairy arms and paws, they were finally warm. They quickly drifted off to sleep.

~

You can imagine Kyrill's surprise to hear that his love was sleeping peacefully between the forelegs of a big carnivore. She never stopped to amaze him. He loved the rapport she had with animals as well as the fairies. The prince listened intently to this day's adventures. He was thrilled to hear that she had finally made it into Larandar. By questioning her, he tried to figure out which mountain Arianna and the sprites were on so that he could narrow down the search. The princess, unfortunately, had no clue. All she could tell him was that the peak was not far from the canyon. She had been too worried about her friends to pay closer attention.

Having a little more information on where to find her was great, but it was still a large area to search. The princess would be better visible on the bare mountain than in the woods but without the horses, she also presented a smaller target. The other problem was the elf. They needed to make sure that the hunter lost the trail and would not end up following the girl to the Aerie. They could deal with the man if he ever did find his way there, but Kyrill was concerned about the evil in him that Arianna had sensed. Was the tracker connected to the foul spirit Cassandra had been attacked by?

The grove had been dedicated to the Elder Gods. As far as the prince knew, only one was left, but his power was still strong in Lothrien. The elf had been following Arianna and would have passed by the copse. If he had set foot therein, the ancient deity could have seen his chance. The scout was said to have significant powers which would have granted the god an entirely new set of abilities. Could the destruction of his wraiths have angered him enough to create that enormous canyon to stop the princess from leaving Lothrien? That would have been an immense expenditure of energy and should have been sufficient to weaken even this vile spirit.

After discussing it more and from the similarity in vibrations Arianna had noticed, the couple concluded that Nor'dur had taken over the scout and was using him to exact his revenge. Kyrill thought that the evil one's powers would be significantly reduced once he set foot into Larandar but he feared that they were still far greater than any mortal could wield.

One thing was for certain. Arianna would have to shield herself at all times from now on to make sure that the elf and the evil possessing him could not find her. The prince felt pretty good about all the precautions his lady had taken and hoped that his men could find her quickly to help get her to safety.

~~~

Chapter Thirty One

The Hunt Continues

*T*ristan felt it immediately when the princess passed the filament to the goats. She had tried to fool him, but the vibration had changed ever so slightly and was no longer fully her own. Fury rose up inside the possessed elf. How dare she try to mislead him! That witch was going to die just as soon as he caught her! He could not wait to put his hands around that slender throat and choke the life out of her. His fingers turned into claws on the reins, and he could almost see the act in his mind. That sorceress needed to die! How dare she kill his children! To make up for what she had done, she would become the first of his new spirit slaves.

All afternoon horse and rider raced back the way they had come until they once more reached the grove just as night was falling. Where the altar had once been, a deep fissure originated, turning into the canyon just a bit further west. What power it had taken to rip open the very earth just to cut off one insignificant human! Fury and hatred boiled up out of the very ground like a malevolent cloud. When the elf rode into the copse, it surrounded him and infused him.

It became part of his very being. Any humanity he had left up to that point was now completely gone.

The tracker crossed through the grove and skirted the very beginning of the giant crack in the earth. To make up time, he headed straight to the north for a while on a nice wide game trail before turning west. The hatred inside him spurred the scout on ever faster. He had been riding all day and was still going. His ire was so great that he never even noticed that he and the horse could see perfectly well during the darkest hours of the night. Once the moon had risen, the gloom around them appeared as bright as daylight.

On and on they went with an endurance and speed far beyond that of any ordinary elf or horse. They were covering an incredible distance in a very short time, and it did not seem to be tiring the man or his beast. They raced on all night long. Tristan was aiming for the place opposite from where he had lost the witch. When they got close and ran out of trail, the elf skirted the outliers of the vast canyon. That was slowing him down but for some reason unbeknownst to him, he was reluctant to cross the border into Larandar. Instead, he kept close to the gorge's edge inside Lothrien.

The hunter had no idea how she had escaped him, but he could feel that she had come this way. He just needed to find some sign of her passing, pick up the trail. When she had handed off that filament, he had felt her raising her shields, shutting him out. His fury had been so great that he felt like he might explode. How dare she do this to him?

~

The bear's den was warm and comfortable even on the chilly morning. The sun was just starting to sneak up the mountain's sides when Arianna awoke. For a second, she felt disoriented but then she remembered the events of the day before. The elf, was he still on their trail? He should be following the goats if he had reached this side of the canyon. Just in case he was not, they needed to hurry and put more distance between themselves and the scout.

The sprites and the bear woke up when she moved and greeted her with affection. Introductions were made, and they discovered that their kind hostess's name was Ursa. The bear was communicating through Blossom since Arianna would have to lower her shields just a little to speak to the large female directly. The fairy had explained to the curious beast that a man was hunting them, and if the princess talked to Ursa directly, he would find them. The female understood about hunters and not giving them an advantage and was pleased to have the sprite relay messages instead.

Now that its jaw was healed the large carnivore was hungry and wanted to go down to the river to catch some salmon. It suggested that the girl and the fairies come along. They could wash, and Arianna could replenish her water. Not wanting to offend their new friend, the princess agreed. Soon Ursa was standing on top of the rapids waiting for the lovely sleek fish to come flying through the air on their way upriver. It did not take her long to catch one, and the large fish was devoured even faster. There had been no pain in her jaw whatsoever for the first time in many days, and that made her happy.

The bear noticed the princess watching it eat with wistful looks. So the little human was hungry! That could be easily taken care off. The grateful female pitched the next fish she caught on the river bank in front of the surprised girl. "For me?" came the thought and the large carnivore nodded its head. "Thank you!" the young woman called to her new friend before taking her knife out and expertly dissecting the salmon. Soon Arianna was hungrily devouring pieces of the delicious fish.

The girl was eating the welcome meal raw. There was no way she would start a fire. It could be seen for too great a distance and would lead the hunter back on their trail. She could only hope that her slip up a moment ago had gone unnoticed. She had been startled by the bear's kindness and had mindspoken without thinking. If she wanted to avoid capture, she would have to be more careful from now on.

After several more fish, the bear was sated. Arianna gently stroked its head and asked Blossom to tell it thank you and good-bye for her. Blossom conveyed this and then turned back to the girl excitedly. "Ursa wants to take us further away from the hunter, wants to help us! She wants us to ride her!" she relayed happily. The princess impulsively threw her arms around the female's thick neck and hugged her. Tears of gratitude were shimmering in her lovely sea-green eyes.

It did not take long for them to be on the way. The girl was sitting bent forward on the bear's neck with her arms over its shoulders, hanging onto the thick fur. The saddle bags were tied over her shoulder. Arianna was aware that the lower a silhouette she represented, the harder to spot she would be, and the faster the bear could move. The two sprites were once again curled up tight against her to keep warm. Their big new friend set off in a comfortable run. This kind of pace the female could keep up for hours.

As they were speeding along, the princess grew aware of a niggling at her consciousness. She had this feeling that something bad was coming their way. Had the elf sensed her? Was he getting close? She would have to lower her shields just a little to reach out and check, and that was not really a chance she was willing to take at this point. That one slip up had been bad enough.

As the day wore on, the bear began to tire, and they had to stop more and more frequently for it to rest. In the late afternoon, they decided to take a longer break so that Ursa could fish. Both the princess and the big carnivore were soon happily devouring the succulent flesh.

While eating, the girl took a moment to look around and to drink in the splendor of the landscape about them. The snow covered mountains were magnificent, and Arianna loved the grand vista of the foothills which gave way to the vibrant green of the forests and then the plains beyond to the east.

The princess suddenly realized that the feel of this land was so much different than that of Lothrien. Larandar felt so much cleaner, purer, and full of hominess. She had only been in a small part of King Vargos's realm and then close to that grove. Was the entire kingdom like that? Sticky, oppressive, with an undertone of cruelty and maybe even downright evil?

What could possibly make it feel that way? Could it be the deities which resided there? Was that the reason the Eagles called it the 'Cursed Kingdom'? Arianna was not sure, but that altar had been ancient and, according to Kyrill, had belonged to the Elder Gods.

The girl knew that long ago, all the lands had been ruled by these Gods. They had been cruel and bloodthirsty and loved human sacrifice. The more deaths, the better they liked it. These deities treated their worshippers with disdain and sowed strife and war wherever they went. Hatred, misery, and cruelty had been what they had fed off.

Finally, the humans had enough. As far as the princess knew, in most of the kingdoms, the Elder Gods had been abandoned. Their worshippers had turned to kinder and more caring gods. Could it be that Lothrien was their last stronghold?

The nagging feeling had gotten even stronger in the last few minutes, and Arianna finally decided that she needed to check, regardless of the risk. Ever so carefully she opened a tiny hole in her shields and sent her consciousness searching behind them. When the princess found the source of her unrest, she let out a loud gasp and quickly withdrew. What she had seen terrified her.

The young woman instantly relayed to her friends a brief description of what was following behind them. They immediately set out. With her appetite sated and energy refilled, Ursa was able to pick up the pace once more.

~

Now that she was shielded he could no longer find that witch; she was just simply gone. The elf had felt her briefly a couple of times the previous day but had been too far away to get a good idea of her location. She had been careless again, later that same evening, but he still had not been close enough. In the morning, however, the scout had felt her again. She had lowered her shields just a little and only for a moment. For him, however, that was enough. He homed in on her location and altered his course heading straight to the northwest.

Not long after that, Tristan crossed the border into Larandar. He and the horse came to a dead stop. Something was opposing them, would not let them take another step on their land. An unseen standoff seemed to take place, and the elf and his stallion started to shiver and then shake convulsively. Their spasms subsided when a dark, furiously roiling cloud boiled out of the pair and back into Lothrien. Now they were allowed to continue.

As much of his essence was repelled back across the border, Nor'dur's grip on the elf slipped for a second. The hunter felt like he was waking up out of a horrible nightmare for just one brief moment. His eyes began to clear and his mind to shake off its imprisonment but enough of the entity remained to get the elf and his mount quickly back under control. On they raced, drawn to the spot where they had marked the princess's last known location.

Neither Tristan nor his horse had eaten or slept since the night in the grove. It was the second day now that they were going without stopping. Both elf and stallion were starting to look ghastly, but they were not aware enough of themselves to care about of their condition. Their sole focus was on reaching the witch and getting their revenge for the injury which had been inflicted on them.

The possessed hunter was heading in the direction where he had last felt the girl early that morning. She was a long way away in the Galandrien Mountains. How that sorceress had gotten so far and so fast was beyond him. Were the other gods involved? They certainly had that kind of magic, but why would they care about this one insignificant human? If not the gods, what power was on her side aiding her to stay out of his hands? Whatever it was, it would not help her for much longer. He was coming for the witch, and he would get her. That wicked child's days were numbered.

With Nor'dur sensing the direction they needed to travel, the stallion and hunter were guided which way to go, what paths to take. All day, they rode through the foothills, covering a distance that would usually take days. All life avoided them, one look at the pair was enough for even the bravest of heart. The animals could feel them coming like a wave of darkness rolling over the land and fled before them.

By late afternoon, the things which once had been Tristan, a handsome elven prince, and his valiant horse, reached the foot of the mountain. The stallion was starting to look more skeletal with each passing league. It seemed that even the dark force driving and feeding him energy could not sustain him much longer. The further from Lothrien they traveled, the more flashes of blue showed in the poor animal's eyes. The hunter spotted a steep path which he felt would get him to his prey the fastest. That trail was too much for most horses, but the elf brutally drove the frothing stallion up the incline.

~

When darkness started to descend, it was time to look for a place to sleep. Ursa had been this way several times before and remembered a cave just a little bit out of their way. The small group was all of one mind, being warm and safe during the dark and cold hours was well worth a few extra minutes.

They soon reached the shelter and finding no one within, quickly prepared it for the night. Arianna piled up branches and heaped what little leaf litter she could find on top of them. She then pulled the entire mass into the cavern. They were all pretty exhausted and after sharing a couple of the biscuits with the bear, princess, sprites, and large beast were soon curled up comfortably on their makeshift bed.

They had been in a great hurry earlier and the sprites, as well as the bear, had only received a brief description of what the princess had seen. Now, the ever curious Blossom wanted to know more. In halting sentences, the princess described the horror which was following them in more detail. The elf hunter had been a force to reckon with all on his own, but he was even more so now since he had been possessed by such evil.

Arianna told the others that she suspected that the entity controlling the scout was one of the terrible Elder Gods. The tracker and his horse were being pushed along mercilessly. The effects this evil presence along with the unrelenting exertion were having on the bodies of both man and beast were frightening. From what she had seen, the two more resembled creatures straight out of a nightmare than the magnificent beings they had once been.

Gasps greeted the princess's description of the unlucky pair. They all knew that the Elder Gods were completely without compassion, without love, without kindness. The girl could not help but feel deep sadness for the elf and his horse. She had tried to destroy the evil in the grove to prevent others from being harmed. The princess had never expected this kind of repercussion when she vanquished the spirits.

Whatever had possessed the pair had fled or hidden so well that even her extended senses had not been able to detect it. For the wraiths themselves, it had been a welcome release. Their enslavement was finally over, and they could now rest in peace. Clearing the copse had been something which needed to be done. After all, how could she have left that trap intact to ensnare the next innocent traveler passing that way?

Blossom, as usual, had several questions. Once her curiosity was satisfied, the sprites bid the princess goodnight and were soon sound asleep. It was not so easy for Arianna. She felt responsible for the horrible fate of Tristan and his once excellent horse. Was there anything she could do to save them? Would her Goddess be able to help?

~

Reinforcing her shields, the girl reached out to the Lady. To her surprise, her spirit was pulled into an airy temple where she encountered more than just Brigit. The Lady politely introduced her to the three deities governing this domain. The God An'dar, his wife La'ra, and their daughter Ri'elle greeted her graciously but very quickly let her know that they were not pleased about the evil she had drawn into their kingdom. They were gentle gods who lovingly tended these lands. Having part of the consciousness of Nor'dur, the malevolent Elder God, trespass on their grounds greatly disturbed them.

The Gods of Larandar wanted to know all the details of what had happened and began asking Arianna a multitude of questions. The princess answered as best as she could. These deities were calm and respectful even in their displeasure. When the gods had finally satisfied their curiosity, they relented.

Feeling that this might be her only chance, the princess bravely spoke up and begged the divinities to save the elf and his horse. She explained to the Lady and her three companions how bad she felt about the fate which had befallen the scout and his stallion. The girl stressed that she had meant to prevent harm not cause it. Leaving the wraiths in the grove had just not felt like a viable option.

The gods were pleased with her request as well as the courageous way the young woman took responsibility for her actions. They would try to protect her and do what they could for the unlucky pair. Recounting that terrible night had greatly upset the gentle princess. After exchanging a silent glance with Brigit, La'ra began to hum softly. The slow and soothing melody enfolded the girl, and her body started to relax. Soon Arianna drifted off into peaceful sleep, but she was too exhausted to dream.

~

Up and up they climbed and the evil driving the scout could feel the place where it had last sensed that witch get closer and closer. Soon it would have her! The girl had to be on foot now and could not have gotten that much further in this steep mountain terrain. They were almost there. It was late in the night when the shaking horse and its relentless rider reached the bear's den. Not having slept for many hours the elf had come to the point of exhaustion.

Nor'dur could feel that they were close to the last location where he had sensed the witch and that she had stayed in this cave the night before. The God, who had been driving man and beast so brutally, realized that the horse could not go on and that Tristan was almost done for as well. This alarmed Nor'dur. Without a body to inhabit, he would be in trouble. He would not be able to remain in Larandar nor get his revenge. To make things worse, his anchor in Lothrien was gone. The part of him which had been forced to return there was hopelessly adrift.

In front of the cave, the elf lost consciousness and tumbled off his steed. For a moment, he lay in the grass unmoving. Then, something started pulling him up. The senseless scout moved like a wooden marionette which was being controlled by an inept puppet master. His shambling, bizarre walk was directed into the cave with some effort. There, he was manipulated over to the bear's bed where he was allowed to collapse. The horse was left standing; it had served its purpose. Nor'dur had no further use for the pitiful creature.

All the God's power was withdrawn from the poor beast and transferred into the hunter. The abused animal was left shaking life a leaf in the wind, its legs barely able to support it. Its head was hanging, and flanks heaving. It no longer even had the energy to graze, most of its life-force was spent. It's once lustrous white coat was now dull and dirty, its chest caked with the bloody froth issuing from its nostrils. The once proud stallion looked more like a skeleton than a horse. His eyes were lifeless and his great heart beating weakly with the last of its strength.

~

The Gods of Larandar had been very upset about the invasion of this ancient evil into their cherished land. They had not been able to completely stop the intrusion but had managed to send a large part of the malevolent spirit inhabiting man and steed back to Lothrien. The wicked God, however, had come well prepared and had suffused the pair so thoroughly with his essence that enough had remained to keep them fully under his control.

The deities had been watching and hoping for a chance to deal with the rest of the malevolent spirit. This kind of an intrusion into their territory could not be tolerated, and if it continued, something would have to be done. To be successful against this powerful entity, they would have to wait for just the right moment. And, they would need some support.

The princess's deeds must have seriously enraged the Elder God to provoke such wrath. The amount of energy he had used to create that canyon had been enormous. What was it about this girl that had the ancient Deity so up in arms? Even before she had killed his wraiths, Nor'dur had taken an interest in her and sent the oppressive heat to slow and trap her. The gorge had been intended to stop her and drive her into the hunter's arms. All this had drained the god of a massive amount of magic.

The reckless use of so much power had serious consequences. The more of his reserves Nor'dur used, the weaker he got and the less he became but for now he was still too strong for the Gods of Larandar. This had kept the Deities from interfering so far. They were waiting and hoping for a chance to drive this ancient evil from the lands once and for all.

Watching the cruel God callously abandon the pitiful steed, they decided that no living being deserved to be treated like that. A gentle wind began blowing over the clearing and the unfortunate creature. A soft light began to infuse it. Invisible hands commenced loosening the straps holding the saddle on the dying stallion's sore back. Slowly the offending item sailed into the grass, the blanket followed and, lastly, the bridle joined the small pile. Strength started to infuse the stallion from the ground up, and he took a shivering step.

Setting one shaking foot in front of the other, he followed the soft, beautiful voice coaxing him along. Ever so slowly he was coming back from the brink of death. At a clear stream, he took a small drink and some life returned to his eyes. Weakly, at first, he began to graze on the lush green grass growing along the riverbanks. With each mouthful, strength started to return to his body and the tremors wracking his wasted frame slowly subsided.

~ ~ ~

Chapter Thirty Two

A Desperate Flight

The first light of dawn spread its fingers across the dark mountains but at the cave, nothing moved. The God was impatient to get going, but he could not raise the elf. It was almost mid-morning when Tristan finally awoke. For a moment, the elf he had once been, emerged. He looked around himself in confusion. Where was he? What was he doing here? Where was his horse? The stallion had been his best and often only friend for many lonely years. What was happening to them? Before he could even try to remember the last days, his eyes glazed over, and Nor'dur's control was once again complete.

Stiffly the elf arose from the bear's comfortable bed and walked to the entrance. The horse was gone but who cared? Without a second glance at the saddle or replenishing the food in his pockets from the abandoned bags, the hunter was on the way. Just as brutally as the possessed Tristan had driven the stallion up the steep mountain paths the day before, the merciless god now pushed the scout. The witch might be shielded, but he could feel that he was getting closer and that the direction was right. Soon she would be his and he could not wait to watch the light leave her eyes. He would absorb all that delicious power. Just imagining this caused Tristan to drool.

~

Further to the north on the same mountain, Arianna awoke with a shiver. Quickly she roused the rest of her companions, her urgency infecting the others. The evil was closer, and they needed to flee. Somehow, they had to stay ahead of it as much as they could. Heading further up the peak, they were soon above the snow line. Knee deep snow covered the trail. This hindered their progress but still Ursa raced for the pass, a narrow gap between steep bluffs. Several times they had to duck falling rocks and cascading snow as they made their way between towering cliffs. The friends breathed a sigh of relief when they finally shot through the far end of this treacherous passage.

The pass had shortened their travel time towards the next mountain by at least a day. The friends could see it loom in all its magnificence in the distance. They would still have to head down and across several valleys and ridges to reach it, but they were much closer than before. Whenever they were heading downhill and towards the next range, the tired bear was picking up more speed.

The princess and sprites were holding onto Ursa's back for dear life. The girl was beginning to grow very weary, and her hands were cramping. The stress of their desperate flight was starting to affect her more all the time and was draining her. The princess was feeling anxious and scared. She could only hope that Kyrill's warriors would find them in time.

When Arianna sensed the distance to the hunter increase, she felt a bit better. She was aware that her life was at stake and did not allow her vigilance to relax. If there were no

392

options left, she would order the others to go on without her, and she would face the evil pursuing them alone.

The young woman knew that she was strong. Her goddess, as well as the gentle gods of this land, were behind her. But what could she do against such a powerful creature? Not even the three gods together had been able to stop the spirit of Nor'dur, and she was just one human. How could she possibly have a chance against one such as him? The evil she had felt when she touched the elf and his horse had filled her with terror. Never in her life had she met or felt anything like it.

She had realized at that moment that King Vargos was no longer in charge of his man. Taking her back to the king had been the goal of the scout but was not the intention of the possessed hunter. That one was out for revenge. The Elder God was in control and from what she had read about those gods, the only thing which would satisfy this horrible being was her death. The cruel deity might not stop there and go after her friends as well if they were close. If all were lost, she would have to make sure that they were far enough away and well hidden.

As they were traversing yet another wooded valley, Ursa came to a stop. A brief conversation with Blossom ensued. The sprite finally turned to the princess. "Our friend can go no further. She is exhausted. We have reached the territory of another bear who might be willing to help us. Ursa knows this one, it is a large male she has had contact with before. She will call the bear for us and tell him of our need but she believes that you will most likely have to talk to him yourself if you wish to gain his cooperation," the fairy conveyed.

Arianna's heart sank. They were just getting away from the menace following them. Speaking to the bear would give away their location once again. This was not to her liking but if it was the only way to gain the male's cooperation, then it would have to be done. She would use the opportunity to check on the hunter behind them.

Their helpful companion let out a loud roar. It was soon answered from the distance. The large male came ambling out of the woods. He was not happy to see them and was still a bit irritable from having been so rudely awoken by the earthquake. He would have attacked had it not been for Ursa. She stood her ground and was ready to defend the princess and the sprites against the much larger beast.

To the friends' relief, he finally backed down. Arianna carefully lowered her shields just a little and touched both bears' minds. First, she sent love and respect to the female and a thank you for all her assistance; then the girl locked eyes with the male. She quickly gleaned that his name was Finn and that he had amorous intents on Ursa. He was willing to do what he must to achieve them even if that meant aiding a human.

After a brief explanation of their dire situation, the bear consented to carry them. Arianna quickly sent her mind flying back the way they had come. There! The hunter was on foot now but racing along even faster than the league eating gait of his people should have ever allowed him to go. He was still catching up and would reach the pass soon! The skin had drawn in on Tristan's face, and he looked more like death than the beautiful, healthy elf he had once been. The force which was driving him on so cruelly was cannibalizing his body, burning him up from the inside. Her heart went out to him in pity. No one deserved such a fate. "Please help him," she sent a silent plea to the Gods.

The bear was ready and after hugging Ursa one last time, the princess tried to climb onto the male's massive back. Getting up on this big animal was different from mounting a horse, and the girl was exhausted. The female ended up having to give her a gentle push up to finally get her securely seated. Rosebud and Blossom were curled up beside her and off they raced once more. Only one valley was left between them and the next peak, and soon they were once again working their way up to the next ridge. Up and up they went until the powerful beast finally needed a break.

Arianna asked Blossom to relay how grateful she was and how much she admired Finn's strength and stamina. The bear seemed pleased and came over and rubbed his large head against the girl's shoulder. She began to gently rub the fur between his ears, and the fierce carnivore closed his eyes in pure pleasure. In just a few minutes, the energetic male was rested enough and prepared to go on. His breathing and heart rate had slowed, and he was ready to start climbing once more. This time, the princess had him sidle up to a rock which made it much easier for her to get on his back.

When they finally reached the top of the ridge, they found themselves on a game trail leading down into a valley and then up the adjacent mountain and north. They had been following this rough path for a while when they came to a river blocking their way. The early spring snowmelt above had filled the streambed with a torrent of wild, churning water and in places, the stream had flooded over its banks. The current was such that large rocks were being carried along. Arianna realized quickly that there was no way for them to wade across. They would have to continue close to the swollen stream but at a safe distance in the hope that further uphill they might find a spot where they could safely get to the other side.

Up and up the bear climbed, always in sight of that violently roiling water. Finally, they reached a place where the river was being forced between two massive rocks. A sharp drop on one side created a cascading fall of water into a rocky pool far below. The powerful male decided he could jump the gap between the stones, even with passengers on his back. Taking a large leap, he solidly landed on the far rock. Everything was perfect until the boulder suddenly tilted beneath them. Only Finn's instincts and strength saved them. The big guy pushed off and just reached safe ground as the stone gave way and a small avalanche of rock and debris began sliding down the side of the mountain and into the pond below.

The spot where they had just been was gone. The swollen stream was rapidly taking up the now available space. Arianna hugged the bear and kept thanking him; he had saved all their lives. She realized that he had not gotten away unscathed but was trying to hide it. The brave beast was moving much slower and more deliberate now. It did not take the princess long to figure out that he had been hurt badly. Still, on and on Finn moved determinedly until they finally reached a high plateau. The vista from up here was breathtaking. The friends were so stressed and weary at this point that none of them even noticed.

They were crossing the plateau when all of a sudden the biggest raptor Arianna had ever seen dove down upon them. The aggressive bird's giant size even spooked the large bear. Up he raised on his rear legs and off tumbled the princess along with the sprites. No matter how frightening the enemy, their valiant protector was not going to give ground without a ferocious attempt at running off this new danger.

Suddenly, the eagle had the head of a man. That had been almost too much for the brave beast, but the shapeshifter's soothing voice and gestures calmed it. "Princess Arianna, I presume?" the birdman said with a smile once the protective bear had been pacified. "Yes, and who might you be?" the girl inquired politely. "Your pardon, your highness! I am Halen, sent by Prince Kyrill to retrieve you. I will carry you away from here now," came the cheery response. Arianna almost collapsed with relief. She might yet get away from the horror which was now so close behind them. Wait! Carry her? "How can you carry me?" she asked the young warrior suspiciously.

"With ease, my lady, in these two arms. Can we go now?" Halen replied. He had changed to mostly human form except for his striking wings. "Please, may I heal the bear before we go? He was injured saving our lives. And what about that thing following us? Will it not just continue to come after me until it finds me one day?" the princess asked with concern. She watched a thoughtful expression cross the warrior's face before it lit up once more. "I think I have a solution, but please go ahead and take care of the bear," came the smiling reply.

Some instinct told Arianna that whatever that young man had planned, she would not like it. But first, she needed to take care of Finn's injury. Stepping in front of the large beast, she had Blossom tell him what she wanted to do. When the obviously hurting male agreed, she gently took his head in her hands and closed her eyes. Lowering her shields just enough to be able to scan the big body, the princess soon found the source of his pain. How this brave soul had sprinted at all was beyond her! Reaching out, she began to weave healing all around the severely pulled tendons, and when it was done, she opened her eyes.

The bear's relief was plainly visible to them all. In gratitude, he gently licked her face. Arianna hugged his great neck and thanked him for all he had done. She told him it was time for him to return to Ursa but to beware of the thing. At first, the large male was very sure of his power. He felt

397

that he could deal with the puny enemy with one swipe of his deadly claws. Arianna sent a picture of what he would be facing to his mind and what it had done to the man and his horse. She described its present location and told him that it was heading straight towards them.

Finn was taken aback and wisely agreed that it might be better to go around. He headed off in a more westerly direction. Mindspeaking to the bear had given away their location, but the girl felt her courageous friend more than deserved this courtesy.

The princess turned back to Halen and, gathering the sprites to her, looked him square in the face. "Ok, I am ready," she told him bravely. She had no idea what he was going to do. Gently, the young warrior picked her up and cradled her in his arms. When she was about to reach up and wrap her arms around his neck for a better hold, he stopped her with a shake of his head.

Carrying her such, he moved towards the cliff. The girl assumed that they would take off from there. Why then was he just standing there looking down into the depth? They were very high up and just glancing down at the ground far below made her head spin.

Suddenly, Halen moved. Before she could grab onto him, he had thrown her far out over the side. An involuntary scream tore from the girl's throat as she fell into nothingness. Kyrill's own man had betrayed her! Had the evil somehow gotten to him as well? Or was the man whom she loved so dearly behind it all? Had he decided that to protect his people he needed to sacrifice her?

Here she had thought she was safe! Instead, she was plunging to her death! The dream she had not so long ago came back in full force as did the memory of the day her mother had died. Terror overwhelmed her as she was plummeting towards the rocks far below.

~

The being which once had been Tristan the Elf was caught off guard and the full force of the princess's scream slammed into his wide-open searching mind. The energy was so intense it knocked him off his feet. The terror and despair the princess was feeling washed through him like an enormous tidal wave and swept away some of the hold Nor'dur had on the man.

Then, all at once, his contact with the girl came to an abrupt stop. The sudden silence was deafening and left the scout stunned. The Elder God used this moment to reassert his control. Within seconds, the tracker was on his feet racing for the place his possessor had last felt the reviled witch.

If the hunter had been pushed cruelly before, it had been nothing compared to the way he was being driven towards the plateau now. He fairly flew up the mountain. Just as the sun was setting, he raced to the ledge and looked down.

There, far down below, was the indistinct outline of a shattered body and blood. A lot of blood! He could just barely make it out in the gathering darkness. The princess must have fallen to her death! The shock was enough to allow Tristan to surface. Realizing his weakness, the elf threw himself back from the edge just in time before his legs gave way. He tumbled into deep unconsciousness.

~

The Elder God was stunned. The witch was dead! No! How could this be? Revenge should have been his! Nor'dur howled his fury at the sight. He had risked all for this vengeance and lost! She had escaped him into death. Her soul was beyond his grasps as was all that incredible power. He had wanted her magic, coveted it. It would have bolstered his own failing reserves for many a year. That silly girl had not even known how strong she really was!

Nor'dur was beyond himself with rage and never even took notice when his vessel collapsed. He was now standing there exposed and for all to see. The God was cursing the day that woman had set foot on his land. His eyes were blazing red with the intensity of his ire.

That the wind suddenly stilled and the stars faded also escaped him in the midst of this fury. He was greatly surprised, therefore, by the sound of a voice. The coldness of tone immediately alarmed him but in his arrogance, he was sure that he would prevail. He was not afraid, he was Nor'dur, the powerful, and since he had put those three incompetent gods in their place coming in, he was sure he could deal with them now.

As his wrath began to subside, his eyes cleared, and he looked at the three feeble little gods with disdain. They wanted to challenge him? Him, the great Nor'dur, last of the Elder Gods, who had survived when all others perished? He threw back his head and roared with laughter. Giving himself over to his amusement made him miss the arrival of more and more of his enemies' friends.

When he finally contained his hilarity and returned his attention to his adversaries, he was in for a shock. Fear suddenly crept into his cold, dead heart. He was surrounded, and not just by the three gods of Larandar but by many other deities from all over the lands.

Putting on a brave front, the Ancient One faced them. "What do you want? The elf? You can have him, or what's left of the thing!" he said with cold, cruel glee. His laughter died in his throat when he noticed Brigit among the assembled gods. The radiant Goddess stepped forward and gazed at him severely. "Nor'dur, we have tolerated your cruelness and bloodlust as long as you stayed in your own lands. You have violated our territory and therefore, put yourself in our hands. Never again will you torment one single living soul or terrorize your kingdom. We have held council and considered your crimes. Your malicious deeds have gone on for too long. We see no option but to condemn you to," here the Lady paused for a moment before continuing with great sadness. "To not be!"

Nor'dur howled with rage and fear at her words. To not be? They had decided his death! He watched as one after another of the gods nodded their agreement. They were about to unmake him! How dare they! As the assembled Gods began to chant, he could feel the first threads of his being unravel. At first, he cursed them, then he began to beg and ask them for mercy. He swore to reform his evil ways. His words fell on deaf ears. He had hurt and deceived them all at one time or another. None of them would believe any promises he made, and they had all had enough.

The last to fade was his howl of despair as his very essence bleed away into the winds. Among the gods, there was no elation. Coming to this decision had been very hard for them. They had seen no option, no course of action left they had not already tried over the years. Having to punish one of their own in this fashion did not sit well with any of the immortals, but Nor'dur had been pure evil. That they would have never been able to change. With great sadness and tears at the loss of this most ancient and powerful member of their assembly, one after another of the Deities departed until only Brigit and the Gods of Larandar remained.

~

"What about the elf, the hunter?" An'dar enquired of Brigit. The Goddess regarded him sadly, her eyes brimming with tears. She was a gentle soul, and her heart was full of love for all beings, even for one as cruel and wicked as Nor'dur had been. His unmaking had deeply upset her. "He has been prayed for, and his healing requested. He was a victim of Nor'dur just as much as that poor innocent horse. Ri'elle, do you care to heal him or should I?" came the soft answer.

Ri'elle had only been waiting for permission to save the dying scout. Her heart was full of compassion, and she could not stand to see anyone or anything hurt. Gently placing her hands on the elf's temples, she infused him with strength. His heartbeat was weak and his skin shrunk in around his very bones. Almost all that he had once been had been burned away. The amount of damage he had sustained was almost beyond repair. Ri'elle was not sure she would be able to save him, but she kept trying.

Tears started to roll down the young goddess face for she could still sense the exceptional person he had once been. She had imbued him with all the life-force she could when she felt a gentle hand on her shoulder and power infused her. Ri'elle allowed it flow through her and poured it all into the elf. He would live, but it would take a long time for him to get back to what he had once been.

Tristan was still too weak to be left on his own. After a brief consultation, it was decided that they would have to take him along. He would need to be nourished before reuniting him with his horse and sending him on his way. An'dar gently picked up the hunter and together the merciful gods took him down off the mountain and to the border of their lands. His horse and supplies were waiting there already and after caring for him throughout the night, the elf was strong enough to be sent on his way back into the kingdom from where he once came.

~~~

Chapter Thirty Three

A Dream Comes True

*A*s she was falling, exhaustion and panic overwhelmed Arianna and her shields crumbled completely. Despair and utter terror filled her heart. After the last few days, she had nothing left. Her mind felt totally blank. Tears were rolling down her chalk-white face. Her two fairy friends were desperately pulling on her trying to slow her fall. All thoughts of saving herself were gone, and her mindless scream trailed behind her as she was plummeting towards the rocks below. To have hope for a moment and then have it so cruelly crushed had taken the last of the princess's resolve and wiped out the last of her strength.

Suddenly, powerful arms embraced her. The sprites were pushed up against her chest. A strong shield slammed around them and for the very first time in her life, Arianna fainted.

~

When the princess came to, they were high on a mountain top. A heated argument was taking place between Halen and Blossom. The tiny fairy was so angry that her face was bright red. "She is coming awake!" Rosebud tried to tell them, but the pair was too busy yelling at each other to pay attention to anything else. "Stop, please!" the princess begged, but the two still did not take notice. Arianna repeated her request louder and was finally heard. Sheepishly, the fighting duo turned towards her.

"He threw you off that cliff!" Blossom said full of indignation pointing at Halen. "I had to! How else was that thing going to think that you are dead? I am going to leave your clothes and some blood at the bottom of that drop-off. That will make it appear like you were killed by the impact. If I had warned you, it would not have worked!" the young warrior explained desperately.

"Now please, would you change clothes so I can go back and take care of things before the elf gets there?" he requested handing her a bundle of clean, warm clothes. "And Lady, please, raise your shields as tight as you can. For this to work you need to maintain them no matter what. Under no circumstances are you to lower them, do you understand?" he asked her intently.

The princess immediately brought up her shields and reinforced them as much as she could. She was not up to full power, but this was easy for her and would most certainly do. Giving the young man an affirmative nod, she let him know that it was done and that he could withdraw his shields. Once he turned his back, Arianna loosened the reins she had used as a belt. It was cold up here, and the horse blanket served as a tent as she took off her boots and pants.

The girl gratefully slid into the new trousers. The exchange of shirts was a little trickier. Pulling the blankets up over her head, she managed this as well while staying covered and somewhat protected from the freezing wind. How nice it was to have clean things! Also, these clothes were so much warmer than what she had been wearing. Halen even handed her a fur jacket, and she gladly traded this for the now filthy blankets. If only she had some way to wash her face and comb her hair!

"Wait here, please, Princess! I will return shortly," the young man told her after making her comfortable amongst the rocks. Spreading his magnificent wings, he was gone. Arianna watched his flight with fascination and was amazed at his speed as he streaked away to the far mountain. As soon as he was out of sight, the girl worked on making herself as presentable as possible. Blossom and Rosebud were happy to assist. They combed out her long hair with their hands and, with some water and a rag, helped Arianna clean off the worst of the dirt on her face and hands.

Her thoughts wandered to the prince. Not that he was ever too far from her mind as it was. Until now they had only met in her dreams. She wondered if the real life Kyrill was different from the one she had grown to know and love over the years. The princess could not wait to meet him in person and hoped that Halen would return soon to take her to him. Slowly her body and mind began to calm. She was still a bit shaky after the ordeal of the chase and then that horrible fall.

Terror had completely overwhelmed her, and that was something that bothered her badly. Deep down she felt she should have been able to handle the situation a lot better. Absolute panic had paralyzed her. Why had she reacted that way? Examining her own feelings further, the princess realized that her mother's death and the dreams of falling had fed this fear substantially. She had lost her nerve, and that could have killed her. She decided right then and there that she would get over that and soon! Letting fright overcome her was weakness and not acceptable.

Becoming conscious that she was mentally beating herself up, the young woman brought this train of thoughts to an abrupt stop. Nothing was to be gained from that kind of self-condemnation! She needed to go back to talking to herself like she would her best friend. Everything happened for a reason and provided an opportunity for growth. It was up to her to make the best of any situation no matter how unpleasant or scary.

Even if she was a powerful sorceress, it was just plain unreasonable to expect perfection from herself. She was human after all and everybody made mistakes. It was time to forgive herself for behavior she would have only had deep compassion for in others. Now that she was aware of the root of her fear, she could examine it further and find the best way to handle it. Tension began to leave her body. The adrenaline which had continued to pump through her system like crazy was tapering off. She was beginning to relax and starting to get very tired. When this was all over, all she wanted to do was sleep for a week!

Blossom was still completely outraged with the young shapeshifter. Arianna continued trying to calm her. After she had gently explained to the sprite yet once again why the birdman had thrown her over the side without warning, the usually quiet Rosebud piped in. "The monster has to think she is dead, my Princess. He did what needed to be done! Please, let it go!" she told the flustered Blossom. The tiny fairy stared at her best friend in disbelief, then shaking her head and throwing up her hands, she gave in.

The princess was starting to fall asleep when Halen returned. The sun was just nearing the horizon. "See that mountain over there, Princess? That is where the prince is waiting. Come, I will take you to him now," the young warrior explained. He wrapped her in a fur blanket and soon

Arianna was comfortably cradled against him. This time, however, with her arms securely locked around his neck. At the Eagle's request, the two fairies were under the covers and nestled up against the girl. This would allow them to stay warm.

Once they were in the air, Arianna glanced around herself eagerly. They were very high up and flying due north. Below them, she saw the beautiful mountains lit up with the reds of the sunset, to their right the already shadowy forest and the vast rolling plains which extended all the way to the Salten Sea. To the left were more mountains and beyond them the plains and forests of Larandar. Their flight was fast enough to bring tears to her eyes, but still, she watched. She saw the shadows lengthen and darkness race across the land until the sun finally sunk below the horizon and night set in.

How would they ever find Kyrill now? Could Halen see in the dark? The books had not mentioned such a thing. She was just about to ask when a beacon flared up on the mountain. The young warrior streaked towards it with renewed speed. Excitement was bubbling up inside her as the far off peak came closer and closer. Would they get along in real life? Did he really look like he did in her dreams? She knew him so well but had never even seen his home. Would she finally be allowed to go there and what would it be like? Could she maybe go get her horses? And what of the sprites? Would they be welcome at the Aerie?

They were almost there now, and Arianna was shaking. She did not remember ever feeling this anxious about meeting any of the young men she had been introduced to over the years. Her stomach seemed to be doing flip flops, and she felt close to throwing up with excitement. The fire was huge, and she could now make out several people waiting for them. Finally, they came in for a landing. Halen set her down gently. The princess released the death grip she had around his neck. She had never even noticed that she was holding on this tight! Squaring her shoulders, she turned to face the man she loved and who had been her best friend for so many years. Their eyes met and next thing she knew, she found herself in his arms.

So much for proper introductions! But who cared? This was Kyrill, her love, her confidante, her advisor, the man who had risked his own life to save hers. Throwing etiquette to the wind, she flung her arms around his neck, and they stood there for a moment, relishing the feel of each other.

Finally, they pulled apart a little and regarded each other solemnly. To Arianna, Kyrill was even more handsome at this instant than he had ever been in her dreams. The love which she now realized she had been holding back, burst forth. A happy smile spread across her face, her eyes lit up, and her entire being seemed to shine with the force of those emotions.

For Kyrill, watching her light up with the love she felt for him was a dream come true. How many years he had longed for this moment! To him, Arianna was more beautiful than anything in this world. The prince looked at this brave young woman with her hair in disarray and tears staining her cheeks and he thought how very lucky he was to have a mate such as her. Finally, after all those years of waiting, she was his!

~~~

Places And People

In this section you will find information on all of the 'Eleven Kingdoms' but some places and characters do not appear in this story. The appendix will be expanded further in the future.

A map showing seven of the Eleven Kingdoms has been included in this book to give you an idea where this adventure takes place.

THE ELEVEN KINGDOMS

The 'Eleven Kingdoms' are an alliance of eleven of the local monarchies. It started with the marriage of Prince Roderic of Maridanmar to Princess Anna of Re'adeen. Working together and helping each other made the realms a force to be reckoned with. Outside attacks quickly dwindled to the occasional hostile excursion.

Life in the Kingdoms was peaceful for many years until King Vargos ascended the throne of Lothrien after the 'accidental' death of his father. He quickly established himself as the de facto overlord. These unfortunate events took place almost seven years before our story begins.

For a while, life in the other monarchies went on as before. Vargos lost interest once he had established his dominance. It was a blessing for the rest of the realms that the tyrant was more concerned with his castle's servant maids and the pursuits of various pleasures than with the governing of the kingdoms. More and more the actual ruling of Lothrien fell to Odessa, the housekeeper of Darkmoor and mistress to the king.

When the self-appointed overlord decided to marry, the trouble really started. None of the other rulers wanted to hand their daughters over to this depraved man. King George of Daladion, father to Princess Sara, flat out refused Vargos's demand for his daughter's hand in marriage.

The tyrant, however, was ruthless once he set his mind on something or someone. To make the princess his wife, the cruel despot ended up destroying her kingdom and killing her family.

This vicious deed inspired enough fear in the region to firm up his rule. None dared to cross him after this blatant show of strength. The unhappy queen soon died a terrible death as did the two unfortunate princesses the tyrant married after her.

King Vargos was very sure of himself and always thought himself in full control. He was aware that Odessa was a practitioner of the Dark Arts and had her use her powers on his behalf many times over the years. The king was too blind to see that his evil mistress would do anything to become his wife. He never realized that the powerful sorceress had her black heart set on creating an empire. To achieve this, she needed to become queen. It is doubtful that the deluded ruler would have survived their wedding night.

Our tale starts when the overlord sets his sights on Arianna, Princess of Maridanmar. What he did not count on was that King Roderic would dare to cleverly defy him and that his intended bride was not what she seemed.

THE KINGDOM OF ANDALEA

Landover Castle: A simple, keep consisting of one large building with an attached tower. The castle is surrounded by the town of Dover.

The Royal Family

King Ralfus: The energetic ruler of Andalea. He is a very artistic person and would have rather been a painter than king.
Queen Anita: The talented queen of the realm. She is very interested in architecture and has been instrumental in reinforcing and beautifying the town and castle.

THE KINGDOM OF ASTORIA

This mountainous realm is located west of Re'adeen.

Harlstone Keep: A heavily fortified mountain fortress.

The Royal Family

King Ketas: A fair but at times quarrelsome king. He is known for quickly taking offense but also for settling down just as fast. He has a kind heart and good mind.
Queen Christina: A true lady with a beautiful spirit.
Princess Micha: Their only child. The young princess has inherited her father's hot-headed disposition but also his warm heart.

THE KINGDOM OF DALADION

The monarchy is located south of Wymara.

Sevenberg Keep: The home of the royal family of Daladion. The keep was completely destroyed by King Vargos's army.

The Royal Family

King Georg: The King of Daladion. He refused to marry his beloved daughter Sara to King Vargos. The once thriving kingdom south of Wymara was overrun by Lothrien's army in record time and before they could even mount their defenses. Thousands died, and the castle and every town in the monarchy were destroyed, the realm laid to waste. King Georg was publicly executed and his body treated with the utmost disrespect.

Princess Sara: The first unlucky princess to become wife to King Vargos. She died 13 months after their marriage took place.

THE KINGDOM OF DRAYDON

Draydon is a kingdom consisting of wide open plains in the east and old forests in the west. It is located west of Noridea.

Draeden Castle: A rather whimsical building reflecting the personalities of its builders.

The Royal Family

King Wern: The very technically preoccupied king of the Draydon. He leaves the running of the monarchy to his wife, Ilsa.

Queen Ilsa: The queen is in charge of the realm. She runs it very effectively and tries very hard to always have the good of all in mind when making decisions.

THE KINGDOM OF THE EAGLES

Eagle's Nest Aerie: The hidden refuge of the Eagles up in the high mountains of Re'adeen. The place is well-guarded and has only one way in and out for regular people and horses.

The Eagles: This is what the shapeshifters call themselves. It started when full humans began to fear and hunt them and in a way was a rejection of the human part of themselves. The Eagles wed for life and have one life-mate. The bond between the pair often comes into existence at birth.

The Royal Family

King Le'onard: The peace-loving king of the Eagles and Kyrill's father.

Queen Eliza: The Queen of the Eagles and Kyrill's mother.

Prince Berin: The oldest son and heir to the throne. A studious and very serious young man.

Prince Kyrill: The middle son of King Le'onard. A handsome young shapeshifter with warm brown eyes and the sharp aquiline profile characteristic among his people.   His dark brown hair nearly touches his shoulders.   He wears it parted on one side, and it often falls across one of his eyes giving him the look of a dashing adventurer.   He meets Arianna in her dreams on her 9th birthday, and they often visit with each other after that.   His people set up a hut away from the Aerie for the princess's spirit to travel to.

Prince Zander: The mercurial youngest prince who likes to explore new areas and try new things.

Other Important Persons

Cassandra: The seeress and wise woman of Eagle's Nest Aerie.   She is their most powerful sorceress.

Halen: The young Eagle warrior who finds and rescues the princess.   He comes up with a plan to stop Nor'dur from following Arianna.

THE KINGDOM OF IRIDOR

This realm is located south of Andalea.

Iredale Fortress: A beautiful castle surrounded by the town of Dale.

The Royal Family

Queen Irella: The ruler of Iridor.   The monarchy is passed down from mother to daughter instead of father to son.

King Jan: The queen's consort.

Prince Da'vid: The couple's oldest son.

Princess Marie: The oldest daughter and heir to the throne.

Princess Aleah: A lively young princess who is fascinated with dragons and drakes.

THE KINGDOM OF LARANDAR

Claradee Castle: A good sized abode consisting of a main building flanked by two towers.

The Royal Family

King Richard: A fair and just king and a good friend to King Roderic of Maridanmar. He was fostering Arianna's brother, Prince Dylan.

Queen Tara: Larandar's spritied queen and a Princess of Andalea.

Prince Albert: The only son of the king and queen. A very quiet young man. He and Dylan are usually inseparable.

Princess Clara: A sweet young princess and friend of Arianna's.

Princess Anika: The youngest of the royal children. She is as spirited as her mother and can be a bit of a handful.

THE KINGDOM OF LOTHRIEN

Darkmoor Castle: The dark and brooding home of the King of Lothrien. The fortress is located close to the Darkmoor, an extensive peat bog and a convenient repository of disaffected citizens.

The Royal Family

King Vargos: The vicious and cruel ruler of Lothrien. Rumors have it that he killed his own father to gain possession of the throne. He has made himself the de facto ruler of the 'Eleven Kingdoms' and has a standing army strong enough that none dare to oppose him.

King Randolf: The previous King of Lothrien and father to King Vargos. He was an honest and peace-loving ruler who was beloved by his people and highly respected by the other rulers. The monarch died under very mysterious circumstances in an unexplained accident. Many suspect that the son grew tired of waiting for the throne and took things into his own hands.

Other Important Persons

Aaron: The young soldier was promoted to lieutenant and put in charge of the camp after the attack by the bandits.

Captain Angus Tremaine: The captain of the column sent from Darkmoor Castle to fetch the princess. The man had red hair and a friendly, open face. Odessa used threats against his family to keep him compliant.

General Darius: The head of the army of Lothrien. The man is completely under Odessa's control. The general does whatever the witch commands him.

Esme: Sebastian's sullen wife. He first encountered her in Wymara in his capacity as an emissary. When the envoy met her, she was dainty and beautiful. The man fell so in love with Esme, he never saw how spoiled and bad-tempered she actually was.

Flanders: Sebastian's huntsman. The retainer also served as his lord's groom as well as his spy.

Gilbert: Sebastian's valet. The competent man also acted as his master's secretary, confidant, and advisor.

Gordro: The captain of the reinforcement column which is sent out to assist the princess's escorts.

Odessa: The housekeeper of Darkmor. She is a sorceress with great powers and practices the Dark Arts. The witch is beautiful and slender and has waist-long raven black hair and pitch black eyes.

Ora and Valentine: Sebastian's spoiled daughters who have unfortunately inherited some of the nasty personality traits of their parents.

Roland: The Lieutenant to Captain Gordro. He is half elf, half human and usually keeps to himself since half-breeds are even less accepted in Lothrien than full elves.

Sebastian: The envoy, a little toad-like man who was supposed to be responsible for the welfare of the princess. He is a pompous and rather short fellow. His facial features and build give him a distinct resemblance of a toad.

Teresa: The evil Odessa's second in command. She is almost as malicious as her mistress.

Squire Tom Buchanan: The owner of the chalet and grounds Flanders decides to 'acquire.'

Tristan: The Elven scout and hunter of humans. He works for King Vargos. Whoever he is sent after, he mercilessly tracks down and returns to his cruel king.

THE KINGDOM OF MARIDANMAR

Castle Maridar: A fortified castle and home to King Roderic and his family. It is a welcoming dwelling, bright and inviting, and filled with cheerful and pleasant people. The fortress is surrounded by the town of Maridee. Fertile fields and lush woods border the place on three sides and the Salten Sea on the fourth.

The Royal Family

King Roderic: A gentle and kind father and king. He had the wisdom to ensure his realm remained defensible even in peacetime. He is a handsome man with startling, light blue eyes and light brown hair. King Roderic is a fair man who usually extrudes a calm and quiet air of authority.

Queen Anna: The late wife of King Roderic and mother to Arianna, Dylan, Dionna, Mareena, and Genna. She was a beautiful woman, tall and slender, with waist long reddish blond hair and mischievous bright green eyes. Queen Anna died in a horseback accident shortly after King Vargos takes the throne. She was a Princess of Re'adeen before her marriage.

Arianna: The oldest Princess of Maridanmar and daughter of King Roderic and Queen Anna. She is 17 years old when this adventure begins and an independent young beauty with honey-gold hair and sea-green eyes. Her name means 'Silver Goddess' 'Star" or 'Pure of Heart.' Her parents had chosen this particular spelling due to it incorporating her mother's name. She was 11 when her mother died.

Dylan: The Prince of Maridanmar and second oldest child of King Roderic and Queen Anna. His name means 'Son of the Sea.' He is just 10 months younger than his sister and is being fostered by King Richard of Larandar when our tale begins.

Dionna: The third child of King Roderic and his Queen. Her name means 'From the Sacred Spring.' She is given a pendant with a beautiful green stone reflecting her sparkling green eyes by Arianna.

Mareena: The fourth child of the King and Queen. Her name means 'From the Sea.' Mareena received an arm ring from her oldest sibling. The ornament is worn on the upper arm, well out of sight, and set with the girl's favorite stone, a light blue aquamarine.

Genna: The youngest of the princesses. She had just turned seven at the time of the tragic accident of Queen Anna. Her name means 'White Wave.' To Genna, Arianna gives a pendant with her birthstone, a sky blue sapphire.

Other Important Persons

Anders: He is the weapons teacher, hunter, and 'Jack of all Trades' at Castle Maridar. He is also in charge of the armory. He was a patient but persistent teacher to Arianna. He trained her to survive on her own out in the woods and taught her a host of other things Anders felt she might possibly need some day. Usually, only princes are privileged to such teachings.

Baladazar: The court wizard who has been training Arianna since she was small. He gives the princess a completely tasteless sleeping powder, leggings, and a powerful ring before she leaves the castle.

Captain Caleb: The second in command at the castle.

Greta: The princess's long-time friend and maid. The young woman is given a pendant by Arianna inset with an amethyst. The princess felt that the purple color would look lovely with the young maid's blond hair and violet eyes. Greta gives a packet of Witchbane to the princess before she departs the castle.

Captain Gunther: The captain of the guards of Castle Maridar. He stashes some of the princess's brother's clothes, a knife, and a bow for her a little way over the border.

Ruth: The loyal nanny was called in to help with Arianna. She is well versed in magic and in dealing with talented children. Ruth is a patient and kind person. She took care of Queen Anna from birth on. The nanny manages to hide or explain away most of the infant princess's accidental magic.

THE KINGDOM OF NORIDEA

Norideen Castle: A small but lovely castle on the plains of Noridea.

The Royal Family

King Wolfle: The patient and very industrious ruler of Noridea. Under his reign, the kingdom has prospered.

Queen Isabelle: Larandar's beautiful Queen and a Princess of Iridor.

Princess Valentina: The only child of the king and queen. A very intelligent but somewhat indulged child. Valentina loves all things fey and is fascinated by the small drakes which like to roost in the eaves of the castle. She is a little like Arianna and enjoys exploring.

THE KINGDOM OF RE'ADEEN

Hidden Castle: A secluded mountain fortress which serves as a refuge for the royal family. Few know of its location, and any who serve there do so for extra pay and for life. Giving away the location to anyone is considered high treason and only the most trusted of soldiers ever get to see the keep.

Kendall Castle: The royal fortress of the Kings of Re'adeen. The castle is well designed and stays warm even in the coldest of winters.

The Royal Family

Queen Margaret: The lady is the ruling Queen of Re'adeen and daughter of King Rudemont and Queen Irena. She is the sister of Queen Anna of Maridanmar and aunt to Arianna and her siblings. Margret and her husband took over ruling the kingdom when her father decided to retire. She lost both her husband and young son in a terrible accident making her the sole ruler. The lady never wed again.

After the death of her sister, Margaret left her trusted steward and parents in charge of the kingdom and took over the raising of the children. She is given a beautiful emerald pendant by Arianna. The necklace had belonged to the girl's mother. The Queen is a beautiful woman, tall and slender like her sister, with auburn hair and cornflower blue eyes.

King Rudemont: The retired ruler of the Kingdom of Re'adeen and father to Margaret and Anna.   After Margaret was married, the king decided to give the running of the realm over to his daughter and her husband.   When Queen Margaret takes over the rearing of Anna's children, the king along with his wife and steward take charge of the monarchy.

Queen Irena: The Queen of Re'adeen and mother to Margaret and Anna.

Princess Selda: The sister of Queen Irena.   She prefers books over marriage and assists Queen Irena with the running of the castle.   She also helped with the raising and tutoring of the young princesses.

Other Important Persons

Olaf: An old family retainer who lives in Road's End.   He is in charge of guiding people to the Hidden Castle.

THE KINGDOM OF WYMARA

Castle Suzette: A bright and whimsical fortified castle and home of the royal family of Wymara.

The Royal Family

King Darian: The King of Wymara and the father of King Vargos's last bride, Princess Alyssa.

Queen Constanza: The Queen of Wymara and the mother of Princess Alyssa.   She falls into a deep depression after the death of her daughter.

Princess Alyssa: The third ill-fated queen to King Vargos. She died a horrible death within a year of her marriage to the tyrant.

THE DRAGON

Galata: The dragon lady Arianna steals a crystal from and tries to send after the bandit leader, Alandor. The dragon is a very large female and greedy even for its kind. She already has an immense hoard but is always looking for more.

THE FAIRIES

Ash, River, Roots, and Silver: The male sprites sent along to protect Blossom and her friends.

Blossom: Queen Liza's daughter. She becomes a companion and friend to Arianna.

Bork, Leaf, and Twig: The sprite brothers assigned to protect and follow Alandor to his keep. They become great friends with Galata the Dragon.

Queen Liza: The Queen of the Sprites. Princess Arianna enlists the fairy queen's help for her escape from the bandits. The queen and her people care for the area the game trail leads through and had been harmed by the brigands in the past.

Petal: The third female sprite who goes traveling with the princess.

Rosebud: A usually very reticent fairy and Blossom's best friend.

Sky: A male sprite who comes to warn the friends of the hunter following behind them.

THE GODS

An'dar: The God of Larandar. He rules together with his wife La'ra and daughter Ri'elle. An'dar is a God of peace, innocence, beauty, and rebirth.

Brigit: The Bright Lady. She is a powerful goddess and Arianna, and her mother both worship her.

Cer'ridwen: The Goddess of the Dark of the Moon and one of the few friends of the Elder God Nor'dur. The elf Tristan starts using her name once the evil god possesses him.

La'ra: The Goddess of the homestead, love, as well as fertility. She is the wife of An'dar and mother to Ri'elle.

Nor'dur: The only surviving Elder God, evil and cruel. He was angered beyond reason by the annihilation of his altar in the grove and the destruction of his enslaved wraiths. Nor'dur wants Arianna's power for himself and risks all to gain it.

Ri'elle: A gentle and sweet Goddess of healing.

THE HELPERS

Arabella: The beautiful mare ridden by Princess Arianna. The horse was assigned to her by Captain Angus when the witch refused to let the princess ride in the carriage.

Azariel: An unfortunate mare belonging to the bandits. The horse's luck turns when the princess becomes her rider.

Finn: The powerful male bear who agrees to carry Arianna so that she can stay ahead of the elf.

Ursa: A female bear who shelters and helps Arianna.

Glossary

Some of the terminology, as well as measurements, are different in the kingdoms, and I have therefore taken the liberty to convert these to make it easier to follow this engaging tale.

Kahve: A restorative similar to coffee.

League: A measure of length. One league equals about three miles. It was defined as the distance a person could walk in one hour.

Mindspeaking: To talk to another person or being by the use of just one's thoughts.

Sending: A cruel incantation which acts as a magical dream trap. It is fed by the captured persons own power. The harder the victim tries to escape, the stronger the spell grows. The enchantment is often designed to use the person's fears against them and end their life. Some 'Sendings' are crafted in such a way that the magical gifts of the dreamer are passed on to the senders.

Shield: A protection placed around or raised by a person which acts as an invisible armor against psychic threats. It can also be used to hide a person's abilities or location.

Soulbond: The bond shared between the Eagles and their mates. It often comes into existence at birth or in early childhood and grows stronger over time. The soulbond is an actual bond between the souls of these individuals and can only be broken by death. The loss of the bond is so devastating to the remaining partner that he/she is often unwilling to go on living.

Woodcraft: The skill as well as the practice of survival in the wild and the knowledge of how to maintain oneself in the woods and find one's way. For Arianna this included hunting, scouting, finding tracks, not leaving traces for others to follow, along with anything else her teacher, Anders, could think of.

Map Of The Eleven Kingdoms

Partial Map of the Eleven Kingdoms

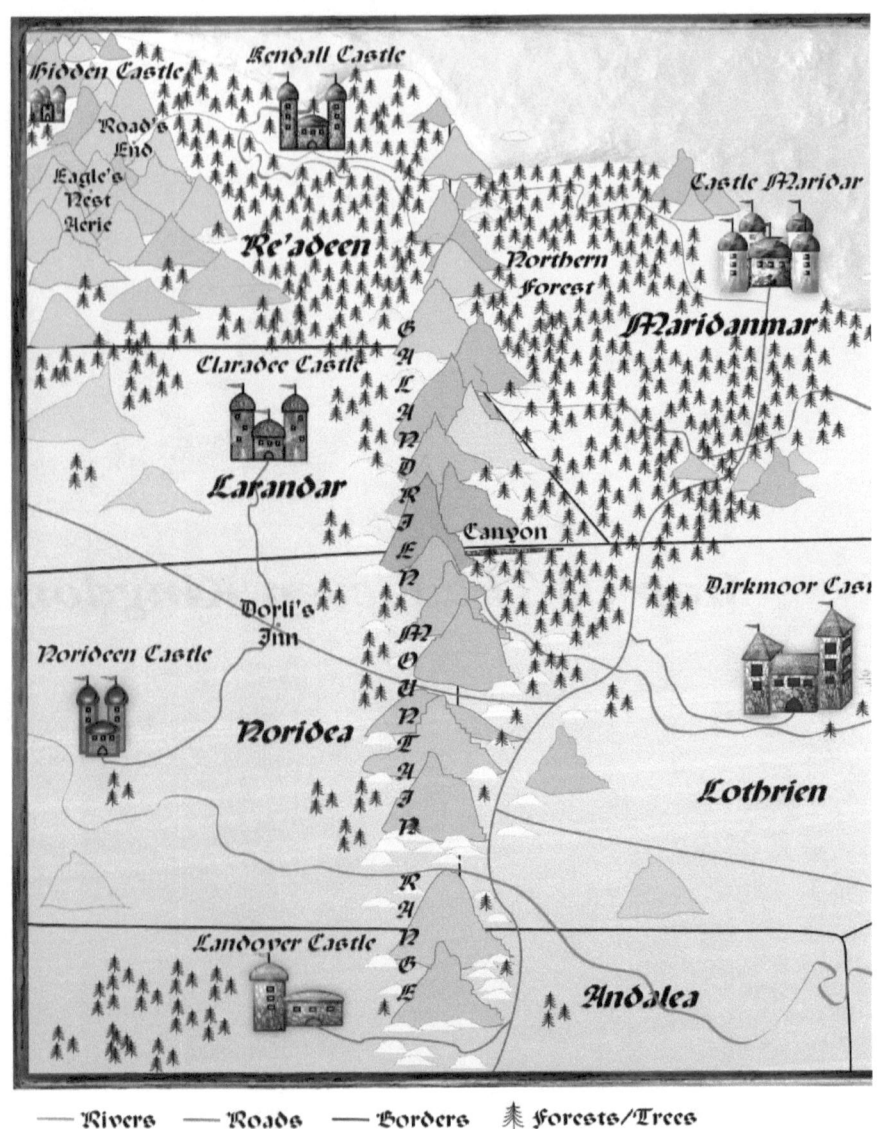

— Rivers   — Roads   — Borders   ✦ Forests/Trees

Not all the kingdoms are shown on this map.
Astoria is located west of Re'adeen, Draydon west of Noridea, and Iridor
south of Andalea.

Daladion is located south of Wymara.

Afterword

I love to write and even the tiniest little bit of an impression or glimpse can give rise to a story or poem. Sometimes a new tale will pop in my head while walking, reading a book, watching a movie, or in a dream. Since I have learned how to look, stories are all around me begging to be shared with the world.

I especially cherish the ideas coming to me in my dreams. The ones I remember vividly feel different. When I put them down on paper, more details flow into my mind, almost as if I had lived them. If there are many universes and many dimensions, who knows, maybe in one of those I did.

Many of my tales started with a dream as did this one. In February of 2015 I was actually almost done writing and editing my latest creation, a book of fantasy love stories, when I had this incredible dream. It was the adventure of a young princess being chased by an elf tracker and being rescued by a winged shapeshifter. The story just begged to be told, and I could not refuse. 'Arianna – A Tale from the Eleven Kingdoms' is the result of this dream.

At first, I thought it would be just a short story. It seemed, however, that this tale had another thing in mind. It soon took on a life of its own and kept growing at an amazing rate. New twists and turns were appearing all the time which I never even imagined in the beginning. But, somehow that is where the story led. This made writing this book incredible fun. If something did not feel right or it felt like I was flailing, I stepped back for a few days until inspiration once again sent me back to the computer to continue this ever growing work.

For me, writing is just as exciting as reading. I know where I am going but, along the way, most of my stories manage to surprise me. As I am writing along, new adventures which I never even expected flow from my fingertips and I can't wait to see where this new notion is going. This is what keeps me enthralled and working away. It is almost like automatic writing or channeling, and I am always eager to find out just what happens next. I had a fabulous time writing this book and hope you will enjoy reading it as much as I loved writing it.

This will be the first of my books to see publication. I believe in divine timing and that there is a reason for everything. 'Arianna' just felt right as my first publication. I am also turning this story into an audiobook and will publish a hardcover version which will include drawings. The soundtrack will include some of the incredible music by the talented Christopher Boscole for your listening pleasure.

Once this project is completed, it is time to start on the second part of Arianna's adventures. After that has been finished, I will go back to some of my other tales. Over the last couple years, I have and continue to grow incredibly both as a writer and human being and will be able to approach these stories from an entirely new vantage point.

Acknowledgements

A huge thank you to my partner. Without him, my writing would have never reached this level. His constant encouragement, help, support, and patience kept me going. He named Arianna, came up with the title, assisted with the editing, and was instrumental in the cover design.

A very special 'THANK YOU' to all my amazing friends and family who loved and supported me during the creation of this book. I greatly valued all your input and ideas. You were always there for me whenever I needed you and often listened to me talk about the book for hours. I love you.

The cover took shape over several months. Thank you, my wonderful friends and family, for helping shape it with your comments and tips.

And last, but not least, a huge thank you to the Divine for sending me this story in a dream and helping me write it.

Author's Biography

GC Sinclaire loves to write and could not imagine her life without it. Her inspiration comes from many places. One of these sources is Sinclaire's vivid dreams. When she writes them down, more facts emerge, almost like she has lived them.

'Arianna - A Tale from the Eleven Kingdoms' is the result of one of these dreams. Several other stories, including a sequel to 'Arianna' are in various stages of completion.

If you would like to read more about GC and her works, please visit her Facebook page, GC Sinclaire, or her web page at www.gcsinclaire.com. You can check on updates there and connect with the author.